A Bolt from the Blue

By Timothy B. Brown

ISBN: 1508884846
ISBN 13: 9781508884842
Library of Congress Control Number: 2015915818
CreateSpace Independent Pub Platform, North Charleston, SC

A science which does not bring us nearer to God is worthless.

Simone Weil

1909-1943

Philosopher and Mystic

Part I

1

The great bells began ringing just as Professor Lisa Duffield reached the top of the long sloping hill and turned onto a brick path. Stopping to look at the bell tower, she reflected on similar mornings long ago when she had played those bells herself as an undergraduate. Unlike most of her friends, she had enjoyed waking early and making the walk from her dorm room to the heart of campus – and then up the many steps to tower's clavier. The rising sun, the bracing, autumn air and the deserted sidewalks all lent this time of day a certain peacefulness. Lisa imagined being at the top of the tower, opening the door to the observation deck and enjoying the first view of the university from far above. It was particularly pretty now that the leaves were changing color – actually nearing their peak – and a red maple leaf fluttered by her face to punctuate the thought. Lisa toyed with the idea of climbing the steps to drink in the sight. It would only mean a few minutes delay in getting to the lab – and she would still be the first one there. She surveyed the tower once more and sighed. "One hundred sixty-two steps," she said aloud, having counted them many times, "that's one reason I don't play the bells anymore."

Lisa carried on walking, concentrating on her work and trying to suppress the feeling that she was on the brink of the biggest breakthrough of her career – possibly the biggest breakthrough in her field since DNA's very discovery. She alternated between "It could be," and "It isn't," and then kept thinking, "I've got to put this out of my mind – one step at a time." She was absorbed in these thoughts as a bicyclist pulled up short at the street crossing right in front of Lisa, and called out, "Hey, watch out!" freezing the young professor just as a black sports car raced by. Realizing that she may well have walked in front of the car, Lisa came out of her fog, amused at what a "typical scientist" she could be.

"Thanks," she called back to the man, raising her eyebrows and exhaling loudly. "He was going way too fast!" The cyclist only smiled in response, gracefully nodded his head, and carried on his way.

Despite the near accident, Lisa's enthusiasm didn't evaporate – yet she became a little less giddy about whether this next experiment might be her defining moment. Within a matter of minutes Lisa navigated – safely – the rest of her pedestrian commute and found her way into the gleaming building which housed her genetics lab. She loved this building for being so modern and clean. Beyond being a comfortable place to work, and a high-tech one at that, it jibed with her preference for newness and orderliness. She loved it when her friends or family, or better yet, some colleague from a different (preferably less prestigious) school would come to visit and she could show off the building and her lab. She wasn't a showy person, and she didn't have an aversion to "old", but Lisa simply believed in science as precise and well-structured and new. This building said all of that in a tangible way.

The fact that the elevator was out of order made a different kind of statement, but Lisa's bright mood was not going to be brought low by this minor inconvenience. In her mind she traced the route to the freight elevator, but then scolded herself and decided to take the stairs. It was only three flights, and if she wimped out on this, after waving off the bell tower, she might have to question her physical state. That would be one more thing to distract her from the work. She leapt up the stairs to convince herself of her fitness.

As Lisa reached her floor, only slightly out of breath (and

that was pretty encouraging), she thought of how she was going to break the news to Jeff, her one-time PhD advisor and now colleague who had been central to her scientific and career success. It was a preliminary question, of course, but what if things worked? Would she toy with him? Make him think it had all dismally failed, then drop it on him like a rock? Or just come out with it "matter-of-factly" and watch him put the pieces together? How fun it would be to see the realization of her stunning discovery dawn on him! Lisa arrested her fantasy – it was probably better to see the results before doing too much plotting.

"Good morning, Lisa!"

Lisa looked up and realized, once again, that she was more self-absorbed than she had thought. Megan Brack, a post-doc in the next lab over, was crossing the hall at the top of the stairs, and now walking abreast with Lisa. Lisa instinctively looked at her watch, surprised that Megan was there ahead of her. "Hi, Megan. I'm used to beating you in here." The words, "by a couple of hours" almost slipped out, but she was fond of Megan and didn't want to discourage the very bright and likable young scientist. Lisa had wanted Megan to work in her lab, but Megan was more interested in ethnic and population genetics. Anyway, they maintained a close relationship and Lisa acted as her mentor.

"How's the cloning going?" Megan asked. "Have you made a copy of Jeff? The two of them could sit around and complement each other."

"Well, funny you should ask." Lisa chose to ignore the jab at Jeff, whom Megan had never liked. "I'm about to look at the newest culture under the microscope. We might have it."

"What's 'it'?"

"A reconstituted nucleus."

"Human?"

"Uh-huh. Today could be the day."

"So what do you do with it?" They turned the corner and

stopped, since their respective labs were in different directions. "Does it count as human life?"

"It's a living cell – but it's hardly human life. Last time you scraped yourself, did you think you were committing genocide?"

"Last time I scraped myself was when a car knocked me off my bike. I *wanted* to commit genocide." Megan reached out her hand and touched Lisa's arm. She smiled. "I'm just kidding. I know this is what you've been waiting for. I hope it works." Lisa smiled; she admired how personable and sweet Megan was. Lisa wondered if she ever touched people's arms like that. "If I drop by later today, will you know?"

"I should know in a couple of hours." Lisa was now beginning to get impatient. She wanted to get in and start warming up the microscope.

"I'll drop by." Megan held up one hand, with her fingers crossed, and smiled.

"See ya." Lisa turned and headed down the hall. Megan watched her walk away and wished she worked in Lisa's lab.

Lisa unlocked the door to her lab and went in. No one was there, which didn't surprise her too much. Grad students were always late risers – at 8:20 am they were all rolling over in bed. *More like rolling over each other in bed.* No, that isn't fair, she thought. I have a good crew, but they aren't so ambitious.

She got lost in the routine of turning everything on, a little faster than normal and did the usual cursing about how messy the lab was. "We've got to talk about this at the next meeting." Which she always said. And she usually did raise the subject. Her students would look sheepish, nod as if they understood, and act no different within a week, perhaps even by the end of that day.

Within a few minutes she was set up at the fluorescent microscope and peering through the eyepiece. "Oh please, oh please, oh please." Her hands were trembling so much she was having trouble finding the right focal depth. She stopped and took a deep breath. "You're not going to see anything if you can't get a grip," she scolded herself aloud. Lisa settled back down and resumed scanning the tissue culture, hoping to see a faint fluorescent glow. "Nothing. Damn!"

Lisa spun around in her chair and closed her eyes, trying to think what she had forgotten. Everyone who knew Lisa admired her ability to separate emotion from work. Anyone else would have flung the sample to the floor after such a disappointment. Lisa was about as fazed as if she had just made a typo on an email. She ran through every step in her mind – isolating the enzymatic reconstituting factor, incubating with the desiccated specimen, drawing off the media, adding fluorescing antibodies. She was most of the way through the process when there was a light tap at the door. A head peeked around the corner.

"Dr. Duffield?" A barely-20ish guy with short, matted-down hair and a gold earring in each ear looked hopeful, and maybe a little apprehensive.

Lisa recollected something about agreeing to meet with an undergrad who was profiling different professors for the university's *Daily Sun* newspaper. "Yes, come in." She was exasperated at the interruption, but she had committed to the appointment. Her experiment could wait, particularly now that it didn't seem to be working. The student entered enthusiastically.

"I'm Elex, Kristina Abbott's friend. She suggested your work would be really interesting for this series I'm writing." He made himself comfortable in the next chair along the lab bench, and swung his backpack to the floor. He had a cup of coffee in his hand and put it down on the bench.

"Please no food right here, Alex," Lisa was a little put off by his presumptuous manner, but she was used to students these days, even their bizarre way of dressing. She wanted to tell him that his pants were falling down, but she figured that he was used to them defying gravity.

"It's Elex," he responded quickly, picking up his coffee. "It's actually just the letters, L – X, but 'cuz it doesn't stand for anything, I just made it into its own word. I hope I didn't mess up anything. I mean, like your experiments. I just needed some coffee to wake me up at this hour."

Lisa chuckled at the suggestion that mid-morning could be described as "this hour." "I'm not as worried about the experiments as I am about you. We use powerful mutagens here." She read the quizzical expression on his face. *He must be an English major,* she concluded. "Mutagens are chemicals that cause genes to mutate. We are pretty careful about how we handle them, but we try not to bring any food into this area." Elex looked regretfully at his coffee as if he was now considering not drinking any more. "I'm sure it's fine," Lisa said. "Let's go into my office. You'll have some room to spread out."

Lisa's office was across the vestibule, just inside the entrance to the lab suite. It was incredibly neat, although Lisa still made excuses for a couple of books and papers on the desk. Elex was indeed an English major, and none of his professors' offices were anything like this. He actually became suspicious of her credentials. As they were settling down he asked her how long she had been a professor.

"I've been an Associate Professor for three years now." She did not fully understand the reason for his question. "I did my graduate work here, though, as well as my undergrad. This very much feels like home to me." She paused and waited for Elex to start off the interview, but he was just smiling and looking around. *Perhaps he'd bought decaf.* "What would you like to know about my work?"

Elex blinked and realized this was his show. He was actually looking at a print she had on the wall of a Renaissance painting – he knew it from his Art History course as the *Annunciation*, but he couldn't identify the painter. All he remembered was some prolonged discussion about the use of lilies as a symbol. He now vaguely recalled falling asleep in the class and realized he needed to pick up the notes from someone. "I'm sorry, I'm still waking up." He opened his laptop and turned it on. "I think I mentioned in the other room that I'm writing for the *Daily Sun* – a series on interesting work, you know, research, science, that kind of stuff – to show how our school is on the cutting edge in all subjects. Kristina and I hang out a lot together and she said you did some really cool stuff. She actually talks about you all the time. I hoped that maybe I could get an overview of it for the next installment in the series."

"Great, I'm happy to do it," Lisa replied. "Before I launch into it, how much do you know about biology and genetics?"

Elex felt a little embarrassed but he tried to put on an air of self-assurance. "Actually I'm an English major." Lisa smiled. "But I took Biology in 9th grade, and genetics was part of the course." *That was convincing*, he thought.

Lisa wanted to reflect on how long ago 9th grade was. She sensed Elex's embarrassment and wanted to put him at ease. Unlike most of her colleagues, she didn't look down her nose at non-scientists. Good thing, too, because her husband, Tom, was a History professor also here at Cornell. "Well, it's not really as complicated as most people think. Let me give you an overview, and you stop me if you have any questions." Elex nodded and smiled, taking a long sip from his coffee.

"What we're studying here is the potential of reconstituting cells that may otherwise be considered dead, and, to some extent, bringing them back to life. The research is really designed to understand the interplay between the biochemistry of DNA, and what we call life.

"Here's what we do. We take special cells from the uterus of sheep and develop a cell culture – "

"Like in a Petri dish?" Elex asked. This was probably the only term he remembered from 9th grade Biology.

"Sort of, that's the right idea – it's called a cell culture flask. Anyway, we believe that there is some powerful factor excreted from those cells that holds the key to life by turning on DNA and thus the cells around them. We call it Ewe Factor. That's E-W-E, as opposed to the letter U. We use a centrifuge to pellet the sheep cells – that is to separate them so we can then draw off the liquid medium now containing this Ewe Factor. Next we take human cells from a piece of flesh – just a small scraping, really, not even enough to make you bleed. After we dry it long enough to make sure that the cells are desiccated – dried out – we put them in that Ewe Factor medium to help them grow and, essentially, reconstitute. After incubating them for several days, we look in the medium to see if there are living human cells."

Elex had been typing away as she spoke. There was a moment of silence as he caught up, then he looked up. "What kind of cells do you have? Skin cells?"

"Well, we're not really sure. What we're hoping for is undifferentiated cells – that means cells that haven't yet decided what they want to be, like stem cells." She was simplifying quite a bit, but he didn't seem embarrassed by it.

"I guess that means I am an undifferentiated person," Elex joked. He looked down at his computer and kept typing.

"All cells are the same when an organism is brand new, and you may remember that all cells in a body have the same DNA material. Then, depending on where in the body they are, they begin behaving in a certain way – being part of the skin or the muscle or an organ. During differentiation, the DNA structure gets modified to prevent unnecessary genes from being expressed. For example, you wouldn't want a cell in your eye excreting an enzyme you need in your liver, right?"

Elex shook his head, "No, that's just gross."

"Right, and it's also a waste of your body's energy and resources. Undifferentiated cells are the Holy Grail of biology. The power of an undifferentiated cell – if you took it a step further – is that its nucleus, containing the DNA, could be implanted into a denucleated egg – that means an egg which has had its original nucleus removed. This *re*-nucleated cell could then be implanted into a uterus for incubation." Lisa watched Elex's expression, trying to figure out if he understood what she had said, let alone the implication of her work, if it was successful.

"Very cool," he commented. Lisa was a little flattered, but she knew she really could have told him almost anything. "You're cloning people here."

He was bright, Lisa thought, but jumping to conclusions. "We are not cloning people exactly. We're a long way from that. But we are trying to understand what makes the conditions right for DNA to become life, what regulates overall cell behavior. It has tons of applications for science and medicine. It's not about 'playing God' which seems to be the normal media phraseology for cloning. Don't put that part in please, about 'playing God' because I will never hear the end of it from the Dean and the Chairman of my Department."

"Cool, no problem." Elex yawned long and leisurely, adding a little audio. Lisa held back a smirk and the urge to ask him if he would like to stretch out on the floor for a little shut-eye. He shook his head and took a long draw on his coffee. "This is very cool stuff," he announced again, almost as if he was trying to convince her of something she didn't know. She hoped he had a broader vocabulary when he wrote. He suddenly began looking intensively at his screen and typing more carefully, and rather than watching him too closely, she picked up her experiment protocol and scanned it again, trying to figure out what may have gone wrong. Suddenly, Elex cleared his throat and she realized that she must have been reading a little too long.

"Oh, sorry, I was a thousand miles away."

"Did you hear my question?" Elex asked.

"No, I missed it." She thought it was ironic that she was the inattentive one, after he had nearly nodded off. "I must be on a different wavelength." She laughed and then stopped cold. Suddenly her mind was racing. When she looked at her sample first thing this morning, had she adjusted the light wavelength on the fluorescent microscope? No, she hadn't. She was sure she hadn't. Perhaps the experiment had worked after all.

Elex cleared his throat again. "Umm, is everything alright?" He looked concerned, and Lisa realized that her mouth was agape, and she was covering it with her hand.

"I'm sorry," she apologized, but could hardly get out more. She was suddenly conscious of being in a cold sweat. Were her hands trembling? She wanted this boy to go away so that she could get back to the lab, but she needed to carry through on her commitment. She took a breath and pulled herself together. "Everything is fine. What was your question again?"

The interview dragged on for ten more minutes, with Elex clarifying a few details on what she had told him earlier – how many people were in the lab, what papers were they publishing. Lisa was helpful, but much less chatty than she had been at the outset. Elex started packing up his computer and backpack, and then, just before she thought he was about to leave, settled back in the chair to finish his coffee. Lisa was anxious, wasn't that coffee cold by now?

"We just studied that painting in my Art History class," Elex said, pointing to the poster over Lisa's shoulder. She spun around in her chair, and relaxed for a moment as she looked at the painting.

"It's the *Annunciation* by Da Vinci – the moment the Angel Gabriel appeared to Mary and told her that she is having a baby. I bought the poster in Florence . . . on my honeymoon." Lisa reflected on those happier days, but briefly. She needed to get Elex out of here so she could get back to the microscope. "So thanks for coming in, Elex." She stood up.

Elex rose to his feet and slung the pack over his back. He was about to leave his empty cup on her desk, but caught her looking at it and scooped it up, looking for a wastebasket. "Thanks so much for your time, Dr. Duffield, Kristina said you were excellent."

She motioned to the basket in the corner. "Excellent in anything specific, or just . . . in general?"

"Oh, you know, like just in a manner of speaking. Thanks again!" He was embarrassed and she was touched by his earnestness. He was a nice guy – had Kristina said she was dating him?

He wasn't moving in slow motion, but it seemed that way to Lisa. And then, just as he was about to leave, he decided to take his sweater off. "He's just torturing me," she whispered under her breath. Finally, after stuffing it into his bag as if he never wanted to wear it again, he made his final goodbye and exited. Lisa bolted back to the lab. She sat down so hard on the wheeled chair at the bench that she actually rolled several feet across the room and had to scoot back using her feet. Her head darted around the side of the microscope, trying to see the setting and smacked into a bookshelf. She winced momentarily, but nothing was going to stop her now. She looked at the dial again and confirmed that the wavelength setting was at the default – she had failed to set it properly and quickly dialed to 485 nanometers. Lisa caught her breath and her hands started trembling again. "Alright, now chill out or you will definitely screw this up. You've already knocked your brains out." She put her hands together and looked up. "Please God. Please God. Let this work."

The cool professional in her took over as she made the adjustments, first to the proper focal depth, and then, reaching around the side to switch over to the fluorescent light source. She looked at the wavelength setting again to make sure it was right, then took another breath. "Please God," she said once more as she lowered her head to the eyepiece and peered through. Her jaw dropped. There were green dots throughout the field. There was no question they were there, hundreds of them. She took a deep breath and closed her eyes, leaning back. Still breathless, and with her mouth hanging open, she looked at the wavelength setting. It was right. She looked again through the eyepiece. The green dots were still there. "I *am* excellent!" she declared loudly, and then, with a little more attitude, "I *am* excellent! In general!" She closed her eyes to hold back the tears that were welling up and to relish the moment of this discovery. This was the most wonderful moment of her life and she wanted to hang on to it as long as possible. Then the tears really started, serious tears, and from her very core. Suddenly she could remember the stress of every test, every experiment, every frustration, every humiliation at the hands of her professors, every challenge from Jeff. Her entire career and the hard work it had demanded came pouring through her eyes like a flood, and she began to enjoy the release. Before long the life-replay was up to this very morning, and she knew she needed to pull herself together. Further, her students might start drifting in any minute and she could hardly be seen in this state.

"Alright, time to pull yourself together," she teased herself out loud. "I am excellent, I am excellent," she sang as she wiped her face with a tissue. Just then, a chill passed through her and she was silenced and perplexed by the sensation. Lisa sat quietly to enjoy the last few minutes of this experience. She still wondered about the chill, but passed it off to a very eventful morning. And then, just before she stood up, she clasped her hands together and looked up. "Thank you, God."

2

At the other end of campus, and the architectural spectrum, from the Biotech building, stood McGraw Hall, housing the University's history department. It made the same grandiose statement in 1880 that the science building did one hundred ten years later. Looming, ponderous, rough-surfaced – it was the perfect shell for the dark-stained oak molding, dusty bookshelves and heaps of paper within. Tom Duffield's office was on the fifth floor, up creaky staircases – or a modern and very out-of-place elevator – and then down a labyrinth of poorly planned hallways. Tucked into the mansard roof and a gable, it provided the perfect contrast to his wife's lab. His was a laboratory of words – old words, fading words, words packed into musty leather books and overstuffed file cabinets. His desk, squarely in the middle of the room, filled up half of it, and had only fit up the stairs and through the doorway, minus hinges, when the legs had been removed. Despite its size, the desk's entire surface was covered by at least one layer of papers, files and pamphlets. He had actually cleared a small spot, however, for a very tired, but obviously favorite coffee mug, which was steaming now with his first cup of the day. This was an earlier start than usual, but Lisa had wanted to rush off to the lab to finish up some experiment, and Tom had more than enough to do at the office. Besides, like his wife, and perhaps only in this respect, he liked to be at the office early and before everyone else had rolled out of bed.

Despite his decision to head into the office early, Tom was having trouble getting started and sat behind his desk looking through his small window at the dorms on the hillside below. He sat quite motionless, but his mind was racing through a hundred different ideas, ranging from contemplating the gothic revival architecture of the buildings below, to the papers he needed to grade, to the book he was supposed to be writing. The latter was most important, and the middle was most urgent, but the first was the most interesting, and he rationalized that, as a professor of medieval History, thinking about the architecture was just exactly what he ought to be doing. In particular, he was thinking about the pointed arch, a topic which would make most people, and all of his students, either yawn or roll their eyes. But for him, the change from rounded, Norman arches, to the soaring, Gothic pointed arches was a defining moment in Western civilization. No more the earthbound, life-on-the-ground, consciousness of the earlier arch. Indeed, the Norman arch was just a better-decorated version of what the Romans created a thousand years before. But the new arch, freed from the ground and pointing to heaven, signaled the intellectual explosion of the Renaissance, of divine inspiration, of man's release from his self-imposed limits . . . .

The door burst open and Tom's overweight boss waddled in. His huffing and puffing, other than being comical, gave Tom a moment to break from his deeper thinking and consider his first snide comment of the day. "Good morning, Professor William J. Rogers. I didn't realize the elevator was out." Tom knew it wasn't, he'd ridden it twenty minutes before. Further, had it been out, he knew that Rogers would never climb the stairs. It would kill him. That set Tom's mind spinning toward interesting possibilities.

"Oh, no. It's working," Rogers replied. "I have just been on a tear this whole morning and haven't had a chance to stop and get my breath."

That would take about a week and a half, thought Tom, judging by how winded Rogers was from just managing the short distance from the elevator to Tom's door. He noticed Rogers was giving the coffee pot a prolonged look and that meant trouble. Armed with a cup of coffee and planted in a comfortable chair, Rogers could blather for hours. The morning would pass without Tom getting any real work done, nor getting a word in edgewise in a conversation-cum-diatribe. Tom reached for his cup, took a sip and grimaced. "Jeez, this decaf is just awful!"

"Oh . . . decaf." Tom had knocked Rogers off his game plan.

Tom tried to seize the advantage. "Are you just making the rounds this morning? Or did you come with a specific purpose?" He suddenly realized his tone was a bit harsh with the Department Chairman, and he smiled to ease the pointedness of his question. He decided to lighten things up a little. "Did you see the game last night?"

Rogers looked troubled. He glanced around for a chair, but they were all covered with papers and books and unloading them was going to be awkward. "Um, I know this is a bit sudden, and perhaps I should have booked some time to discuss this. I had a discussion with the Dean about your career outlook and tenure. Well . . . perhaps we should book some proper time."

This was bad. The only thing worse than Rogers' shoddy scholarship and pointless lectures was his poor management. Without being carefully coached, Rogers would succeed in getting the entire department fired and having History cut from the University curriculum. To Tom, it was a wonder he had ever attained this level. This had to be dealt with now. "No, I have a few minutes before my first appointment. What's up?"

Rogers smiled nervously. "Well, as the Moses Coit Tyler Chairman of the History Department," he began, "I have certain responsibilities with respect to the faculty and staffing decisions, of course, as you know." Tom reflected that Rogers always had to work his title into the conversation – it would have been more efficient to tattoo it to his forehead, but then Rogers wouldn't have the personal joy of hearing himself say it. He continued, "The Dean is concerned that you haven't published in quite a long time."

"Is my getting tenure in question?" Tom thought they should get right to the point.

"Well, it's a bit more serious than that. He raised the question of whether there is a good match between your strengths and the University aims."

Tom realized this situation had already spun out of control. The chances of Rogers appropriately defending any of his people were nil. And given their strained relationship, the chances of his defending Duffield were slightly lower. Instead, Rogers likely took perverse pleasure in protesting loudly but ineffectively, and allowing

Tom's job to teeter on the brink. The only question was whether there was any hope of undoing his boss' ineptitude and malice.

"And the Dean had some concerns about your teaching. Apparently he went through your course critique forms and noted that several students mentioned that you were . . . um . . . 'Crappy'." Rogers paused looking deeply concerned and sympathetic. It was all a put on – Rogers loved this.

Tom fought to keep his temper. "Course critiques from those morons taking their first and only History course?! I should have received arduous duty pay for having to drag them through events they had never heard of before – like the signing of the Magna Carta and the Hundred Years War. Christ, I taught that class as a favor to you, on top of two others! I taught more than anyone else in the department. You know that. Did you mention that to the Dean?! That's why I can't get anything written." Tom took a breath, wondering whether he ought to add that he did three times as much work as his slovenly, fat bastard of a boss. He decided to stop there and spare Rogers any more pleasure. He glared directly into Rogers' eyes and waited.

Rogers tried to hold out, but when Tom leaned forward and raised his eyebrows, he had to speak. "Of course I told him that. But he was very insistent." It was a lame and transparent response. Tom couldn't hold back.

"Insistent? Insistent about what? You said he was questioning my strengths and the University aims, whatever the hell they are. Christ! I am carrying this frigging department. What do you want? What do I need to do to fix this?"

Rogers had looked forward to baiting and torturing Tom, but the intensity of his response had surprised him. He wasn't ready for all of this and hadn't figured out how to close the matter. "Well, how is that book going? Can you have it done this semester?"

Tom had been talking about writing a book for some time, and Rogers must have thought it was much farther along than it really was. It was really still more of an idea than a book at this point. But that was secondary. It was unrealistic to carry his teaching load and have the time to research and write, or even edit. "This semester?! I am teaching two classes again – unlike you. Are you even teaching this semester?"

Rogers was quick to his self-defense. "Of course I am teaching the Senior Seminar. Now don't take this out on me. Let's not lose focus."

Tom was not going to be foiled by this sorry excuse for academia. He pulled himself together. "I am very focused, as always. If I get that book done this semester, will this problem – this concern you seeded with the Dean – go away?"

Rogers was surprised. Despite what he'd asked, he really didn't believe Tom had started the book, let alone be in a position to finish it. If a book suddenly popped out of this scheme, Rogers might be the one to take the fall. Needing to re-strategize, Rogers dissembled, "Well, it would help, of course. I can raise it with the Dean. Yes, we could discuss that."

Ah, now it was all clear. Tom was Rogers' decoy to get himself and his pathetic leadership of the department out of trouble. Duffield was a pawn and had already been put in the vulnerable position. If he produced a book quickly that would be good news for the department. If he didn't, he would be martyred for all the non-publishing faculty. His life had just been turned upside down for the next six to nine months, and he still might not survive. He hated Rogers. He hated that he had followed Lisa to Cornell. "I'd better get writing," he said flatly.

This was an escape opportunity that Rogers couldn't pass up. For all his petty vindictiveness, he really didn't have the courage for an extended argument. "Yes, of course. Let's talk about this next week. I will have Gail set up some time." He began backing out of the office. Still nervous and uncomfortable, he smiled once more, making the entire episode ludicrous. Finally, Rogers turned and lumbered down the hall.

Tom caught his breath as he watched his boss depart. A number of rude comments made their way to his lips, but he was too incredulous about the whole incident to simply be angry. This was just disappointing and bizarre. Suddenly the phone rang and he jumped.

"Hello?"

"Hi, it's me."

Tom was not up for this. "Hi, what's up?" He could tell she was excited.

"I've got fabulous news – the Ewe Factor, it worked. My big experiment *worked*. I can't believe it!"

He was too distracted to catch her energy, but he knew this was big. Now he would truly play second fiddle to his star scientist wife. Tom faked it well. "Honey, that's great! You must be so happy."

"Oh, I can't believe it. I haven't even told Jeff yet. I wanted to let you know first."

"Honey, I am really happy for you, but I have someone here and it's rather important."

Lisa was suddenly embarrassed. "Oh, I'm sorry. Let's talk tonight."

"Tonight it is. Bye, honey."

"Bye."

Tom hung up the phone, clasped his hands behind his head and leaned back. After a moment's reflection he declared out loud, "I guess I'd better start writing." Reflecting just a little more he added, "Christ, I guess I'd better figure out what I'm going to write about."

3

Lisa was too excited by that morning's events to be deflated by her husband's tepid response. He was busy, she reasoned, he was preoccupied with his meeting. Later that evening, they would have a chance to discuss it. Discuss? No, not discuss – celebrate. This was huge! This was Nobel Prize material. Lisa wasn't much of a dreamer, but she let herself fantasize just a little. She and Tom had traveled to Stockholm a few years back, and they had toured the Stockholm City Hall where the Nobel Prize ceremony was held. A severe, dark red brick building, it gave little hint of the beautiful rooms within, and particularly their stunning mosaics. She pictured herself walking down the grand staircase, and turning the corner into the fabulous banquet room, all heads turned her way. Would she have to give a speech?

"Okay, that's enough. One step at a time. I gotta tell Jeff." It was nearly ten and she thought he ought to be in the office by now. He definitely wasn't an early riser, but it was virtually mid-morning. She thought back to when she worked in his lab as a graduate student and would arrive hours ahead of him. In spite of that, Jeff would always tell her she wasn't putting in enough time and effort, and she would respond by working even harder. If not for Tom's counterpressure, she would have slept under her bench.

Lisa left her office and peeked into the lab bench area. *No one's shown up yet? This is ridiculous.* She resolved to have a meeting with her students and challenge their commitment. Turning back through the vestibule and leaving through the main door, she walked forty feet down the hall to the main entrance to Jeff's lab and entered. This lab shared the same floor plan as her own – faculty office to the right, lab office to the left and laboratory bench area straight ahead. She stopped in the vestibule to compose herself before turning the corner into his office. She had been beaming all morning and now wanted to look coolly professional, if not nonchalant, about the stunning news she was about deliver. Lisa was confident that she had wrestled her facial expression under control, but her hands were still shaking. With one last deep breath she stepped forward and turned, framing herself in his office door.

"Good morning, Jeff." Lisa sighed. He wasn't there. She looked around for the trademark leather briefcase which traveled with him to the office every morning and home again in the evening. It wasn't there either. Jeff was becoming as lazy as her grad students. Lisa stepped into the lab area and looked around the benches. In the far corner she spied a grungy undergrad who had recently joined Jeff's lab. Lisa had met her just the week before, but couldn't remember her name. Bad at names under the best of circumstances, Lisa was so distracted by the woman's nose stud and eyebrow ring when they were introduced that she was unable to concentrate on anything else. She approached the student and put on a cheerful smile. "Good morning."

"Hey."

"I was looking for Professor Wolf."

"Mmmm." Although the word on this student was that she was brilliant, she was clearly lacking in conversational skills. It wasn't clear whether she was thinking about answering further, but she intently maintained eye contact.

Lisa wasn't sure she should say more, but she couldn't bear the staring contest. She decided to cut it short. "Ummm . . . I guess he isn't in yet."

"Uh-uh, not yet." The girl kept looking at her. Lisa felt like she was speaking a foreign language and the girl was struggling to understand.

"Well, that's okay. I can come back later." Lisa smiled and turned to leave.

"He had to go downtown this morning to the city offices," the girl said as Lisa stepped away. "You could call him on his new iPhone."

This was a promising improvement, thought Lisa, both the conversation and the information. "Wow, Professor Wolf, got an iPhone?!" For a cutting-edge scientist, Jeff was technologically inept. He actually still had a Smith-Corona typewriter in his office.

A smart phone was a big move, but it would be ages before he mastered it. "That's a great idea. Do you have his number?"

"I think the number's on his desk. Let me help you find it." The girl jumped down from her stool and led the way back into Jeff's office. Lisa was now both amused and baffled by the girl's earlier responses. Perhaps she was just deep in concentration. They entered the office and headed to Jeff's desk, which was cluttered with science journals, mail and a mish-mash of sticky notes. Lisa was concerned that the student would be able to find anything, yet the woman walked right up to the desk and started pushing papers around.

"I saw it here the other day," the student said confidently as she sifted through the papers. Lisa was anxious to get the phone number, but she was a little uncomfortable about messing up Jeff's desk. Indeed, she couldn't decide whether she was amused or appalled by the student's hunting expedition. Lisa had known Jeff for ten years, yet she'd never be so presumptuous as to do this. She was just about to call it all off when she spied an old issue of the Journal of Molecular Biology which was just now being shoved unceremoniously aside. Lisa recognized it as the copy she'd loaned Jeff three months ago and had been bugging him to return.

"Hey, hang on a second," Lisa blurted out. But it was a second too late. The student had actually pushed it over the edge and it toppled into the wastebasket with several papers. "Hold on, hold on!" Lisa shouted. This was bordering on scandalous. Lisa feared Jeff's quick temper might let loose on this energetic, young scientist if he ever discovered what she was doing. Lisa also wanted to rescue her magazine. The student looked up with a quizzical expression. Had she not seen everything fall off the side of the desk? Lisa leaned over and peered into the trash can. Unfortunately it hadn't been emptied for a few days, so in addition to her magazine there were crumpled pieces of paper and tissues and someone's lunch detritus. She hated trash – in fact, at home she always made

Tom deal with it. But he wasn't here to handle it now. Lisa reached down and picked up the magazine and the other papers that appeared to fall with it. With a grimace she picked off one still damp tissue.

"Here it is!" the girl exclaimed. She had continued hunting as Lisa went through the trash, and now held out a scrap of paper with just a number scribbled down, no words. Classic Jeff, thought Lisa, he never labeled phone numbers and would thus constantly lose them. Lisa tucked her recovered science journal under her arm as she copied the number to a blank note. She made a point of writing Jeff's full name on the note.

"This is great. Thanks for your help." Lisa blushed, "I'm sorry, can you tell me your name again? I'm terrible with names."

"It's Allison Irgang. And don't worry about it. It must be impossible with all the kids here. Hey, you've got a great reputation for knowing your students." Allison smiled.

Lisa blushed a little more. "I do? Well, thanks, Allison. I always appreciated it when my professors knew who I was. I really appreciate your help. I'm sure I'll see you around."

"You're welcome. See ya."

Allison smiled again and returned to her bench as Lisa headed back to her own lab. Somehow, the phone number-hunting exercise had taken Lisa's mind off the morning's achievement, and she now tried to refocus on how to break the news to Jeff. While likely measured and thoughtful, he would surely be excited – after all, he owned a piece of this success. Beyond just consulting on this work over the past couple of years, Jeff had been her PhD advisor and mentor. He had pushed her to achieve far beyond what Lisa herself had ever expected, although he never made it easy. He was extremely hard to please, ever critical and perpetually requesting one extra analysis or one more experiment. More grad students burned out in his lab than gained their degree, but those that got through were top achievers. His graduates held faculty positions at the greatest universities around the world, and they would always call him first to inform him of their achievements. To some extent they did it because they regarded him as a father of sorts. However, as competitive and ambitious scientists, they also wanted to show that they had attained status as his peer. Deep down, Lisa felt both these emotions as she tossed the recovered science journal on a shelf, sat down at her desk, and dialed his number. She collected her thoughts as she heard the first ring at the other end.

"Hello?"

"Jeff, it's Lisa. I have the most amazing news!" Lisa was breathless as she spoke into the phone. She waited for his response – when none came she continued. "The Ewe Factor experiment. It worked. Oh, I can't believe it." She waited for his response, but again, none came. *Perhaps the connection dropped.* "Jeff, are you there? "

"Yes, yes, I'm here. I'm just thinking. And driving. The traffic is terrible today. Is there something going on downtown today? Are they redoing this road again? This is just hell."

"Jeff, did you hear what I said?" Her husband, Tom, had already failed to share in her excitement – she really didn't want the same to happen with her closest working colleague and professional mentor. "Did you hear what I said about my experiment?"

"Yes, I heard, of course. I told you that I am thinking about it."

"I came in this morning and took a look through the fluorescent scope. But the first time I looked I hadn't adjusted the wavelength. Suddenly, while I was giving an interview to the guy from the *Daily Sun*, I realized my mistake. I couldn't get rid of him fast enough!"

"Why were you giving an interview to the *Sun*?"

"What does that matter? I want to tell you about the experiment."

"We'll get to that in a minute. As the department chairman, I am supposed to be informed of anything going on with the press.

Were you giving an interview on the experiment?"

"No, of course not. It wasn't an interview about the experiment. It was an interview about me. I mentioned my work. And I guess I mentioned the experiment as part of my work. I didn't think I needed your permission. It's not the press, it's the *Sun*." Oh God, Lisa thought, now I am going to get yelled at.

"Did cloning come up?"

"Did cloning come up?! I'm a geneticist for God's sake. Of course it came up! That's what I do." Lisa was really rattled. The underwhelming response she got from Tom was looking pretty good compared to one of Jeff's irrational lectures.

"Oh, this damned traffic. Just tell me 'playing God' didn't come up. He didn't say that, did he, 'playing God'?"

"I don't know if it came up. It certainly wasn't the focus of our discussion. Can we talk about the experiment?" Lisa heard a car horn in the background. "Is that you honking the horn? Why are you in such a hurry?"

"I'm not in a hurry. I just can't stand these damned idiots. They've shut down the road and they're just standing around drinking coffee."

"Jeff, are you interested in talking about my experiment?" Lisa was really exasperated. This was meant to be a wonderful moment. Jeff was supposed to recognize her accomplishment and praise her, finally.

"Frankly, it isn't what I expected and I am trying to think through what I might have miscalculated. Or, of course, if there is a flaw in the protocol . . . ."

Lisa's patience was not easily tried, but this was too much. It may have been the morning's emotional roller coaster, or simply the years of trying to satisfy someone who just couldn't be satisfied, but Lisa was unable to hold back the torrent of anger sweeping through her. "Goddammit, Jeff. Why can't you, just once, give me a little credit? Just once, have a little faith and confidence in my ability.

There was no flaw in the protocol. And you couldn't have miscalculated anything, since this was my work. My work, Jeff! I thought you'd finally be happy for me, but obviously I was wrong. I have to go. Goodbye!" Lisa hung up the phone. She was so furious that she sat staring at the telephone, wishing she hadn't terminated her rant so prematurely. Lisa had never before had angry words with Jeff – at least not for her part – yet plenty were now coming to mind. Fortunately for her reputation and departmental relations the words didn't come to her mouth, for her students were now in the lab office and would surely be able to hear. As she fumed, the only sound that came out was a strained, "Arghhh," and the anger and frustration began converting to tears. Kristina Abbott, one of Lisa's graduate students, looked in through the window and knocked as she entered Lisa's office wearing a look of deep concern.

Lisa could not bear the thought of being seen in this condition and this new humiliation only amplified her anger. Averting any eye contact with Kristina, who stood frozen in embarrassment, Lisa rose and wound her way around the desk. She tried to pull herself together and say something to the young woman, but nothing came out. Escape, as quickly as possible, was the only answer, and Lisa slipped out the door without a word. She headed for the stairs, as she knew that would minimize the chances of running into anyone else, and quickly descended to the ground floor and charged outside. With all the morning's activity, she had lost track of time. It was now late morning and there were students everywhere – no hope for the privacy and quiet that she needed. She kept her head down and made a bee line for the flower garden in front of the Ag Quad. There was a bench tucked away among the plants where she knew she could gather her thoughts and regain some composure. She crossed the road still seething, only hoping the garden would provide the solace she desperately needed. The bench was partially hidden behind tree branches and chrysanthemums, but it looked as if someone was already there.

"Oh, perfect," Lisa muttered under her breath, yet she continued heading toward her intended destination. Picking up her pace, she considered asking the occupant to leave.

Lisa rounded the flower bed and approached "her" bench. There was, indeed, a lone person sitting there, facing away from her. It was a man, and judging by his hair and clothing, he appeared to be around Lisa's age. In fact, he looked vaguely familiar, yet no one she could place. Curiosity began to replace her anger. The man turned and looked directly into Lisa's eyes, his face suffused with compassion. He smiled, stopping her in her tracks and melting away her anger – then he rose and nodded gracefully as he passed her by. Only as Lisa watched him gain the sidewalk did she realize it was the bicyclist who had stopped her at the crossing that morning. Beyond the mystery of that coincidence, Lisa suddenly found the peace and contentment she had sought.

Jeff was stunned by Lisa's outburst. Given his status, reputation and force of personality no one had stood up to him for years. Frankly, he had forgotten what it was like, and unlike Lisa, he was not blessed with patience. Jeff was angry even before Lisa hung up – her abrupt disconnection nearly drove him into a frenzy. He quickly looked down at the buttons and tried to remember how to dial the number from which the last call came. He wasn't going to let her get away with treating him like that! It was star-something, he recalled. "Damn it to hell!" He yelled looking at his phone.

The instant Jeff looked up, he realized he'd made a terrible mistake. He had begun accelerating as he cleared the road construction, just as Lisa was yelling at him, and had failed to ease up now that he was studying the cell phone. Unfortunately, he was now going too fast to stop at a red light, and entered the intersection far too late. While his brilliant and perceptive mind had always been Jeff's greatest asset, it now allowed him to understand the inevitability of his doom. A heavy truck was coming from the left, and there was no way either driver could avoid collision. Jeff heard – more than felt – the crushing impact. The sound of grinding metal and smashing glass drowned out the scream that came from deep in his throat. He had enough time to realize that his failure to don a seatbelt would surely be fatal, yet mercifully he was unconscious by the time his body was flung from the car. He landed in a broken heap twenty feet away amidst glass and debris. There was already more blood pooled around him than seemed possible, and a crowd of pedestrians and drivers quickly gathered. Jeff came around moments later, dazed, numb and unable to move. The horror and fear on the faces of the onlookers told him he was in a terrible state.

"Someone call 911!"

"Oh my God!"

"Don't move him."

"You're going to be okay"

Jeff refused to believe that his survival depended on these panicked morons who couldn't organize a coherent thought or action. If only one of them would hand him a phone he would call for help himself. Unbeknownst to him, however, his spinal cord was severed, and it was already a miracle that he was still alive, if only for a few moments. He searched the faces around him for someone of action, but only felt despair. And then, as Jeff tried to tell them what they should do, he fixed on a face he thought he recognized. It was a man, about his age, whose expression was nothing like those around him. Instead of tears or panic, there was a sweet peacefulness about him. The man looked deeply into Jeff's eyes and said no words, but commanded the moment nonetheless. Jeff wasn't confused by this man's way, he understood it completely, and for the first time in his life he felt that same peace. Jeff closed his eyes and died.

4

Freed from the morning's emotional roller coaster of anxiety and elation and anger and joy, Lisa spent the early afternoon visiting her favorite places around campus. She had spent most of her adult life at Cornell, and had many distinct and happy memories of particular spots. Now resolved to visit several of them, she was completely forgetful of the experiments back in the lab which needed to be designed and executed. The bench in the flower garden on the Ag Quad was her first stop in this sentimental tour. Not only had it been the joyful site of Tom's marriage proposal, but also a more serious site when she sat and contemplated which Grad school she should attend – whether to stay at Cornell, or to try something new and venture west to Stanford. The peacefulness she discovered during her encounter, if that is what it could be called, with the stranger did not fade as she sat for more than half an hour. Beyond a simple few minutes of planning her brief sojourn, her thoughts were fairly aimless and free. Lisa probably spent the most time thinking of her childhood, centering on the happy memories around the holidays when her older sisters would come home from college. Easter was a special favorite – either for the dainty hats and gloves they wore when she was really little, or for the ham and scalloped potato family banquets of her teen years. And she could never forget the small Episcopal Church and the sunrise service. She was generally sleepy at such an early hour, but the carved, wooden Jesus on the crucifix always seemed to be staring at her. She never dared *not* to pay attention.

When Lisa finally roused from the bench, she walked briskly across the crowded Ag Quad, and passed down the side of Martha van Renssellaer Hall, where steps, now slightly slick with the first downed and dampened foliage of the season, led to a path toward the footbridge over Fall Creek. Lisa loved standing on the quieter of two bridges, and thinking about the contrast between the two sides. Beebe Lake, on one side, was literally a quiet mill pond, and just now one red canoe paddled silently across to underscore its calm. On the other side, those placid waters began a cascade of almost a hundred feet – falling, splashing, misting, breaking into separate streams before recombining once again in peace at the bottom. For Lisa this was just like life, just like this very morning. A peaceful morning like any other held a thunderclap surprise when she simply adjusted a microscope dial. A simple telephone call to relate happy news had morphed into the angriest confrontation ever with her close friend and mentor. And then, in the garden, peace was once again restored. The scientist in her toyed with some means of figuring out this strange rhythm, but only briefly. Her science was one of consistent and predictable biochemical markers – not of life's vicissitudes or human emotions. Far too variable and idiosyncratic. She got on with her walking tour.

Lisa passed up through the Balch Hall archway and lingered in the inner courtyard. This was one of the loveliest places on campus, yet so few students looked up from the flagstone path to appreciate it. Sheltered from the cold winter winds, the trees there had grown to magnificent size and now cast heavy shade on the ivy covered walls and leaded windows. She considered sitting on the wall and really studying the scene, but she was enjoying the walk and wanted to keep going.

Despite the traffic noise, which was picking up as she approached the busy Central Avenue bridge, Lisa could hear the tower's bells strike one o'clock. She was struck at how long she had been wandering and the odd blurriness that had characterized this strange day. *Have I not eaten since breakfast?* The fact that her stomach or blood sugar levels had not signaled this earlier was perhaps strangest of all. But now, because she was thinking about it, or maybe simply because she had only breakfasted on a piece of toast and a glass of juice, she was completely famished. Her original walking plan tour needed some revision. Needing something to eat, she crossed the bridge and entered the Arts Quad.

Lisa slowed her pace and savored the marvelous sight ahead – grand collegiate buildings, stately trees shading the crisscross paths, statues of Cornell's founders, all profoundly punctuated by

McGraw Tower at the far end. Taken in isolation, the grounds and buildings were somber in their earthy tones of deep red and gray and brown. They were squat (with the exception of the tower), smug and proud of their Ivy League status – perhaps conscious of countless brochures and postcards which featured them. Yet there was a second element to this scene which made it complete: the dozens of students moving randomly across the Quad. They were like slow-motion confetti celebrating the marriage of sobriety with fervor, of deliberation with impetuousness, and of age with youth. The tower understood its relevance only in the context of this juxtaposition, and stood as a giant exclamation point to declare that this, *all of this*, was what made a university.

She glanced right to the Stone Row, the University's original buildings which included McGraw Hall, and wondered whether she should find Tom and lure him to lunch with her. She couldn't recall his schedule that day, although she was pretty sure he wasn't lecturing just now. Did he have office hours? Not that any students came this early in the semester. Lisa decided not to bother him. She was enjoying being on her own schedule, and didn't want to have to compromise her whims. She passed by McGraw Hall, and closed on the Library and Tower. Just as the student union was coming into view, Lisa revised her plan once more and opted to visit Sage Chapel, site of her wedding and one of the most peaceful places on campus – a complete contrast to the bustling sidewalks just outside. She turned left on the path and entered the Chapel at the West door.

Normally, Lisa would choose a pew, say a brief prayer, and then contemplate the Chapel's beautiful decoration from that randomly-selected spot. But today she was drawn directly to the altar rail. The mosaic on the apse's back wall was a magnet for her – Lisa considered it the prettiest place on campus. It featured eleven life-size figures in a lush and shimmering garden. She would always try to regard the mosaic differently; perhaps admire the figures' elegant gowns on one occasion, and then their facial expressions on the next. The three female figures to the far left each represented a branch of Science, with Biology the leftmost. Lisa naturally felt an affinity for this figure, but wished she didn't have to have a skull at her feet and a bird's nest in her hand. The objects were appropriate to the subject, she reasoned, but so outdated. What about a double helix or a microscope? Science has come so far, Lisa thought, and just this morning another great advance had been made – by her!

Lisa turned her attention to the seated man at center. He was supposed to represent Philosophy, but she always thought of him as God. The only problem Lisa found with that identity was he seemed so contemplative, if not uncertain. *Was God ever uncertain?* she wondered. *Did he ever have to weigh conflicting possibilities? Surely truth must not be hard to discern for the one who created it. Perhaps he was judging Man, an unenviable and challenging task. Yes, that was it,* she decided – *he was considering condemnation yet trying to figure out how to grant one last reprieve. Truth is easy; love and mercy are hard, even for the Creator.*

The mid-day sun, streaming through the colored glass, and making particularly good use of the few untinted panes, bathed the altar in vivid light. The mosaic shimmered and the golden tiles virtually glowed. In this surreal lighting, Lisa understood the mosaic creator's genius. The artist had likely never seen this particular lighting, as it existed for just a few minutes each day, on just a few days each year. Yet it was to this vision that the mosaic was executed. And that is like life, Lisa mused. We are shaped for moments which no one – except God – can anticipate. She started as she felt a hand on her shoulder. Lisa turned abruptly to see Tom standing by her side, and her godly thoughts evaporated.

"You scared the crap out of me!" she spat out.

"I am so sorry. I didn't mean to startle you. I have been following you for the last couple of minutes, since you passed McGraw, but I couldn't catch up. And I didn't want to call out in the church." Tom looked serious and contrite, and Lisa's irritation subsided. Just then the Tower bells pealed forth in afternoon concert. Tom raised his voice a little to be heard. "I talked to . . . Kristina, in your lab. Are you alright?"

"Oh, it's so embarrassing. I just lost it completely." Lisa was struck by the deep concern on Tom's face.

He reached out to hold each of her arms. "Oh, Lisa, I think people understand completely. The two of you have been so close for so long. I am so sorry."

Lisa was touched by Tom's concern, but also a bit surprised. She thought he would clap her on the back for finally standing up to Jeff. "I'm just not going to take his crap anymore." Now Tom looked puzzled and he looked down at the floor. She sensed they were having two different conversations. "What's going on?" she asked.

"You know about Jeff, right?"

"What about him?"

Tom closed his eyes. He now realized Lisa didn't know, and he was going to have to break some terrible news. He spoke very deliberately and slowly. "Jeff was killed in a car accident this morning."

"But I just talked to him a little while ago," she protested.

"He ran a red light downtown and collided with a truck. He died at the scene." Tom left out the more gory details he'd heard on the radio. "I am sorry."

Lisa searched Tom's face for a sign that this was some odd prank based on his general dislike for Jeff, but no sign was present. She saw only genuine concern. Then she began to think about what Tom had said and the horror dawned quickly. Her hands flew up to cover her gaping mouth and her legs began to shake. "Oh . . . my . . . God!" Tom held her more tightly as she began to convulse and the tears began to flow. "Oh my God!" she repeated in a high-pitched wail. "Oh please, God, no." She suddenly felt light headed and dizzy.

The shimmering mosaic behind the altar had become even more vivid to her and the characters seemed to be coming to life. Their faces were turning to look at her, and they seemed to be chanting and talking. Then, one by one, they began to incline their heads toward the center. Lisa followed their eyes to the middle, and found herself looking directly into God the Judge's eyes, and he into hers. Blackness was closing in from the periphery of her vision and Lisa held on desperately to maintain control. She concentrated on God's face, slightly perplexed by the sense that his mouth was moving. He seemed to be saying something. She leaned forward to hear. His right arm lifted from his lap, and he pointed directly at her. His mouth formed the word again, and he spoke in a deep rumble, "Guilty!"

The blackness closed in, and Lisa's legs gave way. Tom lowered her gently to the floor.

5

The dreariest autumn anyone could remember began the afternoon Jeff died. Dark clouds and rain swept in over Cayuga Lake as Tom and a catatonic Lisa made their way home from Sage Chapel. By dusk, a steady, drenching rain had begun falling and a brisk wind began stripping the colorful foliage from the branches. Lisa had gone directly to bed on arriving home, and Tom, still unaware of what catalyzed Jeff's death, was baffled by her reaction. As he sat quietly in their living room watching the rainwater streaming down the windows, he reflected on the fifteen plus years he had known Lisa. Had he ever seen her like this? When any of her four grandparents passed away? When their first dog was hit and killed by a car right in front of her? No, she was always practical, thoughtful and balanced. Not that she wasn't sensitive and loving. He knew she felt deeply saddened by all those events, and he could envision her calm withdrawal for several days, perhaps to read a book or work in her lab. But this was beyond anything he had ever seen, even their darkest moment together, Lisa's third miscarriage.

Just past midnight Tom awakened from a doze to Lisa's voice from the bedroom. "Tom, are you out there?" Her voice was shaky and weak, but these were the first words she said since she fainted. He jumped from the sofa and ran to their bedroom. He entered the darkened room and could see her tearstained face by the light of the clock radio. "It wasn't just a dream, was it?" She knew the answer to the question, but was looking hopefully into his eyes.

"No, Sweetie. I'm sorry." Tom was anxious to talk to her, but he could see that she was going to begin crying again. He sat down next to her on the bed and put an arm around her to comfort her. Lisa began sobbing again, and pulled away from Tom to bury her head in the pillows. "Lisa, do you want to talk about it?" He was increasingly frustrated by this communication gap between them. Tom repeated the question.

"No!" she wailed between her sobs. Her entire body was convulsing, the movement exaggerated by her shaking her head. Tom realized this was pointless and retreated from the room. His sympathy and patience were being replaced by resentment and irritation, but he knew he had to do something. What if this was a nervous breakdown, or what if she became violent or suicidal? This was way outside of his control, he needed help. "Claire!" he blurted out and headed to the kitchen telephone to call her.

Dr. Claire Prentiss was one of Lisa's closest friends as well as her gynecologist. Most recently she had been advising them on fertility and administering several treatments to assist Lisa in getting pregnant. Both Lisa and Tom were disappointed to be seeing Claire more on professional than social grounds. The phone was answered on the first ring.

"Claire Prentiss"

"Claire, hi. It's Tom. I'm glad you're up. Sorry I am calling so late."

"I wasn't up. I'm just a doctor and I am used to late night calls. I wake up fast. What's going on?"

"Sorry, sorry." Tom had not thought about where to begin. "Umm . . . I need your help. Jeff Wolf – you know Jeff, Lisa's old mentor and now Department Chair – was killed in a car accident this afternoon and when I told Lisa, she fainted and has been inconsolable since. I'm afraid she is having a nervous breakdown. What should I do?" It had all come out in a rush and he now took a deep breath.

"Oh, I am sorry about Jeff. They were very close."

This was really not what Tom needed to hear. "Were they closer than I knew?"

Claire didn't understand his question. "Huh?"

"You know what I mean. Is there something I should know?" His heart began pounding.

"No, of course not. Don't be ridiculous. Is this why you called?"

Tom was chastened by her rebuke. "No, I called because I am worried about her. I need you to either talk her out of this or prescribe something strong. She is a total mess."

Claire knew that Tom was not big on drugs so this must be serious. "I can be over in a half an hour. I have some injectable sedatives in my bag. I'm on my way."

"Thanks, Claire. And I am sorry – sorry about bothering you and sorry about what I said."

"Don't worry about it. I'll see you in a bit."

Claire pulled into the driveway forty-five minutes later, slowed on her trip by the torrents of wind-driven rain. She made a dash for the door which Tom, agonized by the longer than expected wait, held open for her. They were both wet once she got inside and the door was closed. "Oh, it's just gruesome out there. Sorry it took me so long to get here." Claire pulled off her raincoat and gestured outside with it as it dripped on the floor. "Was this forecasted?"

"I don't think so, but I heard tonight that it is going to last for days."

Claire shrugged, her hair still dripping. "There goes our Indian Summer." Claire put on her professional face. "Where's Lisa?"

Tom pointed down the hall. "In our room. She was still sobbing just a few minutes ago."

"So she's awake?" They started down the hall.

"I don't know what is going on. I broke the news about Jeff to her in Sage Chapel and she burst into tears and fainted. She collapsed right there."

Claire cut in. "What were you doing in Sage Chapel?"

"I was heading from my office over to her lab, and I happened to see her walking in. I don't know why she was there. I figured that she had already heard about Jeff and was going in to pray or something. I really don't know."

"But she didn't know about him?"

"No. So then she fainted – she went into a total swoon – and when she came around I walked her to the car. She didn't speak at all, and then, once back here, she's been crying all night. I tried to comfort her, but it seemed to make it worse."

They stopped at the door and could her muffled crying inside. Claire put on her professional face again. "Why don't you let me go in alone," she suggested.

Tom was happy to be off the hook, but didn't want to be seen to shirk his spousal responsibility. "I'll be here if you need me." As he said that, he decided he was going to nip back to the kitchen and pour himself a brandy. Claire opened the door and stepped into the darkened room.

Tom was only just putting the stopper back in the decanter when Claire came into the kitchen. He felt a little sheepish. "How is she?" he asked earnestly. Claire was smiling, but Tom could tell she was troubled.

"Are you offering any of that?" she asked.

"Of course, pardon me." He took a second snifter from the cupboard.

"Not too much, thanks, I have to drive."

"You can spend the night here if you'd like. The roads aren't safe with all the wet leaves down."

"I need to get home tonight. But thanks for offering. Bob is traveling early tomorrow, so I need to get home."

Tom checked his habit of pouring generously. "My freshman year roommate turned me onto this. Good brandy always focuses the mind, he would say."

Claire winced at the first taste, but liked it nonetheless. She took another swig and winced again. "That definitely focuses the mind, but I'm not sure what on."

"So, how is she?" he asked again. Tom was beginning to feel the relief of both the brandy and Claire's presence.

"Well, *her* mind needed a little defocusing – so I gave her a sedative. If she isn't sleeping already, she will be soon." Claire smiled as she took a smaller sip.

"I've never seen her like this before," Tom offered.

"This isn't normal, so I am sure you haven't. Especially Lisa, the great even-keeled one."

This reawakened Tom's concerns. "Is this a nervous breakdown?"

"Let's see how she is tomorrow – and maybe even the day after. No need to diagnose it as anything yet. Give her a little time."

"Will the injection interfere with the other ones she's been getting?" Tom knew Claire would understand the reference to the fertility-enhancing drugs Lisa had been receiving. "This was supposedly the ovulation week."

Claire knew the day had been tough on Tom as well, so she chose her words carefully. "Tom, I don't think anything's going to happen this week. Any extra pressure on her is not going to help. I mean, maybe you'll see a big change tomorrow, but that's," she paused, feeling caught in an awkward place between being their doctor and their friend, "unlikely."

Tom felt his usual bitterness toward Jeff – once again, Jeff had screwed up their life. Even after his death, no less. Well maybe this would be the last time, he thought, and then he felt remorse. He chose not to respond to Claire, finished the little bit of brandy in his glass and considered pouring himself another.

"I'd ask you if you need a sedative, but on top of this brandy you would be out for a day." She was trying to lighten the moment.

"You say that like it's a bad thing." Tom smiled. He, Lisa and Claire had been good friends for many years and he was thankful for her companionship. "I'll be fine. Sure you don't want to stay in the guest room?"

"I'm sure, but thanks." She took one last swig of the brandy – without a wince this time as now she was used to it. "Back into the monsoon." They headed together toward the door, and Claire swung on her coat and readied the umbrella. "Don't worry, I'll drive slow and carefully. At least there's no one else on the road for me to run into." She gave Tom a quick hug and headed outside. Tom watched through the window as she backed out and drove away. Once again he considered refilling his glass, but sat down on the couch and pulled a blanket around himself. Before he could finish another thought, the brandy and the long day got the better of him and he drifted off to sleep.

Lisa was better the next day, but not much. She woke late in the morning from troubling and emotional dreams, and spent several minutes trying to piece together what day it was, why it was so late, and why Tom wasn't in the bed with her. Yesterday's events began to dawn on her, the worst ones first, and her mourning resumed, although now with a deep sadness and depression, rather than hysteria. Now for the first time since she heard of the accident, she thought of Jeff's wife, with whom she had always been close, and his two teenage children. They must be devastated. And how could they ever forgive her? It was her fault that he crashed. If she hadn't called him and then ranted and raved and hung up on him, he would still be alive. How could she forgive herself?

Tom peeked in from the hall. He heard rustling bedclothes and figured she was awake. He knew that "Good morning" would be the wrong greeting, so he offered a tentative, "Hi." Lisa blinked in response, so he continued, "Do you want anything to eat?"

"No, well, maybe some water. Thanks for getting me home yesterday. I don't really remember anything after you told me . . . ." Her expression was very bland and her voice monotone. Tom wondered whether the drugs were still at work.

"I had Claire come over late –"

"Claire?! Why?"

"You were a mess, Sweetie. I was worried you were having a nervous breakdown, or were going to hurt yourself."

"Oh. Sorry. Was she mad?" If there was any extra emotion available, Lisa would have been embarrassed or humiliated. As it was, she just considered Claire one more of her victims. Oddly, she didn't extend that sympathy to Tom.

"No, she wasn't mad. Let me get you a glass of water . . . are you sure you don't want something to eat? When was the last time you ate?" He was worried about low blood sugar triggering the next emotional collapse, but he didn't want to push it.

Lisa couldn't imagine eating. She wanted to sleep more or lose herself in a book or mindless television. "No food now, thanks. And, I still feel like being alone, if that is okay with you. Do you have to work today?"

"No. I have one lecture tomorrow and then office hours in the afternoon. Other than that I am free to work on my book." Tom realized he hadn't had a chance to relate his conversation with his Department Chair, Rogers, and the foolish commitment to finishing a book that hadn't yet been fully contemplated.

"Your book? What book?" Despite her drained state, she didn't miss this odd comment.

"Oh, I just thought it was time to turn my research into something. We'll talk about it later."

Lisa frowned thoughtfully, but she didn't want to pursue this discussion either. "Okay. I'll come out in a few hours."

"Call me if you need me."

It was early evening when Lisa shuffled out of the room and finally satisfied at least part of the hunger that had led her around campus the previous afternoon. She lost her appetite halfway through a bowl of cereal, however, and retreated once again to the quiet of her bedroom. Passing by the living room, she conversed briefly with Tom, but he was giving her room, and simply reassured her that he was there if she needed him.

The next couple of days passed similarly. As if slowly recovering from some terrible flu, Lisa slept most of the time and would rise to eat a little or go to the bathroom. She spent a lot of time thinking about Jeff, and particularly her last conversation with him, if it could be called a conversation. Why had she snapped, she kept wondering. It wasn't as if Jeff hadn't jerked her around in the past – this was really pretty much standard operating procedure for him. And, she knew, he was easier on her than many others. If he hadn't been so damn brilliant, and helped so many people to attain their goals, and further science, he would have been hated by everyone. But Lisa adored him as a father figure. His stern demeanor and incisive mind had pushed her far beyond what she likely would have achieved – indeed, her career was a success. She knew what she was getting into when she first tied her star to his nearly twenty years before. They had both benefited from this partnership, but Lisa more so. Jeff would have succeeded with or without her.

This line of thinking led to Lisa's slow mental chronicling of her entire relationship with Jeff. Perhaps as a final tribute to him, or maybe as a way to take her mind off her guilt about their argument, she began meticulously walking through the chapters of their life together. It did not occur to her that such obsessing was extending the mourning period, nor that it was taking her away from husband, family and friends still living. Lisa simply decided that Jeff deserved to be remembered, and she was going to do it the way he would have liked – thoroughly and exact.

Her chronicle began with the first encounter with Jeff. It was first day of classes during her freshman year; in fact, it was her very first college lecture. She had already heard the old line about looking to the right and looking to the left and reflecting on the fact that only one of the three would make it to the end. Thus, she thought she heard that coming when Jeff breezed into the lecture hall, faced the students silently for a moment, and then began, "Look to your left and look to your right . . . ." Lisa actually did that, exchanging nervous looks with another eager and obedient woman sitting in the front row. Then he continued, "Now look in front of you, behind you, two seats over, three seats down. Stand up and look all around this lecture hall." He raised his voice "You won't actually see another person who understands genetics and will glean anything from the hours of lectures and study that lay before you. Frankly, it is a waste of my time to prepare for these lectures and stand up here and talk at you, because none of you, not a one, will really get anything out of it."

Lisa laughed – just a nervous titter – but in the stunned silence of the lecture hall it was sufficiently audible to catch Jeff's notice. He looked directly at her. "That includes you, miss. In fact, it's grade-conscious, front-row, copious-note-takers like you who'll be in my office next week begging for my signature on the course drop form. Hell, I'll bring some blank forms to my next lecture."

Lisa wasn't the only one whose jaw dropped open in this first five minutes of college.

That was all the ire Jeff would toss in her direction that day, but it left Lisa completely flabbergasted. She did, in fact, take copious notes, but only because that was a habit she was incapable of breaking. However, somewhat uncharacteristically for her, she divided her attention between the lecture and solving the problem of dropping the course without further humiliation. There was no way she was going to be the victim of a bitter faculty member, regardless of his fame or stature. When the lecture finally wrapped up she packed up her backpack and left quickly so as to avoid any interaction or eye contact with Professor Wolf. Unfortunately, she did make eye contact with a handsome and sporty-looking boy who was standing at the door.

"Bummer that you're going to drop . . . I was hoping to get notes from you," he said with a smirk. It was the second half of the one-two punch begun an hour earlier by the professor, and elicited two split-second decisions on Lisa's part. One, she would never give notes to a lazy fathead like this, no matter how good looking he was. Two, she was not only going to take this course, she was going to ace it.

She did ace it, gaining Jeff Wolf's respect day-by-day and exam-by-exam. He was reticent to show it – not because of his first lecture prediction, but because he believed the only way to make someone excel was by pushing them. Yet he began paying very close attention to her progress after she scored 100% on the first exam. On the second exam he added a very difficult extra credit question specifically to probe the extent of her ability. Then he corrected her test himself, just to make sure there was no "funny business" with the Teaching Assistants. She aced this test as well, despite his critical intentions, and answered the special question correctly. This was the moment Jeff decided Lisa would join his laboratory. Ironically, Lisa wouldn't know this for several months, as the two of them had avoided speaking to each other since the first day. It wasn't until the last lecture that they actually spoke to each other. As usual, Lisa was packing up her backpack to make a quick escape. Jeff came up behind her and spoke before she knew he was there. "I'm not usually wrong about people. You've done better than I expected."

Lisa chuckled to herself, thinking he was speaking to someone else, and then turned to see that he was addressing her. She was both surprised and pleased, but didn't want to show it. "Thank you," she responded politely.

"Perhaps you would be interested in working in my lab," he continued.

"Do you have an opening?" she looked hopeful despite her intention not to.

"Maybe. Let's see how you do on the final exam." This was Jeff's way of stringing her along and keeping the upper hand. Later, when she aced that as well, he was obliged to formalize his offer, and thus their working relationship began.

Lisa fleshed out the details of all her other Jeff memories in similar, exacting detail. She would doze occasionally and then awake and resume precisely where she left off. Surprisingly, she didn't critique or evaluate the events. She never questioned the grip that Jeff had on her psyche through the many years she worked with and for him. And that in itself was very telling.

6

Tom left her alone when he went to work, and otherwise spent most of his time reading in the study or watching television. He was facing his own crisis, but he was doing his best not to think of it. If he came clean with Rogers on the fact that he was not going to have a book finished in the next several months, he may lose his job. If, on the other hand, he pulled together his magnificent notes on the Plantagenet dynasty of France and England during the eleventh and twelfth centuries and quickly wove them into a book, the workload would be miserable. It might also tear apart his marriage, already strained by years of failed attempts to have children, and his bitterness at being in Ithaca because of Lisa's career. Tom chose to hang awkwardly in the middle, fearing both decisions and thus not deciding. He was also increasingly concerned that Lisa's reaction to Jeff's death belied some dark secret. Claire's vehemence when he probed this the other night, led him to put that thought away. But as the days of mourning dragged on, he began fixating on questions and suspicions. Would Lisa so grieve for him? Probably not, he decided. A few tears, and then back to work. Tom's fantasy world of jealousy became a convenient hiding place from real issues.

There was one reality he needed to face with Lisa, however, and that was Jeff's funeral. It was taking place tomorrow, Friday, and he believed they needed to attend, both out of respect for Jeff and his family, and to help Lisa find closure. He wasn't excited at the prospect of standing outside in the rain for an hour for a graveside service, but the sense of obligation prevailed. On Thursday afternoon he broke from some light reading in front of the TV and entered their bedroom. Lisa was awake and reading on the bed. He was surprised to see that she had made the bed and thus realized she was making progress.

"Do you have a minute?" he asked plaintively.

"I seem to have a lot of time." A little sense of humor, even if cynical, was a second good sign.

"I wanted to talk to you about tomorrow. Jeff's funeral takes place at two, and I think we should go." He paused to evaluate her expression. "Are you up to it?"

Lisa looked away and thought for a long time. "I am not sure I can face Mary and the kids." She was referring to Jeff's wife.

Tom was perplexed by this response and responded quickly

and curtly, "What!?"

"I don't think I can face Mary. I don't know what I would say?"

They sat quietly looking at each other. Despite his rampant imaginings over the past few days, it took Tom a minute to weave what Lisa was saying into his suspicions. Once woven, however, he felt a sick feeling in his stomach and a deep feeling of betrayal. He decided it was time to make her lay out the whole story. Fortunately he remained calm and resolute. "I think you should start with the truth. I think we all need to hear the truth and then deal with it as best we can."

Lisa was oblivious to where Tom was leading, still consumed by her own guilt. She was still fixated on the cell phone call and the accident. "What are you saying, a simple, 'Gee, I'm sorry, I hope you won't hold it against me'? Do you think that will suffice?"

"Apologies are a good start." Tom was sinking into deep despair. Their marriage was finished after all. "Other people might deserve them as well."

"Oh, like the department and the students? I can put a poster up in the lobby." Lisa wasn't sarcastic often, but it was still a well-honed skill.

"He was the department chairman, he should have known better himself. You don't carry all the responsibility." Tom was angry and disappointed with Lisa, but he reserved his real hatred for Jeff. Jeff was the one who took advantage of Lisa's admiration and respect.

Lisa was still reflecting on the depth of her guilt and the appropriate breadth of her apology. Suddenly it occurred to her that perhaps there was legal liability for the accident. "I imagine the police have already figured it out, but perhaps I ought to confess there as well."

"Jesus, Lisa, it isn't against the law," Tom scoffed. "I mean, it can be grounds for divorce, but I don't think the police really care about it."

Tom's comment had brought her out of her guilty haze. "Grounds for divorce? What do you mean?"

"Adultery."

"Adultery?!"

"It isn't against the law."

She looked incredulous. "What are you talking about?"

Tom was suddenly confused. What was she talking about? "Your . . . um . . . affair with Jeff." It was a statement, but he said it as a question.

"An affair? My God, are you crazy? I never had an affair with Jeff."

Tom believed Lisa's denial based on the expression of surprise and horror on her face. He was chastened for the second time on this topic. "Well, what are you apologizing to everybody for?"

"For calling Jeff on his cell when he was driving and then yelling at him and hanging up on him. It was my fault he crashed!"

Tom finally understood Lisa's depression and mourning. None of the reports of the accident had mentioned a cell phone (most likely because it was smashed into a hundred pieces and swept up in the wreckage), nor had the connection been made or reported by the students in Lisa's lab. With this piece of information everything fell into place. "Oh," was all he could manage.

She continued, "Aren't the Police going to care about that? Aren't Mary and the kids going to blame me? Why in God's name do you think that I have been so devastated by this thing? And you thought I was having an affair with him?"

Tom thought it would be better to focus on the phone-blame topic than the affair topic. "Honey, you don't bear any blame for the accident. Jeff was a big boy. He didn't need to answer the phone in the car. Or he could have just answered and said that he would call you back. You weren't talking when the crash occurred, right? So you don't know how much time passed." He could tell that she was thinking about what he said. "You can't blame yourself. And it would be crazy to say anything to Mary. She doesn't need to hear any details of the accident."

"You don't think I need to tell anyone?" She was almost convinced.

"No. No question in my mind."

"I still think it was my fault."

Tom seized the moment to cross the room and give Lisa a hug. They held each other for a long time, and then Tom pulled away. "Let me make you a bowl of soup and a sandwich and maybe a glass of wine. I am so sorry about this whole thing."

"Thanks," she smiled and continued, "and yes, please, to all but the wine."

The rain continued through Thursday night and by early morning a stiff wind whipped up and blew the last, most tenacious leaves from the trees. This caused a somewhat bizarre scene as the funeral procession wound its way through the hilly cemetery. Despite the perilous footing on wet leaves and slick pavement, many of the female mourners had worn high heels and were now slipping and sliding on their way to the graveside service. After the second person actually fell down, everyone had become more careful, men were helping their companions and the large group slowed to a mincing snail's pace. Lisa was not part of the high-heel set, yet she held Tom tightly nonetheless. At Tom's insistence – and logic – she had decided not to say anything about the cell phone call. But this decision was essentially moot, as the driving rain conspired with the mood to discourage any conversation. Most of the hundred or so attendees hunkered under their umbrellas and only nodded to others they recognized. Lisa and Mary acknowledged each other in this way, refiring Lisa's pangs of guilt and urge to take blame.

Only Megan Brack, standing next to Lisa as the group

encircled the grave, tried to engage them in conversation. "Hello, Lisa. I am so very sorry for you." She had tears in her eyes and looked ready to cry again.

Lisa smiled acknowledgement, but Tom was annoyed. He motioned over toward Mary. "Jeff's widow is over there." This was pointed and awkward and fortunately the service began just then.

For both Lisa and Tom the service seemed to last forever, but for very different reasons. Tom braced himself against the cold wind and driving rain, and tried not to sink into the soggy ground. His arm ached from holding up the umbrella, exacerbated by the weight Lisa was adding by hanging on so tight. However, the physical circumstances were simply irritating. What he found really tedious, and frankly, pointless, were the lengthy prayers for God's intercession. Jeff had considered himself God, so in his world there was really nothing left to be done. *Drop the box and fill the hole*, Tom yearned to call out. He wondered how many other people were there out of sheer obligation and scanned the crowd for signs of the cynicism and detachment he felt. When he didn't see it, he concluded that they were all under the same powerful grip that held Lisa. Out of respect and sensitivity, especially for Lisa, he behaved himself and acted appropriately touched.

Tom's mind wandered from the funeral to his crisis at work. Earlier in the week he had overcome the urge to whine about how unjust it was for him to take the fall for his incompetent boss. Now, he was considering the simple reality that he needed to either give up immediately, or beat the odds and get this book done. There was really no choice to be made. He couldn't bear the thought of being asked to leave, particularly since Lisa would never leave Cornell and he would become jobless, the ultimate humiliation. Speculating on this contingency the day before, he checked for openings at colleges nearby, but unfortunately, nothing was listed. Tom realized he was simply going to have to climb out of this pit. As the first handfuls of dirt were cast upon the casket, Tom resolved that he was going to get this book done. *Teach all the classes and whip out a manuscript* – he was going to perform a miracle.

For Lisa, each prayer and rite was one painful step closer to burying the man who had made her what she was. He was her teacher, her mentor and her friend, yet they had parted on the angriest words that ever passed between them. And that parting had brought on his death. There was nothing so bitter to her as the forgiveness which would never be granted. As the tears flowed down her cheeks she desperately wanted to hear Jeff's voice saying, "I forgive you."

7

As if to match the dull monotony of the continued dreary weather, Tom and Lisa fell into a robotic routine in the weeks following the funeral. They would rise and eat breakfast together, exchange a few logistical details of their day ahead, then head off in different cars only to park a short distance from each other and slosh through puddles to their respective offices. In the evenings they would return home at about the same time, prepare dinner together and then retreat to separate parts of the house to work, read or watch television. They weren't gloomy or unfriendly in their interaction; on the contrary, they were pleasant and polite. Yet they avoided any substantive discussion. Their life took on a matte gray finish, devoid of sunlight and absent obvious emotion or intimacy.

Lisa had said nothing to Tom of the successful experiment, which in her mind, led to tragedy. Further, she'd done nothing with it, neither replicating the experiments themselves nor even beginning to map out the logical next steps. Instead, she busied herself with administrative work in the lab, preparing outlines for next semester's new course and consulting with her students. Megan had begun dropping by for lunch and they would chat quietly in Lisa's office, gossiping harmlessly about different grad students or events on campus. Oddly, her decision not to pursue the Ewe Factor breakthrough was not really a decision at all. She wasn't contemplating and rejecting the work because of the pain it caused. Rather, the pain itself kept the ideas from even forming in her head. She was in a sort of trance, but nobody around her acknowledged, let alone recognized it.

The weekends were equally bland. She attempted to garden in the backyard, only to be chased back inside by rain squalls. She and Tom considered going to the football games, but the much-hyped team had lost three straight and didn't appear poised to buck the trend. By late-September, everyone was already looking forward to the hockey season.

Tom communicated no better than Lisa, but this was by conscious design. He was being used by the department chair, Rogers, to deflect pressure from his inadequate administration. But Tom saw the opportunity, if successful, to be a hero. Not only would he have taught more classes than anyone else, but he would deliver a new publication to rescue a troubled department. And with the material he had been researching over the past years, he had enough to deliver several more publications. His work could propel himself and the university to the forefront of medieval history studies. Tom could finally climb out of Rogers' dungeon. It wasn't even too much of a leap to see himself being awarded Department leadership. And then, despite Rogers' tenure, he would figure out a way to fire the bastard.

Best of all, however, would be his emergence from Lisa's shadow. No more receptions with the University President warmly greeting Lisa and then needing to be reminded of Tom's name and role. No more reading Cornell Chronicle or Daily Sun articles about his wife's work and finding his name in the last paragraph – the "gee whiz", what-a-coincidence, he-works-here-too, honorable mention. This was his chance to break out. And this was the reason he didn't say anything to Lisa. If he told her of his crisis and solution, she would participate in making him successful. He would be obliged to give her credit and within days there would be another article profiling this amazing woman who, in addition to being a brilliant scientist, found time to help her struggling husband. The spotlight on her would shine even brighter, and the shadows, while no darker than before, would seem so for the contrast. This was going to be his triumph, and his alone. It would be a silent quest with a surprise ending for everyone, except him.

By the end of the second week after his confrontation with Rogers, he was getting into a productive rhythm like none he had ever experienced. During the morning commute he would plan each step of the day ahead, and then he would execute them with precision. Reading and answering email, preparing and delivering lectures – Tom completed every task as planned and wasted no time contemplating what to do next. While Lisa was reaching out to others around the office and making time to chat, Tom had withdrawn from most social contact. He curtailed all his coffee breaks and lunches out. Instead, he stayed hunched over his keyboard or organizing the piles of notes and texts from which he was drawing material. Even going to the bathroom or getting water for his coffee maker was preplanned and efficient. Tom started to admire himself for this new level of productivity and started muttering, "I'm a machine," as he moved about his office.

Office hours were a bit tricky. They could burn up a lot of time as students rambled in and made idle conversation. Furthermore, because he was teaching three lectures, he was obliged to offer an expanded schedule. Thankfully, students didn't come in much early in the semester. The serious students weren't yet stumped, and the lazy ones not yet sufficiently panicked. The rush usually happened around Thanksgiving. Regardless, Tom didn't want to chance losing the time, so he left his door just barely ajar, hoping to deter all but the most determined from coming in. He also took down the card which showed his hours. He knew very few students would retrace their steps to the departmental office to check his schedule and then come back.

Tom was in full stride one Friday afternoon during what should have student time, typing busily at his computer, when he heard someone outside his door. He really didn't want to stop at this point, particularly as Lisa would want him to relax with her that weekend and get away from work. He was making serious headway, already five pages since lunch and enjoying the rush of being on a roll. He paused from typing and looked up, trying desperately to think of some way to put off the hopeful student. Should he pretend he was talking to someone, maybe on the telephone? Too late, there was a knock at the door and it began to swing open. Tom tried to mask the scowl on his face. Who would come on a Friday afternoon – weren't they all partying by now?

"Hello, Tom." It was William Rogers, hauling his massive bulk through the doorway.

"Hello, William." Tom could tell the scowl was back.

"Aren't these supposed to be your office hours?" Rogers knew perfectly well that they were, Tom had had these same hours for seven years.

"Yes. That's why I am here." He knew he was about to get the door-should-remain-open lecture. He needed to deflect it. "I have been on those maintenance people to come fix that door for some time. It keeps swinging closed. Do you have any luck with them?" *That will confuse you, you simpleminded fool*, Tom thought. "I guess I should just find a doorstop."

William's diatribe was indeed checked. He needed to come up with something else, but he wasn't very fast. "Um . . . I guess I haven't had any problems to call them for."

Tom smiled, enjoying the fact that he had so easily knocked Rogers off his game. "Well, do you think you could pull any strings for one of the hardest working members of the department?" He had almost said "weight" instead of "strings" but it was too early to escalate this certain confrontation.

"I guess I could make a call or two." Rogers was flattered by the acknowledgement of his position. "But that isn't why I stopped by." This came as no surprise. "I wanted to check in with you on the progress of the book. You know, see if you need someone to help proofread the manuscript." Rogers then paused and looked thoughtful. "Come to think of it, I don't even know what your book is about."

Tom needed to head off too much enquiry until he could get a lot more finished. "Well, things are going fine. I have it out for review – with old colleagues, one at Yale and one at SUNY Buffalo. Yeah, it's going great." Tom nodded and smiled to reinforce his lie. "But thanks for asking . . . and offering."

"Oh, it's done already then? I had the impression you were plugging away at it right now. And you know, nobody has seen you around much."

"Well, I never really stop adding touches here and there. Lisa always tells me I'm something of a perfectionist. Plus, teaching three classes and finalizing a manuscript keeps one pretty busy." Rogers sat down in the chair by Tom's desk, which didn't please Tom at all. He did take a little solace in the fact that this spindly, Victorian chair from his grandmother's estate might explode under Rogers' weight. However, that Rogers was making himself comfortable suggested a long discussion, which might in turn lead to Rogers discovering that the manuscript was far from complete. Tom absolutely had to mask the truth. Rogers would shut everything down now and sacrifice Tom if he knew the book was only twenty percent finished. "I didn't realize I never told you the subject, since it seems we talked about it so much. It's a biography of Henry the Second. I would say 'of England' but that is sort of the point, the migration of the Plantagenet rule from what is now France to solely England. Well, you know all this." Tom was confident Rogers knew very little about it.

"I am a bit fuzzy on that period," Rogers puffed. "Do you think this is a very current subject?"

"How do you mean 'current'?"

"Well, would there be popular or academic pick-up? Who's interested in this period right now?"

Tom was trying not to be insulted since he was, in fact, a professor of medieval history. He paused to check his anger and reflected on his response. "I think that anyone who appreciates the impact that these kings and royal families had on culture and countries, the languages we speak and the traditions we follow, how we pray, how we work . . ." He stopped to size up his effect on his boss. *Should I go on or should I stop there?* Tom couldn't resist the urge to become a little more sarcastic. "Frankly, anybody who gives a rat's ass about European history, and by extension American history would probably consider this fairly important. I guess maybe I am writing it for real historians, if there are any left." Tom decided he should probably stop there. He smiled at Rogers.

"When could I peek at the manuscript?"

"Why?"

Petty tyrant that he was, Rogers hated being challenged. "Because I would like to see it. I am a real historian."

Tom wanted to burst out laughing. The retort, "You're a fool!" almost popped out of his mouth. He knew he was cornered and should now stall. "Perhaps I can print out a copy for you next week. You know I'm really pretty stretched these days."

Rogers enjoyed having the upper hand. "You could email it to me if that would be easier."

"I'd prefer not to have different versions kicking around electronically as I'm making changes. I'll print it. That's no problem." He looked at his watch and pursed his lips. It was time to get rid of Rogers. "Jesus, I didn't realize it was so late. I need to go pick up Lisa." He stood up from his desk.

"Oh, yes, I meant to –" Rogers took a breath, gathered his

strength and rose from the chair. "I meant to ask how Lisa was managing after Jeff Wolf's death."

Tom turned away and rolled his eyes. "She's doing fine. She got right back into her work pretty quickly." He started packing up his briefcase without looking at Rogers. "Christ, I'm in trouble if I don't get out of here."

Rogers began shuffling toward the door and turned back just as he was going through. "By the way, who do you know at Buffalo? I have an old friend there who runs the History department."

"Bob Gardy – we went to grad school together." Tom made a mental note to call Bob over the weekend and make sure he didn't blow Tom's story. He wondered whether William Rogers' friend was any more competent as a department chairman. He hoped so, for Bob's sake.

"Oh. Well, enjoy the weekend." Rogers waddled down the hall.

Tom didn't respond. Instead he was calculating how long it might take him to get the book done on the current pace. He could do it, he reckoned, by the end of November or maybe mid-December. Eight to ten weeks should be enough to get out a defensible quantity of work. But he had to keep Rogers off his case, and he needed to steel himself for an exhausting grind. It was worth it, he told himself – this was going to be the greatest achievement of his life. Tom stopped packing up his briefcase as soon as he could tell that Rogers was safely out of range. Lisa wasn't expecting him, of course. That was all pretense. Tom had no idea what her plans were, nor even where she was. He sat down at his desk and scanned the text he had been writing on his computer screen. Within seconds he was lost in the twelfth century. "I'm a machine," he muttered as his fingers began striking the keys.

8

Friday afternoon was equally quiet at Lisa's end of campus. Most of the students and faculty had wrapped up their work for the week and were either talking about weekend plans or actually putting them in motion. Lisa had spent the last couple of hours reviewing her students' experiments or work plans and was daydreaming at her desk when Megan Brack came in. Unlike every other day that week, Lisa and Megan had not eaten lunch together, so Lisa was happy to see her before the weekend. "I missed you today," she said with a smile.

"Sorry." Megan looked sheepish and shrugged. "I had some social . . . issues."

"Anything you want to talk about?"

Megan shook her head and looked down at a science journal perched on the edge of Lisa's desk. "Not really." She flipped open the cover and skimmed down through the Table of Contents.

Okay, thought Lisa, no need to pry. "Got any plans for the weekend? Going to the football game tomorrow?" She was just trying to get the conversation started.

Without taking her eyes off the journal, Megan answered distractedly, "Umm, no." She concentrated momentarily on the journal and then finished, "I think I'll probably just work."

"You've got to take a break every once in a while. You seem to work harder than anybody else around here. It's great to be devoted, but don't burn yourself out."

Megan looked up from the magazine. "I love the work. I'm not going to burn out, I can assure you."

"Are you dating anyone?" Suddenly Lisa realized that she was getting into more personal ground than she had ever tread with Megan and wanted to give an out to the young post-doc. "I know this isn't any of my business."

Megan shrugged. "It's ok, I don't mind. No, I'm not really interested in anybody. But hey, I'm not anti-social or dull. I like to hang out and party, with guys as well. I just don't want to date them. Maybe I am just married to the science."

"There's not a lot of emotion in science – by definition. Be careful being married to something that doesn't give back very much." Lisa meant this as a warning, but reflected on how it hit so close to home.

Megan reached a broader conclusion at the same instant. "You could say that to a lot of people. At least I won't be let down, or even worse betrayed, by my spouse." She wanted to change the subject, as this was too personal and embarrassing for her. "Lisa, you haven't talked about your work for so long. Nothing since we met that morning in the hall and you were so excited about a breakthrough. You know, scraping skin and genocide, remember that? What's the latest?" Megan was pleased with herself for this professional deflection. She gave Lisa a moment to respond and again began scanning the cover of the scientific journal on the desk.

Lisa's response took much longer than she expected, and when she looked up, prepared to repeat the question, Megan was baffled by her friend's reaction. Lisa was staring down at her hand, apparently studying her fingernails, eyes brimming with tears and lips pursed as if ready to cry. Completely disarmed by this, Megan simply stared at her friend. The silence filling the space between them was becoming increasing uncomfortable and Megan desperately tried imagine what nerve she must have struck with the question. "Did I say something wrong?" she asked tenderly. She reached out and put a hand on Lisa's knee.

Lisa shook her head, eyes still fixed on her hand. She opened her mouth as if she was beginning to answer, but then stopped. The silence began expanding once again. Megan tried once more, "I . . . I'm sorry if I said the wrong thing. I was just . . . trying to change the subject. We don't have to talk about work."

Lisa looked Megan in the eyes and gave the first hint of a smile. She deeply admired this sensitive and mature young woman, but she wasn't quite ready to open up. Gathering herself, she said, "The experiment succeeded in every respect. We were able to reconstitute completely desiccated cells and start a cell line of undifferentiated pluripotent cells."

Megan was perplexed. Had she heard this correctly? This was a stunning advance, but Lisa was acting as if it were the opposite. That contradiction left Megan's brow furrowed and mouth hanging open at the same time as she tried to figure out what was going on. She could muster no words. Lisa was not oblivious to her confusion and went on, "I know it should have been the breakthrough of the century. Really, it is everything I've been working toward."

Megan regained some composure; although her heart was pounding so loud she could hear it in her ears. "Lisa, it's a Nobel Prize! I don't understand why you're talking about it like it's a bad thing."

"I haven't told you the whole story." Lisa resolved to put this tragedy behind her, but not before she confessed to one more person. She gauged Megan's nervously expectant expression and wondered how she would react. "I would like this to stay between us. Tom's the only other one who knows."

Megan couldn't imagine where this story was going, but her curiosity was overpowering. She would agree to anything just to hear more. "Trust me, my lips are sealed."

"Just after I confirmed the cells viability I called Jeff to tell him the news. I was so excited, I tracked him down on his new iPhone – he was driving downtown. Well, he said something – I don't even remember what it was – that irritated me and I just, sort of, wigged out. I told him off and hung up on him." Lisa paused to figure out how to describe the final event. "I think the distraction of the call and our argument took his mind off the road. That's when he ran the red light and was hit." She looked down and shook her head, "I wish I could take back that call, those words . . . those stupid words. He's dead because of that call."

"Oh Lisa, I am so sorry." She put her hand on Lisa's and gave it a gentle squeeze. "I understand why you feel bad about this, but you have to accept what happened. You called him to celebrate a wonderful and exciting event, and I am sure that if you lost your temper, it was reasonable. Look, as much as we all idolized Jeff, he could be really difficult." Megan leaned in close to regain eye contact and make sure her next point was understood. "You can't blame yourself for this. You have to let it go."

Lisa studied Megan's earnest expression and knew she was right. Lisa nodded in assent. "You're right. I need to move on." A huge weight was lifted from her shoulders, and she wondered why this hadn't occurred to her without Megan's assurance.

Megan couldn't contain her desire to discuss the science, despite the painful memories it conjured up for Lisa. "Lisa, forgive me for asking this – and we don't have to talk about it now – but I would really like to work on this project. Would you take me in your lab?"

"You've been in the Pratt lab for more than a year. Do you want to throw that all away?"

There was no hesitation. "I can't bear the thought of not being able to work on this project. I'm tired of working for Nick and the grant is running out. He's fine, but he isn't you. You're . . . you're advancing science and I really want to be a part of it. Is there any way that you would take me?" As Lisa paused to answer, Megan clasped her hands together, partially facetious and partially serious, to underscore her request. "Please?"

Lisa would indeed be thrilled to have Megan join her lab. None of her own students were so devoted to their work, so eager for pure scientific enquiry. Megan was brilliant, hardworking – she reminded Lisa of herself ten years earlier. There was no question that the work would advance faster with Megan by her side. Her only reticence came from the idea of poaching her from Nick Pratt, a good friend and long-time colleague. "I will think about it. I need to talk to Nick."

"He's still in the lab if you want to call him. Extension 8854. Or maybe it'd be better if you discuss it face to face." Megan smelled success.

"Let me think about it over the weekend," Lisa replied. She could tell Megan was not about to abandon her efforts, so she relented further. "Okay you're in – but I'm going to put off talking to him 'til Monday."

Megan jumped up from her chair and gave Lisa a hug. "Thanks so much," she gushed, "thanks so much, Lisa! This is so exciting! Can I read the protocols over the weekend, or look at your lab books?" She was clasping her hands together again, but subconsciously this time. "You don't have to share the prize money with me. Just let me be one of the authors."

"Prize money?! Whoa, slow down. Let's just see if we can repeat it. We'll worry about prizes later." Lisa already knew that Megan was going to energize her moribund team and make things happen. Hiring her was the best decision she had made in the past year. "Go have some fun, we'll roll up our sleeves on Monday."

Megan wanted to make one more try to get things going now, a little more subtly. "Are you going to be in the lab this weekend?"

Lisa considered the question for a moment. She hadn't planned to work, just as she hadn't during any of the last few weekends, but Megan's enthusiasm was nearly irresistible. On the verge of giving in, Lisa caught sight of a picture of Tom on her desk. She had neglected her marriage as much as her work and she needed to fix the home front first. "No, I think Tom and I are going to spend some time together this weekend."

9

The weekend did not measure up to Lisa's hastily-formed expectations, but it was close. After politely rebuffing Megan's increasingly feeble attempts to begin working on the Ewe Factor project over the weekend, Lisa rushed to her car and made a bee-line for the grocery store. If Tom's timing was anything like normal, he wouldn't get home until about 7 pm, and thus there was a good chance of surprising him with a steak and mashed potato dinner, a favorite for both of them. Once at the grocery store, she made her purchases with an efficiency Tom ("The Machine") would admire and even chose the fastest check-out lane, a true rarity. The driveway was empty when she arrived home – still a chance to surprise him, Lisa thought as she unpacked groceries, fired up the grill and started peeling potatoes.

In the midst of these chores, however, she gave in to a bottle of wine beckoning from the back of the refrigerator, and one glass later she had summoned up the courage to select a bottle from their modest "wine cellar" in the basement. This was exclusively Tom's domain, so it took Lisa a few minutes to navigate to the reds, then the Bordeaux. From there she had to depend on intuition, as the names meant little, so she chose based on label graphics – not the nicest, but not the worst. She crossed her fingers that it was good, but not too good. Coming back upstairs, she placed the bottle on the dinner table, and was about to resume other tasks when she realized that her decisiveness would only matter if Tom could not slip downstairs and replace her choice with something else. "It has to breathe," she said aloud and grabbed the corkscrew to finalize *her* selection. She almost decanted it, but not only was that going too far, she wasn't quite sure how to do it.

At 7:30, a full hour after she had rushed home, and no sign of Tom, Lisa began having visions of being the forlorn, stood-up woman eating alone by candlelight. Her enthusiasm was waning and her hunger waxing (despite a few discreet nibbles from the mashed potatoes) when his car finally pulled into the driveway. Lisa tried to act nonchalant as he made his way inside, but when his eyes widened at the nicely set table and delicious aroma, she broke out in a big grin. "Welcome home! Are you hungry?"

He *was* hungry, and he was relieved she wasn't cross about his tardiness. "Absolutely. Sorry I'm running so late . . . office hours were so busy I couldn't get . . . ." The bottle on the table caught his attention. "Oh good, the Clos Rene – I was thinking we'd better drink this before it went bad." He picked the bottle up and scrutinized the label, mostly as diversion from discussing why he was so late. "Let's decant this." He stepped to the cupboard to find the decanter.

Lisa wasn't sure whether to be proud or disappointed for her wine selection, but either way she did not want to discuss his afternoon; she wanted to eat. "The grill's ready, I'll put the steaks on," she said as she slipped out to the back patio.

They spoke little while initially tucking into the hearty meal. Lisa was a very good cook despite not cooking very often, so the food, wine and candlelight became a perfect complement to a successful day for both of them. Both relaxed visibly as they cleaned their plates and contemplated seconds. Lisa decided to pass, but Tom was helpless to the temptation of another helping of potatoes. As he gave in, she took the opportunity to start and guide the discussion. "I think it is time I got back up on the horse."

"Pardon?"

"I need to get my work going again. Do you remember that day I called you in your office raving about a huge breakthrough? It was the day Jeff died." Tom nodded. "Well, I haven't touched it since then. Not a single experiment. Haven't you noticed that we haven't talked about it for the last several weeks?"

This had all the makings of marriage minefield – *Have you noticed the big change? Aren't you interested in what I have been doing?* Tom picked up his wine glass, swirled it and studied the rivulets running down the inside of the bowl. He'd been far too busy with own crisis to pay attention to what she was doing. And now that she'd mentioned it, it was surprising that she hadn't been raving about her work and talking him through some intricate laboratory protocol. The truth was, he hadn't noticed but now that she mentioned it, he realized that something had been out of order. He only had to fib a little. "Yeah, I noticed that you were acting a little different. I just thought you needed some time to yourself."

"I was acting *a lot* different. I'm sorry. Thanks for giving me some time. I'm afraid I've been thinking more about myself than I should've been." Tom relaxed, realizing he was out of danger and that he had actually made some points. He savored a taste of wine and invited her to continue. "Jeff's death devastated me – you know that already. It should have been our greatest moment. *My* moment really, but everything he had guided me toward since he first took me in his lab and started pushing me. I was so excited about the experiment, and I was trying to share the news – first with you, but you were in a meeting, and then with Jeff. I hunted around the lab for him and then got his cellphone number – and called him. He was in one of his moods. The traffic and construction, I guess – you know, when they dug up State Street?" She didn't pause for him to answer. "So something he said, I can't even remember what, just got me and I snapped and hung up on him.

"I haven't touched the work since then. Three weeks now and I haven't done a thing. I'm not even sure that I've thought about it. But just this afternoon, that post-doc Megan Brack came by and we started talking about it, and suddenly I can't pick it up fast enough. I want to take the weekend off – for us – because I know I have abandoned you for the past few weeks, too." She reached out and touched his hand. "But come Monday, I'm going to hit the ground running. That gives us two days to get back in touch with each other." She traced a finger lazily over the back of his hand, and tried to catch his eye. Tom was staring into the candle flame, the reflection of which was dancing across his eyes. He was thinking hard how to free her for the weekend so that he could keep working.

"Didn't Claire say you weren't in the right . . . phase . . . just now?"

"Yeah, but this isn't about conceiving. This is about us."

Tom knew there was no evading Lisa's plans, but decided it was worth one more try. "Honey, don't worry about me." He smiled and flipped his hand over to hold hers. "If you want to get cracking this weekend, that's fine. You could work during the day and then we can go out at night. You know, somewhere nice for dinner. What's that place we went with Bob and Claire?"

"Friary Manor – well, we can go there, for sure. But I don't want to work tomorrow. I already told Megan I wouldn't start 'til Monday. Can't we spend the day together?"

"Of course." Maybe he needed a break after all, he thought. "What did you say about Megan?"

"She wants to join my lab. She was quite insistent that I rescue her from the Pratt lab. Well, those are my words, but I knew she wanted a change, and frankly I could really use her help. Nick Pratt can handle losing her, given all the grad students he has. She's so much like I was at that time – so into the science. She lives for it, for God's sake."

Tom had mixed feelings about Megan. Sure, she was bright, but a little too intense for his liking. Tom never remembered Lisa being quite so manic. "So what do you want to do tomorrow?"

"Let's decide after we get up late." She filled both wine glasses, draining every last drop from the bottle. "Come on, time for bed." Lisa stood up, tottering only slightly from the wine she had already drunk.

"Shouldn't we clean up first? Put away the leftovers?" Tom was not usually the conscientious one at clean-up time. In fact, he generally needed a little push from his very tidy spouse.

"I think it can wait. Come on." She picked up both wine glasses and headed down the hall.

Tom and Lisa awakened earlier than planned on Saturday morning as the sun's rays, undiffused by clouds for the first time in weeks, streamed through their bedroom window. The still-messy kitchen became a convenient excuse for going out for breakfast and by mid-morning they found themselves window shopping in downtown Ithaca and waiting for the stores to open. They still hadn't made any real plans for the day – they were simply enjoying each other's company. Holding hands as they walked, they reminisced about the old stores that used to be in each location. So few, perhaps none, were left over from their days as undergrads.

The morning melted away in a leisurely and comfortable way. Lisa and Tom returned home at mid-day and puttered around the yard, raking and tidying their flower beds. They skipped lunch, both as a result of a big breakfast and in preparation for a bigger dinner, and took a nap in the late afternoon before cleaning up and dressing for dinner. Their evening out, particularly the meal, was splendid and despite having very little room to consume anything else, they came home to glasses of port and chocolates.

The wine, the food and the late night all conspired to make a groggy Sunday morning. The two professors slept late in spite of the a second bright sunrise. As they snuggled close, trying to fight off the urge to get up and be productive, Lisa spoke the first words. "Should we go to church today?"

"Church?! We haven't gone to church in years." Tom desperately wanted to stay in bed longer.

"Exactly. Maybe we should go. It's been too long. Come on." She nudged him and started pulling away the covers.

"I'll do anything if you let me sleep in." He rolled to hold the bedclothes and continued, "I'll cook breakfast and make the bed. I'll even take you out to dinner again." He was sure he had her.

She slipped her hand inside his pajama bottoms. "I'll do anything for us to go." His resistance, both to her and to church, melted in an instant. Slowly and elegantly and for the first time in years, they made love in the daylight. Even with Lisa keeping one eye on the clock to make sure they could still make the service, they reveled in the physical joy of each other. When they were done, Lisa snuggled up close and whispered, "I think maybe it worked that time."

Tom knew better than to cloud the moment with a more practical response. Instead, he held her close for a few minutes and nuzzled her temple. The thought crossed his mind to suggest skipping church, but he decided this morning belonged to her. He was truly enjoying spending time with her again, and despite worrying about getting back to his work, wanted this weekend to continue. Before long they climbed out of bed, into the shower, dressed and were off to church.

"It's a lot like riding a bicycle," Tom thought as he went through the motions of standing, sitting, kneeling and reciting the liturgy – not missing a beat even though he hadn't done it for years. His parents were avid church goers and he accompanied them every Sunday for his first eighteen years. He wanted to make these observations to Lisa during short breaks in the service, but she was very focused on the prayers and did not invite conversation. His mind yearned to wander, but readings and responses kept dragging him back. The Gospel, "Therefore keep watch . . . ." he took as specifically directed at him.

As the service drew on, Tom began noticing how much Lisa seemed to be concentrating on the prayers and saying "Amen" louder than everyone else. As they came back to their pew from Communion, Lisa knelt and prayed rather than watching all the other communicants advance and retreat from the altar. He could only conclude that she was trying to make up for their years of absence, and at the risk of being snide, wanted to commend her for it at the end of the service.

As the service closed and the altar candles were being

extinguished, she turned to him and took his hands. Tom put aside thoughts of making a smart comment. "I was praying for a baby. We have tried everything else. I don't know why we haven't tried praying." She was too sincere for Tom to be cynical. He smiled in response and squeezed her hands.

"Good idea," he responded. "God has made babies happen in much more complicated situations." They rose and departed from the church, avoiding the pastor by leaving through the side door, and drove off home.

Tom was just fantasizing how he could escape for the rest of the day back to the office when Lisa unveiled their next agenda item. "Let's picnic in the Plantations gardens." She paused with an expectant smile on her face and waited for Tom to respond similarly.

Eager to avoid eye contact, he concentrated on the road. "I've eaten enough this weekend for the rest of the month."

"Well, then, let's take a walk to work it off. It's beautiful there, even though the leaves are all gone. Come on, it's been such a great weekend and we still have the afternoon." Lisa still had the hopeful, happy look on her face that made refusal impossible. In a matter of minutes, Tom was parking the car in the botanical garden parking lot and they were strolling down the paths.

Lisa orchestrated the rest of their afternoon in a similar fashion. Their walk morphed into working in the back yard and then dinner out and then renting a movie. The first time Tom had any free choice occurred as he selected his pajamas. Frankly he had enjoyed the weekend and the chance for romance and reconnection. On the other hand he dreaded the fact that he was now even further behind his writing schedule. He drifted off to sleep while planning how many more pages per day he needed to write in the week ahead.

10

Come Monday morning there was no lingering in bed for either Professor Duffield. Lisa was rejuvenated and energized and anxious to progress the work which would transform biology and genetics. She had lost weeks since Jeff's death and couldn't make it up fast enough. Tom was anxious also, as well as panicked and desperate. He had lost two days of writing – and while his work would not transform the study of history, it would save his career. In great contrast to the previous two days, they parted with a perfunctory kiss.

Arriving at the lab that morning, Lisa was amazed to find – for the first time in years – that she was not the first to arrive. Out of sheer habit, she inserted her key in the door and then felt a sinking feeling in her stomach as she realized that it was not locked. She searched her mind for who might have left it unlocked, and rather than going in immediately she stood contemplating what might be stolen or vandalized. Gathering courage, she pushed the door open, ready to face almost anything.

"Morning!" Megan smiled at her from one of the benches where she was hunched over one of Lisa's lab notebooks. "I kept my promise not to work over the weekend . . . other than borrowing the key from Kristina yesterday so I could get an early start today. And I hope that you don't mind me digging around to find your lab books. This work is amazing! Do you know that? I mean, do you actually understand what this means? You can clone anything. Living or dead. Frankly, I can't really believe it works. I see the results here. And by the way, your lab records are impeccable. I hope you don't think it presumptuous of me to say so. But this is just . . . awesome. We have to repeat this last experiment before we do anything else." Megan jumped up from her stool and walked over to Lisa who was still holding her briefcase in one hand and keys in the other. "I have some questions here, in the Extraction protocol, where you precipitate the sample." She held the book up to Lisa and pointed to the pertinent section. Megan stopped talking and took a deep breath.

Lisa's mind was racing as she considered one of many

responses. "Have you had a lot of coffee this morning?"

"No. Do you want to get some coffee?"

"I do, but it doesn't seem like you need any." She grinned.

Megan did not catch the gentle dig. "Um, I guess not. Maybe a muffin or something. I didn't eat breakfast this morning."

"Come on, I'll buy." Lisa dropped her briefcase in her office and ushered Megan out of the lab and down the hall.

Megan picked up speaking at her previous pace. "Do you know much about the Korean protocol? I saw the paper in *Gene*, but I didn't read it very closely. I think there are probably some techniques you could borrow to make it your procedure a little more efficient. If you don't mind my saying so, I think we need to go faster."

Except for the last of the overnight janitorial staff piling bags of garbage at the rear service entrance, McGraw Hall was essentially empty as Tom entered. He was pleased to be getting an early start and after quickly setting up his coffee maker, he settled down to a cluttered desk, booted up the computer, and recentered himself on the twelfth century. Now forty to fifty pages behind his target pace, he needed to make meaningful progress before halting around noon to prepare for an afternoon lecture.

It wasn't hard for him to pick up the thread of Friday's thinking. He knew the characters better than he knew his next door neighbors. Henry Plantagenet – Henry the Second – was impetuous and irascible, a personality to match his bright red hair. Either by fate or personal magnetism he had become close to two of the most powerful personalities of that time, Thomas Becket and Eleanor of Aquitaine, befriending the former and marrying the latter. Unfortunately, just as magnets can attract, they can repel with equal force. In a medieval version of, "This town isn't big enough for the three of us," Henry had Thomas murdered and Eleanor imprisoned. By the 1170's he ruled over a vast empire, stretching from what today is central France and across Great Britain up to Scotland and over to Wales. He spent the last twenty years of his life alternately warring and making peace with his equally impetuous sons. Only his son Richard – Richard the Lionheart – proved Henry's equal; in time Richard was able to bring his old father down. Tom would have loved to meet these powerful and adventurous people. What would they have been like, Tom wondered, had they lived in the twentieth century? Would they be rising to the top of some political party, or directing some multinational corporation? Would they be stuck fighting for tenure in a university History department?

Tom made fast progress that morning, and actually kept writing until fifteen minutes before class. He would have gone longer if he had not needed to cross the Arts Quad to give his lecture in Goldwin Smith Hall. Twenty more pages under his belt. He feared the editing job ahead, but better to have it all down on paper. He used the backstairs to exit, sure to avoid Rogers, who was more likely to remain near the elevator. Tom could not risk running into his boss and having to tap-dance around the truth. It occurred to him that he should have a good new excuse ready for the next and inevitable confrontation. Instead, he fantasized about meeting Rogers on the stairs, pushing him backwards and enjoying watching him rolling ass-over-tea-kettle to the bottom. The sadistic joy of that thought powered him through one of his most inspiring lectures of the semester.

Both Professors Duffield made fantastic progress during the week that followed. Tom resumed his machine-like efficiency, writing whenever he wasn't lecturing and successfully avoiding William Rogers. He was closing in on his goal, and at this pace could imagine finishing in two more weeks. Lisa was amazed at the power of Megan's energy. Not only had their collaboration advanced the pace of duplicating the landmark procedure, but together they had made improvements to the protocol. Megan had spotted several techniques to replace with new and robust methods. Lisa now knew why earlier attempts had failed, and recognized that Megan's genius, combined with her own, represented guaranteed success. She reorganized other students in the lab to start work on portions of the protocol – synthesize more Ewe Factor, and extract and reconstitute desiccated DNA. Even after taking several hours off on Tuesday for an appointment with her doctor and friend, Claire, she and her team had done far more work in four days than she had imagined possible over a month.

By Friday morning Lisa realized that while she didn't have results from this round of work, she needed to discuss it with Wolf's replacement, the Interim Department Chairman. Were this experiment to succeed, they were sitting on one of the biggest news events of the decade, and the University needed to be prepared to manage the story. She was sitting at her desk and just about to reach for the phonebook when the phone rang. It startled her slightly and she jumped. Amused at herself she smiled and answered, "Lisa Duffield."

"Hello, Lisa, it's Claire. How ya doin' this morning?"

"Oh, hi, Claire. I'm great – super busy, but getting tons of work done. As I told you the other day, this new post-doc I brought into my lab – Megan – she has really helped me set things on fire."

"Sounds great. Do you want to have lunch together?"

Lisa thought quickly through what she had planned for the day. "Um . . . sure. Do you want me to come downtown?"

"No, it's alright, we can meet in Collegetown. Do you mind walking down there?"

"Not at all. It looks pretty nice out. Maybe we can grab a sandwich and walk along the gorge."

"Do you think Tom would want to join us?"

Lisa suddenly realized this was not a social call. Claire was working. "Claire, is there something you need to tell me?" A cold feeling washed over her and she felt nauseated.

"I have had a chance to look over the results of some of the tests we did the other day. And I had a long consultation with a couple of people I consider very knowledgeable regarding fertility. I think the three of us should talk it over and figure out what options are open to us at this point." Claire had a great bedside manner, and even over the telephone she succeeded in at least partially comforting Lisa. "Should I call Tom? I am happy to do it."

"No, no, I can call him. I think he was lecturing this morning, so he should be free now. What time should we meet and where?" Even if Lisa couldn't control her world, she could control her calendar.

"How about the Central Avenue bridge in an hour?"

"Okay."

"Lisa, everything will be alright. Trust me."

"See you on the bridge."

Lisa hung up, closed her eyes and uttered a short prayer before relifting the receiver and calling her husband across campus. The phone answered on the fifth ring.

"Hello?"

"Hi, Honey. Are you free for lunch?"

"Not really . . . I've got mountains of work. We're going to have the weekend together. How about dinner instead?

"Claire called me and asked if we could meet her in Collegetown. She said she has results of the tests I had earlier this week. And she talked to some of her colleagues. Can't you just cut out for half an hour?" Tom scanned his computer screen, looked at his watch and sighed. Lisa misinterpreted it in her own context. "Claire promised things would be okay. Are you alright?"

"I'm okay. Sure, I can make it. I just need to be back for office hours by one. Where and when?"

Lisa gave him the details and they spoke for a few more minutes. The two of them tidied up their work in their own way.

Tom hammered out a few more paragraphs about Henry II's illicit romance with Rosamund de Clifford, a sordid and turbulent chapter in Henry's life – and one more chapter of Tom's book. Lisa pulled her Bible out of the drawer of her desk and flipped to the Book of Psalms to find something to settle and comfort her.

Lunch was much less about eating, and much more about delivering stark and difficult news to the Duffields. Claire had come to the conclusion that neither could they conceive, nor could Lisa successfully carry a baby full term. Even if Claire waived her fees, which as their friend she willing to do, the drugs and procedures could be ruinously expensive and still not yield a baby. They had now been trying for three years – it was time to think about surrogates or adoption. Claire suggested that they would be better off getting a baby while they were still young and active, rather than coming to the same conclusion several years from now. Tom and Lisa said little and ate less. Lisa put on a brave face and fought off the urge to break down and cry. Tom felt badly too, especially for Lisa, but nevertheless kept surreptitiously checking his watch out of concern for losing too much working time. They thanked and hugged Claire as their lunch wound to a close, and then walked together as far as the Straight. "You have office hours this afternoon?" Lisa asked Tom, unable to think of anything else to say.

"Yup. 'Til about five. Then I was hoping to finish up a few things that I haven't been able to tackle. Do you want to meet out somewhere for dinner?" He squeezed her hand and forced a smile.

Lisa continued to look down at the ground as she considered the question. She normally loved going out for a meal – anytime, anywhere – but not today, not after their conversation with Claire. "I'm really not up to it. Let's just get a pizza and watch a movie. Is that okay with you?"

Tom stopped walking and hugged Lisa. As professors, they were ordinarily very discreet regarding their public behavior. But this was mourning, not romance, and neither felt self-conscious. "That'll be fine," he answered. He thought he should offer to walk her to her building, but he was starting to get tight for time. Fortunately she beat him to it.

"I'll see you later," she put on a smile, and he knew she would be okay, at least for now.

"Love you. Hang in there." They kissed and parted.

Tom practically ran up the back stairs to his office and settled himself down at his desk, eager to get going before his office hours began at two o'clock. Before leaving for lunch he had left his outline atop the keyboard to assist in starting on the next chapter, but he knew where he wanted to start and tossed it aside. Just as he was about to crack his knuckles to signify his readiness to proceed, he noticed the message light flashing on his telephone. He was inclined to listen to it later, but he received so few calls, he was curious and retrieved it immediately.

"*You have one new message,*" the electronic voice intoned.

"Yes, yes, get on with it." Tom punched in the proper sequence to work as quickly as possible through the voice mail menu.

"*To listen . . . Message one received today . . . Twenty-seven sec– . . .*" Tom wondered whether the electronic voice was frustrated that it could never get the whole recording out before he advanced the menu. The message finally began.

"Tom, it's Bob Gardy. How are you, Buddy?"

"Oh, Christ," Tom exclaimed aloud. He had meant to call Bob last weekend.

"I got a call from your Department Chair, Rogers . . . William Rogers, I guess. What a pain in the ass he must be!" Tom knew what was coming. "Anyway, he asked me what I thought of your book. I guess he understood that I was reviewing something of yours. Maybe I was supposed to cover for you –"

"Of course you were, you nitwit."

"—Well it didn't occur to me until it was too late. Rogers seemed pretty excited to hear that I wasn't reviewing whatever it was. Sorry, pal, I just didn't think fast enough. Give me a call if you want to talk about it. And hey, have a great weekend." Tom was holding his face in his hands. He could see his entire plan unraveling very quickly.

"*To save this message, press –*" Tom picked up the receiver and slammed it down hard, cutting off the next help message.

"Shit! I am totally screwed." Tom replaced his head in his hands and searched for a new plan. Perhaps if he could get to the Dean before Rogers and plead his case, he might be able buy enough time to make it all work out. He stood up and grabbed his jacket. Screw office hours, he thought, time to take matters into my own hands. He pondered whether to call over to the Dean's office and check whether he was even there. Administrators had a reputation for "convenient" hours, and thus Friday afternoon might present a low likelihood of finding him. No, this was just lazy, he concluded. Tom was determined to find him and set things straight. He headed out the door.

"Hello, Professor Duffield," William Rogers huffed.

"Well, if it's not the Moses Coit Tyler Professor of History." Tom actually hid both the contempt and the panic he felt simultaneously.

"You wouldn't be abandoning your office just at the beginning of office hours, would you?" As usual, William was relishing the mere thought of abusing his power and authority. This was a warm up to whet his appetite for the main course he was only beginning to envision.

"I just had to run out for a coffee." Tom covered, badly. Rogers knew he had a coffee maker in his office. "That is, more coffee for my machine. I'm going to be caught here in my office for a while."

"Hmmm . . . pity for the eager students coming to learn from their professor – or maybe those trying to make sense of your lectures."

"Were you coming to see me . . . or can I continue on my way?" The contempt was a little more obvious this time.

"Actually I was. Shall we go back in your office?" Rogers grinned while he wasn't gasping for breath. Tom noticed that even in the absence of exercise, Rogers could never get enough air for his massive bulk. He checked his watch as a means of looking nonchalant and shrugged, then turned and entered his office, tossed his jacket on the only chair open for Rogers to use, and sat at his desk. Rogers looked around in vain for a place to sit, but abandoned that because he was so eager to torture Duffield. "I had an interesting conversation earlier today."

"I imagine you talked to Bob Gardy and he told you he wasn't reviewing anything for me." *That will take the wind out of your bloated spinnaker, you puffed-up bastard*, Tom thought.

He was right. Rogers had been planning to make a point that "real historians" research facts methodically. Now Rogers had to get straight to the point. "I don't believe that you have a book written, and I am not even sure you are working on one. It is astounding to me that you would fabricate such an untruth. It's completely outside the ethics and principles of this department and this university. As you can imagine, I am going to have to discuss this with the Dean."

For what might have been the first time in his life, Tom was speechless. One part of him wanted to mock Rogers' I'm-telling-on-you childishness, another wanted to protest that there really was a book under review, and a third itched desperately to wrap his fingers around Rogers' throat and choke him to death. His indecision led him to the most effective response for the moment; he looked at Rogers and said nothing. Tom simply appraised Rogers with a pitying smile and waited for him to make the next move.

Rogers was confused. Duffield always had a clever retort

and thus the silence shook his confidence in this checkmate declaration. Rogers' brow furrowed as he tried to regain control of the situation. "Well, what do you have to say for yourself?"

Tom fought off the urge to laugh. His boss was a clown, and even if he were a clown with a great deal of power over Tom's life, right now he was beneath Tom's witty derision. He decided to let the farcical scene proceed at Rogers' discretion. Tom moved not a muscle in his face.

Rogers could handle any remark, but the continued silence put him off completely and he became increasingly frustrated as Tom stared him down. His face flushed, reflecting his anger. "Answer me!" he shouted. Tom said nothing and Rogers flushed to a deep purple. "I said 'Answer me' you insolent prick!" A fleck of spittle came out of his mouth as he said the last word which landed squarely on Tom's chest.

This was simply too ridiculous and Tom burst out laughing – deep and from the belly, then laughed harder as he watched Rogers' eyes bug out. Tom finally spoke, "Run along now, before your head explodes. Do what you must." His laughter subsided briefly until Rogers stepped back and collided with the door.

"You're finished, Duffield."

"Only if you make it to the Dean's office without having a heart attack."

"Do you think that's funny?"

"You'd better be damn sure I don't pull a manuscript out of my top hat."

"You haven't got one."

"A top hat?"

"A . . . a . . . manuscript!" Rogers was apoplectic.

Tom shrugged. "We'll see."

Rogers turned and left the office, slamming the door behind him.

Now left alone, Tom looked down at the bubble of spittle still on his chest and brushed it off with his sleeve. "Well," he declared to himself, "I think I handled that pretty well." He chuckled and then, remembering how dire his situation had now become, said, "Guess I'd better get back to this book."

11

Lisa returned to her office with none of the drive or determination of her husband. Beyond the bitterly disappointing news Claire had delivered, she had worked extremely hard in the preceding week. By the time she closed the door to the lab and sat down at her desk, she was completely spent, emotionally and physically. Lisa leaned back in her chair and looked up at her poster of the *Annunciation*. How sad, she thought, that she would never have such an event. She had no expectations of being visited by an angel, of course. But perhaps just a doctor, like Claire, telling her that in less than nine months she would bring forth life. This was the whole point of life. God knew it when he delivered Christ as a baby, da Vinci knew it when he painted fourteen hundred years later, and Lisa knew it now. It wasn't about having a baby – Lisa didn't even like babies. For here they were noisy and needy and messy. This was about creating and continuing life. This was about giving, not having. Tears rolled down her cheeks as she mourned the baby she would never bear.

There was a knock at the door and it opened a moment later. Megan peeked her head in, sporting the same enthusiastic grin with which she had greeted Lisa on Monday morning. "Hey, I have some fabulous news!" Her smile faded as she saw the tears rolling down Lisa's face. "Oh, pardon me." She paused, trapped between wanting to give Lisa privacy and yearning to be helpful, "Should I come back? I didn't mean to barge in, I just wanted to let you know how things were going, and I wanted to make sure I caught you before you left for the weekend. We can talk on Monday . . . if you'd like to wait until then to—"

Lisa cut her off, "No, please come in, Megan. I'm sorry, I've just had a long week. What's up? I'd love to hear some fabulous news." She smiled, motioned for Megan to sit in the chair next to her desk and quickly wiped the tears off her cheeks.

Megan didn't need any further encouragement. She made a point of closing the door before stepping quickly to the open chair and drawing it as close to Lisa's desk as possible. "I think we've repeated the experiment. I just got off the microscope – we have living cell cultures again. Congratulations." She reached out her hand to shake with Lisa.

Lisa shook her hand, and broke into a genuine smile, but could not resist the temptation of a professorial moment. "So, tell me, Dr. Brack, what can we now say about these findings?"

Megan knew the drill and answered without hesitation. "We have been able to reconstitute desiccated human cells in a medium containing sheep uterine cell extract. We know that the cells are alive, but we don't know yet if they are skin cells, or undifferentiated cells." She paused for Lisa's agreement.

"Yup. I think we need to specify that we have done it with skin cells. We don't know how other cells would behave. Where do we go from here?"

"I think we need to determine the type and viability of the cells. I can run a screen using commercial stem cell marker antibodies." Megan was proud of her grasp of this work, but not at all smug. "When should we start?" There was little mystery she wanted Lisa to let her begin immediately.

"I hate to hold you back, Megan, but I want to do this right, and I don't want us to burn ourselves out. What would you think about running this one more time to make sure we are doing it right? This has all the hallmarks of cold nuclear fusion. Remember that? Can't you see our story breaking and then we find we can't replicate the work and someone figures out that we were contaminating the Ewe Factor medium with our own viable living cells? We need to take a sample of someone else outside the lab and then match the cells back to that person." They both knew that this was the right next step. Megan was like a champion racehorse, without a patient trainer she could injure herself in striving too hard. "I know this is the second Friday in a row that I am preaching some patience. I am not asking you not to work, just to sit back a little and think about how you think we should proceed." Lisa could tell by Megan's expression that she was on the verge of giving in. She pushed a little further to close the deal. "Map out a way for us to nail this, a way for us not to miss. We want that Nobel prize, not a place in the Hoax Hall of Fame."

Megan's mind was already racing as she began solving this next problem. Her mind wandered away from the conversation at hand and she absentmindedly stood up and started heading out of the office. Suddenly, she came to back to her senses and blushed seeing that Lisa was watching her with a bemused expression. "Oh, Lisa, I'm so sorry. Please forgive me. I'm just so juiced by this work, I can't stop." She sat back down and reached out to touch Lisa's arm. "I can take it easy for a couple days . . . as long as I am allowed to work on the protocols." Megan paused and leaned forward to look into Lisa's eyes. "Anything you'd like to talk about?"

Lisa let out a small and rueful laugh. "Weren't we here doing this a week ago? Is this my standing therapy session?"

"I'm really not trying to pry. I'm sorry I busted in here."

"No, no. It's no problem at all." Lisa's genuine smile eased any tension. "I just had a tough discussion with my . . . friend, Claire. On a personal, um, health, issue." Lisa noticed Megan's face darken briefly and was quick to add, "Claire's my fertility specialist."

Megan corrected her facial expression immediately and nodded thoughtfully. She was stalling. "You don't have to tell me about pers—"

"No, it's okay." Lisa said that to ease the tension, but she truly was uncomfortable talking about her inability to have a baby, mostly because she was afraid she would cry. She turned away from Megan and faced her bookcase. If nothing else, this would hide the tears. "Tom and I have been trying to have a baby for quite a while now. It looks as if," she paused as she decided how to put it. The word "barren" was stuck in her mind, but there was no chance that she was going to let herself utter it. "It looks as if we can't have a child."

Not knowing what to say, Megan continued to nod. She was only in her mid-twenties, and almost all of it had been focused on her own life – growing up, getting through college and post-graduate work. Intellectually, she knew that someday she might marry and have kids, because that is what everyone seemed to do. But not because she had a specific desire to do so. As a biologist she found babies quite fascinating, but perhaps just a little too much work.

Lisa continued as she did a good job of holding back the tears, "So, she's suggested looking at surrogates or adoption."

This sounded hopeful to Megan and she jumped on it. "Well that sounds like something to think about."

Lisa turned back toward Megan and shook her head. "I couldn't imagine Tom's baby, in another woman. That's a non-starter."

Megan decided listening was a better idea than speaking in this discussion. "I understand."

"Adoption might be okay, but it seems like even more work than being pregnant and having a baby." Mulling over this option eased Lisa's emotional stress. "I guess it is something to think about. But not on a Friday after a week like this." Then, after pausing and looking around her office, "I've let this place turn into a real dump," she self-scolded, shaking her head. "Maybe I ought to stay late and clean it up so it doesn't distract me on Monday." Lisa turned back toward her bookcase and lifted a pile of papers and journals and transferred it to her desk.

It wasn't clear to Megan whether Lisa had terminated the conversation consciously, or had just let herself be conveniently distracted. In any case, there was little point in reprising painful topics. "I think you ought to give yourself a break and head out now. You've talked *me* into that."

Lisa had begun sifting through the stack of papers and now looked up at Megan. "I've brow beaten you into it, let's be honest." They both smiled broadly. Glancing back down, Lisa noticed the *Journal of Molecular Biology* she had rescued from Jeff's office the morning of his accident. While not returning her to her darker mood, she thought back to that morning.

Megan noticed the change. "You alright?"

Lisa considered that question before she answered. But when she said, "Yeah," she meant it. She held up the magazine for Megan to see. "I stole this back from Jeff's office just before we had our fight." As she dropped it back down to one of her sorting piles, something caught her eye. She grimaced as she recognized it as a soiled Band-Aid stuck to the back of the magazine.

"What's that face?" Megan asked.

The grimace remained, as Lisa daintily lifted the Band-Aid off the journal's back cover with thumb and forefinger and dropped it into her wastebasket. "Well, how gross! When I was in Jeff's office, one of his undergrads knocked it into the trash by his desk. I must not have seen it. Blechhh." She detested all things unsanitary, and this surely qualified. Lisa continued her tidying half-heartedly and then came to the decision Megan had suggested. It was time to stop work for the week and go home. "You're right, it's time for us to call it a day. Come on."

It did not take long for the two of them to close up the day's affairs, pack their respective briefcases and close up the lab. They left the lab together and rode the elevator down to the ground floor, where they parted for the weekend. The moods and mindsets of the two scientists could not have been more different as the bid each other goodbye. Lisa was deeply melancholy – her thoughts focused on the lunchtime conversation with Claire, the now-apparent futility of years of fertility procedures, and the emptiness of her childlessness. A bitter cold wind and foreboding sky aggravated that sense of woe, and she pulled her too-thin sweater tightly around herself. It was more of a self-hug than an attempt to stay warm. Alone and depressed, she wound her way to the parking lot, fighting off the urge to walk instead to Tom's office. She consciously dismissed the thought because she knew he was busy; deeper down she knew he would offer no solace.

Megan could not have been more upbeat. In the space of a week she had completely reoriented her field of research, and was now taking a leading role in experiments which would accelerate her career and surely change her life. But it was bigger than all that. This work could change the world, and that idea excited her the most. Her mind raced as she thought through how to revise and perfect the protocol. Lisa (poor Lisa, she thought briefly) was absolutely right. It was too easy to rush forward and claim victory without truly ensuring the science was sound. The science was sound, of course, but she had to prove it. Megan was leaving her workplace, but she was not leaving work.

12

Lisa and Tom passed the next two days together, but with none of the romance and fun that had characterized their previous weekend. They discussed their meeting with Claire, but it was detached. Lisa was emotionally sapped and Tom was distracted by his last encounter with William Rogers. He dreaded the consequences of his insubordination, which would likely begin playing out in the beginning of the week. Reasoning that the more he got done before having to meet with the Dean, the better off he would be, he slipped away whenever he could to work on his manuscript.

On Monday they returned to their respective offices. Tom's office was much as he left it on Sunday afternoon – quiet and cluttered. A half-full cup of coffee sat next to the computer monitor. The evaporation from the dry heat of the building left a dark ring which needed to be scrubbed off. Anxious as he was to keep making progress on his manuscript, Tom was demotivated by the thought of having to face Rogers or the Dean. He thus busied himself with cleaning his dishes and brewing a fresh pot of coffee. It didn't take long, but it took his mind off the pitiful futility of trying to save his job. Even so, once the caffeine began kicking in, Tom was back to the Middle Ages making sense of the Plantagenets and their land holdings in France and England. Wales and Scotland needed to be conquered, but in which order and when. So many wars, so little time. Tom was in his groove.

At 9:31am the phone rang and startled Tom out of his historical reverie. He received relatively few calls – most of them from Lisa – and picked it up cheerfully expecting it to be her. "Hello, what's up?"

"Professor Duffield?"

Oh crap! Tom thought. "Yes, speaking," and then to sound chipper, "Good morning!"

"This is Dean Thatcher."

Tom wanted to keep up the happy façade. "Yes, sir, how are you this fine Monday morning?"

"Well . . . I'm fine, Tom." The Dean paused thoughtfully. "I had a long discussion with William Rogers over the weekend." *Figures*, thought Tom derisively, *Rogers set out across the campus on Friday afternoon and didn't get there until Saturday. I should have raced him after all.* Although he was warming up slowly, the Dean was widely regarded as a gentleman and he must be finding this awkward. On the other hand, he was also known to be resolute. The fact that he had called Tom this early did not bode well. Dean Thatcher continued, "Tom, I think we need to talk – face-to-face.

Are you free this morning? Even now, perhaps?"

Despite the fact that this was the call he had been dreading over the weekend, he had not planned out how he was going to respond to the Dean's certain summons. Duffield had blustered through life reacting to life's crises as they happened, and subconsciously he must have decided that this was no time to tamper with a reliable approach. Yet now, as the moment of reckoning was upon him, Tom was coming up empty. Claims of maltreatment, even abuse, at the hands of an asinine manager, were not springing to mind. Nor was he ready to argue that he had over 150 pages of scintillating and well-researched historical text. In fact, he was even trying to think of what to say. Instead, he was suddenly resigned to his fate. It had been a good effort, but the game was up.

"I'll come over now."

"That will be fine, Tom. Thanks."

"See you in a minute."

"Bye."

Tom hung up the phone and sat silently looking at his computer screen. He was weighing the last few lines he had typed and pondering whether to save his work. He had not done so all morning – almost four pages. "What's the point," he said aloud and flipped off his computer, quickly enough so that he had no time to change his mind. He grabbed his jacket and exited his office, walking down the stairs at a measured pace and acknowledging, albeit not with a smile, the students and faculty he met on the stairs. He stopped by Rogers' office and tried to discern whether Rogers was there. He could not tell, even after stooping to look for light under the door, but doubted Rogers could haul himself in before 10 am. Oddly, he let the sense of cynicism pass without forming a witty or cutting thought or remark. It was what it was, he thought. Tom passed out of the building and crossed the Quad.

Lisa was less surprised than the previous Monday at finding

the lab's main door unlocked, the lights on and centrifuges spinning. Megan looked up from the students' computer area, across from Lisa's office, and greeted her professor warmly.

"Good morning, Dr. Duffield. How was your weekend?"

"Did you work over the weekend? Against my orders?" Lisa asked with a theatrical scowl.

"Actually I didn't," Megan was quick to respond. "As long as pondering some of your questions from Friday doesn't count."

"That doesn't count. But what time did you get in this morning?" Lisa was relieved that Megan was not going to burn herself out, but now she was genuinely curious.

"Um, let's just say the night cleaning crew was mostly finished." Megan's smile verged on sheepish. "Let's not talk about that, let's talk about the experiment." She emphasized these last two words as if to indicate it was a proper noun, an official name.

Lisa instantly became business like. "Yes, of course, let me just drop my coat and brief case." She turned and entered her office and then called back over her shoulder. "Do you have some questions?"

Megan was quick to respond. "I've got an answer!" she shouted out.

"To which question?" The two women were conversing, despite not being able to see each other.

"To the question of how to ensure that we are not contaminating the sample with living tissue."

Lisa appeared back at the door, unconsciously pushing up her sleeves as she was anxious to get to work. "To which question? You've got to let me get my brain in gear. I haven't had coffee yet," she said dramatically.

"To the question of how to ensure that we are not contaminating the culture with our own cells and to *really* test this procedure."

"And the answer is?"

Megan reached behind her back and lifted a small plastic bag off the desk. She held it up with a smile. "This."

As she leaned against the door jam and tied her blond, shoulder-length hair in a pony-tail, Lisa sensed Megan's cheerful, good humor and was eager to play along. She squinted at the small bag and tried to discern what was inside, but could not make it out. "And what would that be?"

"The Band-Aid." Megan continued to hold it up.

Lisa came closer, no longer smiling as she tried to figure out what Megan was talking about. It was not making sense. "Which Band-Aid?"

"The one we talked about on Friday afternoon. That's why I had to come in early this morning before the trash went out. Actually, I almost didn't make it. I had to dig through a bigger bin and it was pretty gross. You would've hated it. Anyway, I was thinking we go after the white blood cells – the leukocytes – instead of skin." Megan realized that Lisa's smile had faded and felt the first pang of remorse. "Maybe it wasn't such a bright idea after all."

Lisa caught on only now as Megan lowered the bag and looked sheepish. "You mean Jeff's Band-Aid? The one I found on Friday afternoon that was stuck to the journal?" Although she wrinkled her nose slightly, she was not as horrified as Megan seemed to think. But even so, she was not eager to clone her deceased mentor. The professor chose her words carefully so as not to demoralize the already chastened post-Doc. "Megan, it's okay. That's the kind of out of the box thinking I've come to expect from you." Lisa paused and her green-blue eyes softened to match a genuine smile. "It's what I admire about you. It's why I am so happy for you to have joined my team. But I don't think that we want to start playing with Jeff's DNA. Not without his family's permission. In some ways it was this experiment that got him killed . . . ." She looked down at the floor and considered whether to pursue that line of thinking, but rescued herself and resumed, "I think we'll work with something a little more conventional right now. Okay?"

"Okay." Megan responded, understanding why she had such deep respect for Lisa. "Well, I guess it's time for Plan B. How about some of those human cell lines you can purchase?" She dropped the baggie on the desk and jumped up, her face suddenly animated by her enthusiasm for solving the next challenge. "I just saw that catalog on the lab bench on Friday and was wondering whether it would come in handy." Megan brushed past Lisa and rushed out into the lab space, "Yeah, here it is. Come here," she called out over her shoulder.

Lisa glanced back at the plastic bag on the table. "I'll be right there." She took a tentative step toward the desk, and then as she felt herself helpless to resist what she was about to do, carried on to the desk and picked up the baggie. She studied its contents carefully.

Megan called out from the laboratory. "Do you have any experience with these cell lines – or this company?" She paused for Lisa's answer, unaware that her mentor was transfixed and had not heard the question. "Lisa?" She started back toward the office.

Without thinking Lisa shoved the baggie in her pocket and turned around. "Yeah, I'm coming."

13

Dean Thatcher's office was tucked away in an unrenovated corner of Goldwin Smith Hall. The 50's-era, white terrazzo floor in the approaching hallway was yellowed and worn, despite the very little traffic which found its way here. Indeed, the wear probably had more to do with the janitor's closet opposite, the door of which was ajar and allowing a musty, dank odor to seep out. Tom paused at the Dean's door, more to catch his breath after walking briskly across the Quad than to gather himself. He considered rapping lightly on the frosted glass which bore the Dean's name and title, but remembered from a visit years earlier that this was only the entrance to an Anteroom where the secretary sat. He opened the door and entered.

The room was much as Tom recalled, minus the secretary, who had not yet arrived for the day. It was neat, but plain; only the decorations on the wall hinted at the power and prestige of both the office and the man he was about to see. Tom's earlier visit flashed to mind – it took place a couple of weeks after he had accepted his faculty position and was being graciously brought into the fold. How ironic, he thought, that this place would bookend his time at Cornell. Tom wondered how many other faculty members did this same hello-goodbye routine. His contemplation was interrupted by a call from behind the door to the inner room.

"Cindy, is that you?" The door jerked open, revealing the Dean in his inner sanctum. He stood looking surprised for a moment, but composed himself quickly. After all, given his position he was as much politician as administrator, and true to the former persona he extended his hand to shake. "Hello, Tom, you must have made a bee line across the Quad."

Tom shook his hand, as not to do so would have been both rude and awkward, and he genuinely admired the Dean as a man of substance and integrity. Yet this was not a mere social call, it was the prelude to dismissal. He wanted to get it over with quickly so he could get back to McGraw Hall and pack up his belongings and maybe toss a lighted match into Rogers' office on his way out. "I used to be a runner – I guess I just like to get where I am going quickly."

"Yes, indeed." The Dean motioned into his office. "Please come in and sit. I've just brewed up a pot of coffee and was pouring myself a cup. Will you join me?" Tom was charmed by his gracious manner, in spite of the circumstances, and entered a more sumptuous office. He sat in a leather chair as indicated by his host and watched the older man fuss at a makeshift coffee station atop a small refrigerator. Surely nearing his sixties, Dean Thatcher still cut a dashing figure. He sported closely cropped, gray hair above a chiseled, handsome face. His tall figure was trim and fit – academically armored in gray flannel trousers and a blue, cashmere sweater. He moved as gracefully as he spoke. "Milk or sugar?"

"Just black, thanks."

"Certainly." The Dean picked up two pristine red and white mugs and joined Tom in the small sitting area around a low table. Unlike William Rogers, Dean Thatcher did not relish making others ill at ease, so once he settled in his chair and took one, testing sip of his coffee, he began. "Your Department Chair, Professor Rogers, has voiced some very serious concerns about your performance and behavior."

"I can imagine," Tom replied curtly.

"Frankly, I find some of them hard to believe, since all of our interactions have been so pleasant and courteous. Further, I know the merit of your historical research and teaching. But, as you know, I am obligated to support our traditions . . . our structure . . . and take these allegations seriously."

Tom was watching the steam rise off the surface of his coffee, but was anxious for the Dean to know that he was earnest. He lowered his cup and looked Dean Thatcher squarely in the eye. "I understand. I'm prepared to answer any questions you may have, or simply to handle whatever punishment you mete out."

The Dean chuckled quietly. "Tom, this isn't about meting out punishment." His expression became serious again. "You are not being dismissed, if that's what you're worried about. But there are some issues we need to deal with." He reflected on his next question. "Did you tell Professor Rogers that you had finished a book and were having it peer reviewed?"

"Yes."

"Is that true?"

"Not . . . completely." Tom wanted to explain more fully,

but decided to let the questioning take its own course.

"What part *is* true?" The Dean was now becoming less genial.

"I am pretty far into a manuscript – nearing 200 pages – probably half-done. And it should need very little editing."

"We could double the size of Olin library with all the books that are half-done by the faculty here. That's far from being finished and under review." His response left Tom little room for rebuttal. The younger man simply nodded. "And were you disrespectful to Professor Rogers?"

"No more so than he was to me," Tom responded directly. He could accept being called on the carpet for his shortcomings, but could not stomach defense of Rogers' asinine and aggressive behavior.

The Dean was not going to be put off this line of questioning so easily. "Did you make remarks about his health – specifically joke about him having a stroke and a heart attack?"

"I don't remember anything about a stroke, and frankly, the heart attack comment was more of a prediction than a joke." Tom chuckled at his wit and then realized the Dean was not amused. He caught himself and apologized, "I'm sorry. It was in the heat of an argument."

"Argument or not, I think we both know that it was inappropriate." The Dean could play the patriarch well, and only Tom's total contempt for Rogers kept him from agreeing. He pursed his lips and attempted to avoid responding. Thatcher continued, "What you probably don't know is that you have a guardian angel."

Tom guffawed, "Well, that would be a first,"

The Dean rose, strode to his imposing, mahogany desk and picked up a letter. "I received this not twenty minutes after my interview with Professor Rogers. It is a letter from John Strater, Class of 1960 – I'm sure you know who he is." He paused only long enough to acknowledge Tom's nod. "He is considering a major gift .

. . I should say, another major gift . . . to the University. But he has specifically called you out as a key player in this process."

Tom was incredulous. "Me? By name? How does he even know I exist?"

Thatcher sat back down opposite Tom and scanned the letter. "Apparently he met you at Reunion last year in one of the faculty receptions and you made quite an impression."

"I do remember that. It was in the Jazz Music tent. Hopefully the impression was positive," Tom said nervously.

"Yes, yes, of course," the Dean replied reassuringly. "Did you know that he is a collector of medieval works of art, especially things with specific royal or . . . um, historical connections?"

"He mentioned that when we met, but I didn't really think he meant that he did it seriously." Tom shrugged and continued, "I thought he was just trying to make some connection with what I said I did."

Dean Thatcher looked up from the letter. "John Strater does everything seriously. He has a few billion dollars. That's not the sign of a dabbler. Anyway, he would like to donate his collection to the art museum, eventually building an extension to house it permanently."

"So what do I have to do with it?"

The older man smiled. "He has asked for you to author the catalog for the collection."

"You're kidding," Tom stated, although the Dean appeared to be quite serious.

"No."

"I'm a historian, not an art historian."

The Dean reviewed the letter again. "That's the point. He wants it described for its historical importance, not for its artistic value. Of course, you would work with the museum staff to get all the details and descriptions right."

"I am teaching two courses and trying to finish this book! I don't have time to suck up to some rich guy who thinks we are at his beck and call." Tom was losing his cool.

Thatcher stood. "You *are* at his beck and call – I'm surprised that wasn't obvious to you. We all are. You will make time to do this, and you will do a splendid job." He left no doubt that this decision was not negotiable. He began walking toward his door.

Tom stood and followed him. He was angry and bitter, but could find no clever argument to buttress his position. "Yes, sir." He nodded at the Dean and passed out of the office.

With his manuscript-ruse blown and the impending humiliation of having to suck up to a self-important billionaire in order to save his job, Tom slunk across the Quad, entered McGraw and slowly climbed the steps to his office. He paused at the landing, at first to catch his breath, but as he stood there he realized that there was no hurry to return to his office. It really didn't matter if he finished the book, he thought, as he was soon to be sidetracked by a completely different project. He shrugged, looked out the window as he leaned against the heavy wooden banister and tried to decide how to make the most of a bad day. It didn't take him long to decide on finding a quiet corner with a cup of coffee and a newspaper. Skipping back down the steps on his way to the Student Union coffee shop, he realized that he was actually relieved by the morning's events. No more secrecy, no more furtive rushing and writing and lying – it was an enormous weight off his shoulders. Tom stepped outside his building and, for the first time in weeks, strolled.

14

Lisa and Megan had a productive day in the laboratory. They ordered the human blood samples which they would first desiccate and then attempt to clone using Ewe Factor medium. In the interest of security they agreed not to discuss the work with anyone else in the lab, and that meant that they would have to do all the prep work by themselves. It was a slow and tedious process, because Lisa had decided they should start from scratch on virtually every part of the experiment, to ensure that no other human cells might be contaminating their work. Unfortunately, it was monotonous work allowing Lisa to spend most of the time thinking about the babies she would never bear. She kept up a brave face to Megan and the other students in the lab, but her heart ached as her mind replayed what Claire had told her the previous Friday. Black Friday, she dubbed it on its fourth pass through her conscious memory, and she embellished on the name several times after that. None of the subsequent dark monikers stuck, but they all reinforced the empty void which was growing within her. During the late afternoon she resolved to call Claire and discuss the "verdict" once more and slipped into her office to make the call. But as she lifted the receiver and began to dial, her dread of hearing Claire say those words again provided just enough pause for her to rethink the plan and simply return to the lab.

Megan noticed none of this. She was oblivious to Lisa's pain – mostly because Lisa pretended well, but also because whatever sensitivity she might have to those around her was drowned out by the joy and excitement of participating in landmark science. While Lisa was playing dark reruns of what had been her saddest day, Megan was creating visions of what she imagined would be the greatest moment of her life. She had never been in a press conference, but had seen them on television and imagined herself standing behind Lisa at the microphone and – no, no, sitting by Lisa at a table where there was a microphone at each place, and a little cardboard placard in front with neat block lettering that read, "Dr. Megan Brack". Lisa would answer most of the questions, but then a reporter in the front would toss one Megan's way. "Dr. Brack, would you comment on the part you played in this stupendous breakthrough?" She would be very careful to turn on her mike before responding and then, looking out across the sea of people, she would tell them that she had run many of the confirmatory experiments, thereby assisting Dr. Duffield – she would be very proper in using Lisa's title – in validating the procedures and thus the findings themselves. It was like being the second man to step on the moon. Sure, being first was better, but no shame for number two. Schoolchildren still learned Buzz Aldrin's name right after Neil Armstrong's. Better yet, she thought, DNA was born of Watson and Crick. Who knew which of them did what – they were just partners. Duffield and Brack had a nice ring to it. Might sound even better in alphabetical order . . . .

The end of the working day came too soon for Megan and too late for Lisa. They had stopped briefly for lunch on the go as they pursued separate errands and then worked straight through the afternoon until 6 pm. Megan wanted to keep going, but Lisa was anxious to get home and spend time with Tom, hoping for solace in his companionship. Lisa had only to deliver the preface to the "Don't Burn Yourself Out" Sermon, before Megan, who was genuinely tired, agreed to a good night's sleep and an early Tuesday resumption.

Any anticipation Lisa had for Tom's company was dashed the moment she stepped through the front door of their house. While she couldn't make out the exact murmur emitting from the family room, she suspected it was a sports program. A few steps farther into the house she knew it was ESPN's sports commentators reprising Sunday's best and worst moments on the gridiron. She found Tom planted on the couch and the two exchanged brief reports on their respective experiences that day. Lisa's précis was accurate and relatively complete – she left out the technical details which she knew Tom would either not understand or simply ignore. Given that she had stood at the bench virtually all day, there was frankly little left to relate. Tom's report was also accurate, but much less complete given the omission of his discussion with the Dean. While he was still relieved that a secret and stressful period of his life was over, Tom saw his new assignment with John Strater more as a Rogers-induced punishment than an endorsement of his reputation and value to the University. Besides, after the first early departure from his office in weeks, a couple of cold beers and the distraction of a hard-hitting sports program, he really didn't feel like launching into it. Tom was ready to be entertained, and conversation with Lisa about the machinations of the University's History Department did not qualify.

Lisa made dinner and busied herself around the house, neatening up the kitchen and then sitting with Tom and going through the mail as he watched the football game. She made a few perfunctory efforts at starting a conversation, more to convince herself that Tom wasn't being sensitive to her needs for companionship than actually to talk. "Have you had a chance to think about our conversation with Claire?" she asked without looking up from a Lands End catalog.

She had timed the question badly. The football game was close and Tom's favorite team, the New England Patriots, were two yards from the goal line and trying to punch the ball into the end zone before the end of the half. Tom tried his best to answer the question despite the distraction, but did not master the opportunity. "Umm . . . well, I've been – come on, drive it in!! Damn!! – I guess I haven't had a chance to really sort through what's next. There's no way that was holding! Christ!"

"So, do you want to talk about it?" She asked, still not having looked up from the Summer Closeout catalog. Lisa knew the true answer to this question, but she was curious what Tom would say.

"Just a sec . . ." he replied, putting his hand on her thigh. "Touchdown!! Great!!" he exclaimed, and then more conversationally, "So, you want to discuss it right now? I mean, tonight? Were you thinking that we would talk it over tonight?" He made an effort to look at her, but just as she noticed and turned to look at him, his attention was diverted away to witness the extra point.

Lisa relented, as she knew she eventually would. "We don't have to discuss it right now. But I want to make sure that we talk through the options. Some of these things take a lot of time."

Tom was relieved. As much as he had wanted Lisa to get pregnant with their own baby, he wasn't very interested in the other options Claire had mentioned. "Well, of course, honey. Maybe this weekend we could really set aside some time to discuss it." He didn't think he could push it off longer, and promising a weekend discussion sounded like commitment. Ironically, now that the referee's whistle had announced halftime, he was actually feeling like talking. At least until the highlights began playing.

The next couple of hours dragged on similarly, with slightly less conversation after Lisa snuggled into one corner of the couch and fell asleep. Tom was deeply engrossed in the game, particularly as his team came out strong in the second half and began blowing out their opponent. Noticing that Lisa was deeply asleep he got a glass of cognac to celebrate the eventual win and watch the recap. It was half past midnight when he finally turned off the television, awakened Lisa and joined her in the tired trudge to the bedroom to commence their bedtime routine. As usual, Tom went right to the bathroom, perhaps with more of a sense of purpose given all the beer he had drunk. Lisa stayed in the bedroom and stood at her dresser, removing her earrings, necklace and watch and carefully placing them in their respective and traditional places. She pulled her sweater over her head and then, as she began removing her pants she felt something in her pocket. Surprised and curious, since she rarely carried anything in her pockets, Lisa reached in to investigate, her fingers probing to the bottom where the object seemed to bunch. As she drew out the baggie she finally remembered her discussion with

Megan that morning – actually yesterday morning, she thought with a confirmatory glance at the clock. Lisa held the baggie close and took a long look at its contents, flipping it over several times and then focusing in on the Band-Aid's gauze center, which was stained yellow, brown and blackened crimson. Her vague and sleepy trance broke when Tom entered from the bathroom behind her and asked, "Are you finished up in there?"

"Not quite." She deftly folded the baggie into her palm and then looking around her dresser top for the right place to keep it, alighted on her wooden jewelry box. She slid out the top drawer, which held only a few gold chains and stuffed the baggie in, closed the drawer and then turned to Tom. "I only need a minute." She was relieved to see that Tom had busied himself at his own dresser and had noticed nothing of her secreting.

By the time Lisa came back from the bathroom, actually only five minutes later according to their bedside clock, Tom was already asleep. He wasn't snoring exactly, as it usually took a couple hours for him to tune up to a full bear's roar, but he had the slow heavy breathing that confirmed he was out for the night. Lisa crawled into bed next to him, dreading the fact (perhaps in a self-fulfilling way) that she would not be able to sleep. She replayed the events of the day, digressing occasionally to think about babies, the Lands End Closeout, Tom's breathing and her schedule for tomorrow. Yet through all of the forty-two minutes that it took her to finally gain a fitful sleep, she kept coming back to the Band-Aid in the baggie like a thirty-second commercial breaking into her favorite program. She wasn't thinking about it, she was simply picturing it – the spectrum of discoloration of the gauze, the pinprick holes of the latex, and the way the adhesive ends were twisted back on themselves and still stubbornly holding tight. It was always neatly contained in the baggie, but as her imaginings wore on, the baggie became ever clearer and less noticeable.

Lisa's dreams that night were disturbing, although not altogether memorable. She woke several times, as was her practice, to tug the bedcovers back from her husband and to make him roll over to stop the snoring. She fell asleep one last time just as the sun was beginning to illuminate their curtains, yet the line between waking and dreaming was particularly blurry since her surroundings didn't change. Tom lay next to her, snoring loudly and hogging the bed, a faint glow shone around the edges of the window treatments, and the water in her glass on the bedside table remained at exactly the same level. However, there was a new sound which hadn't existed in her waking state. It was the sound of a baby, crying. *Oh, not again. I just put him down,* she thought. She rolled over to confirm that Tom was deep asleep and then rallied herself to a sitting position and out of bed. She slipped her feet into her shearling slippers, circled around the bed and headed down the hall to what she knew was the nursery. The baby's cries were getting louder as she neared the door and she began calling out in a gentle whisper, "I'm coming sweetie, shhhh, shhhh, shhhh, I'm coming." Lisa pushed the door open and entered a beautifully decorated nursery, which should have struck her as strange because in real, waking life this was the guest room and normally stacked high with boxes. Even so, everything seemed normal to her as she entered the room, approached the crib and kept up her reassuring coos and whispers to the little baby. "I'm right here, sweetie," she said to the baby which was turned away from her, and she reached down to pick him up.

Only as she tucked her hands under the baby's arms to lift him up did Lisa feel a strange sense of dismay. *Is this my baby?* she asked herself as she hoisted him toward her. *Do I have a baby?* was the second question that shot through her mind. Suddenly the baby's head swung around and Lisa was frozen in terror. Although small in size to match the tiny head, the face was not that of a baby. Instead, it was Jeff Wolf's face, exactly as she had last seen him.

"Hi, Mommy!" the baby said in Jeff's deep voice.

15

Tom arose at 8am that morning and found his wife sitting quietly in the kitchen reading the paper and sipping from her favorite coffee cup. He noticed her breakfast dishes were already soaking in the sink. "You've been up for a while?" he said, half as a remark and half as a question.

"I couldn't sleep," she said, without looking up.

"I slept like a baby," Tom replied, stretching. He was too busy selecting his box of cereal from the pantry closet to notice Lisa's wince, as subtle as it was. "Did I tell you about my conversation with Dean Thatcher yesterday?" he asked. Despite his mild hangover, Tom was feeling more talkative. He looked over at Lisa and she shook her head. "Yeah, he called me over to his office first thing yesterday."

"Why?" Lisa put down the paper.

"It seems that some rich alum – oh, you know, John Strater, the telecom whiz," he said looking up as he poured his cereal. She nodded, her brow furrowed in a mix of curiosity and anticipation. Tom continued, "He's got this huge collection of historical artifacts which he wants to donate to the University's art museum and he wants me to author the catalog." He said the last part as he padded across the kitchen in his slippers and picked up the Sports section of the newspaper.

"Dean Thatcher?" Lisa asked.

"Huh?" Tom was perplexed.

"Dean Thatcher wants you to author an art catalog?" she clarified.

"Well, yeah, because Strater asked for me to do it." The cereal in Tom's mouth muffled his words.

Lisa brightened up. "John Strater asked for you by name?"

"Yeah. I met him last summer at reunion."

"Honey, that's amazing." She was genuinely excited for

him.

Tom was taken aback by her sudden enthusiasm. "You think? I have so much going on – I'll have to head down to New York right in the middle of next week and cancel a couple of lectures. That means I have to rejigger a bunch of material. It just seems like a pain in the ass."

Lisa couldn't believe that Tom was so blasé about it. "Come on, honey. He's one of the most important alums. The fact that he asked for you by name is fantastic." She came over to take a seat at the table opposite him. "It's always good to have friends in high places, you know."

Tom hadn't thought about it this way before and it softened his irritation. He shrugged. "I guess," and then changing the subject, "what are you up to today?" he asked.

"The usual. Megan and I are doing the entire Ewe Factor experiment from the beginning to validate it. We want to make sure that everything is right before we report any results. It occurred to me the other day that you and Megan are the only people I've told about it, so the news is pretty contained."

"And Jeff Wolf," Tom added, neither thinking nor trying to be cruel. As soon as the words came out of his mouth he knew that he'd said the wrong thing, but he hadn't sufficiently awakened to backtrack. Helplessly he watched her smile fade.

Rather than lash back, Lisa pictured her dream that morning and shuddered. "Like I said, it's pretty contained." She got up from the table and headed toward the hall. "I need to get dressed." Tom resisted the urge to apologize. He knew it would take a lot more to dig himself out than simply saying he was sorry. Without too much more reflection he read the recap of last night's football game and finished his breakfast.

Tom and Lisa spoke again before they left for work, but it was mostly limited to planning and logistics – when would each be home, what should they have for dinner. Lisa wasn't cold to him, nor he contrite to her. They were simply efficient and economical in their words. By the time they left, nearly simultaneously, they were each thinking more about the day ahead of them, rather than the morning already passed.

Once at work, Tom began to settle into the routine which had characterized the past several weeks, at least until he remembered the Strater-safe haven. Then, instead of flipping on his computer and launching back into his book from where he left off, he grabbed the latest copy of *OAH Magazine of History*, sat back with his cup of coffee and put his feet up on the desk. He wasn't going to work on the book, he decided, nor review his notes for the lectures scheduled later that morning. Given how hard he had worked over the last few weeks, Tom decided he had several hundred hours in the bank, and now was as good a time as any to begin cashing them in. The "withdrawal" ended abruptly when Tom heard a gentle knock and watched the door swing open, too quickly even for him to pull his feet off the desk. As soon as Tom realized that it was William Rogers, he resisted the urge to move a muscle. He even turned the page of his magazine to underscore his nonchalance. "Good morning, William," he said with a slight smirk. He glanced at his watch. "Already here at nine forty-five in the morning – is someone giving out free doughnuts?"

Rogers, still out of breath from his transit from the elevator, was unable to deliver a swift response. So after a chuckle and a forced smile, timed just long enough for him to catch his breath, he said, "I was out yesterday at a conference, so I didn't get a chance to stop by."

"I missed you desperately," Tom said without looking up as he turned another page.

"Have you had a chance to talk to Dean Thatcher?"

"Yes, thanks to you. We had a little chat first thing yesterday morning."

Rogers couldn't hide a small grin, betrayed by a dimple on his fat left cheek. He wanted to recount how deliberative the Dean had been in weighing the serious matter of Tom Duffield's future, but then he realized it would be more fun to have Tom describe his own meeting. Rogers wondered how long it would take to drag out the fact that Tom should start packing up his office. "Well, would you care to tell me what you discussed?" he asked.

"Not particularly. Haven't you two spoken?"

"Not since Saturday."

Tom suddenly realized that Rogers did not know about John Strater's letter. He closed his magazine so he could focus on this new opportunity to turn the tables on Rogers. "So how did you two leave it?" he probed.

"Well, we had quite a long discussion about your . . . umm, fit with the department."

"Apparently, it's like a glove."

As usual, Rogers had trouble driving his agenda with Duffield. "Look, Tom, I know this is difficult, but it is best to be as professional as possible about it." He couldn't resist lecturing.

"Well, you're certainly the role model for professionalism," Tom retorted.

Rogers was becoming cross. "We're not talking about me, here," he responded, "we're talking about you."

Tom corrected him. "You're *trying* to talk about me. I'm just not playing along."

"If you acted this way with the Dean, it would have made his decision easier."

"I respect Dean Thatcher. My behavior was impeccable." Tom decided it was time to pull the Strater-card. "I think his decision was simple, given the letter and all."

"What letter?" Rogers quickly assumed Tom was talking about a letter of resignation. "You resigned?"

Getting Rogers to start guessing was a sure sign that Tom

had seized the upper hand. He was beginning to enjoy this. "You wish! I'm talking about John Strater's letter. I'm sure the Dean told you about that."

"Strater? What are you talking about?" Dark crimson blotches were beginning to appear on Rogers' already flushed face. Tom noticed this and wondered whether he could drag their discussion out long enough to see beads of sweat forming on Rogers' forehead.

"Certainly you know who John Strater is?"

"Of course I know who he is! What does this have to do with you? What letter did he write?"

"I'm sorry; I assumed the Dean would have told you. I thought you two were close," Tom jabbed. Rogers pulled a handkerchief out of his left pocket and mopped his glistening forehead. *Check*, thought Tom, *and it didn't take long*. "Well, anyway, Strater is donating his collection of medieval treasures to the Johnson Art Museum and he wants me to author the catalog."

Rogers was stunned and his mouth hung open. A thin strand of saliva linked his top and bottom teeth. "Strater asked for you? By name?"

"Yes, isn't that terrific? I think he wrote something in his letter mentioning . . ." Tom waggled his fingers as he feigned searching for the term, "'a real historian'. I don't have the letter, but I am sure Dean Thatcher would share it with you, if you asked him nicely." Tom hadn't seen a picture of the Cheshire Cat for years, but he did his best to mimic the grin as best he could remember.

"But you have far too many things going on to do that!" Rogers was too angry to realize this was not the cleverest line of protest. Tom saw it at once.

"But not so busy that you couldn't try to get me fired!" Tom sneered. He looked down at his hands and imagined them wrapping around Rogers' throat. He wondered briefly whether they would fit around the extraordinary circumference.

"Activity and capability are not the same thing." Rogers said imperiously.

"No, they definitely are not. And sometimes both are completely absent." He said the latter flatly. All traces of his previous grin had evaporated. Tom realized that if he did a good job on the Strater project, his relationship with Rogers, good or bad (and most likely the latter), was irrelevant. Dean Thatcher's admonitions to be civil were suddenly ringing in his ears, however, and he thought he should ease up rather than go in for the kill. "If you will excuse me, I need to get back to work." Tom picked up his journal, leaned back in his chair and lifted his feet atop the desk.

"I am going to have another word with the Dean as to whether you're the best person for this work," Rogers harrumphed, turned and heaved through the door.

"Be my guest," Tom said after him. But for his own labored breathing, Rogers would have heard Tom add, "Better pack some sandwiches for that long trip across the Arts Quad."

Despite launching into work on Tuesday morning with a gusto specifically designed to distract herself from any other thoughts, Lisa couldn't help picturing the Jeff-faced baby. The image made her shudder for the first several hours, but since the vividness of dreams seems to fade at rates exponentially faster than real memories, the creepiness wore off near lunchtime. She finished making one of the last reagents needed to wash the Ewe Factor cells, excused herself from Megan and stepped outside to get some air. Although she had not planned it in advance, Lisa's feet led her across the street to the Ag Quad flower garden, whose chrysanthemums were among the last of the flowers in bloom. The garden was empty that day – indeed, there were only a handful of pedestrians in sight and even fewer cars. Everyone seemed to have been driven inside by the gloomy skies and the chilly breeze. While not a fully-fledged nasty day, one could sense the weather was in a bad mood and aiming to take it out on whomever lingered out of doors.

Lisa didn't really notice this – she was absorbed by the idea she hadn't yet begun thinking about. She had put off pondering it until she sat on her favorite bench by the statue of the girl with the umbrella, and the moment her bottom landed on the cold cement surface, she crystallized her decision.

She would clone Jeff from the Band-Aid and raise him as her baby.

This had been clear to Lisa since Megan held up the baggie, but it was so incredibly perfect a solution to her situation that she had resisted admitting it to herself. It wouldn't be all that hard. Once the cells were isolated from the Band-Aid and soaked in the Ewe Factor medium, Lisa could remove the DNA from any one of the cells and put it into a denucleated human egg. Planted into a ready uterus, it would grow just like a regular fetus. As she let the realization flow through her brain *and* her heart, it brought tears to her eyes. Jeff was a brilliant scientist – perhaps one of the greatest of his time. But his time was cut short and he couldn't achieve his destiny. Many had said that he would someday receive a Nobel Prize. Now, instead, he might be the child of a Nobel laureate and grow up in a household that could foster his scientific passions from Day One. Lisa knew she could give life back to Jeff and have a baby at the same time. A baby which was guaranteed to succeed. Sure, Jeff could be egotistical and obnoxious, but that was likely his upbringing. If she and Tom worked on that, also from Day One, he could be the perfect child. Lisa drew her coat around herself and held her torso in a tight hug. "Thank you, God," she said aloud.

There was, however, one problem. According to Claire, Lisa's uterus was not viable – she needed a surrogate. In fact, the other question that had been swirling about Lisa's subconscious was whether she could ask Megan to do it. The Post-Doc was young, healthy and sensible, Lisa reasoned. Their friendship had lasted a couple of years, and they were now growing very close as they collaborated on this experiment. Lisa knew that Megan idolized her, and while that made her feel slightly guilty and uncomfortable, it meant that she might just say yes if Lisa posed the question. There *was* scientific reasoning for doing it, Lisa rationalized. Skeptics of her science would say that while the cells looked okay, there were too many flaws in the reconstituted DNA to make a viable human clone. Once the cells began to differentiate and become organs, some sufficient number of the 25,000 human genes would be mutated or missing to make the fetus abort via miscarriage. Only if they carried it through delivering a healthy baby (which, by the way, she could take home) would they know that the experiment had truly worked. *Megan isn't going to do this for me*, Lisa thought. *She'll do it for the science.*

A cold gust of wind caused Lisa to pull her coat once more around herself. She checked her watch and realized it was time to get back to the lab. As she broke from her more serious deliberations and contemplated the withering chrysanthemums, another question forced its way into her mind – *What will Tom say?* Lisa imagined hearing the long screech of a needle sliding across a vinyl LP record. *Tom hated Jeff.* She quickly countered that stark realization with the confidence that this would be a great child "prospect" by Tom's standards – smart, good looking, predictable. It was a valiant effort, but she couldn't convince even her willing self. "He thought we were having an affair," she said aloud to herself, and then looked around quickly to confirm no one could have heard. Lisa began biting her thumbnail as she tackled this vexing obstacle. Maybe if she begged him, he knew there was nothing more important to her in the world than having a child . . . *He'll never go for it.* This just would not do. Lisa had the power to undo the wrong of Jeff's death and give them a wonderful baby. And after all, notwithstanding her weird dream, how much would Jeff really look like Jeff – as a baby? "We just won't tell him where the baby came from," she declared as she stood up and began retracing her steps to the lab.

16

The human cell lines arrived by Federal Express on Wednesday morning and Megan and Lisa carefully took samples to desiccate overnight. At the same time, they were drawing the Ewe Factor off the sheep cell cultures. On Thursday, with mounting but well-contained excitement, they extracted a dry sample and put it into the culture bottles containing the Ewe Factor and a culture growing medium. They worked extremely methodically through these two days of the experiment – checking off each step in the lab notebook, verifying for each other the quantities of solution that they were mixing, and calling out and repeating settings on all the instruments. Part of this care was scientific rigor appropriate for two of the greatest geneticists of their day. The last two days had been very long and they didn't want fatigue to cause a silly mistake that would send them back to the beginning. However, the bigger part of their care was a conscious effort to maintain focus as they neared Friday morning's moment of truth. Megan's hands shook as she carried the cell culture bottles into the incubator and set them on a mixer in the rear corner. Earlier that day they had cleaned out and cordoned off this section of the incubator room with masking tape on which they scrawled, "Do not use – ? see Dr. Duffield". They didn't want to risk some careless student knocking over their solutions or taking their bottles off the mixer to make room for their own. Now as Megan retreated from the corner and Lisa replaced the flimsy tape cordon, they exchanged nervous smiles. Megan put her hands on Lisa's shoulders and declared, "T-Minus Fourteen hours. Aren't we supposed to synchronize watches or something?"

Lisa laughed. "This isn't Mission Impossible. Don't worry – it'll work," she reassured her anxious post-doc, "if we just let the Ewe Factor do its thing."

"I feel like a kid going to bed on Christmas Eve. I swear I'm trembling." She withdrew her hands from Lisa's shoulders and held them out in front of her to watch them quiver.

"Well, our present is going to be pretty hard to see without the fluorescent microscope. That will be our Christmas tree. Let's set it up in the morning when we're fresh, ok?" Lisa was trembling slightly as well, conscious that this was the moment that she had chosen to set her plan in motion. "Hey, do you have any plans for tonight?" she asked cheerfully.

"No," she replied as she checked her watch. "Wow, how did it get to be 8 o'clock? There's not so much of a night left to have plans for. What do you have in mind?"

They stepped out of the incubator room and closed the door, stealing one last glance at their cell cultures in the far corner. "I know," Lisa said as if it had just occurred to her, "let's go down to College Town and get a drink. We'll celebrate our success."

"What if it doesn't work?"

"Then we'll get a head start on drowning our sorrows."

Megan had never heard Lisa talk like this, and while it didn't surprise her, she was pleased to see that her mentor had a fun side. "Should we grab anyone else from the lab? I think Kristina is still there."

Lisa was quick to respond, "No, no. Let's just go by ourselves."

"Ok," Megan was excited about letting her hair down with her boss. They reached the end of the corridor and entered the lab. "Let me get my things together – it'll just take a minute." As Megan packed up her backpack and put on her coat, Lisa gathered her things from the office across the vestibule. They met back in the middle and Lisa opened the lab door for her protégé.

"We've worked hard over the last couple of days. Let's go have some fun," Lisa suggested. Megan voiced her agreement and the two strolled back down the hall, down the stairs, and out into the cool fall night.

Lisa had systematically planned this discussion with Megan, right down to when she would transition from small talk about the weather or campus events to discussing their experiment. If she started it too early, they might get to the crux of the matter before they had downed their first drink. If she waited too long, Megan may be too tipsy to make the connections required to land on the conclusion Lisa wanted. So as they walked down the hill and crossed the bridge over Cascadilla Gorge to Collegetown, all while Megan swirled deeper and deeper into a story from her childhood, Lisa became slightly nervous. She needed to change the subject and was trying to think of how exactly to do it, when Megan foiled her plan a second time by blurting out, "Hey, let's bring in bagels and coffee for everyone tomorrow to celebrate our success!"

Lisa's plan for cloning a Jeff-baby hung on their not announcing the results of the experiment until after the baby was born. Despite wishing it were otherwise, she had repeatedly thought through the scenarios and kept arriving at this same truth. Releasing the news before implanting *and delivering* a baby would bring so much attention that the slightest bulge on anyone – okay, any woman – working in the biotechnology building would be aggressively investigated. A pregnancy in Professor Lisa Duffield's own laboratory would be an absolute media circus. Instead, the only logical course was to suppress the news for about a year. That was discouraging, to be sure, but it would give them a chance to assert with confidence (but not proof because the baby would always be a secret) that the DNA was properly reconstituted. Additionally, it would allow them to analyze the Ewe Factor's biochemistry. Right now, the solution was simply a magical mixture of enzymes and proteins and hormones. With one more year of benchwork they could probably understand exactly what was making it capable of regenerating life. Indeed, science" should be more than the "parlor trick" of making old, dried cells come back to life. It was about knowing *how* and *why* it worked – this understanding would advance the fields of genetics and cell biology.

Despite having thought all this through beforehand, Megan's suggestion to buy tomorrow's breakfast took Lisa by surprise and she could only respond with, "Huh, that's an idea." As she gathered her wits, Lisa asked, "Have you thought much about announcing our results?"

Embarrassed by the truth, Megan fibbed. "Not . . . much. I guess I've been so wrapped up in making sure we replicate the results that I haven't had a chance to wrap my mind around it." They had reached the first bar on that stretch of College Avenue, and seeing the table overlooking the sidewalk was free – quite surprising for a Thursday evening – they entered quickly and snapped it up before anyone standing at the bar had noticed the opportunity. The restaurant was both full and noisy, so the two women had to draw their seats close to the table and lean forward to continue their conversation. Megan began, "What were we just talking about?"

"About announcing our results." Lisa was back on her game plan and wanted to move it ahead. She looked around for the cocktail waitress and signaled for her as soon as she could make eye contact. "I haven't ever had results that were so newsworthy," she paused to acknowledge the waitress and order. "I'll have a glass of chardonnay. Megan?"

Megan nodded. "That sounds good." The waitress smiled and turned away without saying a word.

"I think we ought to talk to Peter Evans first, since he took over as department chair when Jeff passed away." The prospect of bringing Jeff back to life eased the pain of mentioning his death. "But, you know, as a plant geneticist, he's not going to understand–"

"Or believe," Megan interjected.

"Exactly! I mean, what are we going to announce? That we're seeing what appear to be viable human cells after complete desiccation and reconstitution?"

Megan was surprised by Lisa's question. "Well . . . that is what we have done, isn't it?"

"Yes, of course. The question is going to be how viable they really are."

Megan felt she was on solid ground and answered confidently. "The cells seem to be dividing normally, that's a big start. If there was some lethal mutation, they wouldn't be able to do that." The glasses of chardonnay arrived and Megan stopped to thank the waitress. Then, raising the glass, she toasted, "To our success!" Lisa smiled and raised her glass, but she didn't respond. Tired and thirsty, Megan took a long draw on her wine. In contrast, Lisa only took a little sip and that caught Megan's attention. "Lisa, is there something bothering you? Are you worried that there's a problem with the experiment?" She reached out and put a comforting hand on Lisa's arm.

"No, I'm sure it's fine. I'm just trying to think through what kind of issues or questions our colleagues are going raise. And you know what, Megan? Our own faculty will go easy on us compared to what we'll get from other Universities, especially once it's fanned by the media." Megan's press conference-fantasies begin to fade. Lisa continued, "The littlest, most picayune, and most unlikely criticisms are going to get thrown at us, and we'll have to take them seriously. Do you think we're ready for that?"

"We're not going to announce anything beyond what we've done," Megan protested. "We're just going to tell people what we've done so far. And Lisa, that's big news! Nobody has been able to do anything remotely like this."

"So you don't think there'll be stories on the news about us cloning a human?" Lisa probed.

"I s'pose." Megan was beginning to feel discouraged – just as Lisa had expected. "But not because of what we're going to say. Right? We'll just talk about human cells brought back to life. It's not like we're going to say there's an embryo swirling around in that cell culture bottle." She laughed as she said this, and then drained her glass.

Without cracking a smile, Lisa asked, "Are you sure there isn't?"

"Huh?"

"An embryo . . . in the cell culture flask."

Megan grimaced. "No way. The environment is all wrong. I mean, it might be viable for a brief time, the initial cell divisions – but it wouldn't survive long." She signaled the waitress for another round. "And plus," she added, "who knows whether all the right genes are in the right place – and getting turned on at the right time – to get a baby to keep growing. Lisa, just think about how many regular pregnancies self-abort up to three months gestation because some gene wasn't there or didn't kick in at the right time." Megan's remorse for her last statement was immediate and painful. "Oh, God, Lisa, I'm sorry."

Lisa hadn't been hurt by Megan's comment, mostly because everything was moving ahead according to plan. Even so, she recognized the opportunity to advance her case by wincing slightly and looking out the window as she bit her lower lip. "It's okay, I know you didn't mean it." There was a long pause as Lisa tried to think of her next move, and Megan searched for something to recover from her gaffe. Lisa spoke first. "But it <u>might</u> be viable. Do you know of any *in vitro* ways to test the genetic makeup?" She knew that this was extremely impractical.

"Only if you had a couple years to screen all the known genes," Megan groaned. She shook her head. "And that's if you worked 24 hours a day. No, there's no way." Their second round arrived and they both drank, still thinking about where to take this conversation next.

"You're right," Lisa said. "We'll just run with what we've got so far. It's good enough."

Megan was not ready to give up so easily. "There is a way to do it in nine months, of course." And then, responding to Lisa's quizzical expression, "We could transfer a nucleus into an enucleated egg and implant it into a ready uterus. It'll either miscarry or survive. And if it's the latter, our experiment is proven."

"I'm a little rusty on human egg implantation," Lisa chuckled. "And I think that's frowned upon on campus."

"I didn't mean you," Megan laughed back, responding quickly to Lisa's lighter mood. "But that's kid stuff compared to what you have accomplished at the lab bench – at least for fertility people. I'm sure your friend, what's her name? Claire? Yeah, she's done egg implantation, right?"

Nodding, Lisa answered, "Of course. We talked about doing it on me, but . . . . Let's talk about something else."

Feeling awkward again, Megan complied quickly and their conversation drifted around for the next 45 minutes and two additional glasses of wine. As Lisa paid the tab and prepared to leave, Megan brought their discussion back to the experiment. "I have an idea, but I'm afraid you'll think I'm crazy."

"Don't be silly." Lisa's heart was racing.

"Forget it."

"Come on, don't worry. Tell me." Lisa worried that her last words were too insistent.

Megan didn't notice. "Let's try the nuclear transfer into one of my eggs. I'd be willing to carry the embryo – the baby. If it works, then the experiment is proven. If it doesn't, then we'll know we need to keep working. It'll give us the answer." Megan weighed her next words, and then leaning close and covering Lisa's hand with her own, added, "And, if there were a baby, you and Tom could have it."

Tears immediately welled in Lisa's eyes, betraying her words, "You couldn't do that, Megan . . . it's too much."

"Yes, I could. I can. I want to. It's perfect. We prove or

disprove the Ewe Factor and you guys get a baby out of it. But, Lisa, you know the stars have to align for the baby to develop and go full term."

"Yeah, of course, but . . . I don't know. It would be so hard on your body. And what about your social life?" Despite desperately wanting Megan to do this for her, Lisa genuinely felt these objections and began to regret her scheming.

Megan scoffed, "I have no social life and I don't really want one. Hard on my body? I'm one of six children and my mother is the oldest of ten. Our family genes are tried and tested for childbearing." She wondered briefly whether she should have said that, but in the context of what she was offering, it seemed appropriate. "Sleep on it tonight and we'll talk about it in the morning. I'll do the same."

"It would give us the chance to work on the Ewe Factor biochemistry."

"Exactly!"

"Then do you think we ought to keep it under wraps?" Lisa's guilt was easing.

"Yeah, I guess we probably should. But I *was* looking forward to bagels and coffee in the morning." Megan squeezed Lisa's hand and then stood. "Come on, let's go."

They left the bar and stood on the sidewalk planning the next day's schedule before heading in different directions. Lisa pledged to bring breakfast anyway, even if they skipped the announcement. They hugged quickly and then as Megan turned to walk home, Lisa called after her, "Thanks for coming out tonight."

Megan spun around and answered, "Thanks for asking me."

"It was my pleasure. Really." Lisa watched Megan walk down the gently sloping hill, glowing as she passed under each streetlight, until she passed out of sight.

As Megan suggested, Lisa slept on the "idea", and slept well. She had returned home to find Tom dozing on the couch in front of another football game. He roused enough to get up and prepare properly for bed, but not enough to notice her poorly-suppressed grin. Lisa had toyed briefly with the notion of dropping the baby idea, yet she knew this might be foolish. Even if she hadn't checked the urge, however, Tom was too sleepy to converse. Alone in her consciousness she lay in bed, flipped through a couple of magazines heaped at her bedside, and drifted into a joyful and dreamless slumber.

Megan and Lisa both awakened early on Friday, nervous with excitement and hopeful for the day ahead. They sped quickly through their morning rituals and hurried out their respective homes, making a bee-line for the lab. Lisa almost forgot to pick up the breakfast she had promised the previous evening, but remembered as she passed the Dairy Store and lucked out on a rare open parking space. The two women arrived at the lab nearly simultaneously and – without digging into the steaming coffee and hot bagels – nearly ran to the incubator room to retrieve their culture bottles. They spoke little as they methodically, but quickly, executed the process of drawing off cell samples, mixing in the antibodies and readying the fluorescing microscope.

Lisa had been first to peer through the eyepiece of the microscope. It took only a brief second to adjust the focal depth and confirm that human cells thrived in the sample. She said nothing, however, and kept a poker face as she stood up from the seat and invited Megan to look. Megan was trembling with excitement, but she too said nothing as she quickly leaned into the apparatus and searched for the tell-tale glowing cells. Spying them in an instant, she squealed involuntarily, and then, looking up at Lisa, squealed again. "It worked! It's real!" She held up an open hand to invite a high five, and then realizing this sold the moment short, stood up from the chair and hugged Lisa tightly. "Congratulations, Lisa!" was all she could muster before choking up and nearly crying.

For her part, Lisa knew all along that the experiment was going to work – again – based on her earlier experience. But she enjoyed the moment for Megan, thinking back to the happy morning in September when she herself had felt the same. So much had happened since then, she reflected – hopefully the tough and sad moments were behind them and this was the beginning of a new chapter. She pulled away from Megan's embrace to look her in the face. "Congratulations to you," she told her protégé. "You're going to be part of something really big!"

17

This had not been a productive week for Tom. He had delivered all his lectures, of course, and puttered forward on his manuscript. But he had lost the drive that propelled him for the last two months and was easily distracted. Late Friday morning, while looking for an accessory program in his computer, he stumbled across a preloaded game he had previously neither seen nor played. He spent the next hour figuring out how to play it, and then the hour after that attempting to beat each new high score he established. He was within five points of setting a new record – at least for him – when his phone rang and the surprise caused him to lose concentration just long enough to lose instantaneously. He was both angry – sheepish, too, for the sense of being caught, as he answered the phone. "Hello?"

"Hello, Tom? It's Dean Thatcher."

Now Tom felt doubly sheepish. "Good morning, sir," he said cheerfully.

"Ah, yes. Actually it's afternoon, Tom, nearly one-thirty."

Whoops, that wasn't a good start. "So it is, and I've been working so hard to catch up on email that I haven't even grabbed lunch." Tom was pleased with this cover.

"Oh, good. So, do you have any questions about my note?" asked the Dean.

"I don't think so," Tom said thoughtfully as he quickly opened his email. It paused while downloading the newest correspondence, so Tom stalled further. "Yeah, I think it was pretty clear. But, you know, while I have you on the line why don't I just read it over once more." *Come on, hurry up you stupid machine!* Tom had the urge to slap the side of his monitor.

Fortunately the Dean punctuated what for Tom was a very long silence. "I appreciate your flexibility in going down to see John Strater. I trust a one day trip downstate won't be too inconvenient."

"Oh, no, sir. That should be fine," Tom assured him as he simultaneously read the Dean's note. *Wednesday?! I have three lectures on Wednesday!* "Are you sure the middle of the week is best for him? I could go down on other days as well – even the weekend if that would be more convenient." Tom crossed his fingers as he waited for the Dean's response.

"This was his request, and you know he's a busy man. We thought it best to work around his schedule."

Dean Thatcher's declaration didn't leave room to push back. While irritated, Tom admired the Dean's use of "we" – it suggested a pantheon of powerful men carefully weighing a difficult decision. In reality, Tom knew at best it was the Dean conferring with his secretary, but more likely Thatcher just speaking royally. "I'll make my arrangements today," Tom responded.

"We've already taken care of that, Tom. We'll send the eticket itinerary over later." Dean Thatcher was leaving nothing to chance.

"Yes, sir. I was just thinking about arranging things with my wife, Lisa." He finished scanning the note. "I'll be on that plane," he said. And then, to be a little more convincing, Tom added, "I'm very much looking forward to it," which, of course, was untrue. Then Tom remembered the only thing about the situation which pleased him. "Dean Thatcher, have you had a chance to discuss this with William Rogers?"

"Yes, Professor Rogers came by to tell me how very pleased he was for this recognition of the department. He volunteered to help in any way that he could."

Stay the hell out of the way, you sneaky bastard, flashed through Tom's mind, but he spoke more diplomatically. "Wasn't that kind. I'll keep that in mind."

"Thanks, Tom, for being open to it. Perhaps in the course of this project you two can strengthen your relationship."

"Yes, perhaps." *But that's only slightly less likely than my winning the lottery.*

"I know you are very busy, so I'll let you go," said the Dean. "Do read my note, again, and let me know if you have any questions. Have a successful trip, Tom."

"Thank you, Dean. Goodbye."

Lisa and Megan spent the balance of the morning further analyzing the cell cultures, checking the controls (which technically they should have done before the test legs, had they the patience) and then thoroughly logging their results. It wasn't until early afternoon – in fact just after Tom finished his call with the Dean – that the energy from the belatedly-consumed bagels and coffee wore off, and they decided to grab lunch. Donning their jackets, hats and gloves to ward off a cold wind that had picked up overnight, they left their building without agreeing a destination and then stood outside in the forecourt quizzing each other about where to go. A fierce gust of wind cut short the third "I don't care, where do you want to go?" and Lisa suggested the restaurant in the Statler Hotel. Although a bit pricey, it was well earned by the morning's success. Further, they could cut through buildings for most of the way to stay inside. As the cold wind intensified, Megan agreed.

The restaurant was nearly empty and the staff was looking forward to the mid-afternoon closing when the two cold and hungry women arrived at the door. It took them longer to take off their outer garments than to be seated in a private table in the corner, and as the hotel school student-cum-waitress poured their ice water and introduced herself, Lisa asked for two glasses of champagne.

"Lisa, it'll knock me out for the afternoon," Megan protested.

"So what, we worked hard this morning. Come on, we need to celebrate a little bit," Lisa urged.

Megan was excited at the prospect of this luxury, but her unstoppable work ethic resisted a final time. "How 'bout at the end of the day? We'll go out for a drink . . . and I'll buy this time."

Lisa reached out and put her hand on Megan's forearm. "Megan, lighten up," she encouraged. "We deserve this."

The waitress had stood patiently by during this exchange and still awaited confirmation of the order. Sensing resolution she interjected, "Two glasses then? And is Asti Spumanti okay? It's, like, Italian champagne." Lisa nodded and the waitress stepped away to retrieve the bubbly.

They studied the menus for the next several minutes, punctuating the warm background music with "oohs" and "mmms". The waitress was back quickly with two glasses and set them down on the table. She was tempted to ask them what they were celebrating, but fought off the urge and stepped away from the table just barely out of earshot.

"To us," Lisa offered drawing back a strand of her brown hair away from her face, "the two greatest geneticists since Watson and Crick."

"And maybe in nine months' time, even greater," Megan responded with a wink.

"Hear, hear!" They clinked glasses and each took a long sip. Then, after a brief pause, each took another.

Megan was anxious to broach the matter she had raised last night. "So, you drank to my toast. Does that mean you agree to the plan?"

Lisa didn't want to seem too eager. "I'm . . . leaning toward it. Yeah."

"Cool. And Tom is okay with it?" Megan asked.

"We haven't talked about it," she replied, and then seeing Megan's surprise, added, "Yet." Megan's silence spurred her to continue a bit defensively, "Come on, Megan, you and I didn't even think of this until last night and by the time I got home, Tom was already asleep and then he left early this morning. Give me a chance to talk it over with him this weekend, okay?"

"Of course," Megan said. "Sorry, it really isn't my business, I guess."

"Don't apologize – it's a fair question. If we were to do that part of the experiment, Tom would definitely have to be onboard." Lisa thought calling it an "experiment" would play better to Megan's professional side. Megan seemed keen now, but what if cold feet were to manifest later on.

"Great, but I'll trust that part to you."

"It's a deal. But don't worry, there's no question in mind that Tom will be excited about it." Actually Lisa had a lot of questions about what Tom would think, but she knew it was her job to convince him of the plan. She also had to keep Megan at a safe distance from Tom and her relationship. Instead, she wanted Megan to see the two of them as blissful in every way but their childlessness.

The toast was the lightest moment of their lunch. Following their brief discussion of the baby, the scientists dug into the Ewe Factor research plan – how to break down the solution into its constituent parts and analyze different levels of hormones and enzymes. They suspected that some combination of the ingredients rather than any individual element led to its incredible power to revive lifeless cells. Lisa wondered – worried, really – how lucky she might have been in her early Ewe Factor solutions and whether it was truly reproducible. Only once the solution was fully characterized would she feel they had the real breakthrough.

As Lisa said this, she realized there was a further sweetener to her deal with Megan. As inventors, she and Megan could probably patent the Ewe Factor formulation – plus all the effective variations thereof – and retain all the rights. Beyond a small royalty they may have to pay the University, the rights could be extremely lucrative. Megan was excited at the prospect; doubly so when Lisa started speculating whether she might be able to open an independent laboratory. Lisa realized this was a way to get Tom to go along with the plan, as well, and salted the idea away for her weekend discussion.

Following a productive hour-long discussion, interrupted briefly by the delivery of a goat cheese salad and a Tuscan panini sandwich, Lisa and Megan paid the check, bundled for the blustery weather and bolted back into the cold wind. Their afternoon passed quickly in Lisa's office with the excitement of planning the next phase of their research. The other students in the lab sensed there was something going on with their professor and the sharp post-doc who had just joined the team – even convening a brief caucus when Lisa and Megan stepped out to the incubator. They agreed that Kristina Abbott, who was both most senior and least unwilling, should ask what was going on when they got back. Within a few minutes of their return to Lisa's office and prodded by her peers, she knocked tentatively on Lisa's door. "Hey, guys, mind if I come in for a minute?"

"Hi, Kristina, what's up?" Lisa said brightly.

"Umm . . . ." Kristina had not planned her line of questioning very thoroughly. "You guys have been super busy and working really late these last couple weeks, and we . . . I was just wondering whether I could help out with anything."

"Thanks for asking. We're just trying to get Megan's work off to a quick start." Lisa brushed her off easily and wanted Megan to understand how important secrecy was to their plan. She looked at Megan and invited her to commit. "Right, Megan?"

"Yeah, right. But thanks for offering, Kristina. Maybe once I'm farther into it – and I have a clue what I'm doing – we could take another look at it. Okay?" Megan's confidence in saying this was extremely encouraging to Lisa and she nodded in support.

"'Kay. Sorry to interrupt." Kristina backed out of the office and retreated to her place at the lab bench, shaking off the inquiring looks of those she passed on her way. She was embarrassed by what she knew had been a feeble effort.

18

"Are you frigging kidding me?! No way!" Tom dropped his silverware and it clattered on his dinner plate. "Lisa, have you lost your mind?"

Lisa had been prepared for resistance, but was startled by the intensity of Tom's response. Not sure which question to answer first, she tried to appear calm, sipped her wine and chided herself for not luring Tom out to a restaurant for this discussion. At least he was waiting for an answer Lisa thought optimistically. Her pause seemed to work – Tom picked up his cutlery and began eating again, albeit shaking his head and rolling his eyes. Lisa inhaled deeply and made her best rebuttal, "Tom, please think about it and don't just fly off the handle. It buys us time to do the biochemistry on the Ewe Factor – and maybe even patent it – and provide us a baby at the same time."

Tom instantly liked the idea of patenting the Ewe Factor, but saw easily through Lisa's argument. "You can patent it without manufacturing a baby! Do you even know where the DNA comes from? It's probably from some homeless, drug-addict who needed money for a fix."

Seeing an opportunity to put Tom on the defensive, Lisa countered, "Oh, that's very Christian." She stood up from the kitchen table and began clearing their plates.

"Come on, Lisa. We're not talking about giving money to a

charity – we're talking . . . no, no, *you're* talking about cloning a baby that might be our child."

"The chances of the pregnancy actually taking hold are slim, you know. Maybe infinitesimal."

"So why bother? It's not going to be free to have Claire do the implantation. Have you even talked to her about it? There are probably professional guidelines that prohibit her from doing it."

Hmmm . . . that's a good point, Lisa thought. She stalled at the sink, rinsing one of the plates particularly thoroughly.

Tom continued, "And what if the pregnancy takes hold but some gene is missing? Do you know that we won't get some weird deformed monster?" Tom was economical with euphemisms, preferring instead to use objectionable terms. Lisa was tempted to call it out, but she knew it would take her down an even more painful line of discussion. He loved to divert her this way. Further, knowing that she could brush this one off gave her confidence.

"We can test it for gross abnormalities. That's easy."

"Gross abnormalities?! What about Megan? How old is she? Twenty-five, twenty-six? She doesn't want to have a baby!" Tom wasn't budging very quickly, in fact, he was digging in his heels.

"It was her idea." Lisa tried to appear convincing as she said this. She left it there.

Tom didn't buy it. "Oh, really? If she came up with it then you planted the seed very cleverly. Lisa, I never took you for a schemer."

She turned away from him as she continued to clear the table, hiding her frustration. "She's an adult. We'd been married two years by the age she is now. Look, if she doesn't want to do this – if she changes her mind – that's her choice and that'd be fine." Lisa thought desperately how to move Tom from his intransigence. Perhaps if the uncertainty of the baby were taken out of the equation, he might feel more inclined. She decided to float that idea. "What if we could pick the DNA donor?" she asked. "That would give us a chance to know what we were getting."

"Like who? Us? Some friend of ours? Don't you think it would be a little odd to have a mini-version of someone kicking around? And that would be a mini-version until they grew up and were a full-sized clone."

"How about someone who's dead? That's the power of the Ewe Factor." Lisa's growing sense of desperation clouded her judgment. She couldn't see that she was quickly weighing into danger, convinced as she was at the good sense of her plan. Worse yet, Tom was intrigued – although no less opposed – at this aspect of what Lisa was suggesting, and she noticed this in his expression.

"Like who?" he asked

Unfortunately she interpreted his curiosity for interest. "I don't know. What if we could get DNA from someone who had everything we would want in a child. Good health, reasonable looks, a great mind?"

"Is this theoretical, or do you actually have someone in mind?' Tom could tell Lisa was choosing her words carefully.

"Well, I don't know," she dissembled. Despite thinking she was on the verge of success, Lisa was really about to plunge into the abyss, "Like Jeff, for instance." That was her step off the ledge.

Tom burst out laughing. "Now I know you've lost your mind."

Lisa was approaching terminal velocity. "Why do you say that?

Tom's laughing stopped and face darkened as he realized this was not just a random example. Lisa wanted to bring his nemesis back to life, and Tom let loose, "Because your obsession with him blinded you to the fact that he was arrogant and manipulative and sadistic. He cared for no one but himself. It was bad enough that I had to share you with him for all the years you worked together, and I was usually on the losing side. I hated his self-absorbed guts. The idea that you would bring him back to life to be a child I'd actually be expected to love is really, totally, fucking insulting." He stood up from the table. "This conversation is over," he said as he left the kitchen and headed down the hall and entered the TV room. The sound of the door slamming shut marked the abrupt end of Lisa's tumble through emotional space.

Had Tom spoken to Lisa on Saturday, he may have remembered to mention his trip to the Strater estate on Wednesday, but on Sunday it truly slipped his mind. Even so, he wouldn't have had many opportunities to tell her. She rose early and went to church by herself. By the time she returned he was raking leaves in their backyard, and when she came out to lend a hand, he retreated back inside to watch a football game. They were civil, but not chatty. He was hurt and angry. She was hurt and angry. It wasn't a recipe for marital harmony. By Monday the chill was passing. They kissed upon parting for work and gave each other an ever-so-slightly prolonged hug.

Tom was relieved to be back at his office, and only then recalled his trip downstate. He contemplated calling Lisa to let her know, but realized that it wasn't that a big deal and just might provoke a tiff over why he hadn't said anything earlier. He scribbled a note to himself, stuffed it in his shirt pocket, and began reviewing his notes for that day's lectures. The energy that had been wanting last week seemed to be back.

Lisa dreaded Megan's questions, fearing her face would betray the disastrous discussion with Tom. The more she thought about it, she convinced herself that she might even start crying, which she knew could unravel everything. If it wasn't already unraveled, she thought. As it was, Megan didn't mention it until the afternoon and Lisa brushed it off with, "Yeah, we had a long talk about it over the weekend, we both wanted to sleep on it a few more days, say 'til Wednesday."

"Do you want me to talk to him about it?" Megan asked.

"Umm . . . not yet. Let's talk about it again at the end of the week. It's not something we have to rush into, you know."

"But we didn't want to go public on the Ewe Factor until we at least tried for a successful gestation. And I don't remember a lot of variability in the length of that," she joked.

"Okay – Thursday, it is. I promise," Lisa said confidently.

Lisa failed to broach the subject over the next couple of days, despite her earnest intentions otherwise. On Monday evening her courage fled as she and Tom were finishing dinner – the situation felt too much like a reprise of Friday (exacerbated perhaps by the fact the meal itself was Friday's leftovers), and she wasn't anxious to see Tom melt down all over again. She promised herself to try again Tuesday, but she and Tom were drawn into a documentary on television, and knowing that she had one more day was sufficient impetus to procrastinate. Only as they were settling into bed that evening – having each turned off their bedside light, kissed each other goodnight and rolled into their nightly sleeping positions, did Tom finally end his own procrastination. "Oh, Honey, did I tell you I am traveling downstate tomorrow?" he asked.

"What? What are you talking about?" Lisa's sleepiness was decimated by an adrenaline surge.

"I'm going down to see John Strater – you know, to meet him and see the collection he's donating to the University. I thought I told you." Tom yawned.

Lisa didn't forget things like this, and she certainly wouldn't have put off talking about the baby again if she knew he was going away. "You didn't tell me. You never tell me about stuff like this," she scolded. "Are you staying the night?"

"No, no, it's just for the day. I get back to Syracuse by seven something – I'll be home by eight or eight-thirty. What's the big deal, anyway? Did we have plans for tomorrow?" Despite his fatigue, Tom was both defensive and cross.

Lisa was relieved. There would still be time for them to have their "discussion". "It's fine . . . whatever. We don't have plans. I just wish you would tell me about stuff like this."

"It's not like I travel that often. I'm . . ." Tom found it hard to say this. "I'm sorry."

"It's okay. Goodnight."

"Goodnight. I'll try not to wake you when I get up and leave. I have a really early flight." Tom looked at the clock and quickly calculated that he was only going to get five hours of sleep. For his sake, he was out within three minutes. Lisa, on the other hand, lay awake for the next hour.

Part II

1

Despite his bitterness at being used by Thatcher and the University to woo a fickle benefactor, Tom's excitement began to grow as he traveled to John Strater's home. While not yet catalogued, the collection he was about to see was rumored to be stupendous – its reputation likely enhanced by its mystery. And Strater certainly had enough money to afford whatever served his tastes. He had made billions of dollars building a network of telecom companies – and selling them off just before one of the periodic busts which plagued the industry. He had then retired to play with his winnings and tease the dozens of people and institutions who believed they needed the money more than he.

Strater did give his money away, but not quickly, and not without extracting certain conditions which generated media attention and debate. Once he had selected a blighted school in the Bronx for extensive renovation (if not total rebuilding) replete with state-of-the-art classrooms and computers at every desk. Plus he endowed the faculty positions and administrators to help attract the best instructors. His condition was that students – and faculty – had to adhere to a strict dress code, and that classes be divided by gender. Liberal New Yorkers, first aroused and then generously exhorted by the media, were aghast at his blatant "social engineering" and condemned him roundly. Strater thoughtfully responded that he was happy to hang on to the money, adding that he was glad they had "considered his gift". In the end, moderate and thoughtful heads prevailed. The gift (including associated conditions) was accepted, the building renovated and renewed and since then, every time the school won another award for scholastic achievement – and there were many – John Strater worked the photo opportunity into his busy philanthropic agenda.

Dr. Thomas Duffield was the only condition so far to Strater's newest spasm of generosity, and this, in its simplicity, was a little perplexing. It likely explained why Dean Thatcher was so quick to accept the offer and send Tom on his way with only a few days' notice. He had not wanted Strater to spend time dreaming up any strange requirements on the University which would either prove onerous or downright unacceptable. As it currently stood, all the Cornell administration need do was task a talented albeit slightly wayward faculty member to help research and catalog a collection of medieval artifacts as they were brought to Ithaca to enhance an already excellent collection. Thatcher couldn't sign up fast enough for that. Tom was not told this, of course. His only briefing had been a short email and phone call from the Dean telling him which flight he was to take and reminding Tom what an honor it must be to be specifically requested for this task. Thatcher's email ended, "Yet while you represent first your own reputation and the body of fine work which built it, and secondly, the tradition of excellent historians eager to learn from generations past, remember, too, that you represent our own Cornell University." This was Thatcher-speak for, "Don't piss off John Strater and come back without the goods." Tom dozed through most of the short flight, and later as his cab wound its way from LaGuardia Airport through the Bronx and up along the Hudson, he wondered whether there was a special school for deans where they learned such diplomatic code.

As the cab ride stretched past three-quarters of an hour, Tom became antsy. While the trip had become progressively scenic and attractive, he knew that he was going to have to do this all over again later that day on the return. Row houses of Queens had given way to deserted industrial parks and empty garages. But it wasn't long before cement and cinder block store fronts were replaced by brick, stone and clapboard houses. Similarly, instead of prohibitions against littering which threatened heavy fines (and which appeared to be either summarily ignored or placed too late to make a difference) there were signs warmly welcoming travelers to towns founded in the 1600's. When Tom saw historic plaques and dates on the houses he knew he must be getting close. But that was twenty minutes ago – since then the plaques were still there, but harder to read since the houses began moving back from the road. Ten minutes later the houses could only be glimpsed now and again through dense trees and rhododendrons, with winding approaches marked either by "Private Drive" or some classy name on a green sign with neat white lettering.

Just as Tom sat forward to ask the driver whether he was sure they hadn't missed their objective, the cabbie slowed and turned onto one such driveway marked "Longmynd". It wound back and forth through artfully tended natural gardens and each time Tom was sure the next turn would reveal the house he was treated to another rolling, yet house-free expanse. At last, the house – country house, that is – came into sight across a finely manicured lawn. It was a well-planned reveal, specifically intended to surprise the visitor with the building's finest aspect, square-on and far enough away to accentuate its grandeur. Longmynd was a stunning gothic revival house from the mid-nineteenth century, certainly one of the finest in the country, if not the world. It had been built by a leading businessman of the day who was trying to relive the glory days when a man's house actually was a castle. John Strater had paid millions for the estate and then invested millions more to return it to its original condition. Tom chuckled at the irony of the modern day magnate recreating the recreator. It struck him like a series of mirrors in which each image was progressively more distant, dim and indistinct.

The cab crawled closer to the house, giving Tom a chance to take in the full magnificence of the building. Its gray stone towers and gables actually represented a number of different periods of gothic architecture – square, crenellated towers mixed with peaked facades. Most dominant was a five or six story tower which appeared to be a mini version of one of the great British cathedrals. Although designed and executed within a decade, Longmynd was built to resemble the rambling great houses of England which were built, rebuilt, expanded and renovated over hundreds of years. Other than the stone color being a bit too uniform and the entire appearance slightly too neat and clean, the effect was very good. Tom hoped this foreshadowed the impending meeting, but he doubted it. Strater hired people to know and interpret – he just showed off their work. Surely he didn't really understand it himself.

The cab pulled under a covered stone portico – a nineteenth century concession to both fashion and comfort – and a handsome, mid-twenty year old man dressed in khakis and a blue polo shirt stepped out promptly and opened Tom's door. "Hello and welcome to Longmynd, Professor Duffield. We have been looking forward to your visit," he said with a genuine smile. Rather than stepping out, Tom paused to look at the cab fare and dig out his wallet from his back pocket. "Oh, we'll get this leg of the trip for you, sir," the man called out quickly. "Please, go ahead in the front door and I will be right with you."

Tom needed no further prompting. He grabbed his computer bag and hopped out, calling thanks to the cabbie over his left shoulder. Circling around the front of the cab, he took in the entryway of the great building while also watching the man negotiate with the driver. Tom couldn't figure out whether his greeter was a security guard or a butler, but in either case was sure his name was Chad or Troy and that he probably doubled as the tennis pro for the estate. Was there a Mrs. Strater? Tom tried to remember – if so, Strater better watch out for this guy. He stepped inside and stood in the hall for no more than a moment before the man entered and extended his hand to shake. "I'm sorry I didn't introduce myself outside, my name is Rob Tucker. I assist Mr. Strater here on the estate. Thank you so much for coming down to visit today."

Tom shook Tucker's hand, squeezing hard so as not to appear intimidated. Now sizing him up, and judging by what he said, Tom decided Tucker was a butler. "Thank you for having me. And what is it that you assist Mr. Strater with?" Tom wanted to suggest "fixing tea" or "getting dressed" but he didn't want to come off as rude – certainly not this early in his command appearance.

"Well, I'm an architect by training and I led the renovation project on Longmynd. Now that it's mostly done, I've been working on helping with the research and cataloguing of his collection. Unfortunately, the few courses I took in medieval history don't quite do justice to it. That's why we're so excited for you to help in the project. And we're grateful, too, for your volunteering to pitch in on this project with all the course work and research you must be doing."

Tucker's earnest expression told Tom that this was no joke or gibe, and so Tom chose not to correct him regarding "volunteering". Instead, he opted for courtesy and tact, which didn't always come naturally. "Well, the collection has become quite a source of interest for historians," he responded. "I'm honored to play a role in bringing it into public view. Will we be working together on this?"

"Unfortunately, I have a prior commitment today," Tucker glanced down at his watch, "and, gosh, I need to leave here in the next ten minutes to make it." He motioned for Tom to follow and led him down the wide hallway to a large parlor. "I'm sorry I won't be able to stay, but," he glanced at his watch again, "I really have to be somewhere else. But I've left my notes with Mr. Strater – and he knows most of what I have uncovered, the little that it is. I hope as the project moves ahead that I can learn from you." Tucker turned and looked out the window at the lawn. "Mr. Strater was working out this morning over in his gym in the old stables but I think he must be done by now. Let me just run over there and make sure he knows you're here." Tucker headed back toward the hallway, and then turned. "I'll have to take off directly, so I'll say goodbye now." He shook Tom's hand once more, saying, "Professor Duffield, it's a real pleasure to meet you, sorry it's so brief, this time, anyway. I really wanted to tell you how much I enjoyed your book on the Norman Conquest."

Tom was now fully charmed. "It was very nice meeting you also, and please call me Tom. I look forward to working with you – I would love to hear more about your work here at Longmynd. It's truly stunning."

Tucker thanked him and stepped quickly down the hall out the front door. Tom watched him jog across the lawn toward buildings in the distance, and then turned his attention to the room into which he had been brought. In the nineteenth century this was the parlor for entertaining guests. It was large and bright, thanks to floor-to-ceiling windows on three sides, and had a massive fireplace in the center of the outside wall which Tom could imagine hosted a grand Yule log in years past. The furnishings were well chosen – Victorian gothic revival pieces to match Longmynd's real period, with a smattering of older pieces which may have been true Gothic from the 15th or 16th century. The walls were painted an austere gray on flat plaster, with a trompe l'oeil border decoration to look like swagged cloth hanging a foot or two down from the tops of the walls. The woven floor carpet appeared to be Aubusson, the finest of European carpets and likely a match to what had lain there originally.

What surprised Tom the most about this room was the art. Rather than original oils, Strater had hung reproductions of Great Masters' paintings from the world's most famous museums. He recognized a Vermeer and a Holbein, maybe a Hieronymus Bosch, and knew he could place the rest with a little time to think about it.

Surely Strater could afford the real thing from these very same artists if he were patient and willing to part with a lot of cash. Tom stepped closer to one he recognized as daVinci's *Madonna of the Yarnwinder*. It depicted a beautiful, curly haired Madonna robed in dark blue sitting outside in front of a mountainous background. Barely constrained within her arms is a nude and squirming Christ child gazing at her long, wooden yarnwinder which he holds up to appear as a cross. Tom knew this painting because it had been stolen in a brazen heist from a castle in Scotland. For an instant, Tom had the horrible feeling that Strater had the stolen masterpiece. But the chill in his spine passed quickly as he confirmed that it was a very good photographic reproduction. On the other hand, the frame caught his attention. It appeared original to the period and was thus quite an expensive way to display a reproduction. *These rich people are very strange*, Tom thought as he caught Strater's entrance via peripheral vision and spun around, only slightly embarrassed.

"Welcome to Longmynd, Tom," Strater announced, "I truly appreciate your coming down for the day. I know you're very busy." They shook hands warmly and Strater continued, "I am glad you had a chance to meet Robert Tucker. He was thrilled to make your acquaintance, but sorry he couldn't stay longer. I am sure you heard what a prodigy he was at NYU – his work in restoring Longmynd bears that out."

Tom appreciated the gracious welcome, and even if he did resent having to make this trip (and do this work, for that matter) he wanted to get off on the right footing with this wealthy and generous man. "It's nice to see you again, and particularly in such a nice setting. This house . . . Longmynd, is truly magnificent. Well done to you and Robert."

"I see that you were taking a look at one of my side hobbies," Strater offered.

Tom wasn't sure how to respond. Certainly Strater didn't mean nicely-framed reproductions. So he paused and then just answered thoughtfully, "Yes."

Strater turned to look at the painting, saying, "And I think it is nice to have these as well, even if they're not the originals. Well, in this case," he motioned at the *Madonna of the Yarnwinder*, "the original seems to be a bit elusive. You heard about the theft, didn't you?"

"I read about it at the time. I thought – hoped, I guess – they'd caught the thieves by now." Tom continued desperately trying to figure out what hobby Strater was talking about and concluded he must be talking about the period frames after all.

"Oh, no," Strater answered quickly. "I doubt they'll ever find the selfish bastards who took this away from the public." He shook his head ruefully and quietly studied the painting.

Tom found the silence awkward and filled it diplomatically. "Well that is a beautiful frame. I assume it's Italian and contemporaneous with daVinci?" He pursed his lips and nodded as if to answer his own question and appear knowledgeable.

"I suppose," Strater answered, shrugging. "It is a nice frame, now that you mention it. I don't know where it came from exactly."

"That's not your hobby then?" Tom was once again at a loss.

"Goodness, no," Strater chuckled. He reached down to a table below the painting and picked up an object Tom had not previously noticed. "I was talking about the 'aspo nero' – the black yarnwinder." He held it up for Tom to see. "This is the original prop for the painting. I found it in a small estate sale in Amboise, France – very close to Clos Lucé where da Vinci lived when he was painting for Francis the First. As I researched the piece, I found that the family from which it came had been in service at Clos Lucé for generations. Further, the yarnwinder is definitely Italian, not French – they were generally longer and turned differently. Like painters of his day, da Vinci used his own possessions as objects in the painting. And this one – and the painting it came from – was likely a favorite. There are at least two similar paintings attributed to his workshop."

He held the yarnwinder out for Tom to hold, and Tom took it gingerly with both hands.

It was an eighteen-inch long spindle, delicately turned at both ends, with perpendicular cross pieces three inches from either end, which themselves were about three inches long and rotated ninety degrees from each other. Tom stepped closer to the image and compared the item in his hands to the one painted by da Vinci five hundred years before. They certainly looked identical, and based on Strater's research, the provenance was reasonable. "Wow!" was all he could muster.

Strater continued, "If you know da Vinci, you know that there is more to the story than meets the eye." Noting Tom's curious look, he went on, "In Italian, the words for black yarnwinder – reversed, of course, as in all Romance languages – is 'aspo nero'. If said quickly, however, as one word, it means 'I will show'. That's what the Christ baby is doing here, holding the cross, pointing to heaven and promising the way to God.

"The joy, the excitement of finding this – and finding out what it was – was what triggered this sideline collection." He motioned around the room, continuing, "These were all everyday objects until chosen by the painters to play some role in what turned out to be a great painting. They were immortalized by the artists." Strater became animated as he continued. "They were given a meaning – a purpose – far beyond what they were originally created to do." He paused to reflect on his words and let Tom do the same, and then added, "Besides, it seems so passé to collect paintings. Every billionaire has to go out and buy a few great paintings to show he has class, and then do his damnedest not to ruin them. I needed my own variation on that old theme."

Tom was intrigued and impressed by Strater's appreciation for the objet d'art and wanted to learn more. He looked around the room for a painting he recognized, and stepped over to Vermeer's *The Milkmaid* and tried to figure out which object nearby was featured as a prop. It was a simple painting featuring a woman in a bright yellow tunic and blue skirt pouring milk from an earthenware jug into a shallow bowl. Tom didn't see either of those pieces, nor the delft jug pictured on the table, nor any of the many baskets. He was stumped and turned to Strater. "I guess I need a little help on this – as you'll soon find out, Art History isn't one of my strengths."

"No issue," Strater was quick to respond, "It's quite subtle". He pointed to a small box-like object hanging on a nail in the wall and said, "It's the foot warmer." He then pointed to the object at the bottom right-hand corner of the painting. "Most people pay no attention to it because the image of the woman is so captivating and the way that she is concentrating on pouring the milk draws your attention to the table. All those objects on the table could have featured in the still life paintings of that day – but Vermeer brought the still life *to life* with the little ribbon of milk and the gentle hands of the Milkmaid.

Yet he put the foot warmer there on purpose – it's not as if it was just there in the room and he decided to paint it in. No, no. Take a look at it. Does anything strike you as strange?" Strater was enjoying putting the Professor into a learning exercise.

Tom was game and stepped closer to the painting to study the image. The foot warmer was a wooden box – about 10 inches square, 6 inches high and missing one side where a pot holding hot embers could be placed inside. A decorative and symmetrical pattern of piercings, through the top, would allow heat to pass through. It took a while for him to notice that a splinter of wood had broken off the base and lay nearby. He looked quickly to the real object hanging on the wall and confirmed that it, too, was missing the splinter. "I see that it is slightly broken," Tom said tentatively. "Is that what you're getting at?"

"Partially . . . keep looking." Strater appeared to enjoy this detective game.

"Oh, and it looks like it fell from the wall. Here's a nail on the floor near it, and a hole in the plaster where it broke free."

"Precisely! And so amid the domestic tranquility and order of the Milkmaid doing her thing, this thing came crashing off the wall and lays at her feet. There's one more detail worth noticing. Look inside the foot warmer." Strater's excitement was leading him to give hints.

"The item inside hasn't fallen out, nor broken. Is it some kind of earthenware?"

"Yes, and good work. A lot of people stare at that for hours and can't see it. So that's the mystery. Did the Milkmaid put the crockery in there as it lay broken on the floor? How did it come down hard enough to splinter the wood, but not dislodge the crock? Who knows? Vermeer certainly meant something by it. As I said, the artists used these objects in much more interesting ways than was ever imagined by those who used the items, or for that matter, those who created them in the first place.

Well, enough about this. If you don't stop me now, I could go on all day and we'd never get to what you came here for. By the way, what time is your return flight?"

"It's scheduled for 6:30, so we have lots of time. Quite frankly I appreciate your showing me this. I didn't realize that you'd dug into these things so deeply."

Strater picked up on this quickly. "So you thought I was a shallow rich guy who just dabbled so I'd have something to brag about?" He chuckled – and Tom carefully controlled his facial expression to make sure that he didn't betray his real thoughts. "Shall we go see the other collection?"

Tom began to nod and then caught himself. "I was just wondering about this painting over here – is it Bosch?"

"Yes, indeed. Good eye. *The Seven Deadly Sins and the Four Last Things* – the original is in Madrid – the Prado. Bosch was a strange guy, as you probably know." Tom didn't know, but nodded nonetheless. "He did all sorts of moralizing and reveled in showing how horrible Hell would be. He almost seemed to enjoy how gruesome it was, but I suppose we can give him the benefit of the doubt and think he was just trying to warn the masses. Anyway, each of these segments of this painting – the arcs of this circle – depict one of the seven deadly sins. See this segment here? He pointed to the lower right hand quadrant, and Tom nodded, truthfully this time. "This shows Pride – the woman is looking into a mirror held by the devil." Strater stepped up to a large, standing court cupboard next to the painting and said, "This is the piece of furniture pictured behind the mirror." Tom stepped closer to inspect it and Strater continued, "I'm sure Bosch was using this expensive cupboard to reinforce the idea of pride and showing off – see the way this creepy monster thing is hiding behind it?"

Tom studied both the cupboard and its image in the painting. It was clearly the work of a master craftsman and the finest type of cabinetry of its time. Linenfold paneling flanked carved doors which were connected by iron, strap-work hinges, and while originally constructed of pale, white oak – and depicted that way by Bosch – it had oxidized to a deep, honey brown. As far as Tom could tell, it was the actual piece so he decided not to challenge Strater on the provenance.

Strater said, "What I like most about Bosch's painting is the saying here," he pointed to the center of the image depicting Jesus with a Latin inscription underneath.

Tom had studied Latin extensively and saw the chance to show he at least knew something. Dramatically, he read it aloud, "Cavé, Cavé, Deus Videt."

Strater translated it equally dramatically, "'Beware, Beware, God is Watching' – come on, let's see the real collection."

2

A short distance down the hall from the gothic parlor was a much cozier room which likely originally served as the Gentlemen's

Retiring Room or Cigar Room. With dark walnut paneling and book shelves from floor to ceiling, it had only one source of natural light, a French door looking out to the lawn and the Hudson River. It was lavishly curtained with green velvet. Tom detected the smell of old and expensive tobacco seeping out of smoke-saturated walls, but knew that was likely his imagination – Strater had sanitized the entire house during the makeover. Pairs of dark leather and overstuffed armchairs conferred in several places around the fifteen foot square room, and were flanked by mahogany bureaux. As a more private room than the parlor, it had given up the medieval pretences and assumed Victorian ones.

Strater motioned for Tom to sit in one of the chairs and then stroked his chin thoughtfully. "Where to start, where to start," he said to himself. After a pause he called out slightly louder, "Anything in particular you would like to see?"

"Frankly, my curiosity is piqued from what you just showed me, but I really don't know what you have. Show me the latest, or your favorite." Then Tom struck upon a better idea. "I know," he added quickly, "show me the item that'll headline the collection. What will be the marquis item? What will be the center spread in the catalogue?"

"Well, there are a couple items that spring to mind. Let me show you what I picked up a couple of months ago." Strater strode to one of the bureaux and slowly and carefully opened the top drawer. He reached in with both hands and extracted a blue, pacific-cloth bag which ran the four foot length of the drawer. Placing it on top of the bureau, Strater stepped to one end of bag and began untying the ribbon which held it closed. Then, with a mix of ceremony and reverence, he extracted an iron sword. Tom judged it to be very early, and the pommel at the end of the handle suggested it was French or English of the 11th or 12th century." Strater was eager to test Tom's knowledge in an area closer to his scholarship. "What can you tell me about it?"

"I'll guess English and 12th century. If the leather handle hadn't rotted off, I would find it hard to believe that it's genuine."

"Oh, it's genuine. No question. And you're right on the money so far."

"Why so little deterioration?"

"I'll get to that in a minute. Any other guesses from your side?" Strater appeared anxious to tell the sword's story.

Tom didn't have much to add. "Some noble carried it at a great battle . . . let's see, what battles do I have to choose from? Hattin? Jerusalem?" Tom knew both of these battles of the Crusades well.

"The noble part is right, but we don't know anything about the sword's battle honors." He couldn't hold out much longer. "What do you know about Hugh de Morville?"

This wasn't the first time that Strater had asked him this question. Suddenly Tom remembered their first conversation during last summer's reunion cocktail party. Like most of the junior faculty, Tom was instructed to attend and schmooze with alumni. His strategy was to spend most of the time standing at the bar, chatting with the young bartenders and keeping his wineglass full. Strater had approached the bar, read Tom's nametag (which indicated he was History Faculty) and asked him his specialty. Finding it much easier to talk about his work than engage in chit-chat with self-important and rich alumni, Tom had launched into a long explanation of his studies. He remembered being surprised that Strater appeared to recognize the key players and periods, and as Tom described some of the more arcane aspects of Henry the Second's rule, Strater had asked the very same question. "Not a lot more than I told you last summer," he now answered coyly. "So all of this now makes sense," Tom said with a knowing smile, "you were interviewing me last summer."

"Oh, don't read too much into it," Strater reassured him. "I had just acquired this sword and it was simply top of mind. I was very impressed by what you knew – and on a couple week's reflection I realized that you were just the person to help me with this project." He paused to let Tom answer, but the professor remained quiet, his attention recaptivated by the sword. "So what are you thinking?"

"I'm thinking that this becomes very interesting if you know when de Morville had it." Tom was replaying Hugh de Morville's violent and troubled life through his mind. As a young and ambitious member of the royal court, de Morville witnessed numerous power struggles between Henry II and Thomas Becket, a close friend whom Henry had installed as Archbishop of Canterbury and head of the Roman Catholic Church in England. Becket's conscience proved stronger than Henry expected – he refused to act as the King's puppet and wrangled regularly with his sovereign. On what turned out to be the last of these showdowns, the King swirled into a rage and yelled "who will rid me of this man?" Hugh de Morville and three others were keen to answer the call, and rode out before the Henry could douse his rage and rethink his words. Within hours the knights had reached Canterbury, and in what has become one of the most infamous acts of an exceedingly brutal age, chased Becket around the cathedral and then scattered his brains on the altar as he was praying. "Was this sword at Canterbury?" Tom asked bluntly.

Strater weighed his response, conscious of both the drama of the moment and the much greater drama surrounding the sword. After a pause, he looked into Tom's grey-blue eyes and said simply, "Yes."

"Christ Almighty!"

"I think those were Thomas Becket's last words."

"Oh, that's terrible," Tom chided. "Seriously, I mean . . . how could you know Hugh de Morville carried this sword to Canterbury? He probably had a dozen swords during his life."

"What did de Morville and his little posse do after killing

Becket?"

"They found out that King Henry was pissed and they hightailed it to de Morville's family seat at Knaresborough Castle in Yorkshire." Tom had researched and written extensively about Henry II's deep guilt over Becket's murder and thoroughly knew the key players and events.

"Precisely!" Strater congratulated him. "And what else – and I'm not talking about their trip to see Pope Alexander begging forgiveness. What else did Hugh de Morville do in England?"

Tom was amazed at Strater's depth in the subject. He had encountered very few people who knew this period of history, let alone enjoyed it, and he was rapidly gaining respect for this rich benefactor. "Let me see. He was stripped of his land and title . . . he built a church with his brother-in-law . . . I think he died in –"

"Back up, back up. Tell me about the church," Strater coached.

"Ah, yes, the Church of Thomas á Becket in . . . um, I can't remember where." Tom was searching his memory for the right village in Yorkshire, but he couldn't put his finger on it.

"Hampsthwaite."

"Yes. The Church of Thomas á Becket in Hampsthwaite. OK, so tell me the story."

Strater continued, "Well, most of the church has been demolished and rebuilt over the last thousand years, except for the original Norman tower which was spared for either its size or its magnificence, or both. Back in 1901 the parish folk decided to add a porch, and a local builder had to tear up some of the foundation. Right below the threshold to the church, he found a lead-covered, completely-sealed, oak box. The builder expected to find it packed with gold. Instead he found this."

"They probably sell a sword a week with that story in Hampsthwaite."

"No, the family traced the provenance pretty faithfully.

Considering the amount of money I was offering, I needed to be convinced."

"Well, I'll be damned!" Tom touched the part of the blade which he imagined had struck the death blow.

Strater continued, "Morville's biography said he finally rested guilt-free after the church was dedicated. Don't you think it's terribly poetic that he made it so that people would tread forever on the weapon as they entered Thomas á Becket's church?"

"Not exactly forever. More like 725 years."

"That seems sufficient," Strater rationalized.

The next hours passed in a blur as Strater produced one spectacular item after another. Any one of them could have been the marquis item of a museum collection, each a witness to the greatest shaping moments of European history. The amazement Tom felt holding Hugh de Morville's sword grew into speechless wonder when he held the helmet of Charles d'Albret, constable of France and slain commander of the defeated French army at Agincourt in 1415. Then he examined a tapestry from the same workshop in Bayeux which turned out the chronicle of William the Conqueror's victorious invasion. In contrast to the battle scenes of its more famous partner, this needlework showed William's consolidation of rule in England, including land grants, building the Tower of London and directing the Domesday Book.

They paused for lunch, and as Tom anxiously gulped down the last of his soft drink so they could get back to work, Strater delicately laid out a printed vellum page. Tom recognized it immediately. "My goodness, a Gutenberg bible fragment. With all due respect, John," Tom called him by his given name for the first time, "I would expect you to haul out an entire Bible, not one page." He smiled to signal he was teasing. "Is this part of the copy broken up in the 20's and sold piecemeal?"

"You've seen enough today to give me the benefit of the

doubt, haven't you?" Strater mocked being hurt.

Tom realized there must be more than met the eye and began to study it more closely. The edges of the pages suggested that it had never been bound, nor had the heading words been hand illuminated like all the pages in known versions. There were notes scribbled at the bottom, but the script and the German made them unreadable – at least to Tom. "Was it a test strike?"

"Well you can be the judge of that. Look again." Strater encouraged him. As Tom stooped to look again and lifted his glasses to see the detail, Strater started giving him clues. "Tell me what you know about Gutenberg's bibles."

"There are about 70 known to exist of the 180 originally printed, most of them are in Germany. Printed in the 1450's – 1455, I think. They were hand illuminated. Umm . . . what am I missing?" He needed a little more help.

"Different versions?"

"Oh yeah, 36- and 42-line versions and the 42's were thought to be first."

"Very good. How many lines is this one?"

Tom counted quickly and reached 44. "I counted too fast, but must be 42."

"Count again."

The professor pushed his glasses up over his head and then counted the lines slowly by two's, inaudibly at first, and then speaking progressively louder. "32, 34, 36, 38, 42 . . . 44. Damn, am I missing something?"

"No, you've counted right each time. You could count it ten more times and still hit 44."

"So it *was* some kind of test strike?"

"Probably," Strater answered. "I have had some people try to decipher the notes at the bottom of the page, but I haven't found anyone who could crack it. They do seem to refer to the bottom lines of printing, however."

"Do you think it is Gutenberg's hand?" Tom had seen enough during the day now to respect Strater's opinion. The benefactor had proven himself both a skeptic and a scholar, and Tom realized he felt comfortable relying on him.

"I think it is, but I could never prove it. I got it in a small town near Mainz, where Gutenberg worked, from the estate of a patron. The family had one of the original bibles before it worked its way into a museum collection."

"So – arguably – this is one of the first products of printing with movable type?" Tom was weighing the importance of this ancient piece of vellum. In the brief moment before Strater could answer, he imagined himself lecturing on this piece in a grand auditorium.

"Well, considering the reduction of lines, perhaps we should call it *re*-movable type."

Mesmerized by Strater's amazing and important collection, the men were completely unaware of the hours that had passed. Only as the late afternoon sun broke through the western-facing French doors at about the same time that a tall-case clock in the hall outside struck four, did their consciousness of time reemerge. The men looked at each other as if they had just awakened from a dream. "I had no idea it was so late," Strater said. "My goodness, I hope I haven't held you here too long."

Checking his watch instinctively despite having just heard the hours chime, Tom reassured him that he would make his flight if he left soon. "I had arranged for that cabby to come back at quarter past four, so I guess we ought to wrap it up. I can't tell you how much I have enjoyed this today. You probably didn't know how skeptical I was about this whole thing—"

"Oh, I could tell," Strater interrupted, sporting a forgiving smile. "But, I don't blame you for that. One of my greatest lessons from all of the research that I've done for this collection is that

History is full of wealthy yet ignorant men whose imagination, what little there might have been, was focused solely on demonstrating how great they were. I'd like to buck that tradition." He paused to let Tom respond, but the guest remained silent, weighing his words. "Sure, I love the media attention and donating this collection will generate a fair bit," he continued, "but I guess I am seeking a legacy beyond money. If this motley collection – well alright, it's better than motley – if this assemblage of fascinating things from medieval history can reignite the tiniest spark of interest for things more meaningful, more sublime than Ultra HDTVs or luxury cars or a pop star's latest faux pas, then I will rest easy.

I knew from the first moment we met that you were the perfect person for this project. And I saw it into your eyes today – I saw true, earnest wonder. Nobody can put that on. You're into History for its purest value – for you it's about why people did what they did back then and how that shaped how we live and talk and think today. You don't kiss ass – mine, your boss. Tom, that appeals to me. You don't get to be a billionaire by kissing people's asses." Strater stopped to let the words sink in.

Tom was flattered, though somewhat concerned about what Dean Thatcher may have shared. He had been so quick to dismiss this man *because* of his wealth and background. Yet now he realized Strater was his equal for both passion and knowledge of history. The potential for this collection to captivate the imagination of the public and scholars alike was astounding. It might well represent the rebirth of history into the mainstream. His head spun with the possibilities, and he was anxious to get started. "Thank you for asking Dean Thatcher for my help. This might be the most exciting and meaningful work I will ever do. I can't thank you enough." While these were not parting words, Tom extended his hand and shook Strater's hand.

The men discussed details for shipping the items to Ithaca, timing for their next meeting, and means for electronically sharing references, citations and other data. They were absentmindedly making half steps toward the door when Strater halted and exclaimed, "Oh shit, I have totally spaced out. I forgot the one thing that would make your trip all worth it." Tom could tell he was only half kidding and felt slightly breathless.

"Every single thing you've showed me today qualified for that, even those first items – the props from the paintings – in the other room. What could possibly top it all?" This was a true question, not a polite challenge. Tom knew Strater didn't over promise.

Strater checked the urge to answer and walked to the bookcase where he extracted a large handled box. It looked like an oversized briefcase, covered with brown leather and polished steel caps on each of the eight corners. He brought it back to the table at which they had stood for the past several hours and gently set it down, deliberately sliding it to the center and justifying the edges parallel to those of the table. Tom's heart began pounding as he witnessed the ceremony, and he took a deep breath as Strater put his fingers on the latches and began to flip them open. Strater then stopped and looked up at Tom. "I can't just bust this open without whetting your appetite a little bit," he teased.

"Whetting my appetite?!" Tom responded instantly. "I'm like Pavlov's dog, here. Every time you open a drawer I start salivating. Believe me, I'm on tenterhooks here. What is this?"

"I know you're a Richard the First buff. So you know which was his favorite weapon."

Sizing up the box, Tom knew it was too small to hold a sword, which would have been his first answer. "His favorite personal weapon?" he asked.

"Oh, no . . . sorry. For his armies, I mean, during the Crusades."

"Then I would say the crossbow. It had good range and accuracy. An arrow – or 'bolt' I guess they were called – was usually lethal, even versus armor. But this case isn't big enough for the kind of crossbow his armies carried."

"No, it isn't," Strater replied, leaning down, flipping the latches and lifting the lid. The crimson velvet interior snugly housed a large golden object. Strater reached in and carefully lifted out the object. Tom could see that it was a medieval reliquary, very common for holding items of particular – usually religious – significance. At a little over a foot in height, the reliquary's base was a flat, quatrefoil plate with a small foot on each of the four lobes. Above that was a decoratively-turned shaft supporting a six-sided, lantern-like housing with very thin glass permitting a view to the prized contents within. Topping off the housing was a rounded gold dome with a spiked finial. Tom bent closer to look inside at what appeared to be a slender, but jagged piece of wood about three inches in length. Strater continued, "It's a little ironic, don't you think?"

"I'm afraid I'm a step behind you." Tom's mind was racing, but he still had no idea what he was looking at.

"It's ironic that he would have been killed by a crossbow bolt. This one, to be exact." He put on an exaggerated grin. "Live by the sword, die by the sword. Isn't that the expression?"

"Christ!" Tom muttered under his breath unconsciously. After a prolonged look at the bolt fragment he broke his eyes away and turned to face Strater. "Are you shitting me?" Finally, after a long day of handling items which previously he could only see as print on a page or vague imaginings, Tom was rattled. Any diplomacy or decorum he had brought to Longmynd that morning was now long gone. "This is un-freaking-believable."

"I told you this would top everything else." Strater was still wearing his Cheshire Cat-grin. "Come on, tell me what you know about this," he coaxed.

"March, 1199. Some farmer peasant in Limousin, France, unearthed a significant horde of Roman treasure and the local lord held back paying Richard the First – Richard the Lionheart, as everybody called him – his full due. So Richard surrounded the local castle, Châlus, where the lord and his few knights holed up, and was riding around it to figure out how best to attack. One of the few besieged knights, who apparently had been fending off arrows all day with an iron frying pan, took careful aim with his crossbow and let one fly at Richard. The King had been pretty cocky that day. He hadn't worn all his armor—"

"And he watched the archer taking aim," Strater interjected.

"That's right, he even taunted the guy! Then Richard failed to duck and whammo, he got nailed in the shoulder. By all accounts, it was a pretty good shot."

"But it didn't kill him outright." Strater obviously knew the story well.

"No, they removed him from the field and summoned the 'surgeon' who botched removing it – is that why this piece is so jagged? I mean, was this the part of the shaft next to the point?"

"I think so, the story behind this is that the wood is not just oxidized, it's stained."

"With blood?"

"What else?"

"Wow." Tom bent down again to look at the fragment and then continued the story as he closely eyed the piece of wood. "Gangrene set in within a few days and then it was just a matter of time. On April 6th he died in his mother's arms. Amazing, isn't it, that in those days – long before telephones or email – word of his impending death got to his mother, Eleanor of Aquitaine who was living in Poitiers, a couple hundred miles away, and she was able get there in time."

"He was her favorite son. Even though she was 77 at the time, nothing was going to keep her from comforting him on his death bed. She was an amazing woman. I wish I could find something from her life," Strater said wistfully.

"And you don't think the bolt which took her son's life qualifies for that?"

"Well, I suppose. Anyway, this came down via Bishop Walter of Rouen who was there at the death. His church connection probably accounts for it being housed in this reliquary."

"This made my day – as you knew it would." Tom's deep appreciation showed in his face.

"Would you like to take it back with you?"

Tom was taken aback, yet very excited at the prospect. "Seriously? I'd love to. You'd trust me with it?"

"I'm trusting you with all of this." He smiled and shrugged, "Of course, it's insured for a lot of money."

Despite his curiosity, Tom fought off the urge to ask how much. He thought knowing that would make him nervous – or more nervous – during the return trip. "This will give me great inspiration to get started. I can put my hands directly on a couple of early texts that chronicle Richard's death. John, this has been a fantastic day – and I can't tell you how exciting it will be to start cataloguing your collection."

"It's Cornell's collection now. I've given it away."

"This is more than a gift. It's . . . it's . . . miraculous – that these things have been saved for us to see and learn from." He checked his watch. "I'd love to stay longer and talk, but I'm afraid I'll miss my flight. Will you forgive me leaving so quickly?"

Strater placed the reliquary carefully back into its shaped velvet housing, closed the case lid and snapped the clips. Sliding it across the table, he handed it to Tom. "No, don't worry about it. I've enjoyed spending the day with you and I look forward to our next meeting. Let me see you to the door."

The men made their way out of the gentlemen's parlor, past the tall case clock that was now chiming four-thirty, and arrived at the front door. The cab was already there, as expected, and the driver made a point of looking at his watch as soon as he saw them.

Tom set the reliquary case down on the floor and shook Strater's hand. "Thank you, again, for everything." He picked up the case and held it slightly higher as he inclined his head toward it. "I'll take good care of it."

Strater put his hand on Tom's shoulder. "I know you will. And you're welcome. Can I prepay the cab fare for you?"

"No thanks, Rob got it for me inbound already." Tom relished the thought of sticking Rogers with a big travel expense. "I've got plenty of cash." He settled himself in the back seat, shut the door and gave Strater a final wave. "LaGuardia Airport, please."

The cabby, who had proven himself short of words that morning, pulled away without comment and guided the car along Longmynd's winding drive toward the main road. Tom meant to look back at John Strater and wave one last time, but his attention was drawn to the leather case lying next to him. He traced his finger along its edges, tapped it gently, and quietly said to himself, "Wow."

3

The moment Tom arrived at the airport, he knew he was in deep trouble. Cabs and livery cars were lined up trying to find a curb to drop their passengers. Private vehicles, mostly SUVs Tom noted, were stacked up curbside, unable to pull out because of buses in the second lane. Lines of people extended outside the terminal, blocking the way for the lost and confused travelers who would otherwise be milling about aimlessly. Thus, they stood in small groups with exasperation registered deeply on their collective brow. Tom swore under his breath and checked his watch. He was tight for time without the lines. "I can get out here," he barked at the cabbie.

The cabby shook his head. "Can no let you here," he answered.

Tom had forgotten that the man didn't speak English – he knew English words, but he strung them together randomly. "Please, here. How much?" Tom barked. Maybe broken English would work better. Tom held up money.

"No here. Ticket. Fine." The cabbie said quickly, again shaking his head.

"I must get out now. Is that price?" he asked, pointing to the meter and swearing again under his breath.

"You must wait." This sentence was grammatically correct, but not what Tom wanted to hear. The cabbie pointed to the drop-off zone ahead. "You . . . out . . . there."

"Christ!" Tom said, audibly this time. He gave up arguing, but checked his watch. No tip for you, he thought spitefully.

They made the drop-off curb in five painfully slow minutes and Tom made good on his resolution to stiff the driver. Tom paid the $79.25 fare with four $20 bills and waited impatiently for the seventy-five cents change, and then he made his way quickly to the terminal. Although not a frequent traveler with the airline, he felt confident he could buffalo his way into the priority line given his clothing and the fine leather case carrying the reliquary. He flagged down an agent and asked sternly but politely for the frequent traveler section. The agent fell for it and immediately escorted him through the mass of humanity to the desk. Most of the holiday vacationers scowled at him as he gingerly carried his things over their sprawling bags. Tom just smiled at the mother whose child complained, "Why does he get to cut the line?"

As Tom expected, the line into which he had insinuated himself was very short, and within minutes he was at the counter. He stepped up confidently, folded his hands on the high counter and smiled warmly to the fifty-ish, female agent on the other side. "Good afternoon. How are you holding up so well in this madness?"

She was flattered, as Tom had calculated. "Oh, thanks," she answered. "The security level changed and it has ground everything to a snail's pace."

"Wow, glad I'm Diamond status!" He chuckled and raised his eyebrows.

"Can I help you, sir?"

"Oh, sorry, yes. My name is Doctor Tom Duffield. I have an e-ticket for the flight to Syracuse."

"Thank you, Dr. Duffield." The agent began typing diligently at her keyboard. It seemed a stunning number of keystrokes for the small amount of information he had offered. At each pause, her brow would furrow as she read the screen and then rapidly tap a few more keys. "I can't seem to find your ticket. There is a T. Duffield, but that record doesn't show a Diamond Level. Could that be you?"

Tom blushed, but was quick on his feet, as ever. "Yes, it is. I've lost my card and couldn't remember my member number when I made the reservation." He put on a confident expression.

"I can't credit your miles unless you have the number. Shall I do a search on the system?"

"No, no. Don't worry about it. I have tons of miles. There must be hundreds of Tom Duffield's in your system."

This agent was unusually helpful. "It's really my pleasure. The search system is very fast."

Given the fact Tom had never enrolled in the program, he knew a search would be lengthy and fruitless, and worse, it would reveal his petty dishonesty. He toyed with claiming to be the first name which she found in the system, but then a better idea flashed into his head. "That security line looks long and slow and I am afraid of getting stuck in it. Really, it's okay."

"Yes, sir." Fortunately, she was keen to please. Upon one more key stroke, the boarding pass spat out of her printer and she handed it across the counter. "It doesn't show your Diamond Level status because we don't have your number, so I am afraid I can't get you through the priority line. Sorry. If you go over to the lines on my left, you'll probably find they are a little shorter."

Tom left the counter and walked briskly in the suggested direction, only to find a decidedly unshort line. He circled back to the counter and then around to the other side, only to find an even larger, slower and more dejected crowd. Tom hightailed it back to the original side and steeled himself for the wait. It wouldn't be that much of a disaster if he missed the flight, he decided, yet he kept checking his watch at intervals of just less than a minute. Serenaded by the muffled plink and thud of gray, plastic bins, and having watched his minute hand advance thirteen minutes, Tom could taste success. He was only three people from the security screener, and from there it was a short leap to the metal detectors. And that is when the next disaster struck.

The small Asian man who next approached the screener seemed completely flummoxed by the whole process, despite having stood behind forty-two people who had gone through what appeared to be a simple few steps – hold out your Boarding Pass and ID and answer a few perfunctory questions. The man was craning his head toward the shabbily uniformed, TSA agent. The man either had a hearing problem or a language barrier, or both, and the agent's response was to become more gruff and clipped. Tom could not hear what she was saying, but he was sure it was neither clear nor polite. Finally the man nodded and started pawing through the multiple zippered pockets in his bag. Not less than three minutes later – Tom actually timed it on his watch, harrumphing loudly – the man triumphantly held up the requisite documents.

Within a couple more minutes, it was Tom's turn with the security woman. Extremely eager, he actually handed his papers over the shoulder of the shuffling woman in front of him. The agent was obviously still angry and appeared anxious to take it out on someone. "Nobody gave you nothing?" she barked out without making eye contact. Tom did not realize it was directed at him at first, and by the time he did, she repeated it. "I said, nobody gave you nothing?"

Her accent was very thick and Tom replayed the question in his mind to make sure he heard it correctly. He figured she wanted him to answer "No", but grammatically the question was a little perplexing. And he was holding the reliquary, which had been given to him. Did that count? Fearful of her wrath, he stammered, "Um . . . no, well . . . I am carrying this for a friend. Does that mean 'Yes'?"

"Sir, I ain't in no mood for games." She turned toward a gaggle of agents grouped by the metal detectors. "Freddy!" she called out, and then to Tom, "Sir, go with him."

Tom followed after Freddy, who was not heading for the fast track. This was the special screening line and Tom rolled his eyes and muttered more oaths under his breath as he stepped to the metal detectors. He unloaded his pockets, took off his jacket and shoes and removed his laptop from the carrying case, lined it all up the conveyor belt, including the reliquary case and walked through the blinking arch. Nothing lit up, and Tom wrongly assumed, but only briefly, he was home free. This was actually just the first pass. Freddy was now going to have him remove more clothes and repeatedly pass a wand over his body. As they headed to the cordoned-off area for this process, Tom could see them hauling the reliquary case back to the front of the metal detector for another check. "Holy shit," he exclaimed over the din, "be careful with that."

Freddy was quick to take charge. "Sir, they are professionals, step this way please."

"Can you please ask them to be careful with that?!"

Freddy called out, "Jason, please be careful with that," with sufficient volume and sincerity that the others might actually pay heed. "Don't worry, sir, it'll be fine. Now if you could step this way, we can finish this up and get you on your way."

Tom could feel his stress level beginning to reach a crescendo. A bead of sweat rolled down the side of his face and he reached up to take his glasses off with one hand and wipe his hands across a very wet forehead. His normally short-cropped hair had grown out and was matted down. Tom followed Freddy and sat down as directed in the chair, looking over his left shoulder as best he could to watch the men at the x-ray machine.

Freddy was trained to engage his subject in conversation in order to take his mind off the frustration and delay of being searched. "So, where are you headed today?" He actually had a calming expression and voice and Tom felt the tension ease.

"I'm trying to make the next plane to Syracuse." Tom looked down at his wrist to check the time, only to remember that his watch was with the men at the metal detector. "It's boarding in a few minutes, so I'm not sure I'm going to make it."

At the same time he was efficiently checking Tom with the metal detector wand, Freddy was genuinely engaged in conversing about the travel plan. "Oh, I think you'll be alright. I can call ahead to the gate when we're done, just to make sure they know you are coming."

This was the first piece of reassurance Tom had received all afternoon, and he sighed audibly. "Thanks so much for that. I really appreciate it."

"It's my pleasure, sir," Freddy responded. He was just about to say something else when the screener called his name out and waved him over. Freddy turned to Tom and said, "We're all done here. Go ahead and pick up your things over there and you should be on your way. Excuse me now, please." He stepped away before Tom could say anything.

Tom stepped quickly to the x-ray space to find the two men peering closely at the video screen. They were pointing to different parts of the screen, which was turned away from Tom. Their conversation was inaudible. Tom's quick glance around the conveyor belt confirmed that everything but the reliquary case had passed through. That must be what they were studying.

The one named Jason finally stepped away from the monitor and approached Tom as the reliquary case was propelled through the opening. "Sir, we would like to take a look at this. Could I open it up, please?"

Tom's profound irritation returned instantaneously. "Yes, if you must. Let me open it for you."

"No, sir, we will do it. Would you kindly step away from the table?"

"I need to unlock it for you."

Jason was persistent, both in his politeness and his procedure. "If you would give us the keys, please, sir, we can unlock it."

"Yes, yes, just a minute." Tom reached into his pockets, only to realize they were still emptied. Looking up, he spied them in the plastic bin on the counter and stepped closer to pick them out.

"Sir, please stand back, I don't want to have to ask you again." Jason was stern.

"What in Christ's name is going on here? Have I done something wrong?" Tom was flabbergasted at being treated like a dangerous person.

"We aren't sure what you have in this case."

"Have you asked me?" Tom asked contemptuously.

"Sir, you will probably understand that we can't just ask people what they have. We have a responsibility to make a positive ID on each item that passes through here." Jason held out the plastic bin which held the keys. "If you could pick out the right key and hand it to me, I would be most appreciative."

"Well, I'll be pretty fucking surprised if you can make a positive ID on what is in that case. There is only one of them in the world and about three people who know what it is." He pointed out the right key.

Jason did not appreciate Tom's tone and was quick to respond. "Sir, please don't take that attitude with us, or we'll have to call our supervisor."

"Fine, open it up. Please be careful." The two men fiddled together with the lock and finally opened the case to reveal the reliquary lying in its satin bedding. As Tom expected, they were perplexed, and as he watched them, he realized that they were concerned about the sharply-pointed finial at the top of the housing chamber. "It is a fourteenth century reliquary display. That piece of wood inside is the bolt which killed Richard the Lionheart."

"That's very nice, sir, but to tell you the truth, we are a little concerned that this metal point could be used as a weapon." Saying this, Jason put his index finger on the tip of the finial to gauge its sharpness. He nodded, as if to indicate that his visual assessment was right. "Do you have a license or document that states what this is?"

Tom could feel the beads of sweat forming once again on his brow and succumbing to gravity as they began streaming down his face. He was measuring his answer and trying to control a nascent rage. "Please get your fingers off my reliquary." Jason complied. "They actually don't issue licenses for these, because this is the only one in the world." His words were clipped and firm. "And I'm the only one who is qualified to document what it is. I'm a Professor at Cornell University, and if you would please let me pass through here, I could get home."

"Perhaps you could check this through as baggage, and then everything would be okay."

Tom's jaw dropped and he blinked repeatedly. "Are you kidding me? That reliquary is worth more than the airplane. I'm not checking that!" This situation was becoming desperate. "Can you please call your supervisor? Is Freddy your supervisor? Can we get him back here?" He looked around to see if he could spot the only rational person he had worked with that day. Unfortunately Freddy was still talking to the security screener. As Tom turned back around, he saw that the two men were putting on latex gloves.

"Freddy's not our manager, he only started today," Jason responded, chuckling a little. "Well, if you don't want to check it, then we are going to have to lift it out of the case and give it a closer look. Are you okay with that?"

Tom looked up at the clock on the wall. His plane was already boarding and if he didn't hurry up, he was going to have to spend the night there or drive home. "Can you do it carefully? Please. Very, very carefully." His heart was pounding, but he reasoned that the reliquary could withstand being picked up and placed on the counter. He held his breath as he watched them lift it from the satin bedding and stand it on the counter. The two men then squatted down and studied the piece very closely, narrowing their eyes as if to make their inspection seem more discerning. Tom couldn't resist taunting them, despite how close he was to clearing this farcical obstacle. "So, Batman and Robin, do you think the skies of Gotham will be safe now that you've solved this mystery?"

Jason's patience was now past exhausted. For him, the only thing better than having power was using it, and he decided now was the perfect time. "Sir, you're going to have to check this."

"I will not check it. That is out of the question," Tom shouted. "I want to talk to your supervisor right this minute."

Bureaucracy chooses its own pace, and just now it resolved to become very slow. Jason shrugged, "It might be hard to find him. He's very busy with this higher security level. Do you see him, Dwayne?"

Dwayne did not appear very bright to Tom, but his readiness to conspire with his partner, without even a word spoken between them, was both impressive and distressing. "Nope," was Dwayne's convenient and all-too-rapid response.

Tom was not going to accept the run-around from these Keystone Cops. He raised his voice and repeated his demand for their supervisor. This caught the two men off guard and Tom noticed it immediately. He raised his voice a tad further and said it once more. "I want to see your supervisor!"

Jason immediately extracted a walkie-talkie from his pocket and commanded, "Sir, please control yourself. I will try to call him now." He held the walkie-talkie in the palm of his right hand and began keying in a number. Just then, Freddy stepped up from Jason's right, and Jason, catching the movement in his peripheral vision swung his body around to see who it was.

"Hey, watch out!" Freddy warned loudly, but too late.

The same walkie-talkie which had promised Tom salvation from a trying situation, now became a curse as its stubby black antenna caught the tip of the metal finial of the reliquary and toppled it in the direction of the leather carrying case.

All four of the men watched the reliquary hover at the tipping point, and had they time to talk it over, they collectively would have agreed that it would recover. Yet they all would have been profoundly wrong. Rather than righting itself and wobbling nervously on the steel counter, it succumbed to its top-heavy design and fell with a thud against the side of the case. The abrupt halt, at the end of its descent, loosed the shard of wood inside the reliquary and it shot from its perch, smacking the glass pane. Despite more than six hundred years of holding its charge safely inside, the paper-thin, hand-blown Venetian glass shattered, disgorging its contents on the stainless steel counter. The relic actually shot across the counter, and came to rest more than a foot beyond the shards of glass under the horrified and prolonged stare of the four men.

No one said anything for what seemed a very long moment. Jason and Dwayne, never long on prose in any case, had the presence of mind not to say, "Uh-oh," but could not think of anything to say in its stead. They had already been slightly intimidated by Tom's aggressive behavior prior to this latest turn of events, and now feared Tom would melt down completely. For his part, Tom was physically incapable of speaking, given the way his mouth was hanging open and he could only catch the shallowest of breaths. He was not sure which bothered him more – the fact that he would now almost assuredly lose his job, or that two morons had just destroyed a priceless piece of history.

Freddy took charge. He grabbed some latex gloves and clear

baggies from boxes near the x-ray machine. "Dr. Duffield, if you would like to pick that up yourself, here is a glove to do it." He handed the glove to Tom. "We can save that glass if you would like, and put it here in this baggie."

Still speechless, Tom put on the latex glove and picked up the wooden relic and studied it very closely. He realized he was probably the first person to actually hold the item in hundreds of years and imagined the chain of handling before him, Walter of Rouen, Richard the Lionheart himself, the surgeon, the Knight of Châlus. If not for these security idiots, Tom never would have touched this piece of history – and he felt his tension and anger dissipate at a rate which surprised him. Despite the need to get on his way toward the plane, Tom felt the strongest urge to continue staring at this fascinating shard of wood. The men noticed his change of character and began eyeing him with curiosity, and when Tom noticed this, he inserted it in the bag, zipped it closed and put it in his shirt pocket. He looked up at Freddy and smiled. "I need to save the glass. It'll be easier for us to replicate the content and thickness." Freddy produced a piece of cardboard and neatly swept the counter clean. He closed the bag and gingerly handed it to Tom, then he replaced the reliquary in the satin bed of the case and closed and locked the case. "Dr. Duffield, I think you can carry this on with you. You go ahead now to Gate 12 and I will call to make sure they don't leave without you. I am really terribly sorry for any inconvenience."

"Oh, that's okay. I really do appreciate your help," Tom said. He picked up the reliquary case and looked up at Freddy. He was puzzled that he felt so calm and relaxed despite what had just occurred. Was he *so* resigned to his fate, he wondered, that all emotion had passed? Somehow this was more peaceful than resignation. "Thank you, Freddy." He turned and headed down the concourse at a brisk pace.

Tom arrived at his gate a few minutes later, only to find the boarding process was running behind schedule. He walked directly into line and boarded the plane, finding his seat quickly and loading the reliquary case into the overhead bin. Tom settled into his seat by the window and watched the other passengers board, making eye contact with several of them and smiling warmly. The seat next to him remained open until they announced the boarding door closing, and then a well-dressed and slightly overweight middle-aged woman, loaded down with shopping bags came huffing and puffing down the aisle. She stopped at his row, studying the numbers and letters above the seat to make sure she was at the right place, and then rechecked the stubby boarding pass clutched in her hand. Had she looked around she would have noticed that there was only one open seat on the entire plane.

Once convinced she stood at the right seat, the woman opened the overhead bin and peered into it. Hopeful of room for her things she reached up and took out Tom's case, then looked around and said, "Whose case is this?"

"That's mine, please be careful with it," Tom was quick to respond.

"Let me just take it out for a second, while I pack my bags into the back." She began lifting her things into the small overhead compartment. Tom did not object audibly. He found it hard to believe that all of her things, plus his case, were going to fit in there, and thus he watched in silent fascination as she began shoving and pushing her bulging shopping bags. Every thirty seconds she would stop and take a deep breath, and try to regain some balance on her awkward spike heels. Then she would pitch into it again, shifting bags here and there as if that might create more space.

Within a couple of minutes a harried flight attendant stormed down the aisle. "We need to have everyone seated and the overhead compartments closed before we can push away from the gate. We are very close to losing our take-off slot!" She pulled up short at Tom's row and glared at the woman loading the bags. "Ma'am, can you close that and take your seat please?" she said with an exasperated tone.

The woman picked up the reliquary case and hoisted it above her head, fighting to keep her balance and not topple backwards. Standing with the case so raised, she answered the flight attendant, "Yes, just this one more case and I'll be done." She pushed it futilely into a space half its size.

The flight attendant was not to be dismissed. "That's not going to fit in there," she spat out, and she quickly began opening other bins, only to find them all packed full. "You're going to have to check that," she said definitively, whipping out a blank bag check tag.

"It's my case," Tom said quickly.

"Sir, you're going to have to check this. Did you check the size before you got on to make sure that it was going to fit in this compartment?" She wanted to bring all her wrath on Tom, but getting the plane away from the gate was a higher imperative. She pulled a strand of her long blond hair back around an ear and made ready to fill in the baggage ticket. "Your name, sir?"

"My last name is Duffield." He paused, and then said calmly, "Do you think you could find a place for it in a compartment up forward – without checking it? To be quite honest, it is a priceless reliquary from the middle ages, and I don't think it can take much bashing around."

The flight attendant was charmed by the way he asked the question, and she turned to look back at the cockpit area. "Yes, I think I can find some room in there for you. Come see me when we land and I can get it out."

Tom thanked her sincerely and settled back in his seat. He reached up with his right hand and patted his shirt pocket, feeling for the reassuring bulge of the wooden shard in its plastic bag. Content that it was safely tucked away, he leaned his head against the side of the plane, and drifted off to sleep.

4

Lisa spent most of Wednesday watching the clock and urging it to go faster. In fact, not counting the ninety minutes she spent dozing after Tom's early morning departure, she checked the clock, on average, every eighteen minutes. And this made for a very long day. She attempted to hasten its passing by busying herself at work and chatting with everyone she saw, yet her attention span was short, and in both cases she would drift away and begin thinking about her impending discussion with Tom. When Megan appeared in the lab just after 10 am, Lisa panicked at the thought of being probed for her progress in gaining Tom's agreement to the experiment, and she decided to preempt it. "Hey, Megan," she called out casually from her office. "Come in when you have a sec, okay?"

"Sure, yeah," Megan replied – and then, peeking her head into the office, "I'm free now. Is everything alright?"

Lisa was embarrassed, but covered it well. "Yeah, of course. No biggie. I just wanted to let you know that Tom and I have set aside some time tonight to discuss . . . the experiment. I mean, it's no change from what we said, you know, a decision on Thursday."

Megan inclined her head slightly and pursed her lips. "Okay," she said. And then she nodded, shrugged and continued, "We'll talk tomorrow."

Lisa changed the subject to some assay results Megan had sent her the night before – long after Tom's pillow-top announcement of his trip. She wanted to scold her for working so late, but became distracted by the science before she remembered to do it.

When the end of the working day finally arrived, Lisa took off quickly, hopeful that Tom might have caught an earlier flight and beaten her home. How long did they really need to meet, she asked herself as she rounded the last corner on the road leading to their house and half expected (yet fully hoped) his car would be in the driveway. It wasn't of course, so once inside she rechecked the note where he'd written his flight details: his flight arrived in close to 7 pm and assuming he didn't lollygag by stopping for a meal, he should be able to make the sixty-mile drive home in a little less than an hour and a half. So by 8:30, or say 9, she would have her second and perhaps final chance to talk him into trying for a baby via the Ewe Factor and Megan. She knew she had to give up the idea of cloning Jeff, and that realization was painful. In the preceding weeks, Lisa had begun imagining an "Infant Jeff" whose brilliance she could nurture, and whose spirit she could tame. He had never spoken of his childhood so she imagined he was raised in a hard and loveless home. Yet she had to put those dreams behind her and think about a baby whose character and characteristics would be a mystery. She mulled this over as she positioned herself at the kitchen table to most easily watch the clock. As Lisa finished the bowl of soup and half sandwich she'd forced on a nervous stomach, she noted that Tom would be home in three hours.

Little did Lisa know that Tom would be stuck on the ground for most of those three hours. A flight traffic control computer managing the eastern seaboard had malfunctioned just about the time Tom's flight was supposed to take off and took long enough to get back on track to stymie operations everywhere. Tom was oblivious to this, too. His incredible day, topped off by the fiasco at security, had exhausted him and he slept for two hours without stirring. While he wouldn't remember it later, he dreamed about King Richard riding around Châlus Castle and shaking his fist at the intrepid knight who shot the fatal bolt. When he did wake, it took him a moment to remember where he was, and then a second moment to check his watch, look out the window, and realize that they were still at LaGuardia. He made the mistake of asking the person next to him what was going on, and then received a detailed description of the last hours, including near verbatim replays of the pilot's announcements. As soon and politely as possible Tom turned back toward the window and fell asleep.

Lisa was frantic by 9:45 and went online to check the flight's status. The ire she was ready to direct at Tom for stopping for a long dinner was – fortunately for Tom's sake – redirected at the air traffic control system and its hapless managers. In any case, she could see that the plane was enroute and would land just after 10. She did the calculation again, and shaving off some time for both the empty roads and her impatience, had him home by 11. Lisa decided that sitting by the kitchen table rehearsing her speech any further would be mind numbing, so she first got herself ready for bed, and then removed herself to their den and turned on the television. This proved mind numbing as well, literally, and within half an hour she was fast asleep. When Tom finally got in at 11:45 (he did get something to eat at a fast food joint on the way) he found her there clutching a pillow, her head lolled over to one side. He gently rocked her awake. "Hey, hey," he whispered gently, "why aren't you in bed?"

She opened her eyes, eyed him strangely and then startled. "What's going on?" she called out.

"You fell asleep in front of the TV. I just got home. Everything's alright," Tom reassured. Lisa relaxed and then asked the time. "It's almost midnight. Come on, let's go to bed." He helped her up and they proceeded together down the hall to their bedroom.

It took only a couple of minutes for Lisa to remember her plan. She was going to begin by probing on whether the meeting with Strater was successful and then, if so, keep Tom on a positive note before re-raising the baby idea. "So how was your day?" she asked.

"It was good. Most of it."

"Did you meet with John Strater?"

"Yeah, we met for a long time."

Lisa noticed Tom smile as he said this and she decided to

anchor him there. "What's he like?"

"He's brilliant, for one thing. And thorough in his research. He puts a lot of historians I know to shame – like William Rogers, but of course that's not saying much." Tom sat on the bed and untied his shoes as she climbed into her side of the bed. "I'm really tired, can we just go to bed and talk about it in the morning?"

"I guess that nap in the den left me wide awake, and I've been sitting alone all evening with no one to talk to," Lisa protested.

"Too bad you aren't married to the person I sat next to on the plane," Tom said under his breath as he went into their bathroom.

"What?"

"Nothing. I was just making a joke," he called from the other room. "Seriously honey, I am really not up to a long talk tonight."

While Tom finished his ablutions, Lisa thought over her plan and decided she had to get right to the point. The moment he stepped back into their room she began Plan B. "Tom, I want to apologize for our disagreement on Friday night. I dropped too many things on you at once and then I was insensitive to your feelings. I hope that you can forgive me."

Tom stopped by her side of the bed. "Lisa, I forgive you. Don't worry about it. Is that why you're still up?" He stepped over to his dresser and began emptying his trouser pockets.

"Well, at the risk of making you angry again, I just wondered if we could talk about it a little more. And Tom," she said preemptively, "it would have nothing to do with Jeff – nothing at all, that's off the table."

Tom stepped out of his trousers and laid them over the back of a chair. He was too tired to fight. "Okay, so what's *on* the table?"

Lisa was encouraged but knew not to take it too fast. She didn't want to screw up this last chance. "Well, we could revitalize cells from the commercially available human cell lines and transfer the DNA to a healthy egg, and then implant that in a uterus. If it took – and actually went full term – not only would we prove the robustness of the DNA reinvigoration, but you and I would have a baby." She had tried to make this as scientific as possible and avoid mentioning Megan's name. Lisa wanted to read Tom's expression, but he had turned to face his dresser as he unbuttoned his shirt. "And as I said last time, it's a long shot for all the genes to get turned on at the right time."

Tom remained with his back to Lisa as he asked, "We won't end up with some weird three-headed . . . child?"

"If something was that wrong, it would probably auto-abort, you know, miscarry, very early."

"So, if the chances are so slim, why are you doing it at all?" Tom started to take off his shirt and felt a light weight and bulge in the breast pocket. Fatigued and distracted, he momentarily forgot what it was and reached up to extract the baggie with the wooden shard he had placed there so many hours ago. He stood quietly looking at the relic while Lisa answered his question, pondering the dark stains running through the wooden shard. *Are they oxidation marks,* he asked himself, *or blood?*

Blood! Desiccated cells. DNA. Tom's eyes involuntarily widened as a thought raced through his brain and shivers shot down his legs. *Richard's blood.*

By the time Lisa finished he realized that not only had he not heard any of it, he couldn't even remember the question he had asked in the first place. He considered asking her to repeat herself, but lacked an excuse for not listening to her answer, so he just stood there and nodded.

"Does that make sense?" she asked to be helpful, fearful that her answer had been too technical. And then noticing his posture asked, "What are you looking at?"

"Nothing," he responded, burying the baggie under some papers on his dresser top. Tom turned, stripped off his shirt and put on a t-shirt. Lisa was repeating her answer to his earlier question, paraphrasing in such a way that she thought he might better understand. When she paused long enough for him to insert a word, he interjected the non-sequitur question, "When you were thinking of cloning Jeff, how were you going to do it?"

Lisa wasn't sure she heard Tom correctly. "What?"

"On Friday night, and then again tonight, you've mentioned something about cloning Jeff. I was just wondering how you could do it."

"Tom, I said that was off the table." Lisa feared another meltdown and wanted to head it off quickly.

"Well, maybe it wasn't such a crazy idea after all. But was it just theoretical?"

Is he trying to lure me into a fight? Lisa wondered. "Do you really want to talk about it?" she asked cautiously.

"Yeah, I'm asking how you were thinking of doing it." he persisted.

Lisa trod as carefully as possible. "I know you think this will be weird, but I found a Band-Aid which Jeff had used just before he died." She thought about what she said and added quickly, "I didn't go looking for it, believe me, it was stuck to a journal of mine which Jeff had borrowed. Anyway, it was stained with blood and fluid from his cut, and I was pretty sure that would yield enough cells to reinvigorate with the Ewe Factor."

"Hmmm. And you have a way to extract them from a Band-Aid? How are you sure you won't make a baby Band-Aid?" He climbed in bed next to her and shut off the light.

Lisa laughed nervously. "Extracting it wouldn't be so hard. We have specific reagents which do that. Band-Aids don't have a lot of DNA – not since they took cotton out of them anyway. But, as I said, Tom, I'm really not asking for that. Let's just go with the commercial human cell lines."

"Well, are you opposed to trying it with Jeff's DNA? I know what I said, and I still hate Jeff," Tom paused for emphasis and then continued, "but maybe if we could raise him ourselves he would be very different. Of course, unlike the old days, I could spank him whenever he pissed me off. There would be some metaphysical revenge ... justice, I mean, in that."

Lisa wasn't sure she should break into Tom's musings. *Is he serious*, she asked herself. "Are you just fantasizing about getting back at him?" she enquired after a long silence.

"No, no, I'm just kidding about the spanking part. You were right that Jeff was brilliant, maybe with a little better upbringing he'd be wonderful – well, at least bearable. There's none of the doubt we would have with the commercial cell lines. I'm still worried about the homeless person who gave blood for a little Thunderbird."

"So . . . what are you saying?" she said as if she were tiptoeing.

"Let's give it a shot."

"Really? With Jeff's DNA?" Lisa couldn't believe where this conversation had landed.

"Yeah, what the hell."

Lisa rolled over to face Tom and snuggled up to him. "Okay." She wanted to avoid saying "thanks" because she didn't want it to appear he was giving her something. "Okay." She repeated, leaning over to kiss him. "I'll talk it over with Megan in the morning."

"Do you think she'll change her mind?"

"No," Lisa reassured. "She's pretty keen to do this."

"And she's okay with the Band-Aid idea?"

Lisa had never intended for Megan to know this part of the plan. How can I keep this away from Tom, she asked herself. "Well, we probably need to talk this through a little more deeply. Technically, I mean."

"I thought you said it was easy."

"It is. It's just a slightly different process. Obviously. No biggie. It was sorta her idea in the first place."

"Alright." He leaned over and kissed her. "Good night."

"Good night. I love you, Tom."

"I love you. And, hey, Lisa?"

"Yeah?"

"Would you let me watch you extract the DNA from the Band-Aid?" he asked. "If it is going to be the conception moment of our baby, I'd like to take part."

"Sure, honey. It might be a little anti-climactic."

"That's okay. 'Night."

"Good night."

Both Lisa and Tom took some time to fall asleep that night. She lay awake wondering how to get Megan, who had never liked Jeff, to accept the idea of cloning him. And if she couldn't, would Tom conspire to keep a secret that big? For Tom's part, despite Lisa's agreement to let him accompany her into the lab, he hadn't worked at a laboratory bench since high school. The secret plan he was hatching required stealth, cunning – and actual scientific capability. When he finally drifted off, he reprised the dream from the airplane about Richard circling Châlus Castle – yet with a minor twist. In this version, Tom was also mounted on Richard's horse and riding in front. Tom felt proud to be at the center of the noble retinue, and as he admired the horses of the knights surrounding him, he relished the idea of riding the finest horse with the finest armor. When he turned back to share this observation with the King, he was surprised to see that Richard had been replaced by a baby – safely strapped and facing backward in an infant car seat.

5

"Tom said yes!" Lisa exclaimed the moment Megan entered the lab Thursday morning. Megan couldn't repress a smile and then looked guiltily around to see whether anyone else might have heard.

She then stepped quickly into Lisa's office and pulled the door closed behind her.

"Great! That's great."

Lisa came out from behind her desk and stood facing Megan. She reached out, grasped Megan's forearms with both hands, and hopped a bit as she blurted out, "I know! Can you believe it?!"

Megan was slightly surprised by Lisa's question. "You said you didn't think it would be a problem. Right?"

Lisa covered quickly. "Oh, yeah. I'm not talking about Tom's agreement; I mean that we're going to try this experiment. This could be the most amazing advance in science . . . if it works." She dissembled well and Megan bought it.

"So what do we do next?"

"I'll call Claire and find out what kind of prep we need for you. She probably needs to extract some of your eggs." Lisa noticed Megan's grimace and added quickly, "Don't worry about that. Claire told me how painless that is – and I heard the same from a friend of mine who had it done. I'll call Claire this morning, and maybe we can all have lunch together today or tomorrow and she can talk us through it."

"Great, and I am free through the weekend, too."

"Okay, I'll let you know." She gave Megan's arms a squeeze before letting go, and Megan pivoted to return to the common office area. Then, betraying her earlier plan, Lisa called out, "Hey, Megan, I've got to ask you something."

"Sure."

"What would you think if we used specific, known source?" Lisa asked.

"You mean, instead of the commercial line we've been working with?" Lisa nodded and Megan continued, "What . . . or should I say, *who* do you have in mind?"

"Jeff." Lisa figured it was best not to beat around the bush.

Megan's brow furrowed as she puzzled on the process.

"How?"

"Remember the Band-Aid?"

The young post-doc grimaced. "I thought I grossed *you* out on that. Didn't you throw it out?"

Lisa blushed. "Almost."

Now that Megan understood the "how" she reflected on the "who". "I wasn't a big 'Jeff fan' you know. He always treated me like shit, if you'll pardon my French."

"I know he pissed off a lot of people," Lisa acknowledged.

"That's an understatement!" Megan was unusually frank this morning. "Lisa, you were about the only person who didn't hate his guts."

"He was close to his mother." Lisa said this with a straight face, and then smiled broadly.

"I need to think about it," Megan responded unconvincingly.

Lisa thought she should sell a little harder. "He was brilliant, Megan, and his potential was cut short when he died. Everybody said he was going to win a Nobel prize for Biology. And, Megan, Tom and I would deal with the baby, the child, the person. We'll raise him right – I always thought he had a nurture problem, not a nature problem."

"Let me think about it."

Considering how thoughtful and deliberate Lisa was about planning everything in her life and work, she was surprisingly unprepared to float her cloning plan to Claire. It wasn't until the phone was ringing at the far end that Lisa suddenly realized Claire might not be so game to participate in a human cloning experiment. She almost hung up after the first ring, and then again after the third, but decided to hold on and think her way through it.

"Dr. Prentiss' office, this is Candy."

"Hi, Candy, it's Lisa Duffield. Is Claire there?" Lisa was still wondering what she was going to say when and if Claire came on the line.

"Hi, Dr. Duffield. You're lucky today. I think she's in her office with a Drug Rep – she'll probably welcome the interruption. Hang on, let me put you on hold for a second." Candy was always cheerful and effective, a rare combination.

There was a brief pause and a series of clicks and then, "This is Dr. Prentiss."

"Hi, Claire, it's Lisa."

"Hey, how are you?"

It was the moment of truth and Lisa still hadn't figured out how to broach the subject. "Great." She paused and Claire filled the silence.

"What's up?"

"Are you there with someone?"

"Yes, but it's okay. She can hang on a second."

"Well, I don't want to bother you now," and then she realized that this was not a matter for the telephone. "Would you and Bob like to come over to dinner on Saturday?"

"Sure, do you have a time in mind?"

"Um . . . Seven? And I'm going to ask a post-doc in my lab, Megan, to come over as well. I'd like you to meet her."

"Sounds great, we'll see you then."

"Great. See you then. Don't bring anything, and I say that knowing that you will anyway." They both laughed and Lisa finished, "Sorry to bother, bye."

"No problem. Bye, Lisa."

Lisa hung up the phone and wondered whether she would have more courage on Saturday night. Having Megan would be a prompt, she knew. And there was a good chance that Megan would bring it up herself if Lisa came up short.

Megan spent most of the day thinking about being pregnant. The idea of carrying the embryo had come to her quickly and, there in the bar, she failed to imagine, let alone ponder, the ramifications before floating the idea to Lisa. Then, persistent to a fault, Megan was unable to abandon the idea once the proposal had crossed her lips. It was *her* idea after all and therefore it was smart and right. Each day she waited for Lisa's answer made Megan more anxious to gain agreement. She even considered calling Tom to make sure he understood how important this was to Lisa's work. Only Lisa's preemptive commitments to closing the deal with Tom, as well as Megan's sense of propriety, held her off.

Now with a green light, however, she could begin the task of dissecting the situation and its implications. Vocationally, even if it slowed her work, it would advance her career. The fact that the baby, if there even could be a baby, would immediately be handed off to the Duffields meant she might not be away from the lab for more than a couple of weeks – not much more than a long vacation, although she'd never taken one. Even better was the fact that she could work on her computer from both the hospital and home. Indeed, it might mean less time away from work than when she had influenza a couple of years ago and had been too weak to lift her head off the pillow for three days. If, on the other hand, the pregnancy didn't take hold and there wasn't a baby, however disappointing that might be for Lisa and Tom, the embryonic tissue could yield fascinating data on the how the genes were or were not expressed. Like so many things in life, there may be more to learn from failure than from success.

The effect on her body would be tolerable. Although Megan didn't work out regularly, she was relatively fit and well-toned. She felt her stomach, which was firm and flat, and imagined it bulging out twelve inches. She wondered a little about stretch marks, but thought there were creams or rubs to manage them. The idea of having to deliver by Caesarian section crossed her mind for a brief and frightening second, but she then remembered that both her sisters and her mother told of dilating so quickly that their babies nearly ended up in the back seats of cars. Her build was nearly the same as theirs, and if anything, her hips were broader. On the other hand her breasts were smaller – both compared to her family and her friends. It would never occur to her to have them enlarged, but she was intrigued at the idea of finding out what it was like to be a couple cup sizes larger – at least temporarily.

As for her family, they were all pretty liberal, she reflected, and while a few of her more "child-oriented" siblings would protest the idea of a) having a child out of wedlock, and b) having it for someone else and "giving" it away, they wouldn't make too much of a fuss. Anyway, they were too busy with their own lives and children to pay much attention. Her parents would likely be even less trouble. They were ex-hippies who on more than one occasion (generally after a couple of glasses of sherry) liked to tell the story of attending Woodstock and having sex under a blanket in the midst of the throng. As comfortable and open in her relationship with them as she was, Megan was still mortified every time the subject came up. She blushed now as she thought about it, yet it provided good evidence that they would accept her choices as informed and rational. Even if they drove the grandchildren around in a minivan and belonged to a golf club, they hadn't really changed.

Megan was just about to close her deliberation and silently reaffirm the baby experiment idea as sound, when Lisa came out to visit her at the lab bench. Listening to her iPod, splitting her concentration between the pipette work and her potential pregnancy, and facing her bench, the young post-doc jumped when Lisa touched her on the shoulder to gain her attention. Megan quickly pulled out one ear bud and laughed. "You surprised me! What's up?"

"Sorry about that – I was just wondering whether you were still free this weekend. I just talked to Claire," Lisa said.

"Yeah, I'm free. What did Claire say?" Megan asked excitedly.

"Well, I didn't really want to get into it all on the phone, so I asked her over to dinner on Saturday – together with her husband." Seeing Megan was let down she quickly added, "I told her I wanted her to meet you, but I might have been presumptuous in assuming you could come."

"I told you I was free."

"I know, I just didn't know if maybe you'd put something together since then."

"Like a date?" Megan laughed.

Lisa had meant to be sensitive, but was now embarrassed. "Well . . . I don't know." She laughed too, to cover the awkwardness.

Megan softened the moment with a smile. "I'd love to come over. What time should I arrive?"

"Is seven okay?"

"Great. Can I bring anything?"

Lisa was excited that her plan was continuing to come together. "No, but thanks for offering. You know how to get there, right? Just off the Plantations in Forest Home." Megan nodded confidently. Lisa began retreating toward her office. "Sorry to interrupt."

"No problem. Thanks for the invite. I'm looking forward to meeting Claire." Once Lisa was back in her office Megan reflected on their exchange. The stark contrast between Lisa's assumption that Megan had a social life and the truth was, frankly, both perplexing and alarming. She wondered briefly whether there was something wrong with her – she was beautiful, intelligent and accomplished (and blonde to boot, she noted) and she had once been socially active. She liked boys – I guess they're supposed to be men at this point, she corrected herself – and she'd had a handful of dates. But no one had ever captured her heart, let alone her intimacy. As her brother liked to put it sarcastically, she was twenty-six and still pitching a shutout. Megan plumbed the depths of her emotion to see if she was denying something – hoping not to discovery anything. The answer came back calm and confident, *No*. She put the matter to rest. Megan was going to have this baby – luck and science willing.

The afternoon passed quickly for Megan. She took a quick bathroom break a couple hours after Lisa had stopped by with the dinner invitation, and next came up for air just before 6 pm. After peeking around the other benches, Lisa's office and the general office across the vestibule to confirm that everyone else had left for the day, Megan packed up her things, turned off the lights and pulled the lab door locked behind her. She took the stairs, as usual, and was just about to exit the building when the Faculty and Staff Photo Board outside the Genetics Department Office caught her eye. Actually it was Jeff Wolf's picture which grabbed her attention – still in its central "Department Chairman" position despite his passing a couple of months earlier. Megan stepped closer to the board and studied his portrait. She noted that he had his usual sneer and tried to decide whether he had been fighting back a disparaging remark about the photographer, or whether he planned this as a means of intimidating everyone who glanced up at the board. "Probably both," she said aloud to herself, just as Sandy Gerber, the Departmental Administrator came out of her office and locked up for the day.

"Hi, Megan," she said cheerfully. Sandy was a thirty-plus year veteran of the department and knew everyone who had ever been there for more than a month. She was efficient, kind, eternally upbeat and enormously capable, and thus they all dreaded the day she would eventually announce her retirement. "You talkin' to yourself?" she teased.

"Evening, Sandy. I was just noticing the picture board needs updating," Megan said.

"Well, I'll be darned! I guess when you walk by something every day you stop seeing it. I'll fix it tomorrow." Then uncharacteristically for her, Sandy added, "I'm surprised I didn't change it the day he died."

Megan was surprised by this and laughed until she covered her mouth out of shame. "Sandy," she scolded playfully, "you shouldn't speak ill of the dead."

"I know it, but there wasn't a nice bone in that man's body, if you'll forgive me for saying so." Sandy looked remorseful, yet unable to stop herself.

"Don't worry, Sandy. I didn't like him very much myself. But don't say that to Lisa Duffield."

Sandy's eyes widened. "Oh, I know. I could never figure that out." She shook her head and shuffled toward the door. "Goodnight, Megan."

"Night, Sandy."

Between Lisa's departmental staff meetings and errands and Megan's diligence at the lab bench, the two women barely spoke Friday. Certainly not long enough for Megan to tell her mentor that she had decided against using Jeff's DNA for the baby. So it wasn't until Saturday evening as they were sitting around the table after dinner that the matter was broached once again. Tom had taken Bob off to the den to watch a college football game, leaving Lisa, Claire and Megan to clear the table, put away the food and replenish their wine glasses before sitting back down to chat. Lisa was pleased that Claire and Megan seemed to hit it off – she thought that boded well for the plan she was about to float to her friend and obstetrician. Noticing that the topic at hand – Claire's upcoming Christmas-time trip to Europe – had just run its course, Lisa took a deep breath, nodded subtly to Megan and launched into the next phase of her plan. "Claire, there's something that Megan and I want to discuss with you."

Claire's smile faded as she assessed the more serious expressions on the other women's faces. "This sounds like a work discussion."

Lisa nodded. "It is. I hope you don't mind."

"It's fine. Go on."

"Megan would like to serve as a surrogate," Lisa stated, "For me and Tom." She smiled at Megan.

"That's fantastic!" Claire exclaimed – and then turning to Megan, "That's a very generous thing to do, Megan." Claire's eyes narrowed as she weighed her next words. "You seem like a pretty level-headed person – you've given this a lot of thought?"

Megan responded without a pause. "Absolutely. I'm sure I want to do this."

"Wow," Claire said, surprised by Megan's confidence and excited for Lisa to have the baby for which she'd tried so hard. "Do you want to talk about the details? Whose egg, whose sperm . . . ?"

Lisa responded without missing a beat. "We'd like to use Megan's eggs," she began, "but we would still like to do in vitro . . . um . . . fertilization."

Claire was intrigued by her friend's suggestion. She knew that Lisa understood the different fertilization processes in great depth, and thus she had chosen this more complicated procedure for a reason. "Are you uncomfortable about putting Tom's sperm into Megan?" She looked at both of them to remain ambiguous as to which woman she was asking.

"We aren't going to use Tom's sperm," Lisa responded quickly.

"Sorry, I shouldn't have assumed that. So you're going to use a sperm bank?"

"Well, not exactly. We aren't actually going to use sperm."

Claire realized she was lost and admitted it, "I'm not sure I am following you."

Lisa felt bad about intentionally baffling her best friend. "Claire, we're actually trying to validate my work. You know for several years I've been working on reviving desiccated human cells through a sheep uterine cell media. I've called it the Ewe Factor. I'm sure we've talked about it." Claire nodded. "We think we've finally gotten it to work – it was actually the day Jeff died when it first worked, and then Megan and I have replicated it several times over the past several weeks. The problem is that while the cells look right and seem to keep dividing, there is no way to ensure that all the chromosomes and genes are there and in working order without growing a full person. That's hard to do in a test tube. If we go public on the Ewe Factor, without at least having proven to ourselves that it is really working, the naysayers will have a field day.

"Instead of using sperm, we want to take the nucleus from one of the human cells from our experiment and transfer it into one of Megan's eggs – without its own nucleus, of course. And then if it's dividing properly, we'd want you to implant it in her uterus."

"You're cloning a person?" Claire asked.

A long silence followed and Megan broke it first. "We're validating an experiment."

Lisa followed with her own rationalization. "We're giving me and Tom the baby we've hoped for." And then, after a pause, "Yes, we're cloning a person. You're not willing to do it?"

Claire closed her eyes as she pondered the question. "I didn't say that. I just wanted to make sure I understood what you were proposing." She ran her finger around the rim of her wine glass, making it sing softly. "It is against the law, you know, as well as current medical guidelines. I'd lose my license if it were ever discovered."

"Claire, we understand perfectly if you aren't willing to do it," Lisa said, speaking somewhat presumptuously for Megan who actually wasn't willing to accept a "no". Megan considered protesting Lisa's remark, yet waited anxiously to see what Claire was going to say.

"Lisa, you know there isn't a thing I wouldn't do for you. But I'm a little concerned about being the test case for violating the human cloning ban." She sat back in her chair and closed her eyes. Lisa and Megan were eyeing her closely, each eager to say something that might nudge her in the right direction. Just before they did, Claire restarted. "How could you guarantee that no one would ever find out? I mean, clone meets – what do you call them, clonee?" All three women chuckled, two of them nervously. "Seriously," Claire continued, "I'd be pretty freaked out to run into myself, or worse yet, a child version of my mother. It isn't someone we know, is it?"

Megan didn't pause for a heartbeat before jumping in with the answer she thought would seal the deal. "No, we're using cell lines that come from California." She shrugged, "And they may even ship from overseas. The chance of the encounter you're talking about is infinitesimally small." Megan held eye contact with Claire to underscore her confidence, as well as to avoid Lisa's stare.

For her part, Lisa was dumbstruck by Megan's answer, but covered it well as she quickly gathered herself. "Do you really think that someone could spot a child-version of someone else? Especially if they grew up forty or fifty years ago? Nutrition differences alone these days would make a significant difference."

Megan was lightning-fast, once again. "Why even chance it? I think Claire makes a great point. The cell line we have been working with has been robust and reliable. Let's just keep going with it. And what's the point of putting any one of us in some kind of awkward situation – either professionally or legally? " Megan felt she was off the hook for choosing against Jeff and hoped that Lisa would fall in line.

Claire could tell the other two women were holding something back, but couldn't quite figure it out. "Lisa, did you have a specific donor in mind?"

Lisa was torn. On one hand her intuition told her that the two most important people to her plan, the fertility specialist and the surrogate mother, were going to insist on using the anonymous and commercial cell line, yet on the other hand her husband had only agreed to the plan on the condition of cloning Jeff Wolf. And there was no way to confer with him now. He seemed so volatile and unpredictable on this issue that he might wreck the whole plan. Further, she was unsure how Bob might react if he were brought into the discussion. He was likely to stop the whole thing to protect Claire and her career. The decision was clear, the only question was how to manage Tom – and as Megan and Claire awaited her answer, she obviously didn't have enough time to figure it out. "No, the commercial cell line is the better option."

"Better than what?" Claire probed.

"Oh, you know, better than *anything*," Megan said, and then looking at Lisa continued, "It's the *only* option. It's what we're going to use for this experiment." She raised her glass, "To the experiment." Megan and Claire raised their glasses as well, the former relieved and excited, the latter apprehensive and reserved. Then all three drank to the toast.

The rest of the evening was spent discussing the timeline and specific plan for preparing Megan and her eggs, and coinciding that with developing viable cloned cells from which to extract the nucleus. The fact that she wasn't on the Pill (or any other means of birth control, for that matter) meant she needed no washout period, and thus it should only be about two months – mid-December – before Megan's cycle would be right for making the first attempt. The men came in a couple of times for beer and snacks, and each time the women would change the topic effortlessly to clothes or shopping, and then change back just as quickly as the men exited the kitchen and closed the door. Finally, near midnight, as Megan agreed to visit Claire's office for an initial examination and they silently passed yawns around the table, Tom and Bob rejoined them for good. Tom tried to talk them all into a glass of brandy to finish off the evening, but Claire and Bob declined, saying they had to rescue the babysitter. Megan seized the opportunity to duck out as well, realizing that if she stayed longer, Lisa might press her on why she had bailed out on the plan to clone Jeff. Within a matter of minutes, a lively party of five was reduced to an exhausted pair who lacked the energy to converse, let alone clean up. They quickly agreed on dealing with the mess in the morning and shuffled off to bed. Lisa was troubled by the fact that she would have to talk Tom into the anonymous baby, but she knew her senses were too addled by wine and fatigue to tackle that now. On the bright side, she had one more conspirator – and an important one at that – and it was time, almost literally, to rest on her laurels.

6

Tom began his work week as he had closed the last – contemplating the reliquary and its long-time captive, the crossbow bolt fragment. He had brought both to the office the previous Thursday – the day after transporting them back from Longmynd – and during quieter moments of each of the past two work days, he had unpacked the fitted leather case and set the gleaming object on the center of his desk. The wooden shard was less gloriously housed. It remained in the clear plastic bag supplied by LaGuardia's security guards, and rather than sealing it in the custom case with its near life-long partner, Tom had taken to locking it in the top drawer of his desk. Now on Monday morning, he had both objects out once again and was savoring his good fortune as Strater's selection for authoring the collection catalog. Staring at the reliquary, he imagined it placed squarely in a larger case smack in the middle of the Johnson Art Museum's biggest gallery. It would be dramatically lit, of course, and people would crowd around all four sides to view with wonder a piece of the arrow that killed King Richard the Lionheart. Tom weighed how in-depth and dramatic his descriptions should read. Would people want to know all the details of Richard's final moments, or just gaze at the offending piece of wood, murmur

"Wow!" and move on to the next item? Tom had been teaching long enough to know that he couldn't make people care. In fact, most people were ambivalent about the past, and were genuinely baffled as to why others would spend so much time reading, thinking and writing about it. Yet there were always a few, a handful of genuine history buffs, like Tom, who felt the drama of real history far outstripped anything they could read in a novel or see in a movie. It was for them, and for himself, that Tom would research and author the collection catalog.

Up to now, however, Tom's research hadn't gone terribly far. He had cracked a few dusty old texts and sent off a few emails to colleagues he thought could shed the most light on the objects. He was beginning with the reliquary and bolt fragment, of course – not just because it was the only item he had in his physical possession, but also because it had most captivated his imagination. Between sipping his coffee and turning over the fragment (still bagged, of course, because he didn't want to contaminate it) in his hand, Tom weighed the idea of cloning the great king. It was probably impossible, he thought. Despite Lisa's confidence that only minute amounts of dried fluids were necessary – and Tom had probed this with her further over the weekend – he found it really hard to believe that enough of Richard's blood had soaked into the grain to be viable, especially after 800 years. "Well, what the hell!" he said aloud, once again committing himself to the plan.

Tom turned on his computer in the middle of these musings and logged into his email. There was one new entry in his inbox, and with its subject line reading *Re: Richard's Bolt?*, Tom knew it to be a response to one of the notes he had sent out the previous week. He quickly scanned across to the sender, *wadams,* whom he recognized as Professor Warwick Adams of All Souls College at Oxford University, England. His heart leapt in anticipation of what Adams had written. Tom had never met Adams, but had read many of his works, one of which, a biography of King Richard, had been the first text he sought when he began researching the reliquary. He opened the email as quickly as his hands could direct the mouse, and he read excitedly.

Dear Professor Duffield,

Gracious me, what a fascinating find! I have found no records of the reliquary, but the bolt fragment is mentioned by Gervase of Canterbury in Twysden's Historiae Anglicanae Scriptores Decem (London, 1652). If you don't have a copy of it, I can scan in the pages and post it to you via email. I would be ever so chuffed if you could send a photo of the item for me to see, since I'm sure I shan't be able to travel to Ithaca. It's amazing that it survived these eight centuries! How exciting for it to be shared with the public.

I would love to discuss it with you further, if you would be so willing. Please don't hesitate to call me at my office if you have any questions.

Kind regards,
Warwick Adams
Professor of Medieval British Studies
All Souls College, Oxford University, Oxon
(1872)816334

"So he'd be 'chuffed', would he?" Tom remarked aloud. "I wonder what the hell that means." Despite the cynical comment, Tom was extremely pleased by Adams' response. The fact that a serious King Richard scholar hadn't scoffed at the relic, and instead had sought and found a legitimate reference to it was thrilling. Tom had read much of Gervase of Canterbury's works – the twelfth century monk had chronicled all the news of the court from the time of Kings Henry II, Richard and John. Tom had drawn from his work many times – at least his work as transcribed and translated by Twysden in the mid-seventeenth century. In fact, Duffield had used that text so many times for his own work that he knew exactly where the book sat on his bookcase and he glanced up at it. Yet he was too excited to go pawing through the book to find the passage, and instead picked up the phone and dialed Adams' number immediately. After a series of mixed pauses and clicks, Tom heard the quaint double-beep of the British telephone system. By the third ring, the other side picked up.

"Eight one six double three four" said the voice on the other side.

Tom did not recognize that this was the number he had just dialed, nor did he know this efficient British custom of answering the phone by stating the number, rather than the American, "hello". "Excuse me?" he said haltingly.

"This is eight one six double three four, Professor Adams speaking."

"Oh, Professor Adams, hello. This is Tom Duffield from Cornell University calling. I just read your email. Thanks for getting back to me so soon!" Tom was talking very loud, as if that helped be heard on the other side of the Atlantic Ocean.

"Hello, Professor Duffield, hello! Thanks ever so for your inquiry. I know your work, of course, and it's very good, I must say. And please don't think me presumptuous in saying so," Adams said in an enthusiastic rush.

Tom was flattered to be complemented by one of the greatest scholars of the field. "Oh, not at all. I appreciate the complement, especially coming from someone of your stature and reputation."

"You're too kind, too kind!" Adams caught his breath. "Well, what a smashing find!"

"It's something, isn't it? I think my knees got weak when it was shown to me."

"I can just imagine. And the provenance, you think it sound? You know the relic business – and I mean that quite literally, of course – in the middle ages could be quite imaginative and resourceful."

"Yes, I've been thinking about that as well. I haven't studied all the documentation that came with the piece, that's being mailed to me shortly. But Strater – the collector I wrote about in my note – he's very thorough. I have to say I was very impressed by his knowledge and the lengths he went to in researching his collection."

"Ahh, good," responded Adams, "I'm rather hoping that it is the real thing. It's so depressing to always be debunking myths and proving that so few of our, emm" he paused, searching for the right term, "'historical souvenirs' shall we say? – are bona fide. The Walter of Rouen connection is very promising, of course."

"I'm very interested to hear what you've found. I hadn't dug into my copy of Twysden's *Historiae Anglicanae* yet." Tom was slightly embarrassed to admit that, but wanted Adams to get right to the point.

"Finding the book itself was a bit of a trick. It's the first place I wanted to turn, of course, but I'd misplaced it. When I couldn't find it in my office I drove home to look in my study and, wouldn't you know it, it wasn't there either. Then I went back to the office and looked again – quite irritated by this time of course – but too stubborn to borrow another copy or go to the library. So, as I was packing up to go home again, there it was in my briefcase. I'd been carrying it back and forth the whole time."

Tom was anxious to hear what he found and restated his question. "I'm glad you found it, but what did you find in the text?"

"Yes, indeed, let me get to the point," Adams chided himself. "Richard's deathbed scene is fairly consistently recorded across a number of texts. Eleanor of Aquitaine was there, of course, having made her way down from Poitiers, and Walter of Rouen was acting essentially as Richard's chief of staff. Most of the records focus on Richard's clarity as he directed his body to be dismembered and buried in a number of places – plus the anecdote about the poor young man who shot him. Richard, gentleman warrior that he was, pardoned him and gave him a small stipend."

Tom was familiar with the story and cut in, "And as soon as Richard's men escorted him out of the room they tortured and killed him."

"Not very sporting, was it?" Adams chuckled. "Anyway, only Gervase's account tells of the moment when, just before dying, Richard handed Walter a small fragment of wood and Walter held it up, announcing, 'soaked with the blood of my slain lord and master, shed to save the people'."

Tom's heart raced. Adams had found real evidence that the crossbow bolt had not only been extracted from Richard and kept, but actually handed to Walter during the last minutes of the great king's life! "Beyond being quite a grand pronouncement, that's pretty good proof that this bolt fragment was there, don't you think?"

"I should say so," Adams responded. "Well, it suggests that some fragment existed."

Tom knew this was a diplomatic way of suggesting that just because there had been a piece of the bolt, it was not necessarily the one Tom was currently holding in his hand. "Of course I need to do a little more examination of the bolt – you know, dating it, identifying the type of wood, et cetera. Plus we need to study the reliquary and provenance from Walter."

"Yes, quite right. But I think you've got something special, Professor Duffield. I really do," Adams reassured him.

The two men continued talking for another quarter of an hour – exchanging information on specific references regarding Richard's death vigil, biographies of Walter, and names of experts on reliquaria. By the time Duffield got Adams off the phone, the American had a long list of robust leads to help him discover – and prove – the truth of this small piece of wood which had changed the course of European history.

Tom spent the next half hour searching the internet and pulling books off the shelf, until he almost inadvertently noticed the time on his watch and realized he was scheduled to begin delivering a lecture in twenty minutes. He quickly rehoused the reliquary in its leather case and placed it on the floor under his desk. Then he slid open the top drawer of his desk and paused to take one last look at the prized bolt fragment before laying it inside. How was this jagged little piece of wood chosen to change the world, Tom wondered. Probably every other piece of the tree from which it came, and every other tree in that forest had rotted or burned in the eight or nine hundred years since it was grown. But it had risen from a humble twig, on a humble piece of land, to kill a king, and because of that was now immortal.

A sharp knock at the door shook Tom from his reverie and he swiftly palmed the baggie with the shard inside as the door swung open, revealing his behemoth boss. William Rogers lumbered in, hoisting his trousers which were slipping down on one side. "Good morning, Tom," he said.

"Hello, William. How are you this morning?"

As usual, William was gasping at the slightest bit of exercise, and walking down from the elevator qualified. He took a deep breath and began, "I was just wondering how your meeting with Strater went. We haven't seen each other since you went down there."

"It was a great trip, even better than I expected," Tom answered. "His collection is amazing, and well researched already."

"Tell me about it." Rogers had finally caught his breath.

"Well, I have to run to a lecture right now, but I can fill you in later."

"Come on, just one snippet. It's been such a mystery. Everyone's dying to know."

Tom squeezed the baggie in his hand. "Okay. How's this? He has the fragment of the crossbow bolt which killed King Richard the Lionheart." Tom paused for effect.

Rogers paused as well. And then he laughed loudly. "The bolt that killed Richard the Lionheart," he repeated. "That's a good one. Ha, ha, ha."

Tom's grin faded. "I'm serious. It's fairly well documented."

"Oh, come on, Tom. Did he also pull out the Ark of the Covenant?"

Tom remained deadpan. "Not that he showed me." Duffield could feel the jagged point of the wooden shard and imagined it piercing his palm. He squeezed a little tighter. "William, this is a serious collection."

Rogers stopped his wheezy chuckling. "I'm sure it is. But the University depends on you to separate truth from fiction. Just because a rich man threw his money at a few mythical treasures doesn't mean we can parrot back the lies to an educated public. We can't risk losing our good reputation."

Tom paused to weigh his response. "Thank you for that helpful advice."

"Is everything alright?" Rogers noticed Tom wasn't acting his normal (and combative) self. Rogers almost longed for it.

"Everything's fine. I have to get to lecture."

"If you need any help researching the collection, don't hesitate to ask."

"Thanks for the offer. I'll let you know."

Rogers took his leave, half-smiling, backing out the office and closing the door. As the door's catch clicked, Duffield opened his fist and looked the relic in his hand. Its imprint was pressed into his palm – its outline clearly visible and tinged in red. He slid the baggie into the top drawer and locked it. Grabbing a sheaf of notes for the impending lecture, Tom stepped quickly out of his office.

7

Lisa spent the first quiet hours of Monday morning, prior to anyone else reaching the lab, trying to figure out whether and how she could challenge Megan's decision not to use Jeff's DNA. She

193

was still undecided when Megan came in, and when the young post-doc launched into thanking Lisa for a wonderful evening, raving about the meal, and bubbling with excitement over Claire's agreement to conspire, Lisa lost her will completely. She rationalized that she had at one point conceded (at least in her own mind) to use the commercial DNA as a means of gaining Tom's agreement. Further, she had raised it only half-heartedly to her young protégé. And finally, when she had the chance to give it one last shot on Saturday night with Claire, she passed. It would be both unfair and risky to raise it again now that Megan and Claire had agreed to the plan. Everyone was aligned, leave it be, she told herself.

Everyone except Tom, that is. She had told him on Sunday that the women were aligned to the plan, yet she had left out the minor detail about whose DNA they would use. The omission repeatedly nagged at her throughout the day, but she squirreled it away in her mind as much as possible so as not to let it trouble her. Knowing she would have to deal with it sooner or later, Lisa opted for procrastination.

As it turned out, the moment of reconciliation came unexpectedly as she placed dinner on the table that evening. She and Tom were making small talk about their working day, when he abruptly changed the subject.

"So when are we going into the lab to soak out the cells?" he asked matter of factly.

Lisa had so completely dismissed the notion that they would still do this, that the question took her by surprise. "Huh?" was her automatic response just prior to realizing that Tom was still working with an earlier version of the plan. She turned away from him and headed back toward the fridge so as to avoid his seeing her panicked thinking.

Assuming that she had not heard him, Tom repeated the question verbatim and added, "You probably have a more technical term for it, right? Extraction? Don't we need to do that pretty soon for you to culture the cells?"

Lisa was searching for the best way to handle Tom's question when a far more pragmatic response took over her lips. "When do you want to go?" she asked, turning back to face him.

"Do we need to do it when no one else is in the lab?"

"Yeah, I guess that's a good idea." Lisa realized this was better than a good idea. She needed to avoid having Megan and Tom discuss the cloning prior to her working through the discrepancy in the source DNA.

"How about Saturday morning? None of your students are likely to be there then, right? Except for Megan, maybe, but she would probably want to help."

"I think Megan takes Saturday's off," Lisa said hopefully. "At least I try to encourage her to do that. I'm afraid she works too hard."

"That's something, coming from you, the Queen of Workaholics," Tom quipped.

Lisa had to acknowledge the irony of her comment. "I want to keep her from making the same mistakes I made."

Unfortunately for Lisa, Tom wanted to pursue talking about the extraction, and he retraced that line of discussion. "So, how do we do it? How do you suck the DNA out of something?" he asked.

Lisa sat at the table, bowed her head over her food for a moment of private prayer, and then started answering Tom's question. "We'd use a mild saline solution to flush the cells from the Band-Aid. That'll give us all sorts of cells, red blood cells, skin cells and hopefully white blood cells – leukocytes – in our solution. Then we'd add microscopic beads coated with antibodies which specifically bind only to leukocytes. We'd spin that in the centrifuge at a very slow speed to pellet the beads and thus the leukocytes – all the rest of the cells remain in solution to be thrown away. Finally, we add a release factor to free the leukocytes from the beads, and draw them off to a clean tube and add a stabilizing solution." She stopped to take a bite of meatloaf.

Tom stopped chewing what he had in his mouth while he thought about what Lisa just said. "So," he began, framing his question carefully, "it might take different methods to extract cells from something more dense, like, I don't know, ummm . . . wood?"

"I haven't really thought about it." Lisa was about to change the subject, thinking that Tom's curiosity was satisfied.

"But, just theoretically, how would you do it from something denser than a Band-Aid?"

"I don't know."

"Would it need a different solution?'

Lisa knew Tom could aggressively pursue theoretical lines of discussion, yet he rarely did that on topics related to her work. She was simultaneously flattered and irritated by his questioning. Knowing that he wouldn't abandon it, she decided to answer thoughtfully. "It probably wouldn't need a different solution, but it would likely have to soak longer."

"How long?"

"Several hours, I suppose, maybe overnight. On the other hand, you'd have to believe that the fluids could have soaked in to the wood in the first place – which is all a function of the porosity of the wood. I don't know, honey. I really haven't thought about it. Is there some particular reason for the question?"

Tom knew he was pushing this too hard. He needed to back off before she became suspicious. "No, no, no. I was just wondering, that's all."

The week passed quickly for both Tom and Lisa. The balance of Strater's collection had arrived at the Art Museum and Tom had spent all his free hours opening the cases with the museum staff and giving them preliminary descriptions and ideas about how to exhibit the treasures. The curator was excited by the prospect of pairing the items with contemporaneous art that depicted the events or key players, and he spent most of the time that Tom was unpacking the collection on the phone with curators from other museums around the world, attempting to borrow some of their most famous works of art. Realizing he had a major exhibit with potential to travel around the country, if not the world, the curator hoped he could piece together the most complementary pieces. Making this more difficult, however, was the fact that Duffield had sworn him to secrecy about Strater's collection, so he had to be somewhat cagey with his peers. On the other hand, unlike William Rogers, the curator never once scoffed at the historical claims tied to the objects, so Duffield began to like him immensely.

Tom had not told the curator – nor anyone else, for that matter – about the relic and reliquary. He was afraid he would have to turn it over to the museum for safe keeping as soon as he made its existence known, and thus he would lose the opportunity to 'experiment' with the shard of wood. Tom was particularly nervous about the reliquary's broken pane of glass and how he would explain it to either the University or Strater. It wasn't his fault, of course. The clumsy, idiot security agents at the airport had knocked the reliquary over while inspecting it and caused one of the panes to shatter. But Tom had not reported it to anyone, and now more than a week later it was becoming increasingly awkward to make an initial mishap report, either to Dean Thatcher and museum staff, or to Strater. Tom decided he would worry about that later.

Lisa made more progress in preparing the commercial cell line than she did in figuring out how to tell Tom that Jeff had been 'deselected'. Over the past several weeks, she and Megan had perfected concentrations of different Ewe Factor solutions as well as the timing and duration of key steps. Megan had found a way to increase the potency of the Ewe Factor, yet she had found as well that when it was too strong, certain chromosomes would begin to mutate. This was worrisome and created several long days of validating the health of the reinvigorated cells as compared to the original cell lines. While it would be impossible to check even a small fraction of the thirty thousand-some known human genes, the women made an educated guess that multiple-site DNA fingerprinting analysis would be a reasonable test. As a means of ensuring objectivity in conducting the test and reading the results, Lisa tasked her most senior Graduate student, Kristina Abbot, with running the comparative screens. Lisa's charge was simple and cryptic, "Tell me how genetically similar these two samples are."

During the middle of the week Megan made her first visit to Claire's Gynecology practice. Lisa took her there as a matter of courtesy and convenience, but stayed in the waiting room to respect Megan's privacy. The exam went very well, and Megan faithfully reported the clean bill of health which Claire took little time to grant. As Lisa was paying for the exam (which had been agreed by the two women beforehand *and* which raised marginally-discreet eyebrows among the office staff), Megan said everything looked good for a mid-December implantation, assuming her periods hit at the end of the next two months. Always proud of a dependable performance, Megan assured Lisa succinctly, "I'm like clockwork". The young post-doc had scribbled a few notes during the exam and related them to her friend and mentor on their way to the car. They would extract eggs in mid- to late-November and keep them frozen until the second week of December when they would be denucleated to begin the chromatin transfer. Once the transfer appeared successful and the cells were beginning to divide, they would do the implantation as quickly as possible. Two items from the exam Megan considered too personal to share were, firstly, Claire's accurate but tentatively-offered observation that Megan was a virgin, and secondly, Claire's now-amplified challenge whether Megan truly wanted to act as surrogate. As before, Megan was unwavering in her commitment to moving "the experiment" ahead.

Lisa had just returned from Claire's practice, when Kristina came to her office with the results of the DNA fingerprinting. Although extremely bright and academically accomplished, Kristina had far less confidence in herself than did others, particularly Lisa, who recruited her permanently into the lab after only two weeks of a planned three-month rotation. "Lisa, do you have a minute?" she asked.

"Sure, come in. Do you want to sit down?"

"No thanks." Kristina looked down at the papers she was holding. "I just wanted to share the results from the DNA fingerprinting you asked me to do."

Lisa was pleased, but not surprised, that Kristina had finished it so quickly. "Great. So soon! What did you find?"

"Is it possible that you . . . umm . . . mixed up the samples?" Kristina asked.

"No, I was very careful with them. Why do you ask?"

"Because they're completely identical."

Lisa smiled and nodded. "Excellent."

Kristina, unaware of the work that Lisa and Megan were doing, wrongly assumed that she was being tested. "Were you trying to see if I would find a difference in the same sample?"

"No, not at all," Lisa protested, and then she fibbed. "We were afraid we'd exposed one of the samples to mutagens and were trying to see if they had damaged the DNA. I guess not."

Kristina was relieved. "Well, not as far as I could tell, and I used a pretty broad panel of probes." She looked back down at her notes. "Did you know it's male? I had a Y-chromosome probe."

Lisa hadn't known this, although the information was likely available through the cell line vendor. She mused momentarily on the contrast between Kristina's laboratory-speak and the lay expression that ran excitedly through her mind, *It's a boy!* She had always thought of *it* as a boy, but probably because she had previously assumed the baby they would clone would be Jeff. This confirmation, despite its unexpected timing, marked a special moment for Lisa and she closed her eyes briefly to savor it. "No, we didn't know that. Good thinking in running that screen. Did you find any other interesting characteristics?"

"No, that was it. Everything seemed pretty ordinary." Kristina took a step back toward the door.

Pretty ordinary?! That took the edge off Lisa's previous excitement, although she knew that was good news in this context. "Thanks for running that, Kristina. You really helped us a ton – and I have lots of confidence in the results when I know that you're doing it."

"Thanks, Lisa." This provided the morale boost Kristina needed. "Let me know if you have anything else you want me to do. See ya." She backed out of the office and pulled the door shut.

On Saturday, the Duffields breakfasted early at a diner downtown and headed into the laboratory by 8am. Their only real risk of discovery that morning came from Megan, and Lisa tried to reduce the likelihood of that by "ordering" her to take the entire weekend off, and Saturday at the very least. The other students were unlikely to appear much before noon, if at all. Lisa had still not found the courage – or the diplomacy – to tell Tom that Jeff was out of the picture. Indeed, going into the lab to do the DNA extraction from the Band-Aid accentuated her anxiety, and she tried to think of it more as a means of spending time with Tom and helping him better understand her work, rather than together creating their child.

For the first time in the twenty-plus years he had known her, Tom paid very close attention to Lisa. From the moment she took the Band-Aid out of the top drawer of her desk and through each step in the process of soaking the sample in a mild saline solution and isolating the leukocytes, Tom tried to memorize everything he saw. Each time she pulled another bottle of fluid off the shelf or measured out some quantity of it, he would ask what it was and what it did and how long that step would last. Once, when Lisa had to go out to the bathroom, Tom grabbed a piece of paper and hastily scribbled down the steps as quickly as possible, and then stuffed the sheet into his pocket when she returned. Fifteen minutes later he excused himself to visit the restroom as well, where, less fearful of interruption, he filled in the remaining details.

Despite her discomfort over the larger issue of deceiving her husband, Lisa was flattered by the attention Tom paid her and hammed up the care and concentration she was taking with each step. Without knowing it, she was actually just intimidating him further and amplifying his worry that he would not be able to repeat this procedure. Near noon, Tom was relieved to hear Lisa announce that they were almost done.

"That's about it," she said. "This solution we made is sort of analogous to body fluid. The next step would be to mix it with the Ewe Factor solution which reconstructs the DNA material in the proper pattern to encourage cell division. Thus it reconstitutes living cells."

"Ok, so can I finally ask how you remember all that?" Tom truly was impressed by her facility in the lab.

"I've done it many times, Tom. I am a Professor of Genetics, after all," she was still flattered by his attention.

Tom wanted to believe that it was more rigorously structured. "But how do you teach anyone else or prove your methods – don't you write anything down?"

Lisa now realized what he was asking and laughed. "Oh, I see where you're going. Of course the protocols are all written down in lab notebooks. We're actually pretty meticulous about it. It's one of the things my lab is known for." She was proud of her lab's reputation for perfect records.

Tom sensed that salvation from his own almost certainly incomplete and inaccurate scrawlings could be found in one of Lisa's neatly-kept notebooks. "Show it to me," he demanded.

"Show what?"

"Show me what we just did. You have it written down somewhere – that's what you said, right?" Tom hoped she would take him directly to the subject notebook.

"Well, I don't have *this* procedure written down," she explained.

Fear crept back into Tom's heart. "You don't?"

"Not exactly. It's not like you would write down a procedure for taking DNA out of a Band-Aid." There was a hint of sarcasm as she said this.

"That's what we did, isn't it?"

He had her on that, she had to admit. "Yes," she answered simply.

"I'm sorry," Tom said. "I don't get it. Were you just making that up?"

Lisa needed to recover her evaporating scientific dignity. "No, no. You're misunderstanding me. Come here." She led Tom back into her office, stopping a couple feet shy of the bookcase on the back wall. Lisa reached up and ran her hand along a mostly matching set of notebooks with consecutive sets of dates neatly hand scribed on the spines. She stopped at two books dated the previous year and alternated tapping each one as she pondered which to select. "I think it's this one," she said to herself, and then to Tom, "I spent much of last year working on a similar process – obviously not using a Band-Aid." She flipped through the notebook, turning pages back and forth until she found the right entry. "See? Here's the process we followed today." She held it out for him to see. "The only variation was that we lengthened . . . this step here," she pointed to one of the line entries. "It says to do it for 5 minutes and I doubled that." Noticing Tom's pursed lips and thoughtful nodding, Lisa thought she had regained her standing.

Tom noted the page and asked, "So you remember this from . . ." he took hold of the book and flipped it over to make note of the date on the spine, ". . . last March?"

"I did it about twenty times."

He read through the protocol. "So what does this line mean, 'Add one hundred eighty ul TE buffer, vortex, incubate fifty-five for 10. . . what's that, degrees? minutes?"

"Just what it sounds like. Put one hundred eighty microliters – that's what "ul" is – of Tris EDTA buffer into the tube. Then vortex it – remember that spinny-thing I kept putting the vial in? And finally, let it sit at fifty-five degrees Celsius for ten minutes. That's what the heat block was for at the back of my bench – the thing with the thermometer that you were looking at. It's really just like making brownies. You just have to follow the directions."

Tom had what he needed, everything but the excuse to get back into the building and copy the appropriate pages from the book. "You amaze me." He handed the book back to his wife. Lisa beamed as she returned the notebook to its place the shelf and led Tom back to the bench where they had been working. From a shelf above the bench she drew a sheet of adhesive labels and neatly wrote "JW 10/16," then peeled off the label and affixed it to the vial. She quickly restowed the other items on the bench top and wiped it down, then picked up the labeled vial and placed it in the rear of the lab refrigerator. Tom made careful note of its location.

They dressed for the blustery day outside and departed the laboratory, locking it behind themselves and took the service elevator to the ground floor where a backdoor to the building would deposit them closest to their car. Just leaving the elevator, Tom spied a door marked, "Glassworks" and asked, "What's that?"

Lisa looked back over her shoulder as they passed by. "Glassworks? They blow special pieces of glass there for laboratories – specialized tubes or needles. In fact, they'll be the ones to make the needle for the chromatin transfer – super tiny gauge."

"Do you think they could do some work for me? A very old

pane of glass broke in one of Strater's pieces and I was trying to figure out how I could get it replaced."

"You should ask them. They are really good and would probably love the challenge."

"I'll drop in on them next week," he said, drawing his coat around him and putting on his ball cap as they left the building. Despite a cold gust of wind which made him wince, Tom smiled inside with the knowledge that his plan was coming together perfectly.

8

The key to Saladin . . . key to Saladin . . . key . . . Saladin

Tom kept turning the words over and over in his head, but couldn't make sense of it. In fairness, he had only been at it for an hour, ever since he had returned from lecture and one of the departmental secretaries had thrust a Fedex package at him – Strater and Robert Tucker's research. He ripped it open as soon as he got back to his office, skimmed the hand written cover note from John (". . . such a pleasure meeting you . . .will call soon to follow up . . . *blah, blah, blah")*, and quickly found the file covering the bolt relic. Tom was impressed by the file's organization. Like each of the other items, there was a pro forma catalog sheet which listed the item and its full provenance. Successive sheets provided additional detail about the acquisition transaction, the location or region, biographies of the protagonists, and bibliographies of pertinent references. "Strater certainly does his homework," Tom remarked aloud as he flipped through the thick sheaf of papers.

Unfortunately, for Tom, however, there was little in the pages which he had not already known or recently uncover himself in his frenzied research of the past week. But there was one phrase, buried in John's interview of the man from whom he purchased the relic, which caught his eye. Tom read Strater's report out loud to see whether hearing it might trigger some other connection, "Subject reported that relic also referred to as 'Key to Saladin' (La Clé à Saladin) in a 13th or 14th century inventory of Bishop Walter's possessions. He could not produce copies of this inventory, but said they were held in Rouen City Hall archives and could be made available via special written request to the proper authorities." Just behind this sheet was the written request which Strater had apparently promptly shot off from his hotel near Rouen, even before leaving Normandy and returning to the United States. Tom flipped to the next page, hoping to find the Rouen archivist's response, or photocopies of the subject inventory – unfortunately there was no more about it. Given Strater's rigorous records keeping, Tom was pretty sure the request was still sitting somewhere in Rouen City Hall – unless, of course, the bureaucrats had already emptied their wastebaskets.

Duffield puzzled over the phrase for some time, and then dug into his most reliable reference texts trying to find some clue, yet even the slightest hint of an explanation eluded him. He even tried Googling "Saladin's Key" on the internet, which yielded all sorts of interesting information about the great Saracen leader and "key dates", "key events" and "key personalities". He reentered the query in French and found even less. Tom's previous productive conversation with Professor Warwick Adams at Oxford came suddenly to mind and he quickly typed a short email asking whether Adams recognized such a phrase. As he hit the "send" button, Tom's eyes lit once more on the note from Strater which he had earlier skimmed and cast aside.

"Why don't I just call him?" Tom asked himself. He picked up the note, reread John's gracious words and thought back to the wonderful day he had spent with the wealthy collector at his estate on the Hudson. Duffield reached for the phone and dialed the phone number scribbled under John's signature at the bottom of the note.

"Strater" answered the voice simply at the other end.

"John?" Tom felt a little awkward calling him this, despite

how well they had hit it off. "It's Tom Duffield, from Cornell."

"Hi, Tom!" Strater seemed genuinely excited to hear from the professor in Ithaca. "Did you get the collection files? Actually, I should ask first about the collection itself. I didn't hear about that. Everything arrive okay?"

Tom pictured the reliquary toppling on the stainless steel table at LaGuardia, shattering one of the panes, yet couldn't help himself from answering cheerfully, "Everything's great. It was packed really well. And I've got to tell you, John – the curator, he was so excited he could barely stand still."

"Glad to hear it. And the research files?"

"They came this morning."

"Sorry I didn't get them to you earlier. I was really busy last week."

Tom couldn't help liking this man. He was donating a priceless collection to make it forever available to historians and the public, and yet was still so conscientious that he would apologize for a week's delay in sending his own research. "Don't worry about it. It gave me a chance to do some independent work without being influenced by what you had already found. I have to tell you, John – and you know I'm not a suck-up – your research is really outstanding."

"Thanks, Tom. I appreciate that coming from you. Any new finds?"

"I've been working on the King Richard bolt relic –"

"No surprise there," John teased.

"I suppose not. Anyway, most of what I have found so far has been supportive. I talked to a guy named Adams at Oxford, who helped me find a reference to the fragment by Gervase of Canterbury. It was written within a year or two of Richard's death."

"Fantastic!"

"I was very excited. So was he, by the way. We talked about it for some time."

Strater was pleased by Tom's progress. "I knew you were the right person for this job."

Tom was too eager to ask about the newest mystery to acknowledge the compliment. "I did have a question about something in your file."

"Shoot."

"You wrote that the person who sold it to you mentioned "The Key to Saladin" as another name for the item."

"Right, that's what he said – in French, of course, 'Le Clé à Saladin.' It was mentioned in an early inventory, which I tried to get copied."

Strater couldn't see Tom nodding vigorously. "Yes, I saw your request to the Rouen archivists. You haven't heard anything back?" Tom asked.

John burst out laughing. "You must have little experience with French bureaucrats."

Tom laughed too. "Don't misinterpret hope as expectation. I didn't think you'd get a response. Sounds like a good reason for me to go over there."

"There you go. I'd be happy to pay for it, as long as you let me tag along."

"I was kidding, but I'll keep it in mind. Anyway, in the meantime, is there any explanation you can ascribe to that name? Does it make any sense to you?"

Strater paused to consider the question. "The only connection I could make links back to the crossbow as Richard's favorite weapon. He believed he could defeat Saladin with an army of crossbowmen, so perhaps it was some ironic reference to that – you know, the key to defeating Saladin."

Now Tom paused to think. "I guess that makes sense," he responded. "I sent an email to Adams at Oxford seeking his counsel. I'll let you know if he comes back with anything."

The two men spoke for another twenty minutes when Tom

glanced at the clock and suddenly remembered he had arranged to have lunch with Lisa. He promised to be back in touch soon and signed off, then quickly dialed Lisa's number.

"Hello, this is Lisa."

"Hi, Sweetie, it's Tom. Do you still want to have lunch together?" His plan depended on a yes.

"Of course. Where do you want to go?"

"How 'bout the bagel place?" If Tom could get her all the way down to Collegetown he had the best chance of success.

"You want to go all the way down there?" she complained. "Why not over at the Statler?"

"Come on, it isn't raining," he looked quickly out the window to see whether that was actually so. "Let's get some exercise. I'll meet you there in, say, 15 minutes."

Lisa was happy for the lunch invitation which came far too infrequently, so she didn't want to push too much. "Okay. I'll leave right now."

That was just what Tom wanted to hear. "Great see you in a few." Tom hung up and went directly to the door where he pulled his coat off the hook on back. He pulled it on as he stepped out of his office and hurried down the hall.

Tom had little intention of going directly to the restaurant. Instead he made a bee line for Lisa's lab, confident that she would be half a mile away in Collegetown by the time he arrived. This would be the first of several surreptitious visits to her lab, likely the shortest in duration, and he gambled that doing it in the middle of the day would be easiest. He arrived at the Biotech building twelve minutes after he and Lisa had finished their conversation and decided to circle around to the back entrance. She would have gone out the other side, he reasoned, so this would minimize any chance of her seeing him in case she were delayed. He took the elevator and entered her lab, coming face-to-face with Kristina Abbott the moment he stepped through the door.

"Hi, Tom," she said with a frown. "Lisa just left about ten minutes ago. Wasn't she having lunch with you?"

"She's not here? I thought we were going to meet at the lab?" Tom was a good liar. He peeked through the small window into her office. "You sure she's not there?" He tried the handle and was very pleased that she hadn't locked it upon leaving.

"No, I walked part way out with her. But I don't think she mentioned where she was going." Kristina appeared very troubled by the mix-up, and this made Tom uncomfortable. He had to get rid of her.

"Don't worry about it, Kristina, I'll just call her mobile and we'll work it out. I just need to use her office phone since I left my cell phone back in McGraw." He edged through the door, leaving it closed enough to dissuade Kristina from coming in behind him. This seemed to work, he thought, noticing she wasn't behind him, but even so he walked directly to Lisa's desk, picked up the receiver and pretended to dial. He turned around to the bookcase on the rear wall and tried to orient himself quickly to the different lab protocol books neatly lining the shelves. In his haste to shake the pesky Kristina, Tom had neglected to turn on the lights and was now struggling to read the dates marked on the spines. Thanks to the light coming in from the cracked door and its small window Tom could just make out the dates and he stepped closer to render them more readable. He ran his finger along the notebooks. *November-December* . . . *January-February* . . . *March* . . . *This is it.* He began to extract the protocol book from the shelf when suddenly the lights came on full bright. *Christ!* Tom swung around to see Kristina at the door.

"Sorry." She held up a hand apologetically and whispered, "It looked dark in here."

Tom fought off the urge to betray his surprise and hoped he wasn't blushing. "Oh hang on, Lisa," he said into the receiver. "Thanks, Kristina, I couldn't find the switch."

"You got hold of Lisa?" she asked helpfully.

"Yeah, she's on the line," he answered. *Now get the hell out of here.* "Can you give us a minute?"

"Oh, sure, sorry." She backed out, leaving the door open to Tom's dismay.

"Great, I'll meet you there," Tom said loud enough for Kristina to hear from the vestibule. He turned back to the bookcase, and now that his mark protruded two inches from all the others, it was easy to pluck the notebook quickly and stuff it into his backpack in one fluid motion. Tom was pleased at how quickly he had taken the book and was sure that Kristina hadn't seen it. He checked the shelf to make sure the other books filled in the hole, pushed a couple here and there to finish the job, and then squared them all up the way he knew Lisa would keep it.

Hanging up the receiver, Tom left the office, flipping the lights off on his way out. He waved goodbye to Kristina and walked briskly to Collegetown to meet his wife for lunch.

Other than the few minutes Tom needed to explain why he was late, he spent most of the mealtime with Lisa trying to figure out how to return the protocol notebook to its rightful place in her office bookcase. Kristina Abbott's pesky presence and near discovery of his petty theft – well, just borrowing, really – had unnerved him. Not only did he have to make up a silly excuse about forgetting where the two of them had agreed to meet – which Lisa privately found hard to believe – he also depended on the young grad student not mentioning anything to Lisa about him phoning from her office. It had been a clever ruse at the moment, but threatened to unravel his plan if Kristina couldn't keep her mouth shut. Thus, just in case Kristina did blab, he needed to think of someone else he may have had to call from Lisa's office. As for the notebook itself, which sat zipped inside the backpack at his feet, Tom figured he only needed a few minutes to copy the few pages required. He could do that on his own scanner-printer back in McGraw Hall, but then he needed a plausible excuse to get back into the Biotechnology building.

Lisa solved the dilemma for him when near the end of their meal she asked, "Have you called the glassblowing lab yet?"

Bingo! Tom smiled and answered, "I actually tried them from your office, but I don't think I had the right number, or I didn't dial it right or something. I'll try again this afternoon."

"Just come back with me," Lisa suggested. "It won't take long. I kinda know the guys there, I can introduce you."

Tom needed some way to beg off so that he could copy the notebook and then get back to Lisa's building to return the book. He was a master at fibbing and this one came quickly and easily. "I promised to meet a student at the Library to give them a book from my collection – that's why I brought my backpack." Tom reached down and lifted the pack a little for Lisa to see.

"You're such a great guy. Someday you'll get the credit you deserve."

"Thanks," Tom said. "I'll call the glass guys later today, though. How about if I drop by in the afternoon? That is, if they have the time to see me." Tom then thought of an additional reason to go back to his office – and his face brightened on the realization that it was much better than the lie. "Going back to my office will give me a chance to get the glass and the . . . you know," he held up his thumbs and forefingers to show the shape of the pane, "dimensions."

"Fine, give me a call when you're coming over."

Tom's afternoon progressed exactly as he hoped. After copying the key pages from Lisa's protocol notebook, he used his own notes from the morning in the laboratory to supplement Lisa's semi-cryptic directions. The locations of the different solutions she had used, even the descriptions of the flasks, the colors of the solutions and any labeling he could recollect – he knew all of these cues were vital to his successfully navigating the lab bench efficiently and effectively. He read through the steps several times, closing his eyes occasionally to visualize the way Lisa carried out the procedure. This was the first of many practice sessions, Tom assured himself. His goal was to memorize it so thoroughly he could carry it out without referring to the written protocol.

Duffield had to lecture mid-way through the afternoon, but that took barely more than an hour and as soon as he returned to his office he called Lisa to let her know he was headed over to her office. He packed the notebook into his backpack along with the baggie full of the reliquary's broken glass and a slip of paper with dimensions of the pane and hurried off to meet her – this time at the agreed place and time.

Lisa was standing at her bench in the laboratory when Tom arrived. He couldn't have scripted her greeting any better. "Hi, Honey. I'm almost done. Do you mind hanging out in my office for a minute?"

Tom was too happy to oblige, smiling broadly and stepping quickly into her office. He noted with relief that there was no one (particularly Kristina) in the break room opposite Lisa's office and wasted no time in moving quickly to the bookcase at the far side. In a clean and fluid motion he unzipped his backpack, removed the purloined protocol notebook and slid it back into its place on the shelf. He lined up the books as before and then turned around, feigning nonchalance just in case there was anyone looking. There was not. Tom patiently held the bored expression on his face for the next thirty seconds, expecting Lisa to come in and when she did not, exhaled a tremendous amount of pent-up breath. He laughed at himself briefly and then, suddenly certain that he hadn't confirmed the chronological order of the notebooks, swung back to look at them. He laughed again when he could see that they were right.

"What's so funny?" Lisa called out, walking through the door.

Tom exhaled again. "Nothing. Just something that happened earlier today." *Which was technically true,* Tom thought. Rather than wait for her to enquire further, Tom asked, "Do you have time to go down to the glass shop with me? I can go alone if you're busy. Really."

"I have time. I like those guys and I haven't been down there in ages. Let me call them first." Lisa came across the room to her desk, picked up the receiver and ran her finger down a list of numbers taped to her desktop. She paused near the bottom, tapped twice on the desk and quickly dialed. "Hey, Neil. It's Lisa Duffield . . . no, I didn't forget about you guys. Do you have a few minutes if I stop down? Great . . . Yeah, well, it's actually some work for my husband." Lisa winked at Tom. "Come on. You knew I was married. He's a professor in the History Department." She blushed slightly and drew a strand of her long blond hair back behind her ear. "So can we come down? Great, thanks. We'll see you in a few minutes."

"Who's this Neil guy?" Tom asked as they left the lab.

Despite Tom's initial impression of Neil as either flirtatious or threatening – and very likely annoying – he came to like him within moments of stepping into the glass lab. Neil had jumped up from his desk as the Professors Duffield stepped into the room and shook hands warmly with each of them. Even then Tom still half expected Neil to make some macho remark about what a lucky catch Lisa was – instead, Neil professed his eagerness for a professional challenge, "I've been trying to figure out what the History Department might want from me, and it hasn't come to me yet. What d'ya got?"

Tom explained the background of the Strater project and talked about the reliquary in excited detail. He was impressed that Neil seemed to know who John Strater was, and Tom was pleased further at Neil's widening eyes and "Wow!" interjections as the details of the collection unfolded. He rolled his eyes and shook his head as he heard the story of the security agents and the damage they inflicted in the airport. When Tom dug the glass filled baggie out of his backpack and lifted it up for inspection, Neil let out a gasp which won Tom over completely.

"May I take a look at it?" Neil held out his meaty, workman hands. The scarred fingertips betrayed his thirty years of hot glass work. Tom handed him the bag and Neil turned back toward his workbench and unsealed it to examine the contents. Extracting one of the larger shards with one hand, he put on his "readers" with the other and leaned in for a closer look. He was quiet for a long time, and then said, "Man! How old did you say this was?"

"I'm not exactly sure – probably about six hundred years. Maybe seven hundred."

"It's beautiful glass. What a shame."

"Can you replicate it?"

"I may not have to. Did you say it is all here in the bag?"

"Ninety-nine percent."

Neil turned back around from the bench to face Tom and Lisa and took off his reading glasses. "I'll just use this to melt it down and recreate the pane. You have the exact dimensions?" Tom held up the slip of paper where he had copied it down. "Great. It's not going to be easy, but I need a good challenge. Leave it with me." He smiled confidently.

Accustomed to departmental bureaucracy, Lisa quickly volunteered to do the work order and have it charged to her lab.

"That's okay," Neil responded. "This one's for King Richard. I'll trade it for a personal tour of the collection once it opens." He held his hand out for Tom to shake.

"It's a deal." Tom fought off the urge to grimace as Neil warmly crushed his hand.

"Give me a couple of weeks and we'll see how we're doing."

Tom was excited by the prospect of having the glass work

stretch out over several weeks. It was the perfect excuse to get him into the Biotech building for a reason other than visiting Lisa. "There's no hurry, Neil, really. The collection doesn't go on display until August or September of next year." Tom paused, as if finished, and then recognizing the value of an overt invitation to the glass lab he blurted out, "You don't mind if I stop by once in a while to see how it's going, do you?"

"Not at all, Tom, you're welcome here anytime."

Tom's break came with far less scheming than he had expected. He had already completely memorized the protocol to the point that he could write it out by hand verbatim. Now he simply needed to get himself into the lab to do the procedure and make the switch. The "simplicity" of that task, however, was unnervingly elusive. He glanced at the calendar hanging on the wall near his door and could see that mid-December was only six or seven weeks away. If he didn't substitute the vial in time he would end up raising his nemesis as his son and regretting his fate immensely. Tom's eyes drifted over to a framed picture of King Richard – a detail from a painting which he had recently scanned in from a book, printed out at the highest possible resolution and framed. It now hung on the opposite side of his door from the calendar. Tom's eyes found the picture often – when his consciousness caught up to them he wondered whether his boy would look anything like the crude portrait. He slid open the top drawer of his desk and stared for a few moments at the dark shard of wood in its plastic bag. It was time to advance the plan, he resolved, rather than sitting around and worrying about it. "Time to visit Neil," he announced to himself and struck off for the Biotech building. Visiting Lisa seemed a natural and courteous thing to do and he conveniently opted to tackle that first.

Once there, Tom lingered at Lisa's lab bench, half listening to his wife talk about her day and half scoping out all the materials he would need for extracting DNA from the bolt fragment. He could see almost everything he needed, but the bottle of TE solution seemed a tad low. What a disaster if he were to get himself into the lab and not have all he needed. He butted into her monologue with a question. "Who's your lab tech these days?"

This was not a Tom kind of question. "Huh?"

"Who's your lab tech?"

"Sylvie. Why?"

"Is she any good? I see your TE is low. Isn't she supposed to keep that kind of stuff topped up?"

Lisa looked up at the bottle and laughed. "You're just showing off that you paid attention that morning you were here. Sylvie's great – I just used this today. It's not like she's standing behind me ready to fill everything up." Lisa took the bottle down off the shelf and walked to a much larger bottle where she refilled her own. Tom made a note of the larger supply and could see a few other solutions stored there as well. He was glad he had asked the question.

Tom's biggest problem was getting into the lab for a couple of hours without the risk of discovery. He knew he could go in the middle of the night, but hadn't worked through his explanation to Lisa. Should he pretend that he was going away on a trip and just hide out in a local hotel? What if one of Lisa's students stayed late – Lisa often told him that they pulled all-nighters here. How could he ever explain walking into the lab at 2:30 in the morning and running into Megan, or worse yet the nosey Kristina? Like the TE supply, the answer to his dilemma came miraculously simply.

"Hi, Tom. We've been seeing you a lot lately." It was Megan.

"Hey, Megan. Yeah, the guys downstairs in the glass lab are doing some work for me." He noticed her quizzical look, and added, "For the Strater collection – they're remaking a glass pane for a reliquary. I was checking on how it's going."

216

"Cool – they're great down there. Is it Neil?"

"Yeah. Anyway, I was in the neighborhood, so I thought I should stop by." He shrugged.

Megan was about to continue toward her own bench when she stopped and turned back to Tom. "Are you coming out with us Thursday?"

Lisa intercepted the question. "Tom, I'm not sure I've had a chance to mention this to you. We've hardly seen each other over the past week."

"What's going on?" Tom wasn't so keen on hanging out with Lisa's group, but a team outing presented certain possibilities.

"You're more than welcome, really," Lisa assured him. She was embarrassed.

"Fantastic," he replied with an exaggerated smile. "Why don't we start with what you're doing and when?"

Megan reapproached them and answered the question on Lisa's behalf. "We're going out to dinner and then bowling. You should come," she cajoled, "Lisa told me about how she always beats you." She added a wink.

"Fibber!" Lisa called out. "Seriously, Tom, I thought everybody was working too hard and that we needed to have some fun – together and away from here."

Tom liked the sound of this. "What a great idea! Good for you, Lisa, looking out for the troops. Is everybody going?"

Lisa turned to Megan, "Did Kristina make up her mind yet?"

"I talked her into it," Megan said with some pride. "I think she was the last holdout."

Tom remembered why he liked Megan so much. "Well that sounds great," he said.

"So, you'll join us?" Megan pressed.

"Ummm . . . let me check out my calendar. I think there's a football game I was hoping to catch." As soon as he said this he realized how feeble an excuse it sounded.

Having forgotten to mention the event to Tom in the first place, Lisa was reticent to browbeat him to make a decision now. She let it drop there and changed the subject by asking Megan a question about one of her experiments. Tom stayed a bit longer and then slipped out as soon as another student tied up Lisa. He wanted to get away before she could raise Thursday's outing. Tom had a date already – a date with an ancient piece of wood and a test tube. Tom forgot to drop by the glass lab as he hurried back to McGraw Hall.

<h1 style="text-align:center">9</h1>

Tom Duffield, Associate Professor of European Medieval History, did very little to advance his career over the next two days. Sequestered in his fourth floor office, consultation hours cancelled due to urgent work on the Strater collection (at least that's what the note on his door said), Tom rehearsed the DNA extraction protocol. Using stained coffee cups as stand-ins for beakers, Gatorade and water for the different solutions and a broken pencil for the crossbow bolt, Tom repeated the process until he convinced himself he wouldn't miss a step. He considered blindfolding himself and doing it one last time, but realized that he was getting cocky and such self-absorption would almost certainly cause him to screw up. "Pride goeth before a fall . . . knucklehead," he chided himself.

Just before leaving for the day on Wednesday, Tom began the procedure. During his visit to Lisa's lab a couple of days previously he had purloined a test-tube and pair of latex gloves. Hands trembling slightly, Tom now removed the items from the top drawer of his desk where he had secreted them away, along with the bolt fragment in its plastic bag. As he donned the gloves, he looked across the room at his picture of King Richard and then held up the fragment in his line of sight. "I'm sorry this arrow took your life, Richard. But now it's giving it back," he said grandly. *I hope this thing soaked up a lot of white blood cells,* he thought next, but he didn't say it, fearful that it would detract from the moment. He inserted the fragment into the tube, and then using a bottle of deionized water – actually contact lens solution (which Lisa told him was the same as what she used in the lab) – he carefully filled the tube. Over the next twenty-four hours, the water would soak the human cells out of the wood. Tom applied the screw cap tightly and then lightly tapped the tube, watching the water swirl around the shard of wood. He worried that soaking the wood overnight might permanently alter its appearance, yet he knew that Strater was probably the only person who might notice the difference. Tom had already decided that he was going to take this risk, and as he imagined the wood yielding Richard's cells to the water, he was excited about that decision.

On Wednesday evening Tom brushed off Lisa's single entreaty to join the next day's group outing. He was almost hurt that she didn't push him harder, but not so much to be distracted from his meticulous planning. His only remaining obstacle was getting his hands on Lisa's keys and that problem had vexed him all day, and particularly that night. Indeed, her key chain lay on the kitchen counter the entire evening – just inches from his fingertips. Tom toyed with the idea of lifting them after Lisa went to bed, sneaking out to a hardware store and having a copy cut. Unfortunately, that plan had two fatal flaws. Firstly, Tom couldn't think of any all-night hardware stores. Secondly, like all other University door keys, it was prominently marked "Do not copy." This plan was a non-starter, he concluded. Instead, he needed to either borrow Lisa's car – whose keys shared the same ring – or get her to use his. A much more plausible plan, he thought. He and Lisa swapped cars on a regular basis. His was slightly bigger and more comfortable. Perhaps she would have to ferry part of her crew, he hoped. Tom realized he couldn't broach this until Thursday – being so thoughtful was so out of character it would arouse Lisa's suspicion. Even though putting it off to the last day threatened his plan, it was a risk he would have to take.

Fate smiled on Tom the next morning, even before he swung his legs out from under the bed clothes. Ordinarily, he and Lisa cherished their last few cozy moments abed by pulling the covers tighter around themselves and listening to the news and weather forecast. Today, however, thanks to the cold rain pounding the window, they had to concentrate hard to hear the radio. It was to rain the entire day, predicted the faceless voice that spoke to them each morning. It added that it may even sleet in the evening. Lisa rolled over and spoke her first words of the day, "Great! It would have to rain on the day of our team outing."

"It's rained every day since September. What's the difference? Were you going to bowl outside?"

Lisa gave Tom a playful shove. "No – it's just that a couple of the undergrads don't have cars and they won't come if they have to walk in the rain."

"So give them a ride. Take my car and you'll have room for a couple extra," Tom offered.

"Plus your car has the seat warmers." She cuddled up to him. "Are you sure?"

"Wait a minute, I forgot your car doesn't have seat warmers," Tom teased. And then, just to make sure he didn't snatch defeat from the jaws of victory, he closed the deal. Throwing an arm over Lisa and pulling her close, Tom kissed her forehead. "Take my car, honey. Your group deserves some fun together."

"Thanks, Tom." She kissed him tenderly. They listened to the radio for a couple more minutes and then, as if on some inaudible cue, simultaneously rolled to their respective sides of the bed and stood up. As they readied themselves for the day, both Tom and Lisa had more energy than usual. She was excited at the prospect of getting away from the lab that evening. He was excited at the prospect of getting into it. Tom was also spurred on by the need to get into the kitchen before Lisa so he could hide the extra set of keys to her car which hung by the door. It wasn't her car he wanted, of course, it was the other keys on her key ring. If she gave him the spare set, he'd be closed out of the lab. Tom strode down the hall just a few steps ahead of her and stuffed the extra set in his pants pocket.

It was a full half hour later, as they queued up at the kitchen door to sprint to their cars through the driving rain, that Lisa noticed her other key set was missing. Tom was quick to suggest that she should try harder to put them in the right place – advice which Lisa didn't fully appreciate. Then he came up with a fix to their nearer term problem. "I'll come by your lab in the afternoon and we can swap keys."

"You sure? In the rain?" Lisa was touched, once again, by Tom's thoughtfulness.

He held up his umbrella. "I'll be fine. I'll come around four, okay?" Tom leaned forward, lips slightly pursed, to invite their customary, daily, farewell kiss.

Tom's fixation on his evening rendezvous with a test-tube betrayed itself several times during his lectures that day. Instead of the "salient events" during the establishment of the Holy Roman Empire, he referred to the "saline events". Much to the confusion of his students, he didn't hear himself say this, and the more attentive in his lecture hall dutifully wrote down that word and pondered whether it related to salt commerce with Mediterranean countries. He did, however, hear himself substitute "first milliliter" for "first millennium" and he chuckled as he corrected himself. What lingered longest in Tom's consciousness was the question a graduate student asked during a discussion of twelfth century.

"Professor Duffield," spoke the shaggy haired but incisive young man, "do you think Richard revolted against his father, ummm . . . Henry the Second, because Henry was such a bad King or because Richard was so impetuous and violent?"

Impetuous and violent? In thinking about bringing him back to life, Tom had always pictured Richard the historical and kingly figure – not the warrior. Indeed, Richard was known for his battle frenzies, after which, when he finally stopped swinging his razor-sharp sword, he was reputedly drenched in blood. Tom imagined a "Chuckie-like", red-headed child standing by their bed in the middle of the night, wielding a huge knife. For his own peace of mind, Tom had to refute that Richard was inherently violent. Finally, after a pause so long that the student considered asking the question again, Tom said, "I think the former, and you have to remember that Richard's mother, Eleanor, was always egging him on against his father." *Note to self,* Tom thought, *keep a close eye on Lisa.*

The cold rain had eased by the time made his way across campus to Lisa's lab. Tom carried his umbrella, but didn't bother opening it up against the cold, yet infrequent drops of rain. Lisa asked him once more whether he truly minded not having his car that evening. He assured her that he was happy to help out. It was the least he could do, he said, if he wasn't going to join them that evening. As Lisa handed him her key ring she paused, considering whether to simply remove the car key. Tom saw the thought cross her mind and pointed out that he needed her house key as well as her car key. She quickly agreed and handed over the set. Tom confirmed that they were headed out at 6pm. He also did a visual check of the solutions, glass ware, and instruments that he would need. Everything looked completely in order. In fact, Lisa even pointed out that the microcentrifuge had just been serviced and was working like new. Ordinarily, Tom would have reacted to such a comment by asking why he should care. Today, he simply nodded and said, "Awesome."

He returned one last time to his office, both to wait until it was safe – he reckoned arriving back at the lab at 7pm would minimize chances of running into any late "leavers" – and to pick up the test-tube of bolt-soaked solution. Tom read through the protocol one last time, but he knew it so well that his eyes didn't really see the words on the paper. Instead, he thought about the child he was creating – or re-creating – and whether this Richard would be larger than life on his second pass through it. How would childhood in a bucolic, Upstate New York, university town modify the genetic tendencies of a man whose claims to fame included slaughtering thousands of Saracens? Was it Henry the Second and Eleanor who made him violent and grand, or was it the complex arrangement of microscopic nucleotides? A little after 6, Tom's patience wore out and he unlocked the top drawer of his desk and removed the test-tube. Holding it close to his face and swirling it one last time, he studied the solution closely to see whether it looked any different after twenty-four hours with its wooden captive. It wasn't quite as crystal clear, he judged, and he hoped that suspended in that solution might be just one good leukocyte from the long-dead king.

"You in there, Richard?" Tom asked the tube. "Yes," he answered himself in falsetto. Then, glancing across at the medieval portrait of a magnificent king-warrior, he said it again in the deepest bass he could muster, "Yes, I am." Tom carefully unscrewed the cap and laid it gingerly on his desk, and using a pair of tweezers he'd spirited from home, extracted the wooden shard and put it in a fresh plastic bag. Earlier, Tom had gathered a handful of desiccant bags from around his house – they always came with electronics – and he now packed them in the bag next to the wooden fragment, hoping they would draw off all the excess water and return the shard to its original appearance. He was relieved that the bolt didn't look all that different from before – hopefully the desiccants would do their thing.

Recapping the tube and sliding it into his shirt pocket, Tom then neatened up his desk, including locking away the prized relic. He grabbed his coat and umbrella, switched off the lights and left his office, locking the door behind him, and then began making his way toward the massive, dark oak staircase. He was so lost in his own thoughts – mostly about the procedure and how he could get it done in three hours or less – that he failed to see William Rogers standing in the hall.

"Hello, Tom. What keeps you so late?" William called out.

Tom was startled by William and his question. "William, hello." He instinctively felt for the tube through his coat. "Why are you here so late?" It was the only response that came to mind.

"That's what I asked you – or are you playing that child's game where you repeat everything the other person said?"

Ordinarily Tom would have observed how little time it took William to become petty and irritating. However, this evening he was scrambling for an alibi. "Umm . . . Lisa's got an event tonight. I'm going over to meet her at the lab." *Dammit, why did I tell him I was going to the lab?*

William smiled broadly. "Splendid, I am heading that direction myself. Do you mind if I walk with you? I was hoping you could give me an update on the Strater collection."

"It's going really well. But, I'm –"

"Shed any light on the Richard artifact? Or should I say, hoax?"

Tom felt for the tube in his pocket once more. "My friend at Oxford stands behind it. I suggest you talk about it with him." Tom continued toward the stairs and William began walking with him.

"So, I'll have to educate both of you," William said chuckling.

Educate me on what!? How to be an enormous idiot? flashed through Tom's mind, but he answered more politely. "He's held a chaired position at Oxford for over thirty years. I think he probably knows what he's talking about." Tom was now several steps ahead of William and beginning to look back over his shoulder. William was lumbering down the steps as fast as he could. He was already breathing through his mouth.

"You know, Tom . . . I am happy to help," William said,

gasping.

"I know, you mentioned it before. Thanks, I'm doing fine."

"I heard there's a Gutenberg test strike. You know I have published quite a bit regarding him."

Tom knew this was an exaggeration and he squashed it quickly. "Only one paper with your name showed up and it didn't add much to what I already knew. I've finished the write-up on that piece. But thanks for offering."

Rogers had fallen several more steps behind. As usual, he was exasperated by Tom's disrespect. "In fact, Dean Thatcher was concerned you may come up short once again – like with your book. He suggested my help might ensure the collection meets the planned opening date in September."

This gained Tom's attention. He stopped at the landing and wheeled around, surprising Rogers who needed more notice to arrest his gigantic momentum. When Rogers finally caught himself, he was practically nose-to-nose with Duffield. "Did Dean Thatcher actually say those words? Or were those words *you* fed the Dean?" Tom asked coldly.

Caught in his lie, Rogers sought to dissemble but was too intimidated by Duffield. He shuffled back half a step. "I don't recall exactly, who said what."

Tom turned back around and continued down the next flight of steps. "I don't need your help, William. I'm doing fine by myself." He reached the bottom of the stairs and pushed open the massive oak door. "William, I'm really in a hurry. I'll see you later." Without waiting for Rogers' response, Tom stepped outside into a blast of cold rain and wind.

The Biotechnology Building was open when Tom arrived, and it provided a dry and warm respite from his soggy sprint across campus. He made his way quickly to Lisa's lab and was pleased to find it dark and locked when he arrived. Even though Tom could see through the small window into a shadowy vestibule, he knocked loudly on the door several times. No one answered, as he expected, so he swiftly unlocked the door, entered, and closed the door behind himself, pushing hard against the hydraulic arm which seemed oblivious to his impatience. When the door finally clicked closed, he depressed the button on the end of the handle. Not as good as a throw bolt, Tom knew, but at least no one without a key would be able to stroll in.

Tom took a deep breath and advanced further into the lab. Lisa's bench, where he planned to work, was around the corner from the main door, and the individual lights on the bench obviated the need to turn on the general overhead lights. Looking in from the outside it would be dim, but not pitch black – dark enough so as to appear deserted. The somber lighting was sufficient for Tom to see what he was doing, but it also changed the room's overall appearance. The hoses, tubes, flasks and other high tech paraphernalia took on a rococo flair – the flourish of their shape, but no hint of their purpose, survived the gloom. It lent the room a serious but decorative air, Tom observed, and not at all creepy. Yet, however visually intriguing Tom found the lab this evening, he was not prepared for the silence. This was the first time he had ever been there alone. The voices, music and rattle of tubes he associated with this space were completely absent, replaced only by the hollow whirr of the hood fans and the gentle hum of machines left on standby. He briefly considered turning on the radio which Lisa had tucked behind her equipment, but beyond the risk of giving him away, it would also degrade the peace which had descended there.

Tom began gliding through the protocol at a measured and confident pace. He anticipated each step perfectly, yet checked on his printed "cheat sheet" before commencing, and then checked it off as he completed it. His methods were meticulous, and notwithstanding the abject betrayal of Lisa's trust his present work involved, he was certain she would be proud of his facility at the lab bench. Tom found the many short incubation and centrifuging periods profoundly unsettling and painful. Unlike his wife, who during such periods could busy herself with other tasks or flip through a scientific journal, he simply divided his nervous stare between his watch and the test-tube. He willed time to move faster, but not so fast that the lab team's evening activities elsewhere would draw to a close before he was done. Despite his deliberate exterior, Tom's stomach churned with the stress he suppressed.

He rinsed and spun, drew off the excess solution, and then did it again. And again. He prayed there was just one leukocyte bound to the special beads, and that when he applied the release solution it would dutifully come away from its chemical captor. Freed back into the solution, these isolated leukocytes held the DNA he would need to recreate one of the most famous figures in western civilization. Just as he raised the tube to pour in the release fluid, he felt a strange tingle on his leg, which paired quickly with a cell phone ring. The sensory contrast to the quiet of the lab caused him to start and he missed his pour, generously dousing the lab bench.

"Shit!" He exclaimed. And then to make his point, "Shit! Shit!" Tom put down the tube and the flask of solution and fished the cell phone out of his front pocket. The mini-screen glowed with Lisa's name and number. "Christ!" He calmed himself, flipped open the phone and answered. "Hi, honey."

"I called our home number and you didn't answer. Where are you?" Lisa asked.

Tom was as quick as ever. "I was in the bathroom – I heard the phone ring, but I was . . . indisposed."

"You still . . . indisposed?" She chuckled.

"No, I'm out now. Thanks for asking."

"You must be psyched about the game."

"Huh?"

"Your team is up by thirty-something points. You must be psyched." Lisa was chatty like this when she had drunk a couple of beers.

Tom had completely forgotten about his excuse for not joining the lab outing. "Oh, yeah," he covered, "it's always fun to watch them hammer the opposition." He needed to change the subject. "You guys having fun?"

"We're having a blast. I'm so glad we did this. I was calling to tell you that we're going to bowl one more game and then I'm going to drive people home. I'll probably be home in an hour and a half."

"That's great," Tom was relieved. "Make sure you drive carefully. Take a little extra time to metabolize all that beer you're drinking."

"I'm fine, don't worry."

They conversed for a couple more minutes before Tom convinced her to rejoin her friends. Fortunately he was not on a timed step of the protocol, and as soon as he signed off, Tom cleaned up the spilled solution and recommenced his work. Knowing that Lisa wouldn't make it home for at least ninety minutes and that he had no more than thirty minutes of protocol remaining, Tom became even more deliberate. The added sense of relief that he was going to get away with this deed nudged him toward the theatrical. He recited out loud the directions for the step he was performing, saying it with different voices and accents. A deep sonorous chant pleased him the most, and he used that to narrate the rest of the procedure. Within twenty minutes Tom had finished the final step – and now only had to substitute this tube with the one Lisa had set in the back of the refrigerator-cooler on the other side of the lab. He neatened up the materials and wiped down the bench. No one would notice that he had been there, he was sure.

Tube in hand, Tom crossed the midpoint in the lab, and through the corner of his eye he caught the shape of a head silhouetted in the small window panel of the door to the hall. He stopped mid-stride and swung his head toward the door – precisely the opposite of what he should have done, he knew a millisecond too late. Due to the backlighting from the hall he couldn't make out the face, but remembered that only someone with a key could get in. Tom turned away and carried on toward the refrigerator.

Whump, whump, whump. The person was knocking on the door. *Whump, whump, whump.* The second set was more insistent.

"Go away!" Tom whispered. He opened the refrigerator door and spied the tube Lisa had put there several weeks ago. Although it was tucked far in the back and turned slightly, he could make out the sticker marked "JW 10/16" in Lisa's hand.

Whump, whump, whump. Tom heard a faint "Hello?" in accompaniment.

"Jesus Christ, get the hell out of here!" Tom reached back, grasped his target tube and pulled it out. The label was firmly affixed and he had to dig on one corner with his fingernail to lift enough to get a purchase.

Whump, whump. Tom noticed it was just two knocks and hoped the intruder was losing patience. "Hello?" The voice called out again.

Tom carefully affixed the sticker to his new tube. Other than the slight marring on one corner of the sticker, it looked perfect. He placed the tube where the other had been, slipped the original tube into his shirt pocket and closed the door. Tom hoped the person at the door had given up hope and walked away. He could try to wait him out, of course, but if Lisa got to the house before he did, Mr. Duffield would have a lot of explaining to do. Tom sneaked his head around the corner. The person was still there. And saw Tom peeking.

"Hey, let me in," he called out. Tom could see a handsome but slightly disheveled young man at the door.

Tom put on his game face and strolled to the door. He opened it and said in his most patient and gracious voice, "Can I help you?"

"Didn't you hear me knocking!?"

"Just now I did, of course, that's why I came to the door."

"Man, I stood there for . . . like . . . ten minutes, hammering on the door."

Tom repeated his earlier question. "Can I help you?" Despite the fact his heart was pounding, he appeared very placid.

"Yeah, my name is Elex – I'm a friend of Kristina Abbott's – I was just trying to figure out where she is."

"She's probably out with the rest of the lab team. They had a group event tonight."

"Do you know where they are?"

Tom checked his watch. "I'm not sure where they'd be at this point," he bluffed. "I think they were going to wrap up about now."

Elex suddenly looked perplexed. "Who are you?"

Best tell the truth in case we ever run into each other again, Tom reasoned. "I'm Professor Duffield's husband, Tom." Before Elex ventured into asking why he was there, Tom added, "I was bringing a little romantic surprise for my wife when I knew she wouldn't be here. Can you keep it a secret?" He winked.

Elex winked back. "No prob," was his eloquent response. "I interviewed your wife for *The Sun*. She's excellent."

Tom didn't know quite how to interpret that, so he simply smiled and thanked Elex. "I really need to get going. I've got to lock this up of course."

"Sure, okay. Well, tell Kristina I was looking for her – if you see her."

"I surely will," Tom responded, nodding. He pushed the door closed, once again straining against the hydraulic closer. As soon as Elex stepped away, Tom exhaled forcefully and prolongedly. "Figures it would be Kristina's friend," he said to himself. "If she can't meddle herself, one of her idiot friends has to do it." Tom pulled on his coat and picked up the umbrella which had been draining in a corner. One last look around the lab confirmed that he had covered his tracks. He flipped off the light above the bench and exited. Rather than heading back down the main hall and staircase which he had used coming in, Tom descended the rear stairs and emerged at the back door, close to where the dumpsters sat. Even before opening his umbrella into the wind-driven rain, he approached the closest dumpster and lifted the lid with one hand, while with the other he extracted the test-tube containing Jeff Wolf's cultured leukocytes. With a swift and fluid motion Tom flung the tube to the far side of the dumpster. He didn't hear it smack against the metal wall, however – the noise was drowned out by the clanging lid, which Tom let drop under its full weight. Its jarring clatter reassured him that Jeff Wolf would remain forever in the past.

10

Lisa held up the backs of her fingertips to survey the damage she had done to her nails over the past half hour. She only gnawed on them occasionally and never in public. Her mother had nagged most of the habit out of her while growing up, and the little that remained was impractical, if not dangerous, once she began working in the laboratory. Even so, when stress got the better of her *and* she knew her fingers were sufficiently free of dangerous chemicals, her left hand would find her mouth and she would trim the nails' ends with her teeth. Lisa did not reflect on what caused her stress today. If she had, she probably would have chalked it up to being excited about performing the chromatin transfer of cultured DNA into Megan's just-harvested eggs. Or she might have attributed it to the fact that Megan and Tom were at least almost an hour late in coming back from Claire's office. It was unlikely, however, that Lisa would put her finger on the real reason she was nervous – her guilt over deceiving Megan regarding the DNA source for their impending clone.

Megan had not raised the issue a single time since her

decision at Lisa's dinner party that they should clone an anonymous and unidentifiable source. From Megan's standpoint the issue was settled and there was no need to bring it up. The post-doc and surrogate-mother-to-be simply powered through the process of obtaining leukocytes from a lab supply company, desiccating them and then reviving them in the Ewe Factor solution. Simultaneously, Lisa prepped her cell culture in the vial marked "JW 10/16" to provide DNA for the transfer. Most recently, given Megan's frequent trips to Claire's office, Lisa didn't even have to operate in secret. In fact, Lisa had put the deception so completely out of her mind that she didn't even feel the need to rationalize. The argument that bringing back a brilliant scientist was better than cloning – well, anybody else – never had to be used.

Now, on a blustery Saturday in mid-December, as Tom took Megan to Claire's office for the egg harvesting, Lisa went to her lab to perform the final preparation for the chromatin transfer. At the same time Megan's medicated and now superovulating ovaries were being prodded to release several fertile eggs, Lisa drew undifferentiated cells from the "JW 10/16" sample and readied the microscopes for the very fine work of extracting the cells' nuclei and injecting them into Megan's eggs – minus their own DNA. Lisa was nervous about doing this work. Although she had worked with extremely fine needles in the past and removed cell nuclei and other organelles, she had never done it on a human cell. One slip could be lethal to the egg or damaging to the DNA material, and the number of eggs she could afford to kill would be very limited. Claire was the best trained to do this type of work, yet Lisa wanted to protect her from any suggestion of wrongdoing. The two women decided that doing the transfer away from Claire's office would reduce intrusion from nosy staffers as well as provide Claire with plausible ignorance of all they were doing. If things blew up, Claire could honestly state that she harvested eggs for a client and then reimplanted blastomeres – the quickly-dividing ball of embryonic cells – into the same client a few days later.

The microscopes were ready and all Lisa had to do at this point was wait and wonder. *Had Megan's ovaries responded to the treatments and produced enough eggs for them work with? Would Megan change her mind after the last month of injections and the discomfort of the egg harvesting? Would the procedure leave her reproductive tract, and particularly her uterus too traumatized to receive the embryos in a few days' time and let them take hold?* As time and the waiting dragged on, Lisa's questions and concerns seemed to multiply faster than a cell – and chewing her fingernails provided the only outlet for all that nervous energy.

Finally, just as Lisa decided to walk down to the vending machines and buy a soft drink, Tom and Megan entered through the door. Lisa betrayed her anxiety by asking "Where have you *been*?!" instead of greeting them or asking how Megan felt.

Cheerfully oblivious of Lisa's lengthy, nervous wait, Tom answered, "Claire was held up by a delivery at the hospital. They didn't get started until at least an hour past schedule."

Megan held up an insulated bag, "We have seven eggs to work with. They're in here."

Lisa remembered her patience and her compassion for the young woman. "How are you feeling? Are you alright?" During her wait, Lisa had done a good job of imagining Megan as traumatized and permanently injured from the procedure. The woman now standing in front of her seemed very different.

"I'm fine. It was a breeze," she answered without missing a beat. Megan looked over Lisa's shoulder toward the microscopes. "Is everything ready?" she asked.

"Don't you want to take a break?" Lisa asked.

"No way! Come on, that little fella's DNA needs a new home." She walked past Lisa to the microscope station.

"Fella?" Lisa said, "How do you know it's a fella?" she asked, following behind. The question had popped out without her even thinking about it – and she kicked herself for asking. Tom wanted to kick her as well.

"Oh, I have always just imagined it as a boy. I picture him having dark hair and dark eyes."

Lisa knew the baby wouldn't look anything like Megan's description, and the guilt over her deception came into blinding, crystal-clear focus. How could she so brazenly cover up what was really going on here, she wondered. She struggled with what to say and do. Lisa was forming the words to come clean when she suddenly remembered her deal with Tom. It was especially easy to remember this, since Tom had sidled up next to Lisa, put his arm around her shoulder and begun to speak. "I have always thought of him as a boy as well," he said confidently, "but, hey, it's 50-50. It could just as easily be a blond-haired, blue-eyed girl. How about you guys stop fantasizing and get on with the science?" He gave Lisa's shoulder a squeeze and winked at her. Just as quickly as Lisa had considered telling Megan everything, the notion faded from her brain.

The women sat down at the microscopes side-by-side and began readying each instrument. Megan would remove the nucleus from the egg as Lisa would draw up the nucleus from the cloned cells in a microscopic needle. Then Megan would pass over the egg to Lisa, who would inject the nucleus directly into the egg. They would do this seven times and then incubate the eggs for a few days as they formed into multi-cell blastomeres. In three days' time, they would take them back to Claire's office where she would pass them up a small tube into Megan's uterus, where, God and science willing, at least one of them would take hold and grow into a fetus.

Part III

1

Megan had mixed feelings about staying in Ithaca for the holidays. Even though she was well past her student days with its semester-end, all-nighter exam cramming and paper writing – the air of relief that came with fall term's eventual completion seemed to permeate campus and relax everyone – students, faculty, administrators and post-docs alike. She'd had her own stresses, of course. Three weeks earlier, Claire had harvested seven eggs from Megan's ovaries, and then, once Lisa had replaced the eggs' own haploid DNA with the full complement of forty-six chromosomes from the cultured and cloned specimen, they reimplanted them into Megan's uterus. It wasn't painful, just slightly uncomfortable – both physically and emotionally. Until all of this started, her body was her own guarded space – her little fortress from which she planned and executed an ambitious assault on any challenge that faced her. Men had gotten close but never breached the defenses; doctors were accepted only on her terms, and definitely only as often as necessary.

Since deciding to use her body as part of the great plan, Megan had needed to see the doctor very often. In all, between mid-November and mid-December, she had been to Claire's office at least once every week, yet even by the sixth and last visit she was not used to swinging her legs up onto the examination table and hooking her feet in the cold metal stirrups. Now two weeks past the implantation she was just beginning to reclaim her dignity, hoping that at least one of the eggs would take hold so that she wouldn't have to go through it all over again. If she were pregnant there would be more examinations, to be sure, yet perhaps with a baby inside Claire wouldn't prod and poke so much.

Claire had left to Megan the choice of going home to visit her parents for Christmas and New Year's. The doctor had said that either the eggs would take hold to the uterine lining and begin growing further, or they would fail and be flushed out with Megan's next menses at the end of December. There wasn't a lot that Megan could do either way, Claire said, other than taking it easy and laying off the alcohol during the innumerable holiday parties her ex-hippy parents were sure to host. However, Megan thought it would be too strange to be home among her parents and siblings. She hadn't told them that she was serving as a surrogate mother to her friend and mentor (not to mention, employer) as well as acting as a living test-tube for one of the most exciting experiments in the history of science. Sure it would be awkward to be turning down the spiked eggnog and goblets of wine, but that wasn't what kept her in Ithaca. Instead, it was the prospect of missing her period and thus launching her quest to serve both Lisa and science – but being too far away from the only people who could celebrate with her.

However, as she passed the morning of December 24th, quietly and alone in her apartment, Megan felt blue about her decision to stay in Ithaca. Lisa's invitation to Christmas Eve dinner with Tom and her brightened the outlook a little, but Megan didn't need to start getting ready until 3 or 4pm. That left all of the morning and the better part of the afternoon to kill, so she made the most of reading the Ithaca newspaper – scouring the classifieds, obituaries and even doing the puzzles. Craving company, she turned on the radio, but that only amplified her loneliness as the local station played Christmas songs and carols non-stop. Just before noon, as she filled in the last empty box of a challenging Sudoku, her eyes caught the unexpected movement of fluffy white snowflakes swirling by the window. Amazingly coincidental but for the fact that some version of the song played every twenty minutes, *Let it Snow* barked out of the radio at the same time. Propping her chin with both hands, elbows planted on the table, Megan gazed out the window and slowly pursed her lips as she contemplated how unfestive it all seemed. She longed for home.

Over the years, Megan's hippy mother had gradually given in to decorating the house for Christmas. The evolution had been slow. Megan's earliest memories of the December holiday featured decorating a tree outdoors and gathering around it to open presents. This was fun with sun or snow – but not so jolly under driving sleet. After a particularly wet year this gave way to a small balsam fir in a pot in the living room. They decorated it with strung popcorn which went outside after New Years to feed the birds. This, too, nearly became a tradition until their dog tipped the tree over, spilling a slurry of dirt and rocks on the carpet. A cut tree followed the next year, and a couple of years later, strings of lights replaced the popcorn. By the time Megan was in high school, the Brack's holiday celebration was indistinguishable from their suburbanite neighbors on either side.

Megan came to love these new holiday traditions, but had never taken the time to recreate them in her home since moving away to college. She was always busy with her studies until the last minute – and then she would travel home and partake in her mother's festival. It seemed pointless to decorate her own place and then abandon it a few days before Christmas – only to return in mid-January and deal with putting everything away. Megan took stock of the decorations in her house. There were a couple of old Christmas cards taped on the kitchen cabinets, and inside the entry foyer, a large cardboard Santa from the 1960's which she had purchased in a yard sale. And with that, the inventory was complete. As if to rebut the obvious conclusion that this was lame, she recalled the Christmas cardigan buried in her dresser. *Maybe I could wear that tonight . . . .* The young woman really knew that the only way to extinguish her holiday doldrums was to buy some decorations, maybe even her own tree, and spruce up the place. She grabbed her coat and headed out the door.

Snowflakes continued to swirl lazily from the leaden sky as Megan made her way into Collegetown. The sidewalk was too warm for the snow to accumulate, but not so the grass and trees which began to collect the fluffy white crystals. Within fifteen minutes, the dingy brown ground had transformed itself completely and the trees were quickly following – the conifers first and then the leafless deciduous, less able to seize the descending flakes. The transformation of the landscape had a lightening effect on Megan's mood and she realized a broad smile had spread across her face, replacing the morning's lonely frown. She noticed the same grin on the faces of the passengers in the few cars that passed, most of which were loaded up with students and likely headed away for the break. Megan reached down to the ground and scooped up a handful of snow to make a snowball. It was perfect for packing. She formed it into a tight ball, and while she had the urge to fling it at the next passing car, picked out a "For Sale" sign in the front yard of a house nearby. "Bulls-eye!" she called out as it hit the mark with a loud clang.

Megan figured the drugstore would have a ready selection of Christmas decorations, and found them stacked high in the first aisle as soon as she entered. She selected two boxes of colored lights which featured a variety of blinking options, and one box of silver tinsel garland. That seemed like enough for her first foray into home Christmas decoration, but a strategically-placed display of candy canes called out to her and she grabbed a box, rationalizing that as both food and decoration it was an efficient purchase. Megan stepped to the register to check out when she realized she didn't have anything to take to Tom and Lisa's house that evening. She ordinarily brought wine, but since Claire suggested she stop drinking Megan had run down the home inventory. Chocolate or some other fancy candy seemed better – at least she could enjoy it too – and

Megan turned back into the store to see what she could find. She passed the clock radios and coffee makers and soon found herself in the cough and cold aisle. She quickly turned the corner and found herself looking at the condoms and "Intimate Lotions". Megan giggled as she imagined gifting one of those items and began to hasten her pace to find a different part of the store when something caught her eye.

". . . as Early as 5 Days Before Your Missed Period"

Megan backtracked several steps to read the claims on a tray of pregnancy tests, neatly wrapped in cellophane and stacked side-by-side. She reflected on how often this shelf must be visited by nervous and frightened students – customers whose needs, but perhaps not their hopes, would be satisfied. How funny that she hadn't thought about buying a pregnancy test – how funny, too, that Claire had never said anything about it. Perhaps the doctor didn't think the experiment was going to work. Or, Megan thought giving her doctor the benefit of the doubt, Claire might just wait until she had actually missed a period. In any case, Megan was surprised to learn that she might be able to test herself already. She began working the calendar in her head and landed on the 28th as the day she expected her next period to start – maybe the 29th – but in either case she was within the five days mentioned on the display. She picked up a "2-pack" and continued her quest for a present for Lisa and Tom, but was now so anxious to get home that she subconsciously decided to pick up the first thing she saw – a box of chocolate-covered, after-dinner mints.

Once back in her apartment, Megan dropped her shopping bags on the table and fished out the pregnancy tests. The decorations had become less important and appeared likely to stay in the box for the rest of the afternoon. It wasn't that she didn't want to follow through on her desire to create the holiday spirit. Instead, she now had a way to cut through all the waiting she had been resigned to endure. She now had a way to answer one of the most pressing questions of modern science. Had she and Lisa tamed the genome? Megan tore open the pregnancy test box and read the very simple directions – twice – even though all she had to do was open it, pee on it and wait. This was an experiment protocol, after all, and there was no point in messing it up. There was, however, one hold-up – Megan's bladder was empty. She had urinated just before leaving for Collegetown, and had not drunk much during the morning (against Claire's direction). She bore down a little to test whether she might have enough but concluded otherwise. "Can't blame the lab tech for this," she said cynically, and went to the kitchen sink to pour herself a glass of water.

Megan broke open the colored lights and garland as she waited for the water to absorb into her blood stream and then filter through her kidneys. She may as well be productive, she thought, and she strung the decorations around her apartment. Once she was busy she didn't feel like stopping, but she worked fast knowing that it wouldn't be long before she had enough urine to do her test. Just before 3:00pm, as she surveyed her newly decorated apartment and sucked on the long end of a candy cane, Megan once again tried to sense her bladder and realized the time had come. Test kit in hand and heart thumping, she walked to the bathroom.

Waiting for the test's pronouncement seemed to take far longer than the three minutes billed on the package. Megan needed no more than two minutes to complete the test and return to the kitchen and now her eyes were fixated on the spinning digital hourglass. As if to build the anticipation, the colored lights blinking behind her reflected in the plastic window, bathing the hourglass in alternating green, blue, red and orange lights. Megan's eyes had actually broken their stare to look at the kitchen clock when the word "PREGNANT" appeared, and when she looked down to see it, she at first wondered where the hourglass had gone. Eyes now wide, she waited for "NOT" to appear, and then realized that the test was done.

Just like that, a $3 home pregnancy test had just proven one of the greatest experiments of all time. And Megan was the keeper of that miracle.

"We did it! We did it!" Megan hopped around her apartment waving the test in the air proudly repeating those three words. Finally, breathless but no less excited, Megan realized there was one other person with whom she needed to share the news. She looked around for her cell phone, but her eyes lit instead on the box of mints she had bought for Tom and Lisa, and the wrapping paper she was just about to use in turning it into a proper gift. As a sly smile slid across Megan's face, she reinserted the test stick in the box and decided that Tom and Lisa would get two wrapped presents that evening.

2

Megan had always hated visiting the gynecologist, but she was excited to be there today. Although she hadn't visited Claire's office since the implantation nearly three months earlier, the staff greeted her by name – as if they saw her every day – and ushered her quickly into one of the examination rooms. She was almost sorry to miss the waiting room experience. Not only were there all those magazines she never had a chance to read – such a contrast between *People* and *Gene* – Megan also liked to watch the other patients. There were the prospective young moms, occasionally a toddler in tow, who seemed pleased to be inconvenienced by their checkups. Less pleased seemed the teenagers, especially the pregnant ones. They avoided eye contact and never picked up anything to read. They would simply sit and stare at the floor with sour and dejected expressions which would clear only when their cell phones buzzed with a text message. If they did smile while reading the message and replying, it would fade as soon as they put down their phone.

Yet today Megan would miss this small human spectacle as she followed a chatty nurse to an examination room. Between questions about how Megan was feeling, the nurse complained about how busy each of the several doctors were and that half of them were over at the hospital delivering babies – blowing up all the scheduled appointments. No worry for Megan, however, Dr. Prentiss, was there and picking up the slack, although she may be running a little late. Oh, and the staff was all turning over, too. The nurse had never been this busy. *Not too busy to waste ten minutes bitching about it,* Megan thought.

"So, it's just an ultrasound today?" the nurse asked.

"I think so. That's all that Dr. Prentiss said I needed."

"Okay, well no need to get undressed. Just jump up on the exam table here and get comfortable. If you want something to read there are some magazines on this shelf," she said pointing to a small heap of dog-eared journals.

Megan glanced down and saw the banner, *People,* amidst the pile. "Perfect. Thanks." As soon as the nurse excused herself and exited, Megan looked for the edition with the most gossipy headlines and lost herself in a celebrity daze.

A brief rap at the door alerted Megan that someone was coming in, and she slapped the magazine closed and tossed it back on the shelf next to her. The door swung open and a man stepped in. Megan did not recognize him.

"Hi, Megan, my name is Michael." He strode across the room and shook her hand. "How's our favorite patient?"

Megan was charmed. "I'm good." Megan reconsidered her answer and decided to tell the whole truth. "Actually, I have been feeling really great."

"No morning sickness?"

"No, not really." Megan felt guilty that her first trimester had been so easy.

"Well, that means you have an agreeable baby."

Megan laughed. "I've never heard that before."

"Oh, it's been said once or twice." Michael smiled warmly.

"So we're going to do an ultrasound?" Megan nodded. "Have you ever had one?" Megan shook her head. "Well, it's simple as can be. No need to be nervous." Michael asked Megan to undo her jeans and slide them down a couple of inches to expose her abdomen while he swung the machine into place and rolled his stool into position at her hips. She was happy to relieve the pressure on her belly. Megan had resisted the sensible urge to change over to maternity clothes and had begun regretting it over the past few days.

"Are you one of the doctors here?" Megan still didn't understand why he was doing the ultrasound and not Claire.

"No, I'm just an assistant. I've just started here." He lifted the tube of gel for Megan to see. "We try to keep this as warm as possible, but it'll still be a little cold when I put it on." Michael applied the gel (it was less uncomfortable than she expected) and drew the head of the transponder across her tummy. It tickled a little and Megan laughed nervously, which embarrassed her. Michael, however, didn't seem to notice as he was peering up at the display screen from the low stool and concentrating on the fuzzy and rapidly changing images. That calmed her and she, too, began trying to figure out what they were looking at.

"Can you see anything?" she asked.

"Not yet, it'll just take a minute for me to get my bearings." He continued patiently lifting the transponder and then placing it down on her taut abdomen and sliding it several inches across. He varied the pressure with each pass and continued to watch the screen intently. "Ah, here we are." He began moving the wand in a smaller range. "Yes, indeed."

Megan still couldn't make sense of the rapidly changing variations of gray showing on the screen, but she was taken in by Michael's confidence. She, too, looked more closely at the screen, but before she could ask Michael to point it out to her on the screen, he spoke again. "Yes, very good. It looks to be . . ." he paused and leaned so close to the screen that Megan thought she could see his breath condensing on it, "a boy. Yes, indeed." As Michael said that, he used his free hand to press several buttons on the console. "Let's make a recording of that for you, okay?"

"Can you show me what you're looking at?" Megan asked, still looking at the screen and hoping that just one recognizable anatomical feature would reveal itself.

"Sure, let me start over here." Michael first squeezed a little more gel on her stomach to create a slick and bubble-free surface, and then replaced the wand where he had last met success. Before Michael could say another word, Megan saw the nondescript image suddenly focus into a tiny face.

"I see it," she exclaimed, and then she corrected herself, "I see him. Wow!" Michael moved the wand slightly, bringing his hand into focus. "Look at his tiny fingers." Michael shifted the transponder again, no more than a quarter of an inch. Megan lost her perspective, and frowned, trying to make out the new image. "What's that?"

"His heart." Michael was leaning forward again, concentrating on the image. "And it looks very good. Wonderful. See it beating?"

"I guess." Megan said tentatively. She could see something moving rhythmically. The physician's assistant patiently pointed out each of the four heart chambers. "And everything looks good?"

"Very good. Never seen better." Michael continued to survey the other organs as he slowly moved down the fetus' body, explaining as he went. Suddenly the buttocks came into focus. "Looks like he's modest now. He's turned away from us."

Despite the fact Megan knew the baby was a boy, she was anxious to have actual, visible evidence. "But you could see his . . . you could see it before?"

"Oh, yeah, he's a boy." Michael was comfortingly confident.

"How did you know that I wanted to find out the sex?" Megan asked. Her smile told him that she was only curious, not unhappy.

Michael shrugged. "Well, that's about it. Everything looks fine. The nurse will be back in just a minute and she can give you the DVD which you can take home – I can't ever figure out how to finish it properly. Do you have any questions?" Megan shook her head. He handed her a towel. "Here, you can wipe off the gel with this." He checked his watch. "Goodness, I need to get going." He rose from the stool. Outstretching his hand he said, "It's been a pleasure seeing you."

"Likewise, thanks so much," Megan responded. She began wiping off the gel as Michael headed for the door. "Bye." He turned and smiled as he vanished into the hall. Megan pulled up her jeans, buttoned and zipped them. She looked back at the shelf where her *People* magazine lay and was just about to grab for it when a quick rap on the door froze her mid-reach. She watched as the door swung open and Claire stepped in.

"Hi, darlin', sorry I'm running so late. Things are really crazy today – crazier than usual, which is pretty crazy as it is. I hope you didn't mind waiting so long." Claire said all this in a rush as she advanced across the room and sat at the rolling stool next to the examination table.

"No problem, Claire. I'm fine. I enjoyed meeting Michael," Megan said. "He seems really nice."

Claire had flipped open Megan's file as Megan spoke and was clearly distracted by the contents. "So, Megan, how many weeks since we did the implant?"

Megan inclined her head to one side and glanced up at the ceiling as she counted them out in her mind. "Ummm . . . I think about twelve. Isn't the date in there?"

Claire was also counting, using a photocopied calendar inserted in Megan's chart. "Looks like twelve and a bit. I guess we're closing in on thirteen now. You're almost a third of the way, Megan."

"It's gone really fast. And I haven't been sick at all," the young post-doc said with some surprise and excitement.

"Well, let's see if I can remember how to work this thing," Claire said, wheeling her stool a few inches closer to the console. "Every time I figure it out they bring in a new one and then I never have a chance to attend the in-service training." She looked back at Megan. "Do you mind unbuttoning your jeans and sliding them down a few inches?" Megan was perplexed. *Didn't I just do this?* She shrugged and complied anyway. Claire was still looking at the ultrasound control panel. A frown was forming on her face. "I asked the nurse to set this up for me, but it looks like she didn't do it. It's still waiting to be closed out from the last patient. Darn it all!"

"Michael said the nurse would come in and finish it for me – that was right before you came in." Megan was hoping she could make sense of what was becoming a very strange visit to the clinic.

Claire looked at Megan as if she had just noticed her for the first time. "Huh?" was all that came out.

"Michael said that I could leave as soon as the nurse finished the disk for me."

"We haven't done the ultrasound yet," Claire protested.

"Michael did it."

"Who's Michael?"

Megan didn't see this question coming and was at a loss as to how to answer it. She tried anyway. "He's a new physician's assistant here." And then to lend him some credibility, she added, "He seemed to know what he was doing."

Claire continued staring in suspicious disbelief and then shook her head slowly. "My partners are changing their staff way too fast." She shook her head one last time. "Sorry, Megan, I was going to do this for you. My staff obviously mixed things up."

"Don't worry about it. He said everything looked great – he even pointed out a bunch of things to me. I saw the baby's heart beating."

"I guess we can just look at the recording." Claire extended her index finger and began punching buttons on the console. Despite the perplexed look on her face, the sequence must have been right – within seconds the two women were viewing the recording made ten minutes earlier. Claire remained silent throughout, nodding occasionally, until it stopped abruptly. "Everything looks great," she pronounced. "You can button those jeans back up, you're done."

"Easier said than done. I think it's time for maternity clothes."

"So, did Michael happen to tell you his last name? Was he wearing a name badge?" Claire asked, still troubled by this unknown employee. She held out her own badge, thinking that might stir Megan's memory.

Megan thought about it briefly and then shrugged. "I don't remember at all. He said he was new and then got busy with the ultrasound."

The more Claire thought about it, the more concerned she became, particularly when she realized that Michael hadn't made any notes in Megan's chart. "Did he bring this in with him?" she asked, indicating the thick medical folder.

Megan's eyes narrowed as she tried to picture his entrance. "No, he didn't – his hands were in his coat pockets."

Claire was now alarmed. How could a new physician's assistant go into the wrong room and do a procedure on one of her patients? And to have gone in to the exam room without taking the chart –

A quick knock on the door, followed by its abrupt opening quickly diverted Claire's thinking. The nurse who had brought Megan to the exam room stood breathlessly at the door. "Dr. Prentiss, Calley Ryan just went to the emergency room – her water broke and the baby's totally breech. There's a foot coming out."

"Aren't Doctors Hayden and Jackson already there?"

"They're in the middle of delivering babies themselves."

Claire turned to Megan and said, "They say things always happen in threes. Sorry, Megan, I have to go." Turning back to the anxious nurse at the door she said authoritatively, "Tell them I'll be there in 10 minutes. You'll have to cancel all the rest of the appointments this afternoon." The nurse was relieved to have Claire take charge and relaxed visibly. Now content to have marching orders, she backed out of the room. Claire was just a few steps behind, apologizing further on her way out, but reassuring Megan that the baby looked healthy and every other sign was positive.

The chatterbox nurse came back a few minutes later, undoubtedly after passing the bad news to all the waiting women that they would have to come back another day. Megan didn't even try to insert more than "wow" or "hmmm" to the stream of snarky commentary regarding the state of healthcare. Finishing the disk and ejecting it from the ultrasound console seemed a matter of only two button pushes – which made Megan wonder why Michael could master everything but that – and within a few minutes Megan was back on her way to campus.

3

Tom made rapid progress on the catalog after the Christmas break because he had negotiated a lighter course load with Rogers. In point of fact, it was not exactly a negotiation. Rogers had initially tried to pile another heavy load on Tom, probably in hopes of having Duffield throw a little bit of the catalog research and authorship his way. At first, Tom had been inclined to grouse loudly and face-to-face with Rogers, yet over the last several months Tom had figured out how to leverage Strater, his high-placed friend, and save himself the irritation of fighting with the idiot boss. One quickly-placed phone call to the estate along the Hudson triggered another back to Ithaca, and by the end of the day, Dean Thatcher had worked things out to Tom's satisfaction.

The one item on which Tom was not making progress was

the reliquary and its broken pane. Despite the enthusiastic spirit with which Neil, the man in the glassworks, had accepted the job, it quickly found its way to the bottom of his stack of work orders. Each time Tom took advantage of Neil's invitation and stopped by to check the project's status, the artisan would treat him to a long explanation of how he was thinking about melting down all the glass shards and then reforming it in a pane of the original size and thickness. He was even quite confident of being able to replicate the nearly imperceptible waves and bubbles. Indeed, it was a project that enervated every fiber of Neil's glassmaking capability – except for the actual "making" part. As he was still stuck in the theory, Tom was beginning to lose his patience – not yet outwardly – waiting for work to begin. So far, Tom had stalled successfully with the Museum director, who was busy designing layout and building cases for all the other items. Tom, Lisa and Neil were still the only ones (other than the airport security nincompoops) who knew the pane had been broken. Tom was very keen to keep it that way.

A mid-March phone call to Tom's office shattered his confidence in maintaining the secret. As always, the ring jangled his deep concentration and brought him – light speed – from the days of castles and crossbows to the era of electronic communication and airplanes. He had been rereading Twysden's translation of Richard's post-crusade life and searching unsuccessfully for other mentions of "Saladin's Key". Tom looked disparagingly at the intrusive and annoying telephone and picked up the receiver. "Hello?"

"Tom? This is John Strater. How are you buddy?"

Tom reflected on how being a billionaire seemed to give one a permanently cheerful approach to life. Yet he also admired this man enormously and was happy to hear his voice. "Great, how are you? Gosh, it's been a while since we last talked."

"I'm good – just back from some work in the Philippines. Hey, I thought I'd fly up to Ithaca tomorrow and check in. You know, see how things are going with the collection. Do you have some free time to join me at the museum? I'll buy lunch if that'll make it worth your time."

"Yeah, John, that would be great. I'm pretty free—" Tom suddenly remembered the reliquary. There was no way he could keep the reliquary out of sight – and no way he could cover up the damage. He tried to cover his tracks. "Oh, hey, did you say tomorrow?"

"Yeah, tomorrow . . . Thursday, right?"

Tom was thinking fast. "Next week looks a lot better," he said. "Could you come up then?"

"Nope, next week is Africa. Tanzania or the Congo. I've sorta lost track to be honest. But tomorrow was going to be Ithaca. How 'bout this? I'll come up and meet the Museum Director. Don't you worry about it. You and I can connect when I'm next back 'stateside'."

There was no way to avoid it. Tom had to get the reliquary fixed by tomorrow. He decided to roll the dice. "I can make it work, John. Late afternoon would be best." Every moment was going to count over the next twenty-four hours.

"Great. How about 4? That'll give me the whole morning free. I'll be coming in my new helicopter and landing at the airport."

"I'll pick you up there at 4. See you then." Tom had already begun looking up Neil's number. The moment he hung up the phone from Strater, he began dialing.

"Glassworks, Neil speaking."

"Neil, it's Tom Duffield. How's that pane of glass going?"

"Tom! Hey! How are ya?"

Duffield was not game for a cheerful chat. "I'm fine, Neil. I was wondering if you've got that project wrapped up yet."

"I'm almost to it, Tom. You know, I was thinking about how to get those ripples right and I think I've got a new idea."

Tom decided to cut to the chase. "Whatever you think, Neil. I need to have that done by tomorrow, or my life is going to get very complicated. Can you make that happen, or should I jump out the window right now?"

"Whoa, Tom, steady up, pal. How's Friday sound?"

"Tomorrow, Neil. Can you hear this? I'm opening up the window?" Tom had actually risen from his chair and noisily opened the old, oaken sash window. The pulleys groaned under a forgotten strain.

"I'll give it a shot. It's a complicated job, Tom, but I'll give it a shot." Neil loved to underpromise and overdeliver.

Tom could sense the confidence but wanted to give one more push. "Please, Neil, the best shot you can take. Otherwise it's a long drop to the Arts Quad."

"Come see me in the morning. And for God's sake, close that window."

Tom took the reliquary in its fitted leather case home that evening, just so he could head straight for the Biotechnology Building first thing in the morning. He almost forgot the relic itself, but remembered it just as he was locking his office door for the night. He reentered his office, removed the wooden shard (still in its baggie) from his desk drawer and slipped it into his pocket. Later that evening, though he chose not to share his dilemma with Lisa, he asked her what time she thought Neil would likely show up at the glassworks in the morning. She guessed 8am.

The next morning, at precisely 8am, Tom waited at a locked door for his savior. Neil arrived less than ten minutes later and the dark circles under his eyes told Tom that he'd had a late night. Tom only hoped that the late night had something to do with recreating the glass pane. Neil was chipper in spite of his fatigue. "Good morning, Tom, it appears you didn't take that leap."

"Not yet. How's the project going?"

Neil unlocked the door and stepped inside. "I think you'll be pleased," he said smugly, waving Tom in behind him. He stepped over to his work table and pointed to the small glass pane, laid out on a soft, white cotton cloth. "My idea worked perfectly. Take a look."

Tom was stunned, the glass looked exactly like the other, unbroken panes in the reliquary. "Fantastic! You are a master!"

"Hold your horses, let's see if it fits." He pointed to the case. "Is that the piece it goes in?" he asked. Tom hoisted the case, laid it on the table and unfastened the closures. As he drew back the lid, the bright work lights shimmered off the glass and silver of the ancient reliquary. "Wow!" Neil remarked involuntarily.

Tom lifted the piece out of the box with the same solemn reverence which Strater had shown several months before. The relic lay inside – he thought it would be tacky to pull that out of his pocket in a plastic bag, so he inserted it the night before, perched in the same position he had originally seen. He hoped Strater didn't have any pictures which might betray its removal. Neil took the new, rectangular pane carefully in his meaty fingers and held it up against the open light. The fit seemed good, but after looking at it for a few moments flipped it upside down, explaining that the side now at bottom looked slightly thicker. He used a pair of fine pliers to pry open the metal clasps, inserted the pane and then bent the clasps back to secure the pane. It was, as Neil had said several minutes before, perfect.

"I can't thank you enough. Sorry I put the heat on, but I really needed it done today." Tom felt relieved, but a little bit sheepish.

"Sometimes a little push can be helpful. I'm glad I could contribute." Neil bent down to look at the relic more closely, cocking his head upward so as to look through his bifocals. "What did you say this thing is?"

"The arrow that killed Richard the Lionheart." Tom said.

"It doesn't look much like an arrow. It's so thick." He moved his head around the side to view it from a different aspect.

Tom bent down to get a closer look as well. "Well it's really a bolt, the arrow they used for crossbows. They're much thicker than longbow arrows. And it's so jagged because they broke it off when they tried to take it out of King Richard's shoulder."

"It certainly looks nasty," Neil allowed. He wiped off his fingerprints using the cotton cloth, and then Tom placed the reliquary back in its satin housing. When he closed the lid and secured the fasteners, a deep sense of relief washed over him. The reliquary now looked exactly as it had the moment he left Longmynd. His tracks were covered.

4

April was always a swing month in Ithaca. It was as likely to be cold, overcast and rainy as it was to bring glorious sunshine and temperatures in the mid-seventies. The Friday before Spring Break was the best example of the latter. The daffodils were giving way to the earliest tulips and both the grass and the trees were beginning to green. The Frisbees came out in earnest, and even the professors were tempted to cut class and stay outside to soak in the long-missed sunshine. Lisa and Tom fought off the urge to play hooky – but met for a bagged sandwich lunch on the Uris Library terrace overlooking the Arts Quad. They sat and ate in a contented silence, enjoying both the antics of the students below them as well as their own mildly cynical commentary on what they observed. Lisa was scandalized by the co-eds' scanty clothing – Tom made a point of thoroughly assessing each case she brought to his attention to judge whether he felt similarly.

Neither Lisa nor Tom was conscious of the point at which they began holding hands. It could have been the example set by so many passing couples, who, like someone who yawns, triggers subconscious mimicry. Or it could have been that their hands, now freed of holding sandwiches and resting near each other, felt the magnetic tug of a twenty-year relationship. In any case, Lisa noticed first after nearly five minutes, looked lovingly at Tom, and squeezed his hand. She was inordinately happy. Megan's pregnancy was right on track – the ultrasound had shown a growing and viable fetus. In fact, since Megan had given her the ultrasound DVD, Lisa had watched it more than twenty times, pausing to cherish the sight when the baby's face or heart or fingers came into focus. Even more exciting was the fact that within the week they would have the results of the amniocentesis – a sampling of the fluid in the amniotic sac in Megan's womb, drawn carefully through a long needle. This was a direct examination of the fetus' DNA and would signal any abnormalities that didn't show visually on the ultrasound. While the chances of a major issue seemed low given the state of the pregnancy and the ultrasound findings, there was no way to be sure without this test. Lisa couldn't wait to get the news. It would tell her both the health of the baby and the quality of the experiment. In Lisa's mind the rest of the pregnancy was virtually academic once they cleared this hurdle.

And then there was Jeff. Thanks to Lisa he was going to have another shot at life, another shot at making his mark on the world. How exciting that this time around DNA would be discovered *before* he was born, that Polymerase Chain Reaction techniques could now speed screening and analysis, and that the human genome would already be characterized. With her help he could hit the ground running. Jeff #2 wouldn't have to wait until college to begin learning about biochemistry, Lisa would carve out a corner of her lab for him to dabble as soon as he could walk. He was going to be twice the science superstar his first self had been. And she was going to raise him to be kinder, gentler and more generous to others. Lisa couldn't wait for Jeff to begin his second life.

Tom was vaguely conscious of Lisa's joy, but he spent little time contemplating it. Jeff had virtually disappeared from Tom's mind the moment he dropped the dumpster lid on that cold, wet night in November. In fact, Tom had spent so much time thinking about Baby Richard that he imagined that Lisa did the same. Unlike Lisa, however, he wasn't excited about managing a baby. That seemed difficult and laborious – instead, he was thrilled at the prospect of reincarnating one of the greatest personalities in medieval history. Despite a heavy workload, Tom spent every free moment researching Richard and his fantastic life – his unusually close relationship with Philippe of France, his revolt against his father, his exploits in the Third Crusade, his long imprisonment in Austria after the war, and his sporadic rule in England. Richard had captivated the imagination of millions since his birth nine centuries before. Tom couldn't wait to meet the real man.

The end of the midday chimes concert told Tom and Lisa it was time to break up their picnic lunch and make their way back to their respective offices. They squeezed each other's hand as they stood up in unison and stretched. "Don't forget we have Claire, Bob and Megan coming over for dinner this evening," Lisa reminded her husband.

Tom had completely forgotten about it. "Of course not. I've been looking forward to it."

"Six o'clock." She leaned in to kiss him goodbye.

Tom's memory was restored extraordinarily quickly when he turned into their driveway at 6:30 and saw Claire and Bob's car. He had more than enough time to think up a good alibi by the time he stepped through the kitchen door, and gained a little more time when he found the house empty. A quick glance through the window over the sink confirmed his suspicion that they were gathered in the back yard – Tom dropped his briefcase and passed through without stopping.

"Here he is!" Lisa announced happily as Tom emerged through the door into their colorful spring garden. "Hi, honey, you're just in time. I was about to offer everyone – except for Megan, that is – a glass of wine." She winked at her pregnant friend, who didn't seem to mind the exclusion. Lisa didn't seem the least bit irritated by Tom's tardiness, and instead made her way past the company to approach and hug him. "What are you pouring?" she asked.

Tom quickly greeted the company and turned to head inside when Claire stopped him. "Hang on, Tom," she called out, "we have the first drink covered tonight." She reached down into her tote bag and produced a bottle of champagne. "I guess we need some glasses," she said a little sheepishly. "And get five, a little bubbly isn't going to hurt Megan or the baby." Tom was back within a couple of minutes carrying a tray of champagne flutes. He set it down on the teak patio table and cheerfully took over the duties of opening the bottle from Bob, who seemed to be struggling. Cued by the hollow pop of the cork, Claire continued speaking. "We have a lot to celebrate this evening. Lisa and Megan's experiment seems to be working perfectly – the embryo took on the first try, Megan's pregnancy has been totally uneventful and the ultrasound looks excellent." Bob and Tom handed out the glasses. "And on top of all that, we have survived another Ithaca winter and spring has finally arrived in all its glory." The others muttered their assent and superstition.

"Here, here."

"Don't jinx us."

"It's supposed to rain tomorrow."

Claire continued, "Wait, wait. That's not all. I have one more piece of good news. It's the real reason I'm giving this toast." She looked around at the quizzical and anticipatory looks of her audience. "I got the results of the amniocentesis this afternoon. I put a rush on them at the lab so I could tell you tonight." Claire looked back and forth between Lisa and Megan, who knew from Claire's build-up that the news must be good, but waited for her to say the words. "Everything is fine. No problems whatsoever," she announced. Claire held up her glass. "Here's to a healthy baby boy." Lisa and Megan both squealed with joy and hugged each other, and only afterwards remembered to sip their champagne. Tom was pleased as well – his Baby Richard was on the way. Bob, the one member of the party who lacked a personal reason to celebrate, circled around the patio and congratulated everyone else.

The weather remained glorious for the evening, although as the sun slunk down over the wooded hills to the west, a cool breeze began blowing which made them edge their chairs in a tighter circle around the still-warm barbecue. The cheerful mood kicked off by Claire's toast was amplified by a splendid grilled steak dinner and a couple of bottles of burgundy. Tom opened a bottle of vintage port to complement the cheese and chocolates which Lisa brought out for dessert. Sated, relaxed and happy, the five friends began speaking less and relishing more the cool April air perfumed by the flowers in Lisa's garden. The conversation paused for what appeared to be an "it's-time-we-were-going" length of time, when Megan suddenly piped up. "Claire, can I tell them about my experiment?"

"Do you have results already?" Claire shot back.

"What are you talking about?" Lisa asked.

"Claire gave me some of the amniotic fluid and I ran some population screens on it to see the baby's ethnicity from its Y-chromosome."

"Why would you bother doing that?" Lisa asked. She momentarily forgot that as far as Megan knew, the baby was cloned from the purchased laboratory samples. She had spent so much time thinking about Baby Jeff that it didn't occur to her that she and Tom were the only ones who were aware of the switching plan.

Tom covered her lapse quickly. "Well those lab samples are unknowns, right?" he asked.

"Right," Megan answered looking at her friend and mentor with her light blond eyebrows furrowed. "Aren't you interested in knowing what the baby might look like before he's born?"

Lisa's heart was thumping as she realized that she almost

gave away her secret. "Yes, yes, of course. I'm sorry. I guess I've had a little too much wine. What did you find?"

"Hang on, let me guess," Tom said. "I'll bet he's from England, or maybe Northern France."

Megan scoffed, "You can't tell it that exactly – not down to a country. More like a big region. Anyway, that's wrong."

Lisa was shaking her head. *Jeff's father was German, not English. Doesn't Tom know that?* "I'd say . . . maybe more central European, like German or Slavic." She was pleased at the prospect of showing up her husband.

Now it was Megan's turn to shake her head. "Wrong again. Any other takers?" After two incorrect answers Claire and Bob simply waited for the answer. Tom and Lisa were eyeing each other nervously. "Well, to be honest, I don't have the exact answer, but I know what the baby is *not*. I ran a couple screens on what I would expect, and none of them came up positive. I can tell you he's not European."

"He *is* European," Lisa attempted to clarify.

"No, he's not."

"Are you sure?" Tom asked.

Megan answered directly, "Very."

Tom and Lisa contemplated Megan's news for a moment and both shook their heads very slightly. *This was impossible*, they both thought. Their minds were racing. "Wow," they both said.

The dinner party was over at that very moment, although it took a while for Megan, Claire and Bob to take their leave. Lisa and Tom were no less hospitable for the genetic quandary Megan had created. They brought in the dishes, cheerfully refused any help in cleaning up and parceled out the leftovers. Lisa noticed that Tom appeared shaken by Megan's news and unsuccessfully tried to catch his eye. She wanted to tell him that everything was alright. So what if Jeff wasn't from European stock? You wouldn't know it by looking at him. The more she thought about it, the more Lisa looked forward to some sleuthing to determine Jeff's lineage.

Tom thrust the remainder of the bottle of port into Bob's willing hands as he and Claire headed out the door. Tom wasn't finished drinking for the evening – as soon as Megan departed he was going to pour himself a head-clearing glass of brandy. He was not shaken or upset as Lisa perceived – instead, he was overflowing with intellectual excitement and curiosity. Megan's news was neither good nor bad. For Tom, one of the foremost experts of the high middle ages, the news was simply earth-shattering. Although his knowledge of genetics was sketchy, Tom knew that Y-chromosomes only came down from through the father. He ran through Richard's father's line – Henry II, Geoffrey Plantagenet of Anjou, Fulk V of Anjou. As far as history knew, these men had been planted in western France for hundreds of years. *What about Richard's mother, Eleanor of Aquitaine?* She had stunned the English court with her dress and her free thinking. She had been one of the foremost advocates of "courtly love", and had famously looked the other way from Henry's many dalliances. Perhaps that was because she had her own. And further, maybe while she accompanied Henry on the Second Crusade she got a taste for Middle Eastern men. That might explain Richard's revolt against Henry – the King wasn't his father.

At long last, Megan and Lisa finished gabbing and the young, pregnant woman set off on her walk home. Lisa had tried to offer her a ride, but Megan was determined to stay active and fit during her pregnancy. She might be giving up her body for science, but it was a nine month sentence, no longer. She planned to go jogging the day after her delivery. The moment the door latch clicked closed, Lisa spun around to face her spouse, "Can you believe Megan's news?!" She didn't wait for him to answer. "It's really not a big deal, but Jeff was always so snooty about being from noble German stock."

"Jeff was snooty about everything," Tom muttered just loud

enough for Lisa to hear. "Did you know what experiment she ran?" he asked.

"Sure, it's not that complicated. You just probe the Y-chromosome for certain mutations that happened over time. There are a few original mutations, those men passed them on to their sons, and so on. Each successive mutation was carried by all the sons after that. By studying large sections of the population you can create a sort of family tree of different groups of people. It tends to break on ethnic and geographic lines."

This confirmed what Tom had understood. "Do you think she ran the experiment correctly?"

Lisa looked up from the sink where she had begun rinsing dishes. "Megan?! Are you kidding me? Not only is she one of the best scientists I've ever met, she worked in a population genetics lab as a grad student. Megan did it right, I promise you." Lisa nodded confidently and resumed her work at the sink. "I just talked to her about it before she left. She felt sort of bad about testing it behind my back."

Tom wanted to extract as much information from Lisa before he struck out on his own detective work. "So what does it mean? Where is . . . Jeff's Y-chromosome from?"

"Who knows? Eastern Europe? The Middle East? It doesn't really matter." Despite saying this, Lisa had already begun thinking about how she might take advantage of Tom's trip next week to travel up to New Hampshire and meet Jeff's mother who might cast some light on the question. Tom was making plans of his own. He was leaving for England the next day and had a couple of days free after his conference. That might provide enough time to contact some "Eleanor scholars" and take a fresh look at what she did in her spare time. As they privately schemed, Tom and Lisa finished cleaning up from their dinner party in silence.

5

Sitting alone in his London hotel room, Tom tried to figure out why the conference seemed so much less interesting than he had anticipated. Billed by the University of London as one of the premier meetings of medieval scholars, Tom found the presenters dull and the papers a tortured rehash of what everyone already knew. One of the speakers had the audacity to introduce "new findings" which bore an uncanny resemblance to work Tom had published a decade earlier. Tom made his way to the microphone during the question period, and despite the blinding urge to call the presenter an idiot, simply provided the full reference to his own publication and suggested the audience might find a similar yet more thorough, thoughtful and well-articulated analysis there. During that afternoon's final plenary session he wanted to shout out, "Isn't there anything new to talk about?!"

There *were* new things to talk about, but only Tom knew it. King Richard the Lionheart was *in utero* and would pop out in less than six months as Tom's adopted child. Tom would be able to chronicle his every point of development. He would be able to describe his likeness with exactitude. Even if he couldn't prove it to others, the certainty of knowing would all be worth it. And if that wasn't enough, Tom had discovered just before his trip that Richard's lineage might be very different from what everyone thought. Richard's Y-chromosome did not point to European lineage, and that fact brought both his mother and his paternal grandmothers into a suspicious light. One of them must have dabbled outside their marriage and Tom was anxious to figure out who it was. He sniffed out a number of experts on Eleanor of Aquitaine during the meeting, and planned to contact them the next day, the final of the three-day conference.

For now, however, Tom sat in his room and paged through one of two texts on Eleanor which he had brought from home. It seemed slightly anti-social to stay holed-up in his hotel, but he feared getting stuck next to the wrong person at one of the dinners. Armed with a few cold beers and some bags of potato chips, Tom could think of no better way to spend his evening than tracking down Eleanor of Aquitaine's lovers. Duffield felt like a seedy gumshoe private investigators working on a nine-hundred year old adultery case.

Tom was not so much startled by his cell phone ring as he was mystified by the noise coming from somewhere in his luggage. As soon as he figured out what it was, he began frantically digging through his bags to reach the phone before the caller gave up or received a voice mail prompt. He answered it just in time. "Hello?"

"Hi, Tom, it's Lisa. How're you doing?"

Tom felt a pang of guilt for not having called Lisa already. Frankly, he travelled so little without her that he didn't have any "checking in" habits. "Great, fine. The trip was easy and I am having a great time at the conference. How're you doing?"

"Fine . . . it's very quiet here," Lisa answered. Tom was about to cut in and apologize when she continued. "Have you had a problem checking your email?"

"No, I just haven't bothered."

"Well, someone named Warwick Adams is trying to get in touch with you. Do you know him?" she asked.

"Yeah, for sure. He's the Professor at Oxford I've been working with on the Strater catalog. Did he say what he wants?"

"He emailed us at home today. He wrote that he had tried to reach you at work, but that he hadn't heard back. Apparently he has found something very exciting." Lisa was always a little bored with Tom's field of study. She couldn't imagine anything 'very exciting' when it came to medieval history.

Tom could imagine all sorts of things. In fact, he had been imagining them all evening – even more so after a couple of beers. "Well, what was it?"

"He wouldn't say – or write, I should say. I didn't talk to

him. But I sent him an email and told him you were there in London. I also had the conference schedule so I told him you would be done tomorrow afternoon. I hope that's okay."

"Yeah, that's fine. Is he going to come down here from Oxford?"

"No, he suggested you go up there. He sent me the directions to get there by bus and the name of a hotel you could stay at."

"This sounds like a lot of effort," Tom complained. Although he respected Adams' work, Tom had really planned on doing his own research at the close of the conference and not schlepping around England.

"I can write him back and tell him you're busy. But you should know that he wrote, 'Smashing great discovery regarding your relic, can't wait to tell you the news face-to-face. Please come to Oxford to meet and discuss.'" Lisa was fairly certain that short passage from Adams' note would melt away Tom's resistance to making the journey.

It did. Tom knew Adams was not given to overselling. Extremely intrigued by the summons, Tom grabbed a pen and asked Lisa for the travel details.

"They're in your email. Just check it," she said.

Tom was too anxious to fuss with trying to connect. "Come on, just tell me," he begged. He also asked Lisa to write Adams back and say that he would arrive in Oxford the next evening for a meeting the morning after that.

Perhaps, after all, there *was* something new in medieval history to talk about.

Despite the ease with which Tom had made his way from downtown London to Heathrow, and then quickly found the express bus to Oxford, he fretted about how to locate his hotel. His phone had been misbehaving the entire trip, and the map function kept trying to place him in Oxford, Ohio. Rather than admiring the rolling countryside as he left the London suburbs, he spent the journey studying an Oxford city map, turning it ninety degrees every few minutes to consider the approach from a different entry point. He did not want to get lost in the middle of the city and have to the play the helpless tourist, begging for directions from random passers-by, and thus he began memorizing the street names and trying to make sense of the major thoroughfares. Yet miraculously, despite the failing light as they finally entered Oxford city center, he was increasingly relieved to see the bus nearing where he wanted to be. When it finally stopped, he was only a hundred or so yards from the Macaulay Hotel where Professor Adams had booked him a room. Tom alighted from the bus and crossed the street, only realizing halfway across that he had looked the wrong way. He admonished himself for being so American – better figure this out, he said to himself, or you won't survive the trip.

He entered the hotel, crossed the lobby and approached reception. The gothic décor appealed to his taste and sense of history. Frankly, unlike Strater's mansion in New York, it was perfectly appropriate here. A smartly uniformed and charming woman standing behind the desk greeted him cheerfully, "Good evening, sir, can I help you?" The English were so polite, Tom thought, although her accent sounded Australian or South African – Commonwealth anyway, and they were basically all the same. Her nametag read "Emily".

"Yes, thanks. My name is Tom Duffield and I think a room has been booked for me."

Emily reached down and picked up his paperwork as if she knew he was coming at that very moment. "Yes, Mister . . ." she looked down at the form and corrected herself, "Doctor Duffield, we have you booked into a single for two nights. Is that right?"

Tom was pleased to be both expected and welcome. What else could she know about him?

"And I have an envelope here for you left by Professor

Adams. He seemed quite excited about your visit." She held the envelope in both hands and presented it across the reception counter.

Tom waited for the next insight into his visit. Did she know that as nice as this was, he really did not want to be here? He looked at his neatly scrawled name on the envelope and tore it open. The single sheet inside bore only two handwritten lines – "Professor Duffield – will meet you tomorrow in hotel lobby at half nine. Very exciting news for tomorrow. Rest well. W. Adams". Tom looked up at Emily. "What time is 'half nine'?" he asked sheepishly.

Emily smiled, but her brow furrowed slightly at such a silly question. "That's half past nine. Nine-thirty."

"Well, yes of course it is. I was just testing you."

Emily pretended to be amused. She slid the registration form across the counter and pointed out all the blocks to be filled in. Tom winced as he saw the rate – one-hundred fifty pounds per night. He was not terribly quick at mental arithmetic, but he knew this was over two hundred dollars. Rogers would have a cow over his expense report, he thought, and that made him fill in the form very fast and sign it with a flourish.

Tom made his way to the room through a rabbit warren of hallways. Upstairs and downstairs, left, right, right again – when he thought he was completely lost and just before he whipped out his mobile phone to ring the reception number on his card and ask for a rescue party, his room appeared before him. *I wish I'd dropped breadcrumbs* he thought as he entered the room and dropped his things.

6

Megan had been wracked by curiosity about her baby's ethnicity ever since striking out on her surreptitious Y-chromosome screen. She previously had no reason to believe the baby was European, of course. And she understood genetics well enough to know that even though the baby was growing inside her, it had none of her DNA. Even so, she had carelessly assumed that the baby would be white, perhaps looking something like the Gerber baby. The realization that his ancestors came from somewhere other than Europe surprised her entirely. And the others, too, she remembered. When she had announced her findings at the Duffield's house the previous week , she was sure she saw Tom's jaw drop open. Lisa looked equally shocked – it was more than surprise, it bordered on consternation.

For the child's adoptive parents-to-be the baby's race had more implications, Megan knew. Lisa and Tom were anything but racist, but there was more to think about when your baby didn't look anything like you. Maybe that's what was flashing through their minds. Further, she might still be jumping to conclusions. The baby could still have blond hair and blue eyes, despite not having a European Y-chromosome. The chances of that were simply quite low.

But Megan's curiosity about the Y-chromosome drove her back into the laboratory. Using her connections with population geneticists she had been able to obtain several probes for other common ethnic markers and had spent the week setting up multiple blots using the remaining amniotic sample she had squirreled away from Claire. Though chastened by her very unscientific assumption that the boy was European, she needed nonetheless, for the sake of efficiency, to hypothesize the next most likely origin for the baby. She knew the commercial lab for the cell line was in California and thus she opted for some of the proto-Asian mutations. This would catch any of the migrations through Central Asia over forty-thousand years ago. Not only did virtually every Asian man carry this mutation, but so too native Australians and Native North and South Americans. If Megan confirmed one of these early markers, she could then work forward in the historical chain to find more specific ethnicity.

Yet on Tuesday, all of these blots had come up negative, and

Megan was back to square one. She considered abandoning the work – it was both expensive and time consuming, and frankly, somewhat moot. The baby was going to be both a miracle of science and a blessing to Lisa and Tom – chasing the genetic roots was simply a matter of curiosity. The race would likely become clear once the infant was born. However, Megan was not easily put off a vexing scientific question. The baby was *in* her, after all, and she still had a little more of the amniotic fluid sample and plenty more time on her hands.

Megan decided to perform at least one more set of genetic marker screens, starting all the way back at the first three mutations. Every male of the human species had one of them – no more and no less. Mutation M168 was the most common, it occurred in one man in East Africa about fifty thousand years ago, and was carried north by that man's male offspring, through the Middle East and into Central Asia. From there, the offspring branched in several directions – some went east through the rest of Asia, Australia and the Americas, while others returned west, into Europe. A second "original" mutation, M60 was carried by fewer men, mostly Africans who also hailed originally from East Africa, but then headed to West and North Africa. Finally, there was M91. The men carrying this mutation had ventured south from the Great Rift Valley and made home in southern Africa. As time passed over the next fifty thousand years, each of these three genetic lines had successive additional mutations. So M168 might also have M89 and then M9 and so on. Yet every man carried one of these three originals to show where his great-to-the-nth-degree grandfather originated.

In terms of genetic sleuthing, Megan decided it would be easier to start at the trunk of the great human family tree, rather than guess a branch from up in the canopy. Once she had narrowed the search on one of these three original mutations, she could zero in on one of the later mutations particular only to that genetic branch. The young post-doc made a second decision that day – she wouldn't tell Lisa about any more findings, nor even her choice to continue screening the baby's DNA. Lisa had not brought up the Y-chromosome screen since the dinner party, and Megan assumed that Lisa was simply happy that the baby was strong and healthy. This population and ethnic screen was Megan's quest. She would keep it to herself.

Megan spent most of Tuesday evening setting up the three blots. She was certain one of them would "pop" and kicked herself for not doing this screen in the first place. Cutting corners always gets you in trouble, Lisa perpetually told her. As someone soon vying for a faculty position and lab of her own, Megan needed to practice the right, high standard. She made great progress over the next several hours without the usual distractions, particularly the undergrads who normally pestered her with questions. Oddly, Lisa had gone home relatively early, and this had struck Megan as strange since Tom was still in Europe and Lisa had only an empty house waiting for her. Megan appreciated the solitude and finished her work just before ten, which was good since lately she had been tiring early and falling asleep hours before her normal bed time. Additionally, the blots needed several hours to incubate and would only be readable in the morning. Megan locked up the lab and went home to crash.

7

Tom awakened before his travel alarm rang, and he showered and dressed quickly. He had planned to call Lisa the night before, but had mistakenly reversed the time differences between England and the U.S. and thus pictured Lisa already abed. Now after a good night's sleep, he was thinking more clearly and realized it was only 2 am back in Ithaca. Lisa was most assuredly asleep – he could not check in with her now, either. With two and a half hours before the appointed meeting time with Professor Warwick Adams, Tom decided to take a brisk walk around the city streets and see a few of the sights. He greeted the friendly staff behind the desk, then the eager Concierge by the front door and exited to the sidewalk. The first stop on his tour was Beaumont Street, just outside the hotel's front door, and named for the palace which stood there in the middle ages. He needed only a few minutes to find the gray slate plaque marking the palace site and read it several times.

NEAR TO THIS SITE
STOOD THE KING'S HOUSES LATER
KNOWN AS
BEAUMONT PALACE

KING RICHARD I
WAS BORN HERE IN 1157
AND KING JOHN IN 1167

Tom was disappointed that every trace of the palace had been wiped out over the last millennium, and try as he could to imagine how it might have appeared, he was too distracted by the nineteenth century buildings now lining the street. He had a vandalous urge to scratch "FIRST" between "WAS" and "BORN", but he fought that off and returned back toward his hotel.

When he reached the first intersection, Tom made a quick right turn toward Broad Street, just where the bus had dropped him off the night before. Despite approaching 8 am, the city was just rousing and he reflected on how similar that was to Ithaca. Oxford and Ithaca might have very different histories, but a university town was a university town. Tom soon found himself in a semi-pedestrianized zone in the middle of Broad Street. To his left was one of Oxford's countless, ancient, honey-colored colleges. He imagined that the name was charming and old-fashioned– some string of letters that never made it across the Atlantic. It wouldn't sound good with an American accent anyway, he thought. A coffee shop on the opposite side of Broad Street beckoned and he crossed to satisfy his hunger and need for caffeine. He was embarrassed to find he had no British currency, yet the keen young student manning the register was happy to take dollars, making the conversion to the third decimal point in his head in seconds. Tom concluded he was studying mathematics.

Recrossing the wide street, Tom found a bench near the gate to Trinity College (this name – and college – *had* made it across the Atlantic) and sat to watch the morning unfold while enjoying his coffee and croissant. Things were beginning to pick up in Oxford and he watched street cleaners rumble along the curb and students cycling by on their way to work or lecture. Craning his head around to gaze through the gate at the inner courtyard of Trinity College, he wondered what advances in science or philosophy had been made within these walls. Too bad he did not teach here, he lamented. These people actually knew who Kings Henry and Richard were. Their descendants still wielded power, of a sort. And even if they didn't wield power, they were fantastically wealthy.

As quick as he was, it took Tom a moment to let the next most logical thought enter his brain. For the first time, Tom realized that Baby Richard was not just an interesting science experiment, as Megan and Claire thought, nor just the baby they always wanted, as Lisa thought. Nor was he even a history experiment which Tom was conducting. By all genetic rights, he would be ruler of this realm. In Ithaca, and certainly in America, where birthright was an arcane and charming artifact of history, it never occurred to him. But here, in the center of one of the great reminders of England's glory and tradition, this fact was starkly obvious. Their son would be "closer" to William the Conqueror than the current ruler given the latter's one thousand years of dilution. The question was not whether Charles should succeed Elizabeth, but rather whether Tom and Lisa's baby, Richard, should. *Now this is getting interesting*, Tom thought.

He rose from the bench and continued his stroll down Broad

Street. His son would own all of this – maybe only theoretically – so trips to England would now be homecoming. Tom's eyes fell on the massive, carved stone heads lining the walls outside the Sheldonian Theater and their bulging eyes seemed to follow him. Unable to discern whether the carved faces' grins were friendly or hostile, he began to feel uncomfortably paranoid. He had an urge to call out, "Don't watch me," but he knew he was being stupid. He glanced at his watch just as nine o'clock rang on a bell in the distance, and he decided to make his way back to the Macaulay.

Tom paused briefly outside the Museum of the History of Science and mused at how the role of science and religion had shifted. Oxford University was founded and flourished under the protection of the church. While there had been periods of terrific tension and conflict, science owed its advancement to religion, because men of God had created an environment where inquiry and learning was fostered. Now hundreds of years later, much more progress had been made in understanding science than God. Perhaps that was why modern man and universities had focused on science – it was more likely to yield success. Man had virtually given up on God as too impossible a mystery to solve. Tom had. He shrugged his shoulders with that thought and continued back to the hotel.

Professor Warwick Adams was not hard to spot. Tom had never seen so much as a picture of him, yet as the dapper man stepped through the hotel's front door, his identity was clear. The first clue was that he was precisely punctual, the second was that he was dressed as Tom expected – an old blazer of nondescript beige coloring, and a poorly matched and too-short tie. Finally, despite the absence of a single cloud in the sky, the man was gripping an umbrella. Unlike the tourists and business people staying in the hotel, this was a local who knew the weather. Tom rose from his chair to greet him.

"Professor Adams?"

The man flashed a toothy smile and shot out his hand. "It's so very nice to meet you, Professor Duffield. Thank you very much indeed for coming all the way to Oxford." He shook Tom's hand enthusiastically and for an extended time. "I'm sure my email raised all sorts of questions for you, being so cryptic, as it were."

"Well, yes, but I had a couple of days free after the conference, so this is perfect." Tom respected Adams' outstanding reputation and was eager to please, even if he had been put out by Adams' reticence to explain the meeting request. "And Oxford is such a fabulous place, I would visit it any chance I could. I already took a walk this morning around Broad Street and some of the colleges."

"Ah, very salubrious. Good for you."

Tom was anxious to solve the mystery of his summons to Oxford. "Shall we have a seat in the lounge and have a cup of tea? We could talk over why it is you wanted me to come."

"It's too early for tea, I should think." Adams looked around the lobby and down the halls into the restaurant and the lounge. "You have had breakfast haven't you? I've heard the cooked breakfast here is very nice indeed."

"Yes, yes, I've eaten already, thanks." Tom did not want to admit that he opted for a dry croissant instead. He feared Adams would drag him into the restaurant.

"Would you like to come with me?" Adams swept back his thinning, gray hair from his forehead.

"Well . . . yes. Where to?" Tom's hope of quick resolution to the mystery was fading.

"It's a bit of a cock-up, really, I am embarrassed to say. I meant to take you over to my office in All Souls College, but last night I took home the documents I meant to share with you and shot away this morning without them." Adams looked sheepish, and then added, "Would you mind popping round to my house with me?"

This was becoming complicated and frustrating. All Tom

wanted to know was why Adams had insisted on a meeting. Couldn't they talk that over here, he wondered. Rather than beat around the bush, he decided to just come right out with it. "Do you think you could just tell me what this is all about and we could decide what to do next?" Tom then softened it with, "I really wouldn't want to put you out by driving me all over town."

Adams held up his hand to stop Tom from saying more. "It's no bother whatsoever, I assure you. And I think you are going to want to see these documents. It'll spoil the fun if I tell you now. Shall we away? Do you want to collect a briefcase or anything?" He was very persuasive and Tom gave in. He wouldn't leave for home until tomorrow anyway and thus he might as well make the most of getting to meet Adams. Besides, perhaps Adams could solve the Y-chromosome mystery. The only trick was figuring out how to ask those questions and not sound crazy. The idea of Eleanor of Aquitaine sleeping around with men from the Middle East might just give this gentle old man a heart attack.

Tom answered, "I'm ready now. If I could just borrow a pad of paper from you to take notes, that would be great."

"Smashing! Lots of paper in my cottage, I can assure you," Adams said cheerfully. "Shall we, then?" He turned and motioned for Tom to follow him out of the hotel and into the now bustling street. They turned a few corners walking to a city parking garage and quickly found Adams' tired old car. Tom absentmindedly walked to the right front door and then stood looking at Adams, who stood patiently next to him. "I think you'll find the passenger seat on the other side," Adams said quite seriously.

The drive to Adams' house was longer than Tom expected. They made small talk at first about the city and the history of the college, but Tom became concerned as they passed out of the near environs and joined a divided highway. "So where is it that you actually live?" Tom asked politely, using curiosity to hide his growing sense of being kidnapped.

Adams responded quickly, "Oh, it's quite a ways still. I live in Chatterford, the north-west edge of Oxfordshire. Some people think I was crazy to live so far from the college – especially before the A-44 was dual carriageway – but I love it there. I must admit that it is a bit cluttered. I hope you don't mind."

"Don't think twice about it. I'm a history professor as well, it goes with the territory. My wife, on the other hand, can't stand it. What's that expression she always says? A cluttered desk goes with a cluttered mind . . . cluttered mind, cluttered desk?" He chuckled, "Whatever, it doesn't bother me."

Adams picked up on the reference to Tom's wife. "I understand your wife is a very accomplished scientist," he said earnestly. "You'll have very bright children. But they'll be pulled in opposite directions." Tom just smiled in response.

They exited the highway and followed progressively narrow roads until they joined a track so narrow in places that Tom assumed it must be Adams' driveway or a one-way road. For all of his conservative and retiring style, Adams seemed to be driving very fast for a winding road with blinded curves. Tom hoped Adams had very fast reflexes. Their conversation trailed off as both Adams and Tom concentrated on the road, the former holding the steering wheel and the latter digging his fingernails into the handle above the door.

Tom's hopes for Adams' reflexes were satisfied when an enormous bus emerged around the corner and Adams applied the brakes so hard that Tom lurched forward in his seat. The two opposing drivers began checking their mirrors and assessing how they could pass safely. "I should have remembered the mid-morning bus to town," Adams said, chagrined. He put the car in reverse and began scooting back much faster than Tom would dare. "Mrs. Adams is probably on board. Good thing, too, as she would not be chuffed to find I brought you home without warning. Would you be so kind as to roll down the window and pull in the side mirror?"

Tom complied, watching in fascination as Adams maneuvered the car so close to the bank on the side that small branches came through the still-open window and brushed Tom's shoulder. After a few nervous moments (for Tom, of course, since this seemed an everyday practice for Adams) the bus passed within inches, if not fractions thereof, from their car. They were soon back on their way and reached the modest and very old house within a few minutes.

Adams explained that this home and the surrounding small village historically housed the staff for the Jacobean manor just another two hundred yards farther along the track. Tom followed Adams' pointing finger and could see where the manor house stood, as well what appeared to be the stubby tower of an ancient church. The manor had recently become a museum and now local traffic was much increased, although it brought jobs and money to the local economy. Adams paused as he watched an elderly woman walk down the road. "Morning," he called out cheerfully, supplementing it with a wave. The woman, clothed in a cream cardigan and plaid skirt, wore a kerchief on her head. She looked up, smiled and waved back and then returned her gaze to the ground in front. She seemed quite lost in thought. "Spinster Grindall," Adams said confidentially, "she was evacuated as a child from London during the War, unfortunately right afterwards both her parents were killed by a V-1 rocket. She stayed here after the war ended and has lived alone since then. She's quite dumb."

"Excuse me?"

"She doesn't speak," Adams clarified. "No one has ever heard her say a single word. Even so, she's quite cheerful and well liked. It's terribly sad, I must say."

They entered Adams' home, a small stone building, through the front door as Adams made more apologies for clutter. Tom had the urge to stoop, even though at 5'8" he was no taller than Adams and well short of the ceiling's open beams. The ceiling was lower than he was used to, however, and the cramped nature of the rooms reminded him of passages from *Alice in Wonderland*.

Adams flipped on the electric kettle as they passed through the kitchen and he led Tom to his ultra-cramped study where stacks of books and papers made Tom's office at McGraw Hall look the picture of tidiness and order. The stacks appeared to be racing each other toward the ceiling, with several in contention for winning the contest. Tom noted that three of them were higher than the two men's heads. Adams motioned to a chair near the desk for Tom to sit down and took his own seat at the desk. Folding his hands on the few uncluttered square inches, he looked around at the room and cleared his throat. Tom's expectations for a great revelation were cresting. "Well," Adams began, "shan't be a moment then."

"Excuse me?" *Would this guy ever get to the point*, Tom wondered. More than an hour had passed since they met in the hotel lobby, and they still had not touched a word on the reason for their meeting. Suspense was evolving into frustration.

"'Til the kettle boils, I mean. Shan't be a moment." Just as he said this, an urgent whistling spurred Adams to jump to his feet and rush back to the kitchen. "English Breakfast Tea alright?" he called out.

"Yes, fine, thanks," Tom called back. And then, as Adams seemed out of earshot, he added, "Oh dear God, he's killing me." With the clatter of china and the ring of cookie tins in the background, Tom sat looking around Adams' study and through the small leaded window into the flower garden. Quite unlike the room in which he was sitting, the garden was exquisitely neat and well-tended. A flash of blooms and bright colors, it must surely be his wife's work.

Adams came back into the room with a loaded tray of porcelain cups and saucers, a full tea set and a plate of assorted cookies. Despite losing his patience, Tom thought this looked quite tasty. He watched quietly as Adams prepared and served the tea and then proffered the cookies, all with great concentration. Tom took only one to be polite although he wanted more. He hoped the plate would be set down within easy reach. As Adams savored the first taste of his morning tea, Tom turned his head in an exaggerated way to look out the window and remarked, "What a beautiful garden. Your wife has quite a green thumb."

Adams looked thoughtful for a moment and responded. "Actually she hates gardening. It's my work . . . and my passion, for that matter. I often wished I had studied horticulture instead of history – much less tragedy and controversy, if you know what I mean. A little fertile soil, a titch of warm rain and everybody's happy." Adams contemplated this point as he, too, looked out the window.

"Well, it's very lovely." Tom remarked, unsure as to whether he had insulted his host. "This tea is just perfect. Thanks so much."

"I imagine you might be wondering why I have summoned you all this way from London." Adams brushed back a graying lock which had fallen across his forehead. His grey-blue eyes twinkled and he allowed a thin smile. Adams was not the kind of man given to smugness or self-congratulation, but the pronounced pause after this by-now rhetorical question replaced Tom's impatience with curiosity. When Adams took a sip of tea, and thus further dragged out the moment, Tom answered.

"Well, of course," was all Tom mustered, but then seeing Adams was not about to continue, he filled the silence. "I imagine you've discovered something about the crossbow bolt. I am only hoping that you aren't going to tell me that it had nothing to do with Richard."

Adams interjected quickly, "Oh, goodness, no." He chuckled and savored another sip of tea and bit of biscuit. "It has a lot to do with Richard, I assure you." Adams chuckled again. "But yes. I have discovered something about the cross—" Adams stopped briefly and reflected on his words. "I have discovered something about the relic." He paused again and sipped his tea. Rather than drag the words out of Adams, Tom just waited and enjoyed his tea. He had a mounting sense that he was going to be very disappointed with his trip to Oxford.

"The text from Gervase of Canterbury's *Chronicle* was quite appropriate to the relic." Adams nodded enthusiastically, "But there was something –" Adams broke off his sentence, put down his cup and saucer and started sifting through the papers on the desk. "There was something . . . ah, yes, here it is . . ." he lifted a piece of paper and held it out at a distance from his face and read it silently, his lips moving with the words. "There was something . . . ." Adams paused again and looked at Tom. "Can I pour you a little more tea?"

Tom could barely stand this any longer, and his patience began to crack. He shifted forward in his seat and closed his eyes, fighting the urge to scream out *Dear God, please get to the point*. "No thank you, I'm . . . fine. I . . . really would like to know why you've brought me here." He swallowed hard, and then remembering his manners, smiled weakly.

"Yes, of course. Let me get right to the point." Adams looked back to the paper he was clutching. "There was something about the text which struck me as very strange. Gervase described the scene of Richard's death and then the relic itself. Well – you know the words, as Walter took the shard of wood from the fading Richard and lifted it aloft he declared 'soaked with the blood of my slain lord and master, shed to save the people', and then he tells of the last hours, how Richard pardoned the bowman and dictated where his own body – I should say his body parts – would be buried." Adams lowered the paper and looked directly at Tom. "Does anything there strike you as odd?"

Tom knew these words well as he had studied the text many times. Neither had it struck him odd in any previous reading, nor did it now. However, Adams seemed so confident in his demeanor that Tom was afraid to dismiss the question. He gazed thoughtfully out the window, his eyes focusing on a patch of pansies which were almost distracting in their vibrant color. Nothing odd came to mind and Tom looked back at Adams and shook his head silently.

"Well, two things seemed quite out of place for me," Adams continued. "For one is the timing of relic's mention." Adams paused and raised his eyebrows, as if he were expecting Tom to figure it out. Instead, Tom pursed his lips and shook his head again. "Well, why would Walter describe Richard as 'slain' – in his presence, when he had several more hours to live?"

This struck Tom as interesting, but probably just semantics. "Don't you think it was a matter of certainty that Richard was going to die? He had gangrene in his shoulder; he was probably delirious from infection and fever. He probably even looked dead to everyone who was there." Tom tried to imagine the scene and Richard's gruesome last moments and he grimaced.

"And secondly, blood 'shed to save the people'? Which people was Richard saving? He had surrounded the castle of Châlus and was going to imprison, if not execute, the Vicomte Limoges for not sharing tax money. 'Save' is a strange word to use in that context."

"I always interpreted it to mean saving – I don't know, *uniting* maybe – the people of Anjou and Limousin. How ever we might now think about it, that was Richard's mission."

"Perhaps," responded Adams, "but it spurred me to track down some of the original documents, which you may know are in the Bodleian – you know, the library here at Oxford."

Tom was now instantly re-engaged and interested in Adams' discovery. Like most historians, Tom used Twysden's seventeenth-century translation of Gervase, and while accurate, it wasn't perfect. And he didn't know Gervase's originals were right there in Oxford. He would be very anxious to see them. "Can I look at them as well?" Tom blurted out.

Adams began sifting through the papers again and grasped another which he scanned quickly. "Umm . . . yes, we can look at them together, of course, but let me tell you what I've found. I have done my own translation from the Latin, a trifle hastily I should add, but it should serve. May I read it?"

"Of course, yes, please."

"It appears that Twysden mixed up some important text. Richard had become quite a popular legend by the seventeenth century and maybe Twysden wanted to honor him instead of . . . . Well, let me read how Gervase put it." Adams held the paper as far away as his arm could reach, and then, acknowledging his frailty, reached into the inside pocket of his tweed blazer and extracted a pair of reading glasses. "Let's see, yes, here we are. 'The King stretched out his hand and gave a lump of wood to Walter of Rouen, saying, "soaked with the blood of my slain Lord and Master." Adams stopped reading and looked at Tom over the top of his reading glasses. "We can check the translation, but I reckon you see the big difference."

Tom mulled the words and their meaning. "Well, I guess it doesn't surprise me that Richard would speak of himself so glowingly, especially in his last moments. His ego was bigger than life." He remained thoughtful, not sure that he understood the revised passage completely. But also uncomfortable that his hasty trip to Oxford was only to uncover that the famous quote he had linked to the reliquary were uttered by Richard instead of Walter.

"You're missing the point," said Adams insistently, forgetting his English manners. "I don't think Richard would make a fuss about the piece of the crossbow bolt that killed him. I can't imagine that he would even have retained it the many days from when he was shot on March 29th to his final moments on April 6th. He was talking about *his* Lord and Master."

"Do you mean his father, Henry the Second?" Tom interjected.

"No, no, of course not, Professor Duffield," Adams shot back. "He was talking about his *supreme* Lord and Master. Jesus of

Nazareth." Adams waited to see if the point had sunk home. "Jesus Christ!"

Tom did not understand this latest interpretation. The reliquary was well documented as a piece of the crossbow bolt which killed King Richard. Tom had extracted the blood and DNA and substituted it in Lisa's lab to now clone it into the baby that was growing in Megan's womb. What was Adams talking about? What did Jesus Christ have to do with King Richard's deathbed? "I'm not sure I understand your point."

"Too right, too right," Adams muttered. He began shuffling through the papers once again and found yet another document. "Your question about 'Saladin's key' was very intriguing, and I thought it might help me get to the bottom of it. I began rereading Blondel – Richard's troubadour – for some hint of what Richard was talking about, and I found this reference to Richard's imprisonment in Austria. As you may recall, that's when Blondel and company found Richard after three years of mystery and silence. Blondel wrote," Adams peered down through his glasses and read,

"My liege had kept his spirits bright,
though stripped of steel had no less might,
for bathed in holiness was he,
Saladin's gift the perfect key
to free him from the prison strong,
transport him where he doth belong,
at God and Christ's right hand to be,
defending Christianity.
A smallish part of Hattin's purse,
was all required to lift the curse,
of Saxon bonds and hellish keep,
and fill the King with God's love deep."

Adams looked up again from his reading and smiled at Tom.

"You know what Saladin took at the Battle of Hattin, don't you?"

Tom wanted to answer that even his worst students could recount that the True Cross – the cross on which Jesus Christ was crucified – was taken by Saladin and his Saracens at the Battle of Hattin. Yet he found himself unable to answer as he wrestled with the understanding that was forming in his mind. On one hand he was reasoning through it and on the brink of seeing it clearly, on the other hand he was fighting it off, fearful of its powerful truth. His hand began trembling slightly, causing the teacup to plink softly against the saucer. His other hand found his forehead, where tiny beads of sweat were beginning to form. He managed a "yes."

Adams jabbered on cheerfully. "It all makes sense to me. Richard discontinued the Third Crusade after meeting with Saladin. Many couldn't understand why he broke it off – other than the problems in England and France – for he was on the very brink of annihilating the Saracens. But he broke off the Crusade just the same and made peace with Saladin. Obviously, as only Blondel has ever recounted, Saladin gave him a piece of the True Cross as a ransom for the Holy Land, and Richard sailed home with the greatest prize of all. A piece of the True Cross soaked in Christ's blood. And now you've got it – Saladin's Key. Well done, I must say. That's quite a treasure."

Tom felt as if the floor gave way underneath him and he was cast into a void. The hand that had been pressing his forehead dropped down to cover his mouth as he exclaimed "Dear God!" The hand holding the saucer began shaking so hard that the cup tipped over, toppled to the floor and shattered. He was now doubly mortified and quickly reached down to recover the mess. "Oh, shit, I'm sorry," he blurted out. His thoughts raced back to the True Cross, and the blood he had cloned. "Dear God," he said again, "*Dear God!*"

Adams jumped up from his chair to grab a towel and broom from the kitchen. He was back in an instant, taking over cleaning the small mess from Tom who was fumbling clumsily with the broken shards of porcelain. Fortunately the cup was virtually empty, so the mess was well contained. "Never mind, not to worry," Adams kept muttering reassuredly. "All neat and tiddly in a jiffy. Just a Marks and Sparks cup, not Mrs. Adams' finest china, thank goodness."

Tom kept up a competing banter of apologies and excuses, but his mind was racing in a different direction. His little experiment at home had suddenly spun out of control, and he was trapped four thousand miles away in a quiet village in England. Now the lack of the European Y-chromosome markers made sense. He and Lisa were bringing about the Second Coming in upstate New York. Tom needed air. "Could you excuse me for a moment please?"

"Yes, indeed," answered Adams quickly, "the loo is just there to the right, past the kitchen."

Tom did not need the loo, except perhaps to throw up. He needed to get out of this stuffy room and breathe fresh air and clear his head. He needed to wake up from this strange dream he was having. He couldn't make eye contact with Adams, and thus couldn't see that his host was beginning to eye him strangely. Tom pushed back his chair and stood up. "I was thinking more about talking a quick walk outside," he said, "if you don't mind." He began making his way to the door.

"Something in the car, then?" Adams queried after him. And then, answering his own question, "No, I suppose not. You didn't bring anything." He was baffled and gave up, "I'll be right here when you come back. No need to ring the bell, come in directly. And no hurry, of course."

The American heard none of this as he passed through the kitchen, into the cramped foyer and out the front door. It occurred to him that he should apologize more directly for the broken cup, but once out in the fresh air he could not bear the thought of the returning to the stale and confining study, or having Adams grill him on why he was so shaken. Tom looked around for a direction to walk and his eyes alighted on the stubby church steeple he had noticed earlier. Without a second thought he had found his way.

8

Megan opened one eye to spy the time on her bedside radio. Lately, she was finding it equally as hard to remain asleep in the morning as it was to stay awake at night. And early it was, according to the red LED numbers on her clock, 5:48 am. *Ughhh, not again.* But for the excitement of getting to her lab bench and reading the blots she had set up last evening, Megan would have tried going back to sleep. Most recently this meant lying awake in the dark for thirty minutes before rising in frustration. However, today, Megan's eagerness spurred her to get up quickly. She threw off her covers and stood up far faster than normal. As a result, she felt slightly woozy and clutched the bedpost to steady herself. Her sense of balance soon restored, Megan spun through her morning routine including a quick breakfast, an energizing hot shower and a steaming cup of tea for the road. With her wet, long blonde hair tied in a ponytail, she departed her apartment and wound her way through the deserted streets of Collegetown and up to campus. At 6:45 am the lab was most assuredly empty, so Megan didn't have to waste time in greetings and small talk as she made straight for the bench to uncover the baby's Y-chromosome mystery. Although all she had left to do was go to the darkroom to lift the film off the blots and develop it in the machine, last evening's remonstrations about not cutting corners were ringing in her ears. Further, given that she had nearly used up the last of her amniotic fluid sample, there was little room for error. Megan was more careful than ever.

Megan's final step was feeding the film into the developer and waiting the few short minutes for it to come back out. She planned her patience as it sat inside the machine. She wasn't going to stand and read it at the machine. No, instead she would carry it back to the bench, pull up a stool and thoughtfully analyze the probe bands. A whirring motor told her it was starting to come back out, and though her heart began to race, she gently took the film in hand and strolled back into the lab. As if to underscore her patience, Megan took the last drag on her now-cool tea, and studied the probe instructions one last time.

Her film had six vertical lanes of dark and light horizontal bands, a pair of lanes for each of the three original Y-chromosome mutations she was seeking. The control lane was on the left of each pair and the track for the test sample from her amniotic fluid appeared on the right. Reading them would be simple – find the dark band in the control lane which represented the mutation and see if there was a dark band in the corresponding position in the test lane. Only one of the three would hit, and from there Megan could zero in on the specific ethnic group from which the fetus came. She began on the left where she was testing for M168, the original mutation of virtually everyone outside Africa. The instructions said the mutation appeared at the 7.2 kb band – Megan traced her finger down the control lane and found the band and then tracked across to the test lane. *Nothing, no wonder none of those other blots worked.* Megan was glad she had gone back to the original mutations, she could have been fruitlessly chasing branches of the M168 tree for some time.

M91, the South African mutation, came next in the middle pair of lanes. *11.2 kb band – here it is – Nothing!* Without a match here either Megan, was zero for two. *I should have known it was M60.* Hailing from West Africa there was a high likelihood that anyone descended from slaves would carry this mutation. Megan smiled at the thought of a dark-skinned fetus growing in her womb. She looked to the directions to find the position for the M60 band – the 9.4 kb band. "Here it is," she said aloud finding the thin black band at the proper position. Even before her finger tracked to the test lane on the right, Megan could see that the corresponding position was blank. "Huh?" She looked back at the probe directions and confirmed the band position, then reconfirmed it was the one she had just compared. "Huh?" she said again, this time a little louder and matched by a perplexed expression on her face. Megan now worked in reverse order, rechecking M91, and then M168. Her test was negative for all three mutations.

These results made no sense! Every male of the *Homo sapiens* species carried one of these three mutations – the baby could be no different. Megan began running through her methods over the past two days, trying to figure out where she had made a mistake. This was bread-and-butter work for her – she'd run these blots for years and trained dozens of others how to do them as well. Given her experience, it was pretty hard to screw up. Besides, the control lanes looked perfect. "Holy shit!" she exclaimed as this last thought sunk in.

For a brief moment, Megan landed on a simple explanation. The fetus wasn't a boy at all – he was a she, and there was no chance of finding a mutation on a Y-chromosome because she didn't have one. But she dismissed this notion immediately; not only had the amniocentesis confirmed the sex, but Michael had seen his genitalia via ultrasound. He said it was unmistakable. Megan's neurons were now firing full speed. What if there was something about the Ewe factor which undid mutations? Maybe it returned DNA to some kind of proto-man state. Instead of the Gerber baby, Megan suddenly visualized a baby with a prominent brow and a thick neck and she shuddered. *No, this can't be right.*

Megan's confidence in her lab methods, her procedures, her ability as a scientist came rushing back. She'd done the test right, she knew it and chided herself for doubting. With a mixture of excitement and worry, Megan concluded this male fetus belonged to an as-yet unidentified genetic line. Instinctively, she patted the small bulge under her elastic waistband. "I'm sorry, but I need to tell Lisa about this," she said, and then added, "Boy, you're going to make history in all sorts of ways."

<h1 style="text-align:center">9</h1>

"Dear God, what have I done?" Tom declared aloud as he strode down the narrow track. He looked down to notice that he was clutching his hands, as if in prayer, and this struck him as appropriate. God knew exactly what he had done; indeed, God helped him do it. But did God really want this to happen? Did he want his son, Jesus Christ, to be cloned on earth in an odd cross between an experiment memorializing a dead scientist and a desperate parenting need? *Why settle for Jeff Wolf when you can have Jesus Christ*, Tom thought to himself and chuckled ruefully. Baby King Richard was academically interesting. Baby Jesus Christ could – no, *would* – change the world.

Tom stopped as he crossed a farm track and looked up to see the church he had spied earlier. He entered the churchyard and followed the narrow gravel path among a variety of gravestones until he stopped at one that was tilted at such an exaggerated angle that Tom half expected it to topple over as he stood there. He looked up at the small church, its honey brown stone mottled with flecks of green and gray lichen. Closest to him stood the square and squat crenellated tower. It was very plain – a door at the base served as the main entrance to the church; mid-way up were louvered openings which allowed for air circulation to the belfry, as well as an aperture for the bell's ringing tones. What kind of sound would emerge as those century-old bells finally rang out the Second Coming, Tom asked himself. "Second Coming, dear God," he said quietly, and then corrected himself, "More like the Second Cloning. God, I'm sure it's not supposed to be this way." He felt nauseated again and unclasped his hands to wipe the sweat that continued to bead on his forehead. Tom looked at his moistened fingers and noticed how much his hands were shaking. He took a deep breath and continued on the path toward the church's heavy wooden door. Reaching out tentatively with his right hand, Tom tested the ancient iron ring latch and jumped as it clunked open. It almost felt as if it tugged him forward and Tom's anxiety and confusion briefly morphed into fear, but not enough to keep him from stepping into the church's cool and damp embrace. He passed through the small porch area cluttered with notices of clothing collections, book meetings and teas and entered the simple and austere nave. Had Tom been visiting this church as a tourist, he would have recognized its similarity to so many other Cotswold country churches – small and unpretentious. A glazed, stoneware-tiled floor bore deep wear marks tracing the paths from the oaken pews to the altar. The few leaded windows were colorfully stained or painted, dimming the interior light to a somber evenness barely sufficient to read the memorials covering the walls. The baptismal font and the pulpit, hewn from enormous blocks of grey stone, were still capable of performing their roles despite a thousand years of service.

Tom immediately noticed another person in the church. It was the Spinster Grindall, the mute woman he had seen earlier, and she was sitting quietly in one of the rear pews, closest to where Tom had entered. While he desperately wanted to be completely alone and sort through the dilemma of his life, he also sought the peacefulness of the church. She hadn't turned her head as he stepped in, and Tom wondered if she was deaf as well. Even so, he trod lightly up the center aisle, past the pew where she was praying and took a seat in the front pew.

Now at his destination, Tom set about the job of solving his enormous crisis. He wiped his forehead once again and noticed his perspiring had eased, though not completely. In the cool air of the church, his skin felt clammy and he wiped both damp palms on his thighs. His hands had stopped their shaking, he observed – perhaps he *was* prepared to think clearly and objectively. Tom began by taking stock of the facts. That was his job, he told himself. He was a historian, and it was a profession grounded in truth. The evidence that Adams presented was compelling. The relic made much more sense as a piece of the True Cross than a fragment of a crossbow bolt. Bishop Walter of Rouen had treated it so, safeguarding it in a priceless reliquary. The fact that it remained in France, where the memory of Richard quickly faded, allowed it to be forgotten. Tom knew as he dove further into the early texts, the truth would become even more obvious. Could it be part of the True Cross, but soaked with someone else's blood, he asked himself. Now this was interesting – there had been many battles fought for and around the True Cross. Could they be cloning one of its defenders who gave his last full measure for God? Or alternatively, was it a Saracen attacker who denied the Cross' significance so vehemently that he would sacrifice his life? The Battle of Hattin was a bloodbath, after all, as more than 10,000 Frankish soldiers were slaughtered by Saladin's Muslim army. These were very plausible hypotheses, Tom reasoned. He knew that a few moments' quiet reflection would shed light on the situation. Sighing deeply in relief and looking up at the silver cross on the altar, he imagined miniature armies locked in a death struggle around it on the holy table.

Without much additional contemplation, Tom's desperate mind improved this new hypothesis to certainty and he began weighing his next steps. What was the point of having a child who lived and died anonymously in the 12th century? Megan was barely three months along in her pregnancy. It might still be early enough to call the plan to a halt now rather than deliver a baby who bore no resemblance to Jeff. Of course, this would have been the case with the infant Richard – especially given his red hair if English legend held true. But that was an explainable substitution – Tom knew he could talk his way out of that. To have substituted Jeff for a hapless, nameless warrior was totally unacceptable.

As Tom once more reviewed the facts, he began to doubt this new explanation. The blood matter which had yielded the DNA was soaked deeply into the wood. That could only have happened when the wood was young and green, not after a thousand years of oxidation created an impenetrable surface coating. The Y-chromosome marker supported non-European lineage. King Richard seemed certain enough of the blood's origin for it to dominate his last coherent words before gangrene killed him. Further, there was little doubt that these words were uttered, even if attributed to the wrong person, since they figured in several independent accounts. Tom had never been given to prayer. In fact, most of the time he'd spent in church had been dominated by wondering whether the idea of God even made sense. Yet at this moment, that more fundamental question seemed secondary to the quandary at hand. Prayer seemed more than appropriate and he pressed his eyes shut. "God, please reveal the truth," Tom whispered earnestly, and then repeated, "The truth . . . please, God, whose blood is it?

The first thing that Tom saw as he opened his eyes was the cross on the altar. Its appearance had changed subtly in the few minutes Tom had been praying, and it now seemed to be glowing red. Were his eyes playing tricks on him? He blinked and looked again. The red was unmistakable – it was deepening and focusing on the center of the cross, although it had a trembling and lively quality as it shimmered on the metal. Tom concluded that someone must be beaming a colored light from the back of the church and swung his head around, only to see just the Spinster Grindall, head still bowed in prayer. He looked back to the altar cross, still bathed in red light, and then realized the sunlight must be toying with the stained glass. Tom followed the beam through the still dust hanging in the air to an ancient leaded glass panel depicting the Holy Family. At center, a seated Mary held a swaddled baby Jesus, with Joseph standing behind carrying a grumpy and disaffected expression. A bright ray of sunlight pierced Joseph's red robes and landed directly on the altar's cross. Tom wanted to think this was a coincidence, but he knew instead that God was answering his question.

Tom imagined himself as that stained-glass Joseph, ever

aware of the baby's true identity and regretting eternally his foray into Lisa's laboratory. He resolved that calling everything off was the only responsible thing to do – although he had not yet reasoned how to answer Lisa's inevitable "Why?" He would telephone his wife right now, tell her what they needed to do and brook no disagreement. Tom reached into his blazer pocket, grasped his cell phone and drew it out as he stood and wheeled toward the door in the rear of the nave.

Miss Grindall was still there – her eyes were closed, her head bowed and her hands clenched in prayer. In the dim light, Tom could see that her lips were moving, and as he slowly stepped closer, he thought he could make out "Avé," the Latin word meaning "hail" which began the original version of the Rosary prayer, Avé Maria. Funny, Tom thought, it hadn't occurred to him that this church was Catholic. As he passed her pew, he realized he could hear her speaking and he stopped altogether in amazement. Hadn't Adams said that she had never uttered a word? Trying not to disturb her private miracle, Tom leaned slightly closer to discern whether she was indeed speaking. It was faint, but he was certain he could hear something as she began to say it louder and faster. It wasn't "avé", but rather "cavé" the Latin word for "beware". She was saying it over and over. Suddenly her hand shot out and grabbed Tom's wrist, causing his cell phone to loose from his hand and clatter to the floor. Her head bolted upright and spun around and her eyes, wide with surprise and fear, met Tom's in a cold stare. The grip on his arm tightened. "Cavé, Cavé," she said in a deep and gravelly voice, "God is watching you!"

Tom couldn't breathe. A deep chill pierced the nape of his neck and shot through his core – every hair on his arms and legs stood straight. Tom shook his arm loose and bent quickly to pick up his cell phone, his eyes fixed on hers. Miss Grindall stared back without blinking, but didn't say another word. He backed away from her pew and then made a run for the door, fumbling briefly with the iron latch before freeing himself from the church and its terrifying clarity. As Tom burst outside into a chilling rain, the church bells loudly pealed forth.

10

"Hello, Mrs. Wolf?"

"Yes"

"My name is Lisa Duffield. I'm an Assistant Professor at Cornell and worked very closely with your son, Jeff"

"Oh . . . yes."

"I'm so sorry about his . . . passing."

"That's kind of you to say, thank you."

Lisa was puzzled about where to take this next. Telling Jeff's mother that she was just in the neighborhood was a bit of a fib, since she was still 350 miles away in Ithaca. But the old woman would never know. "I was vacationing nearby and I remember Jeff saying you lived in New London. I would love to stop by if that wouldn't be inconvenient for you." That came out easily, Lisa thought.

"Well, I would love to have some company. Where are you?"

Uh-oh, thought Lisa, she had not planned the ruse well enough. She looked quickly at the map and picked out a town nearby. "I'm in Darbury."

"Darbury?" the old lady paused, "I not familiar with . . . ."

"Umm . . ." Lisa looked closer at the map. "I mean Danbury. Sorry."

"Oh, Danbury," she chuckled, "well, you *are* very close. When were you thinking of stopping by?"

Lisa was impatient to solve the Y-chromosome mystery, and Tom would be back from Europe soon. If he knew she was chasing this piece of information he would be even more convinced that she was obsessed with Jeff. She had to make the visit today. "Well, is today too little notice?" Surely this old widow wouldn't shun the opportunity for company.

"Today? Well, if you don't mind a little bit of a mess. I haven't tidied up for some time. Is tomorrow a possibility?

"Oh, I don't want you to fuss. And, unfortunately I have to leave tomorrow." That should push her to yes, thought Lisa, enjoying her clever but uncharacteristic scheming.

"Oh, what a shame you left it to the last day."

Lisa wondered why old people always felt a need to chide. Would she be like that when she got older? "Yes, I am sorry I waited so long. Well, if it is too much trouble, then . . . "

"It's no trouble at all, my dear. I would love to meet one of Jeff's friends." Mrs. Wolf was not about to miss a visitor so quickly. "What time would you like to come by? I have a few errands to run this morning." Now the old woman was fibbing. She wanted to pick up her small house, as well as run out to the grocery store to pick up some treats for her caller.

Lisa glanced at her watch. It was just past nine in the morning and her rough calculations made it seven hours, if she drove without stopping – and she had gassed up the car yesterday. Adding a half hour for safety, she replied confidently, "How about four-thirty?"

"Half-past four would be just fine. And then perhaps you could stay for dinner?"

"Well, that's kind." Lisa questioned whether she could bear several hours of Jeff's mother. "Shall we play it by ear?"

"That would be fine. And, my dear, would you mind telling me your name once more?"

"It's Lisa Duffield. Thanks, so much, Mrs. Wolf." Lisa was excited to get her trip started.

"Please call me Mildred."

"Thank you, Mildred. I'll see you this afternoon. Oh, could I trouble you for directions?"

"Of course. Well, from Danbury I imagine you will be coming down Route 4. Follow that to New London then when you come through Potter Place you'll swing around onto 11. Take a left there, even though it is just technically a right from the direction that you were originally coming . . . ."

Mildred kept talking but Lisa had lost the thread and had failed to equip herself with a pencil. She decided to just "Google Map" the address, but how could she cut back in?

" . . . that's where the ski area used to be, but you wouldn't know that place, of course. Follow up that hill and the road comes to a four way stop with the old County Road. Well, it's not Old County Road, that's somewhere else . . ."

When the old woman paused to catch her breath, Lisa jumped in. "I think I see it on the map, can you just tell me your house number?"

Mildred laughed, "Oh heavens, we don't have numbers here. I'm the third house on the left on Mock Turtle Lane, a little white cape with blue shutters and an American flag in the front."

"Well, four-thirty then. See ya later."

"Goodbye, my dear. Drive carefully."

11

Tom had composed himself by the time he returned to Adams' house, but was still working up a passable excuse for his hasty flight. In truth, less than twenty minutes had elapsed since he bolted out the front door, yet the cataclysmic revelation, accentuated by the clutching ex-mute woman and near-complete weather change all combined to make it seem like hours. Now stepping up to Adams' front door, his brown hair already matted by the thick drops of rain, Tom was mortified that the English professor would brand him as a crazy and have nothing more to do with him. *What if he won't drive me back to Oxford,* Tom worried suddenly. He decided bluster and confidence were the best way out of this predicament –

he rapped roundly on the door and opened it far enough to poke his head in. "Professor Adams?" he called out. Tom could hear a rustle of papers in the far room and a distant voice answer.

"Yes, yes, come in please."

Tom did just that and brushed off the rain drops which hadn't yet soaked into his blue blazer. Adams appeared at the other end of the short hall, and Tom could tell he was struggling with what to say. The American chose to rescue him from the awkward moment. "Please forgive me for stepping out so quickly. I suddenly felt really sick to my stomach and needed some air. I'm much better now – other than being a little wet."

"Perhaps it's all the travelling, or some food didn't agree with you. Well, never mind that now. Can I get you a towel to dry off?"

"No, thanks, I'm fine, really."

Adams was anxious to resume their discussion about the relic. "Shall we go back into the study? There are a couple more items I'd like to share with you.

Tom's hands began trembling slightly. He was not keen to see any more evidence that the child developing in Megan's womb was the son of God, rather than a great British monarch. He looked at his watch and grimaced. "I'm afraid it's getting late. I have to check out of the hotel by noon and then get to Heathrow for an evening flight back to New York." Tom saw the disappointment register on Adams' face and added quickly, "Professor Adams, this is really stupendous work you've done. You have no idea . . . really . . . how important it is." This comment seemed to repair Adams' mood. "Is there any way you could scan these documents and send them to me?" Tom asked.

"If I can master the technology," Adams half-joked in response. "Well, then, where did I put the car keys?"

The trepidation Tom felt hearing these words was well placed. Adams spent ten minutes hunting for them, which was astounding given the size of the tiny cottage and the fact that Adams had only visited three of the rooms. He found them tucked safely in the pocket of the battered tweed jacket he was wearing. Apparently he never put them in that particular pocket.

Adams spent most of the commute back to Oxford describing how he found the crucial documents which cast new light on the relic. Tom found that light painful and penetrating – white hot. He desperately wished they could talk about the scenery or local history, and he found himself unable to do anything but nod and emit little "ah yesses." The Englishman was rightfully proud of having redefined several great historical events. Not just the circumstances around Richard's death – perhaps also the diplomatic moment of the twelfth century when Saladin and Richard found a way to halt the slaughter. The shard of wood, the piece of the True Cross was the key to everything. In the minds of the Christians it was the key to Saladin's power in battle. To Richard, it unlocked his spirit during his interminable imprisonment at Durnstein Castle. And now, to Tom, it had unlocked a sort of holy Pandora 's Box. He was so deep into a world of worry and confusion that he failed to realize Adams had pulled up to the hotel and stopped the car.

After a short pause Adams cleared his throat and said, hesitatingly, "Well, there we are then. This is your hotel and its only half eleven – plenty of time to pack up before check out. Shame you can't stay another day. I'd love to show you the originals of those documents. Never mind then. I'll scan them in and email them, shall I?"

Tom had his chance to slip in a word, even if it was a little wooden. "Yes, that would be great."

"I daresay you're not yet feeling yourself. Shall we pop 'round to the Chemist for a Bromo?"

"Pardon me?"

"A Bromoseltzer – to settle your stomach."

Tom shook his head. "No, thank you, I'm . . . I'm fine.

Really. I do want to thank you for sharing your findings with me. It's all quite stunning."

"A smashing centerpiece to the new museum collection, I must say."

Tom had been so fixated on the cloning subterfuge that he hadn't even considered how this reframed entirely Strater's collection. "Yeah, for sure," he answered. "Thanks again, Professor Adams." Tom swung around in his seat to face the Englishman and extended his hand.

Adams shook it warmly. "A pleasure, a pleasure, Professor Duffield. Safe travels. I'll be in touch. Cheerio then."

Tom was happy to escape the small blue sedan and step out to the curb. He waved once as Adams motored off and as his eyes followed the car they fell once again upon the historical marker for Beaumont Palace. So much had changed in the last several hours, Tom thought. No more a paternal glow for the erstwhile birthplace of his coming child. Tom now considered Richard a peer, at least in having wielded the cross fragment for their own, personal purposes. It emboldened Richard to think he was invincible, both in judgment and in body – and led him to disaster at Châlus. Tom wielded the fragment in ignorance. He hoped there was some way he could avoid disaster.

Duffield leapt up the few steps to the hotel and strode directly to concierge's desk to ask for help in changing his travel plans. In truth, despite what Tom had said to Adams, he was booked on tomorrow's morning flight back to the States. However, when he had arrived at Heathrow the previous evening he heard an announcement for an evening flight to New York. Tom needed to be on that plane – he needed to return to Ithaca as quickly as possible, and somehow sort things out.

The concierge explained that he didn't normally manage flight bookings, but agreed to do it nonetheless when Tom's exaggerated look around the deserted lobby made it obvious the man had nothing else to occupy his time. As the nattily-uniformed man began working his ancient, black Bakelite phone, Tom jumped across to the Front Desk where he asked to shorten his stay and depart immediately. While happy to accommodate the request, the desk clerks were mortified that the hotel had somehow fallen short of Tom's expectations. They were just about to summon a suitably contrite manager when he finally convinced them that he simply needed to return home sooner than expected. Their cooperation secured, Tom sprinted up the neo-Gothic oaken staircase and down the labyrinthine hallways until he reached his room. It took him several attempts to operate the electric key – mostly because he was using the wrong end – but once inside he threw his clothes and toilet kit into the suitcase, smacked the pockets holding his passport and wallet to confirm they were there, and charged back down toward Reception. Tom was slower on this half of the journey. The roller suitcase he trailed behind himself kept fishtailing and flipping over, which forced him to stop and right it. Tom cursed the first time this happened, yet newly sensitized to the Maker, he immediately felt guilty and apologized heavenward. From then on he simply *thought* the curses emphatically but didn't verbalize. Tom hoped God noticed the difference.

Everything was falling into place for Tom when he arrived back at the Lobby. The concierge was able to rebook his seat to the 5:45 pm flight to JFK, and the Front Desk clerk had printed up his bill and already inserted it neatly into an envelope with his name hand-scribed across the front. Even better, the concierge informed him that a direct motorcoach to Heathrow would be leaving from the bus depot in ten minutes. A porter stepped up smartly to assist Tom with his luggage. *Why don't we have these guys in Ithaca,* Tom thought as they left the hotel and crossed the main street toward a queue of buses. Just before boarding, Tom fished deep in the front pocket of his khakis for some money to tip the eager young man. Having forgotten to exchange money the previous evening, Tom found only a small wad of US bills – he peeled off a \$5 note, and then after a moment's hesitation, peeled off another and pushed them in the young porter's hand, along with profuse thanks for the assistance.

Although the bus was nearly full, the front row remained open and Tom was happy to slide in there. He sat on the edge of the blue, velour seat until the driver switched on the ignition and pulled out into traffic. The American's journey home had begun – glancing at his watch and performing some quick math, Tom figured he had about twenty-four hours to think his way out of this holy Gordian knot. He was going to need every second of it.

12

Lisa pulled over again to check the map. She was used to navigating, but not driving as well – that was Tom's job. What had Mrs. Wolf told her? Was it right on Route 11 or left? In her mind, she replayed the telephone conversation while sitting in the idling car and staring at the map on her phone. It was already 4:30 and she was embarrassed at the idea of being late. She reoriented her phone to the direction she thought she thought she was going and took a deep breath. It had been a long day crossing upstate New York and Vermont and now halfway into New Hampshire, yet fortunately the weather was beautiful and the roads dry and empty. She had enjoyed the drive except for the growing nervous feeling that she was tricking poor Mrs. Wolf. Lisa put the idea out of her mind as she studied the network of lines on the map and finally found the road she sought. "Mock Turtle Lane," she declared as she found it and then counted out the number of preceding turns, "one, two . . . three." She measured the distance by eye, squared herself behind the wheel and pulled back onto the road.

Mildred Wolf's blue-shuttered cape came into sight as Lisa rounded a bend at the second house. Lisa had been expecting it to be neat and prim, with an annual garden beginning to bloom along the front fence. It may have once been so, but no longer. The house was sadly dilapidated – the white paint was peeling and two of the shutters were hanging askew.   The lawn had not been mown in so long that the grass was going to seed, and the once-beautiful garden was overgrown with weeds. There was one purple iris peeking out from behind the weeds in testament to tidier days. Apparently Mrs. Wolf lacked a green thumb.

"Speak of the devil," Lisa said aloud – but inaudibly to her hostess – as she spied the plump and white-haired woman standing behind the front screen door. Unlike the house, Mrs. Wolf looked exactly as Lisa anticipated. Lisa smiled at her as she parked the car, stuffed her phone into her purse and stepped out. This was the first time Lisa had stood since setting off seven hours previously – not only was she quite stiff, she was desperate to visit the toilet. She stretched as surreptitiously as possible, and stepped stiffly toward the white-haired woman who had pushed open the screen door and was stepping out to greet her.

"Hello, my dear," the woman said in a voice Lisa found vaguely reminiscent of Mrs. Claus in *Rudolf the Red-Nosed Reindeer*. "So nice of you to come see me. Did you have trouble finding my house?"

Lisa wasn't sure if this was a real question, a conversation starter or a dig on being fifteen minutes late. She took it as the former, however, and answered, "Not at all. I got a little bit of a late start."

"My directions were okay then? My Jeff refused to listen to my directions – in fact, he used to state that he would do the opposite of what I said and find his way perfectly," she chuckled warmly and Lisa could tell that she was reflecting on her deceased son.

"They were just fine. I made it here didn't I?" she asked rhetorically with a smile.

"There you go. I can see why Jeffy liked you. Come on inside, I've got some refreshments for you."

The women headed inside the charming white house. It was neater on the inside than Lisa expected from the outside, although she wondered whether Mildred had spent the day tidying up. Lisa fended off a few questions about how she liked Danbury and in which part of town she was staying. Unfortunately for Lisa, Mildred had lived there for a time and knew virtually every building in the town. On the other hand, the old woman admitted that there were so many new houses on the lake – "nifty little cottages" to use her wording – that she found it difficult to keep up with them all. Coincidentally enough, it turned out that was precisely where Lisa was staying.

Mildred brought Lisa through the center hall and guided her left into a formal sitting room which ran the length of the small house. The sitting area was framed by a colorful Persian carpet, the center medallion shaded by a mahogany butler's table. A plate of brownies and a second plate of what looked like chocolate chip cookies lay on the table – both were covered with several layers of clear plastic wrap.

"Please have a seat, my dear. Can I get you anything to drink? Tea or coffee or Coke?"

Lisa took a seat on a rose-colored camelback loveseat. "Ice water would be wonderful. Thanks so much." As Mildred retreated through a door at the far end of the room, Lisa took in the room around her. Despite a gnawing hunger that made her stomach ache, she resisted the urge to rip the wrap off and stuff several brownies in her mouth. *If only she hadn't wrapped them ten times over I could slip one out without her noticing.* She hoped Mildred wouldn't take too long to come back and help her break into the food.

So happy was Mildred to have a guest that she was mercifully swift in returning with a tray of drinks. She, too, was anxious to talk about her deceased child and reconnect with the life that was taken away from her. Releasing the baked treats from their plastic cocoon and offering them to her hungry and grateful guest, she asked, "So tell me how you met Jeffy."

Lisa was happy to launch into a long recounting of her relationship with Jeff. She began with the fateful first lecture which made them both laugh heartily. When the two women finally caught their breath, all four eyes glistened with tears. Lisa continued for twenty minutes until her bladder made an urgent call for the restroom and she excused herself. The few moments of quiet reflection helped Lisa remind herself why she had taken the long journey. As she stood washing her hands and looking at herself in the mirror, she spoke softly to herself, "Don't be sad, he's coming back." Then she issued herself instructions. "Find out what he was like as a baby."

Mildred was perched on the edge of her chair holding up the plate of cookies when Lisa reentered the room. Although her actual words were "Please, help me eat these up," Lisa instead imagined a claymation Mrs. Claus exhorting, "Eat, Papa, Eat," and suppressed a laugh. She took another brownie.

"What was Jeff like as a baby?" Lisa asked abruptly.

"Ornery."

"Really? I imagined him being quiet and thoughtful."

"No, he was just ornery. I loved him nonetheless, of course, as his mother. But he was a darned irritating baby. And he didn't get much better."

Lisa was shocked. Mothers weren't supposed to say such things about their children, particularly if they were dead. Were they? "What do you mean?"

"He was always difficult. When he was six he began correcting my grammar. And not just correcting me," she recalled, "he would also do that to his teachers. He got in a lot of trouble for calling them stupid. The dickens . . . ." She half-smiled, half grimaced at the recollection.

"Did something bad happen to him?" Lisa remained horrified. Surely Jeff wasn't mean-spirited from the start.

"Not that we ever knew. His two older sisters were totally different. Pam was a happy baby, and Jessica too. Oh, Jeffy would tie them in knots." She chuckled wistfully.

"What are they doing now?"

"Pamela is a nurse in Boston. Jess is a social worker. They live in the same neighborhood and see each other all the time. And fortunately they're only two hours away so I see them and the grandchildren all the time. Ithaca was always such a long trip. Is it six hours?"

"Seven." Lisa said this with certainty.

"Jeffy came a little more often after his father died. But not often enough." She pursed her lip and Lisa suddenly feared she would cry. She had to get back to her visit's objective.

"Do you have any pictures of him as a baby?"

Mildred stood. "Oh my goodness yes!" She stepped over to a cabinet under the bookcase and fished out a brown leather album. "He was a beautiful baby – and our first boy. They say the youngest never sees the camera, in Jeffy's case he never saw the camera because he was blinded by the flashbulbs." She sat next to Lisa on the loveseat and opened the cover. After flipping through a couple of pages of Pam and Jessica as toddlers, Mildred found a page Jeff's newborn shots.

Lisa gasped. "He *was* beautiful!"

"I told you so."

"Is that blonde hair?" Lisa asked leaning closer to see the detail.

"More white than blonde. And it stayed that way for years. It only got darker when he was in his mid-thirties. That's his father's side of the family – German through and through."

German!? I looked at the Y-chromosome screen Megan ran. Jeff definitely wasn't from Germany. "I thought Jeff mentioned that his father's family came from farther east – Hungary or Central Asia maybe?" Lisa was fishing hard. *Or else great-grandma was messing around with the proverbial mailman.*

Now it was Mildred's turn to gasp, or at least to feign it. "Bite your tongue, my dear. Jeff's father will turn over in his grave." She laughed at her own theatrics and continued. "No, no. They had reams of genealogy tracing the Wolfs back to the thirteenth century. They were quite an influential family. We made pilgrimages to the ancestral home and church – oh yes, German through and through. On that side of course," she clarified. "My family was Scotch-Irish." Mildred continued with her own multi-century ancestry, but Lisa was lost in Jeff's baby pictures – and there were pages of them. The first Christmas, the first tooth, the first solid food, Baptism, beach vacations, birthday parties. If a week of Jeff's first three years had passed unphotographed it would have only been for the film shortage that Mr. and Mrs. Wolf created in documenting their son's life. Despite the fact that this was a family album, there were very few pictures of the sisters by themselves. Most often they were flanking their celebrity brother – occasionally standing in the background. Lisa reasoned this might explain Jeff's ego, but not his sharp edge and apparent lack of empathy which Mildred described. *I'll need to manage the doting,* Lisa noted as Jeff's new mother-to-be.

Mildred nattered on as Lisa continued flipping the pages. When she reached the end of the book, the elderly woman jumped spryly to her feet and collected two more thick albums from the cabinet. "Oh, you probably don't want to look at these," she said, handing the leather books to her guest.

"Of course I do. I didn't get to meet Jeff until his thirties, so it's wonderful to see what he was like as a child." And this was the truth. It occurred to Lisa that she was the first person in the history of the world to see exactly how her child was going to look – days one through ten thousand. She wished she could take the albums home with her, but knew that there was no way she could ask Mildred for that. The old woman would think her obsessed or crazy.

Further, these books might be all the woman had left of her cherished child. As if to make that point, Mildred picked up the first album and began paging through it as Lisa waded through books two and three. Lisa stole a glance now and then to watch the old woman and could see Mildred's eyes welling with tears. Finally, one large drop rolled down her cheeks and splashed on the plastic page cover. The two women's eyes met and Lisa felt her heart wrench. *If only I could tell you that we've brought him back to life,* Lisa thought.

"I'm sorry. This is just making you sad." Lisa apologized.

"The sadness is always there, my dear. You never expect to outlive your own child. You certainly don't *want* to," Mildred answered softly. She pulled a tissue from the cuff of her cardigan and wiped her eyes. "Do you have children, Lisa?" she asked.

"No," Lisa answered. "Not yet." She turned her face back to the album and resumed paging through, hoping desperately that the old woman would leave it there.

"Well, don't wait too long," Mildred said.

Ughhh . . . drop it, Mildred! "We won't. I'm pretty hopeful that it will happen soon." Lisa decided to change the subject proactively. "Where was this taken?" she asked, pointing to a picture of a small cottage amidst tall conifers. Little Jeff was standing outside the front door.

"That was our summer cottage on the coast of Maine. Oh, did we have fun there!" Mildred became more wistful than sad.

"Tell me about it," Lisa asked.

This launched Mildred into the full detail of their summer vacations. She explained each of the photos on that page, took a deep breath to continue on to the next, and was dismayed to see a venue change back to their home in New Hampshire. "Now isn't that funny," she said, checking to make sure that she had not missed a page. "The rest of those pictures must be in the overflow boxes." She stood again and returned to the photo cabinet, huffing and puffing slightly as she dug through the contents. She came back to the sitting area with three shoe boxes saying, "I couldn't always get all the photos in the albums, so I put the extras in here." She lifted one of the lids, displaying a mass of unsorted black and white photographs. Lisa noticed at once that there were many pictures of Pam and Jessica, although Jeff still figured prominently. "Would you like a little more ice water, or tea, maybe?"

"Water, please. Thanks so much." As Mildred left for the kitchen, Lisa suddenly recognized her opportunity. While she could never take the photo albums, Mildred would never miss a few photos from these boxes. Indeed, the chances of the old lady ever getting into these boxes were very low. Lisa quickly rummaged through the open box to find a few close ups of the little boy, extracted three, and then quickly opened one of the other boxes. "Paydirt!" Lisa exclaimed quietly seeing a pile of Jeffy's baby pictures. Again, she took out several as quickly as she could, and then repeated the process with the third box. In all, Lisa had taken ten snapshots of her mentor and baby-to-be, stuffing them into the back pocket of her jeans. Lisa tried to look as nonchalant as possible when Mildred returned a few moments later.

"Would you like to stay for dinner, my dear? It's almost six o'clock."

Lisa knew that the woman was desperate for companionship, yet she had a very long drive ahead of her. Quickly doing the math, she realized she wouldn't get home until well after midnight. Further, her mission was complete, particularly with the photos stashed in her back pocket. "That's very kind of you but I really have to be going."

Mildred protested the rejection, but not too much. She could tell from Lisa's response that she wasn't going to be talked into staying much longer, particularly when she noticed Lisa studying her watch.

The women chatted warmly for another half hour – about Jeff and his family, about Lisa's work, about Tom and the special collection he was researching. Mildred was envious about his present trip to Europe – she hadn't been there in many years and admitted she was now too old to make the journey. The pause in their conversation after that sad statement provided Lisa the chance to take her leave. Mildred saw her to the door where they hugged and Lisa thanked the older woman for her hospitality – particularly on such short notice. Dreading her long drive, Lisa slid reluctantly behind the wheel and started up the car. She waved one last time to the kind woman who was standing in the doorway – her baby's real mother – and backed onto Mock Turtle Lane. Lisa stopped several hundred yards down the road to extract the photos from her back pocket and, after flipping through them quickly, seal them away in her purse. As she began retracing her way to Ithaca she wondered whether she would tell Tom about her petty thievery.

13

Sitting at the kitchen counter with Jeff's baby pictures spread out in front of her, Lisa savored the steam from her chamomile tea and tried to unwind from her whirlwind trip to New Hampshire. She held the mug close under her nose and inhaled deeply. Her shoulders were hunched and taut from gripping the steering wheel for the last seven hours, but with each breath they seemed to ease. The outbound trip had been exciting – she had felt nervous and tingly about what lay ahead. Would Mildred Wolf be friendly and welcoming? Would Lisa be able to find out Jeff's roots? On the other hand, the trip home had been exhausting. It had been dark since she crossed back into New York and by that point she was already tired from navigating small, windy roads. And though she had "obtained" wonderful pictures of her baby-to-be, the geographic origin of Jeff's Y-chromosome remained a mystery. Too keyed-up to sleep, Lisa decided to study the pilfered snapshots.

Lisa didn't hear Tom's car pull into the driveway, nor the door and trunk lid slamming shut. Not even the sound of Tom's shuffling feet and his wheeled suitcase on the wooden stoop broke Lisa from her overstimulated stupor. Only when the door's opening brought a rush of cool air did she swing her head around to see Tom standing on the threshold. He was as surprised to see her awake as she was to see him at all, and they stared at each other without speaking.

He broke the brief silence. "Why are you still up?"

"What are you doing home?" Lisa reached back and scooped up the photos on the counter. "Didn't you have to visit that guy at Oxford?"

"Yeah, I saw him." Tom pictured Adams' study and suppressed the urge to shudder. "But we finished early and I caught an earlier flight home."

Lisa was desperately trying to figure out how to explain why she was still up. "Was it a good trip?"

"It was fine. Why are you still up?"

"I couldn't sleep."

Tom resented that when he was home Lisa couldn't stay up past nine-thirty and here it was almost one in the morning. "Busy day at work?"

"Yeah, I guess."

"How's Megan?"

"She's fine. Why?"

"Just wondering whether she's doing okay. It's a big thing, you know, being pregnant."

Lisa wondered why Tom had to say things like this. "Uh-huh."

"I'm whipped. Let's go to bed." He stepped forward and kissed her quickly.

Lisa waited for Tom to pass by and head down the hall before glancing down at the top photo in her stack. A tow-headed toddler wearing a sailor's suit grinned back at her. Lisa wondered where she could buy such an outfit.

Lisa couldn't shake Tom the next morning. He tagged along when she decided to walk to work, and once they reached her building, offered to buy her a cup of coffee from the cart in the lobby. When he followed her to the elevator, rather than bidding goodbye for the day, she was surprised, but didn't object. Only as she opened the main door to the lab did she finally query his plans. "Aren't you going to your office?"

"I haven't been up here for a couple of months," Tom answered. The night he had extracted the DNA from the shard of wood flashed through his consciousness. Although it wasn't the last time he was here, it was now the most memorable – by far. "Come on – let's have our coffee together. You can't drink at the bench anyway." He looked around for Megan as they stepped into the vestibule. She wasn't in the student office; unfortunately her lab bench was around the corner and out of sight. There was no way Tom could sneak a look for her without arousing Lisa's suspicion. They entered Lisa's office and Tom sat down in front of desk while Lisa shed her jacket, took her seat and switched on her computer.

"You haven't told me much about your trip yet. And that weird message from what's-his-name? Adams? What was that all about?"

Tom's efforts to insinuate himself into the lab had just backfired. "It was some new findings regarding Richard's death. Some previously undiscovered descriptions. For someone who's spent his whole life studying the man, it was all too exciting. He needed someone to share it with and I was the lucky guy."

"You say that as if you don't care about Richard. You once said he was the most fascinating man in world history," Lisa teased.

Tom shrugged. "One of them, certainly."

"So what did these new documents show?" Lisa thought Tom would appreciate her interest in his work.

"Well, it was similar to what has been recorded already."

Although he still hadn't figured out how he was going to lie his way out of this, Megan's abrupt entrance into Lisa's office saved him. The young post-doc was halfway to Lisa's desk before she realized Tom was sitting in the chair to her right.

"Lisa! . . . oh, hi Tom." Megan tilted her head to one side as she looked at him, and tried to figure out why he was there. She recalled Lisa saying he wouldn't arrive home from Europe for a couple more days. Then again, she didn't recall Lisa saying that she would be away yesterday. Maybe it was something about being pregnant that messed up one's memory, she thought.

Tom and Lisa greeted her in unplanned unison, each looking at her midsection and asking her how she was feeling.

"I'm doing great," she responded to both. "I feel wonderful." She eyed Tom again, and tried to figure out whether she should break her exciting news in his presence. She feared he might react badly to the news – he was as unpredictable as Lisa was even-keeled. Lisa would accept the news as another piece of data to be assimilated into everything else they had learned over the past several months. And then, like the brilliant scientist she was, Lisa would make sense of it all. Tom might start yelling and make a scene. Not only might he condemn the whole experiment, he might do it loud enough for everyone to hear. On the other hand, he was, after all, destined to be the baby's father – she probably had an obligation to tell him. She contemplated all of this faster than Lisa could ask why she had barged into the office, and made a split-second decision. "Do you guys have a couple of minutes to talk?"

"Sure," responded Tom, "I'm back early so I could even play hooky all day." Lisa just nodded.

"I was dying to tell you this all yesterday," Megan continued, "but I guess you were out." Tom's gaze shifted to his wife, and Lisa could see that in her peripheral vision. Her eyes remained fixed on Megan, who she hoped would not pursue that line of discussion. "Anyway, and I hope you guys don't mind this, I did some more genetic screening on the Y-chromosome after that first test came out negative." Tom sat forward in his chair. Lisa leaned forward and cut in.

"Let me guess. Did it come out Middle Eastern?" Lisa asked.

"No."

"North African?"

"No."

Lisa paused. The ethnic choices were becoming farther and farther afield from the Wolf's native village in Germany. "Central Asian?"

"No."

"Did you have a good control?" Lisa wouldn't normally question Megan's techniques, but these results were becoming increasingly unlikely.

Megan laughed. "Of course. What do you mean, did I have a good control?"

"I was just kidding," Lisa covered. "Perhaps you should just tell us."

Tom wanted to jab that Lisa wasn't up to twenty questions yet, but he was too fascinated by what Megan may have found. He waited patiently for the news and hoped it might refute what he had learned in Adams's study.

"Well, before I tell you the final results, you need to know that I checked those ethnic groups. I actually traced most of the branches off M168 – I did Europeans first, of course, and that is what I mentioned at your house last week. Then I looked at a number of Indian and Asian groups. Native Americans would have popped out there too.

"So when all those came up negative, I decided to start back at the first three, M168, which I hadn't checked, M91 – from Southern Africa – and M60 from Western Africa. Every male of the human species has one of those three, and from there I would trace it down the tree. What do you think I found?"

Lisa – and Tom for that matter, but he wasn't going to answer – found it very hard to imagine that Jeff's Y-chromosome had come from Africa, but sensed that Megan was leading her in that direction. "M168," she said despite her intuition.

"Wrong." Megan's own surprise at that finding showed in her response. Her blue eyes widened and her head remained thrust forward, mouth open. Before Lisa could choose between the other two, Megan cut through the suspense. "And don't bother picturing a dark skinned baby, because the other ones came up negative as well. The baby doesn't carry any of the known mutations on his Y-chromosome."

While for Tom this made perfect sense and provided a neat but nauseating scientific underscore to Adams' revelation in England, Lisa rejected it completely. "That can't be," she declared sharply, shaking her head from side to side.

Megan had expected resistance. "I know it sounds incredible, but I checked and rechecked everything. I can run it once more, I think, with the little bit of amniotic fluid I have left. But I know it won't show anything different."

"But this is impossible. You said it yourself, 'Every male of the human species has one of those three.'"

"It's not impossible," Megan countered. She emphasized the word 'impossible' to suggest that it was darned unlikely just the same. "Assuming someone in his male line carried that mutation, which they believe was spontaneous, it is possible that it spontaneously mutated back to the original. Plus, it's not like every man has been tested. We just say that every male has one of these three based on statistical sampling. It's not exhaustive. There could be other Y-lines around that have never been sampled."

"Come on, Megan, give me a break." Lisa said. "You know the chances of either of those are infinitesimal."

"Lisa, do *you* want to rerun the screen?" Megan asked. Lisa wasn't sure whether Megan was offended or simply doubting herself. Science hangs on repeatability – her findings needed to meet that standard.

"I trust your results, but they don't make any sense. I've got to think about what might have gone wrong."

Tom alone knew that the results were not flawed and wished that they would drop the whole matter. He also knew that these two scientists would never be thwarted. He stood up, dropped his half-full coffee cup in the wastebasket and announced, "I've gotta get going. Lisa, I'll see you at home. Bye, Megan." He left without hearing either of their absent-minded responses.

Tom arrived home hours ahead of Lisa. He'd spent much of the day researching the True Cross, but traveling and jet lag left him wiped out by midafternoon. Lisa's noisy entrance through the kitchen door awakened him from a nap on the sofa, for which he was very thankful – he'd been dreaming he was trapped in an old Cotswold church with Adams preaching from the pulpit. Groggy and slightly disoriented, he made his way into the kitchen, both to greet her and pour himself a glass of wine. Lisa needed little encouragement to join him, and it took only a few sips of a fruity Zinfandel to prompt her guilty conscience into admitting her sojourn of the previous day.

"I have a confession to make," she said.

Do I look like your priest? Tom thought. "Yeah?"

"I didn't go to work yesterday."

Do I look like your boss? "So I gathered from Megan's comment. Where were you?"

Lisa couldn't look at Tom as she came clean. "I went to see Jeff's mother."

"In New Hampshire!?"

"Yes."

"Why?"

"I wanted to find out what he was like as a baby." Her intonation made this more of a question than a statement.

Tom clutched his forehead. "Oh my God!"

Lisa decided not to tell him about the photographs she had stolen. "I'm sorry. I know it was indulgent. But it occurred to me that no one ever had the chance to learn about their baby before it was born. It was weird, yes, but I think it meant a lot to Jeff's mother. You should have seen how happy she was showing me the pictures."

"You made her show you pictures?" Tom's eyes were still obscured by his hand. The other hand clutched his glass of wine a little more tightly.

"It was *her* idea. She loved it, Tom, she got to relive so many happy memories. And we hit it off, really, she's the sweetest old thing." Lisa considered her next statement. She knew it might set Tom off into a tirade, but she didn't like operating in secret. Much as she treasured the pictures of her baby, keeping them away from her husband troubled her deeply. She needed to ask his advice and thereby gain his tacit agreement to the next phase of her investigation. "Do you think I could ask her help in tracking down a male relative from Jeff's father's family? I'm wondering whether they're from a whole new Y-chromosome line."

Tom did not answer her question at once. Instead, he finished his first glass of wine and refilled his glass at the counter. "Do you want some more?" he asked, brandishing the bottle. She nodded and he refilled her glass equally generously. Lisa knew he was still pondering her question and she patiently awaited his answer. What Tom said was not at all what she expected. "You can do whatever you want, but there's another explanation for that Y-chromosome." Tom was halfway across the Rubicon.

It was so unexpected, that Lisa was certain she'd heard it wrong. "What?"

Tom sat down at the table across from Lisa and weighed how

bluntly to clue her in. "I switched the DNA. You know, the night you were out with your team? I had your keys and went into the lab and substituted a different sample for the one you did of Jeff."

Lisa's blue eyes were wide – the rest of her face frozen. "Whose DNA?"

This was the tough part. "I thought it was King Richard the Lionheart. I took it from the shard of wood in the reliquary. Remember the glass was broken?"

"And what do you mean by 'thought'?" Lisa was still breathless and hadn't blinked.

"That's why Adams summoned me to England. He found out that the shard of wood isn't part of a crossbow bolt after all."

"So what is it?" Lisa could hear her heart pounding in her eardrums.

"A piece of the cross on which Jesus died."

Lisa gasped. "Jesus Christ?" Tom nodded. "You're not making this up." He shook his head. Lisa felt nauseated. "Jesus . . . Christ." This began as an oath, and finished as simple repetition when the thought sunk in. Lisa's rational mind fought its way into her consciousness. "But you told me yourself that a lot of those relics were hokum. How could we really know that it is Jesus' blood?"

"I've been trying to convince myself of that over the past two days, but too many weird things have happened." Tom described his flight from Adams' house and his encounter with the Spinster Grindall in the church. Lisa listened in rapt silence. "Megan's Y-chromosome screen puts a fine point on it all, don't you think? He has no male line – other than God – and that's the one line without mutations."

They sat in silence for a long time. "So what do we do?" Lisa asked at last.

"What can we do? It's not like you can abort Jesus – that would really piss off the pro-lifers," Tom chuckled briefly before resuming a serious tone. "We carry on and tell no one. It's not like he'll pop out with a halo above his head. Who'll know?"

Lisa contemplated Tom's suggestion, and then shook her head. "We need to tell Megan," she declared.

"Every additional person who knows about this is a potential breach," Tom pleaded. "She'll never know the difference. All Megan wants is to validate the experiment and be part of this scientific breakthrough. She wants a faculty appointment. Please, Lisa, you don't have to tell her."

Lisa was immovable. "It was bad enough that we were trying to clone Jeff against her will and not telling her. This is way too big for us to keep it away from her. The baby's inside her, for God's—goodness sake." She waited to see if her point had been made. "We'll tell her tonight."

Tom realized arguing would be futile, but he wanted to minimize the damage. "Then at least skip the part about Jeff. There's no reason to damage your relationship, blame it on me."

"She's carrying a baby for us, Tom. Now we've done this to her. From here on," Lisa drilled the table with her index finger, "no secrets." She picked up her cell phone from the table and dialed Megan's number.

14

Later that evening, and only halfway back to her apartment from the Duffield's house, Megan's feet and back hurt. She wished she hadn't eschewed Lisa's car ride offer. Even worse, she rejected dinner, too, and now felt her stomach growling. Or it could be the baby kicking. *The Holy Kicking Baby. How did this spin so out of control?* Megan asked herself. *We were just trying to validate the science and give Lisa the baby she longed for.* Her head spun with the events over the past hour – Lisa's phone call, the request to come directly to the Duffield's house, Lisa's and Tom's tandem explanation of the DNA substitution, and finally, the bizarre story of

Tom's visit to Chatterford and its ancient church. *What a fucking mess!*

Megan had always scorned her girlfriends who complained about being 'confused' about boys or college choices or fights with their parents. Now, and for the first time in her life, she was confused. She felt guilty for being so curt with Tom and Lisa – after they broke the news, of course. Indeed, on her way to the Duffields' house Megan had fantasized that Lisa was going to offer a faculty appointment. Instead Megan found out she would be a modern-day Mary. *I don't even own a Bible.* She was angry with Lisa, and furious with Tom, but the two of them had admitted something they could easily have kept hidden forever. If they said they were sorry once, they said it thirty times, and she never acknowledged it. She had yelled at them and called Tom an 'idiot' – they just kept on apologizing. Sooner or later she knew she'd have to forgive them, or at least Lisa. Forgiving Tom might take a little longer – but then again, he wasn't any more deceptive than Lisa. And the fact that he had memorized the protocol and done the extraction by himself – that was equal parts impressive and devious. *Shit! It's the second coming!*

Although a cool breeze rose up from the lake, it was warm for an April evening. Megan could see the western sky gearing up for a spectacular pink-golden sunset, so rather than turning east near the athletic fields, she continued down Tower Road toward the sweeping overlook at the crest of Libe Slope. She passed the Biotech building, thought about her recent finding of the mutation-free Y-chromosome and then epiphanized. *I actually discovered this myself – why did the real explanation escape me so completely?* She wondered whether she was too closed minded, or was this whole . . . situation . . . simply so absurd that no reasonable person, much less a PhD scientist, would ever contemplate it. *Hmmm . . . no mutations. Must be Jesus. Yeah, right!* The baby's genetic purity suddenly became very interesting to her and she began thinking about what other analyses she could do. *How about comparative screenings? I could tell people how close to God they really are.*

Megan carried on across East Avenue, through a parking lot and was just skirting the north side of Sage Chapel when the urge to enter washed over her. Despite the wonderful things she had heard about it, she had never been inside – in fact, she hadn't been inside a church in at least a decade. As socially conformant as her hippy parents had become, publicly worshipping God had never made it into their routine, and thus evaded hers. Even her few college friends who had been married did it on beaches or in hotel ballrooms. She pulled the door open and, with both feet planted squarely on the outside, peered into the dim interior. Her eyes adjusted quickly to the light and the neogothic painting on the ceiling – particularly the golden highlights – dazzled her. Megan's reticence to enter evaporated in wonder and curiosity, and she walked in with her head inclined upward and her mouth agape. "Wow," she muttered to herself.

She spied the altar to her left, yet rather than go there directly, she circled the interior counter-clockwise so as to finish there. Each step of the way led Megan to ask herself more insistently why she hadn't visited the chapel before. The stained glass windows, the Cornell Mausoleum, the organ framed by the Rose Window – any one of them were beautiful in their own right, yet concentrated together transformed the place into something like a museum. But that moniker somehow cheapened it. There was a common direction, a theme to it all which lent it both relevance and grace. As she approached the altar and apse, her awe deepened and heaved analysis and introspection aside. Megan stood with her fingertips touching the altar rail and drank in the beauty.

Megan didn't hear the man behind her clear his throat the first time he tried to get her attention. Even after amplifying it slightly the second time, he barely penetrated the silence of the nave. The young woman remained standing with her back to him, emitting quiet "ahhs" as she surveyed the finely detailed mosaic on the apse wall and ceiling. The man circled around toward the pulpit to catch her peripheral vision and resorted to words, "Good evening, young lady." His voice was warm and melodious.

"Hello," Megan said softly. She had seen him just before he spoke and was not at all startled. However, she turned her head back to the ceiling, not realizing that he wanted to do any more than greet her.

"It seems you like the chapel," he said.

Megan turned and regarded the man more carefully. He was nicely dressed, with a priest's collar and blazer above black trousers and shoes. A balding pate and graying hair on his temples suggested he was her father's age – perhaps a little older. The dimples by his smile extinguished any concern Megan had of his approach in the deserted building. "It's beautiful! I was thinking it's like a museum with a purpose."

He laughed. "I've never heard it put that way, but it's true. It's all to celebrate the glory of God. It's from him, and it's to him." He took a step closer. "Can I help you with anything?"

She was surprised, as much by his question as her desire to answer 'yes'. Yet after a pause she answered otherwise, "No, I was just passing by and thought I'd come in and look around."

"Sometimes we enter the Lord when the Lord has entered us," he said thoughtfully.

Megan tried not to smirk at the irony. "I think it's fair to say the Lord is in me."

"Then, my dear," he paused, nodded his head gracefully, and smiled, "you are blessed." The priest waited for these words to sink in, and continued, "Thank you for coming to visit us this evening. You are always welcome and we are here to serve you." His eyes twinkled, "Good night, my child."

"Goodnight," Megan responded as the man turned and walked down the center aisle – his footsteps curiously silent – and left the church. She followed slowly in the same direction. Pausing for a final glance around the church before exiting into the now-dark April evening, Megan failed to notice the absence of the confusion and concerns she had carried inside.

Part IV

1

When Tom happened upon his *The Crusades and its Leaders* Page-a-Day calendar, he almost had trouble remembering what it was. It laid buried under three inches of miscellany, and while digging for a reference on Hugh de Morville's sword, Tom suddenly revealed the neglected four-inch cube calendar. He was irritated with himself for so carelessly misplacing the de Morville reference – finishing the Strater Collection Catalog that day was now going to be challenging – but the historical note on the calendar's page caught his eye and he ceased shifting papers. *April 6 – Richard the Lionheart dies of infected crossbow wound at Châlus Castle in France – 1199.* Tom suddenly remembered the last time he had revealed that page (on that occasion by simply tearing off April 5) and how he had reached into his top desk drawer and extracted what he believed to be the offending bolt. In fact, not long after that – and possibly even as Tom still held the relic – Lisa had called requesting him to come home and help ready the house for a dinner party with Claire, Bob and Megan. It was a dinner party planned to celebrate the positive results of Megan's amniocentesis. Thanks to Megan's secret DNA screen, it ended up as the evening that turned their lives upside down. Tom had shot off to Europe within the next two days, and four days later found out the real history of the jagged wooden fragment.

Tom held the calendar in his hand and recalled the amusement he felt when he found it in the bookstore. The time was mid-March, a morbid period for all unpurchased calendars and this copy – along with several cousins – had been relegated to the close-out table as a sort of hospice prior to the recycle bin. Tom read the title twice, first because he couldn't believe his good luck, and second because he couldn't believe anyone would invest in publishing such a calendar. He seized it without hesitation, and then spent five minutes searching for another copy for his yet-to-be-born son. Once back at his office he ripped quickly through the first three months of the year, setting aside anything related to Richard so that he could later enter it into his electronic calendar for perpetuity. How silly all this seemed now.

As desperately as Tom had wanted to finish the catalog that day and send it off for printing ahead of the Collection's opening in two weeks, he was distracted by the calendar. Nearly five months had passed since he last tore off a page and he figured that he would need only ten minutes to pull off one hundred-fifty or so pages. Tom noted that Saturdays and Sundays were combined on one sheet, and while he couldn't do the math in his head to figure out exactly how many fewer pages that would mean, it helped rationalize his procrastination.

He began ripping off the pages one by one, and after reading their historical connection, tried to remember what had happened in his recent life. The days just after his hurried trip to Europe were easy to remember. *April 13 – Constantinople is sacked in the Fourth Crusade – 1204.* Tom recalled this as the day they had told Megan "the big news". She had freaked out, as Tom expected, hurling a fair dose of expletives in his direction before storming out of their house. Her anger seemed to blow over quickly, however, and notwithstanding her occasional pointed remarks, their relationship healed in the following weeks.

May 20 – Philip of France forms alliance with Leopold in the Siege of Acre – 1191. Tom remembered this as the day on which he, Lisa and Megan had finally agreed to fully suppress not just what they had done, but also any clues to the relic's origins. Tom gambled that Adams was far enough away and too disengaged from current events to notice Tom's omission of any reference to him or Gervase in the catalog. By sheer luck he had never mentioned Adams to Strater and he thus became confident that they could get well past the museum's opening – and the baby's birth – to arouse any suspicion.

June 8 – Richard the Lionheart lands his army at Acre to begin the Third Crusade – 1191. June was a blur, Tom thought, and so was July. With the academic year behind him, he was able to concentrate fully on the Catalog. He relished the time he had spent with Strater and Rob Tucker during those months, although he regretted deceiving them about the relic.

July 10 – Saladin surrenders Acre after two year siege and Richard the Lionheart's banner adorns the ramparts – 1191. Just after the Fourth of July Lisa had declared that it was time to begin readying the nursery. Despite valiant protestations that they could do the work in August, Tom was tasked with emptying his storage boxes, painting the room and assembling a crib.

August 12 – Godfrey of Bouillon wins the Battle of Ascalon ending the First Crusade – 1099. August had been wonderful. It lived up to its reputation as Ithaca's best month weather-wise, and Tom, Lisa and Megan had made the most of the long, warm evenings. After long days at the office and a couple of extra hours of do-it-yourself home improvement, picnicking in the Plantations or grilling in the back yard fully recharged all three of them. Tom even had the energy to run back and forth to the museum several times a day to help supervise the exhibition's installation.

Tom had now nearly caught up to today's date and although it had required a little more time than he had anticipated, he enjoyed the brief reflection on the summer passed. With the baby on its way, Lisa had abandoned efforts at conceiving. The drugs, the constant monitoring, and the required sex on a schedule – all of these had been replaced by a comfortable intimacy that was its own end.

It wasn't like their newlywed years, but it mercifully lacked the manic focus of the past several years. Megan's pregnancy was going very well. Although she remained trim and petite, the swell in her abdomen had recently bulged out like a basketball under her blouse. She was tiring more and more during the days and having trouble sleeping at night, but nothing out of the ordinary. The three of them never spoke about the baby's identity. After the blow up in April, the Duffields avoided talking about it and that had become a habit. None of them wanted to be the first to raise the issue – certainly not Tom, who bore the most blame. At work, Tom had managed to keep William Rogers at arm's length, and this pleased him most of all. Rogers was still poking his fat head into any place it would fit, notably by showing up any time Strater came to campus. Fortunately John saw William for the fool he was and consistently declined his offers of assistance.

Tom tore off yesterday's expired page, revealing *September 2 – Saladin and Richard the Lionheart agree to a three-year truce, ending the Third Crusade – 1192*. Tom emitted a loud "hah". "We know about that, don't we?" he said aloud, "Now." He wondered how he would have thought about this entry had Adams never dug deep in the Oxford archives. Tom was sure he would have torn off the page and tossed it in the wastebasket without a second thought. Shrugging, he flipped the cube on his desk and glanced up at the clock. It was close enough to quitting time that he resolved to do just that and finish the Catalog in the morning.

"Excuse me, Professor Duffield?"

Tom looked up to see a meek expression on a young man's face, poking through the door opening. "Yes, can I help you?" he answered. It was too early in the semester for students to visit his office. Unless they were kiss-asses, of course, and while Tom was flattered by their pandering, he found them irritating – especially when they later argued over grades. "Come in."

"Thanks. I hope I'm not catching you too late?"

Grammatically it was a statement, but his intonation suggested otherwise.

"I guess that depends on what you are here for." Tom thought the young man looked familiar. "Are you one of my students?"

The young man entered. "No, I'm not – but we've met before. Remember that night at the Biotech lab when you were leaving a surprise for your wife?" He paused to see if that jogged Tom's memory. "My name is Elex. I'm a friend of Kristina Abbott's – she works in your wife's lab."

Tom worked hard not to let the sudden memory of that previous meeting register too dramatically on his face. "Oh yes, I do remember that." He drew out each word as pretense that he was digging into the memory banks. "Nice to see you again. And hey, thanks for keeping that surprise to yourself." Tom flashed a warm smile. "What can I do for you?"

"I don't know if you remember that I write for the *Sun*, in fact, I'm the Editor this year. But I still write a lot of pieces, like the profile I did of your wife last year. Did you read that?"

"Yeah, of course. It was very good." Tom had not read it – he couldn't even remember its publication. "What brings you here?"

"I'm doing a piece on the . . ." Elex flipped quickly through a small, spiral notebook in his hand. "Strater Collection, and I wondered whether you could help me with it."

Finally, a little recognition for my work, flashed through Tom's mind. "Oh my, I'd be happy to talk about it. Have a seat."

"Great! Thanks!" Elex dropped his backpack on the floor and flopped onto the spare chair at the side of Tom's desk. He pushed aside a stack of papers near his elbow to make room for his notebook and then swept back the unkempt black hair which had fallen across his eyes. His attention remained focused on the scribbled notes which already filled the pages Tom could see but not read, and his lips moved almost imperceptibly as he read to himself.

"Yeah, so I think most of my questions have been answered already, but I needed a few dates, data points, you know, that kind of stuff."

"How did your questions get answered already," Tom asked, perplexed by Elex's comment.

"Ummm, yeah, from my interview with . . ." He looked down at his notes. "Professor Rogers. I spent about an hour with him earlier today. He was super helpful." Elex nodded enthusiastically to underscore his satisfaction.

"Was he indeed?" Tom asked. He now understood why Rogers had insisted on having a draft of the catalog by the end of the previous day. "Did you happen to set up the interview yesterday, say around lunch?" Tom remembered the mid-day chimes were playing when Rogers phoned with his catalog request. Elex thought about it for a moment and then nodded. "And how did you get Professor Rogers name?"

"The *Chronicle* said the exhibit was hosted by the Museum and the History Department, so I just called the Departmental Office and got put through to him."

The hairs on the back of Tom's neck felt prickly against his shirt collar. "So what did he tell you?" Rage and amusement are rarely within reach of one person at the same time, but Tom firmly grasped each as he prodded Elex.

The young man was oblivious to the trap being set; he quickly reviewed his notes. "He talked about the great partnership that had been struck between Mr. Strater and the History Department—"

"The History Department?" Tom cut in. "He said the 'Department'?"

"Yeah."

"Okay, go ahead."

"So he talked about how Strater did a lot of his own research and that folks here helped him organize it, write it up, that kind of thing."

"'Folks here'"? Tom asked leaning forward as if he couldn't hear what Elex had said.

"Right."

Duffield's face felt warm and he wondered whether he was visibly blushing. "Did he mention anyone specifically?"

Elex scanned his notes. "Not that I wrote down." He then checked himself. "Not 'til then end, that is, when he mentioned that you also worked on it – that's how I got your name."

"Did he use the word 'also'?"

The young journalist was beginning to sense that something was awry. He read through his notes more closely, flipping quickly to the end and then pointing to the word he'd scribbled on the page. "Yes." Elex was perplexed as to why Tom now sat quietly with his eyes closed and his lips drawn hard against his teeth. "Was that a mistake? Did you *not* work on it?"

Tom remained silent a moment longer and then opened his eyes. "What's your name again?"

"Elex."

"Elex, do you know the expression 'off the record'?"

"Of course. I am Editor of the *Sun*." He said this with pride.

"Then the following is off the record. Do I have your word on that?"

"Yes." He put down his pen.

"*I* did *all* of the work on this project – all of it. In fact, John Strater asked for *me* by name. *I* travelled down to meet him. *I* was the one who got the Richard the Lionheart relic fixed after the airport security guys broke it. *I* was the one who connected with external experts, like Jean Flaubert at Rouen or Warwick Adams—" Duffield caught himself and both redirected and amplified his monologue. "Rogers doesn't even know about that. He doesn't know about any of it. That fat fucker didn't lift a finger on this project, so the fact that he led you to believe he did – *that* just pisses me off entirely."

Elex was amused that Tom had cursed, but was afraid to smile. He was trying to remember if he had ever heard a professor say that word before. He remained motionless as Tom carried on.

"As long as you don't write what I just said, I don't care what the hell you publish about this thing. But, please, in the spirit of journalistic truth – if such a thing still exists – don't give credit to Rogers for any of this. It's just like him to screw me out of recognition for all I have done. This was a major piece of research." Tom felt better for having vented so thoroughly. He would have been embarrassed for his candor, except that he was still furious at his boss for trying to steal credit for the exhibition. He inhaled deeply, preparing for Round Two, when the telephone jangled. It surprised both men, and they sat staring at the phone for two rings before Tom hoisted the receiver. "Hello? Oh, hi." It was Lisa calling to remind him of their evening plans. He swiveled his chair to afford some privacy, and with his back to Elex, tried to hurry his chatty wife off the phone.

Still stunned from Duffield's diatribe, Elex sat in silence and attempted not to hear the monosyllables emitted on the other side of the desk. He contemplated his pen, which still lay next to his spiral notebook and wished desperately he could make some notes on the conversation just passed, notwithstanding his 'off-the-record' pledge. Duffield struck him as a little too volatile, however, and he dared not incur any more of the wrath he'd seen exercised. Instead, he let his eyes wander around the desktop, marveling at the mass of confused papers and notes. He didn't know that it was messier than normal, however, having just suffered Tom's hunt for the de Morville citation and his own search for elbow room. Suddenly one word popped off a sheet of paper and aroused Elex's consciousness.

leukocytes

This was not a word Elex expected to see in a History professor's office and he brought his head closer and inclined it to correspond with the orientation of the page.

–binding leukocytes

The page on which these handwritten words appeared was mostly obscured by a jumble of other papers, yet trailing words on the lines above and below also peeked out.

– ml release fluid

–binding leukocytes

– crocentrifuge

"Whatcha looking at?" Tom asked.

Elex had not heard Tom conclude his phone call nor swivel back around in the chair. His eyes darted to a brochure on the desk. "Just this hotel brochure. The . . . ummm . . . Macaulay Hotel is it?" He had covered well.

"In Oxford. I was there in April. Great service." Tom's mood had lightened during the telephone interruption, and he recognized it himself. "Look . . . what's your name again?"

"Elex."

"Right, sorry. Look, Elex, forgive me for hitting you with all that spite. It's not your fault, no it's William Rogers and all the silly games he feels the need to play. That's my cross to . . . bear." Duffield had stumbled into that expression and smiled at its irony. "Anyway, how can we set you up for a good story?" he asked rhetorically. "Did Rogers show you the Catalog?"

"No."

Duffield fished through his briefcase and pulled out a stapled deck. "Here's a draft copy. It's close to being done, but there are a couple of holes. Why don't you read through it and then get back in touch if you have any questions. In touch with me, that is," he winked, "and not Rogers."

Elex took the catalog and stuffed it in his backpack. He began to do the same with his notebook and pen, but then decided to keep it handy. "Thanks for your time," he said, and then passing through the door added, "I'll let you know if I have questions."

The young journalist barely made it out McGraw Hall's front

door before he had to stop and make forbidden notes of his conversation with Duffield. His curt manner at the tail end of the interview was not a reflection of being upset or intimidated by Duffield's ravings. Instead, he was memorizing the words he'd seen and heard during the last ten minutes – they all seemed a little too noteworthy to go unrecorded. Sitting at the top of the stone steps, Elex now jotted them down as fast as he could before the memory faded any further.

2

Elex hadn't much of a chance to think about his meeting with Duffield since leaving the McGraw Hall steps. He needed to finish a paper for one of his classes, and then had to write an editorial for the *Daily Sun*. It was nearly midnight when he declared tomorrow's edition ready for printing and headed off to Dunbar's for a beer. He went more for the ethanol than the company, so while he bodily joined a few friends in a booth, his mind returned to the afternoon's events. Rogers' monologue was the most informative and Duffield's tirade the most striking, but those few science words scribbled on the paper on Duffield's desk were the most intriguing. Elex couldn't figure out why he found them so beguiling. Duffield was, after all, married to one of the University's leading scientists. Perhaps it was one of her papers, picked up inadvertently by her husband and now forgotten on his desk. It wasn't hard to imagine losing something on that desk. Elex wanted to show that desk to his mother – it might help reset her expectations of her son.

But the handwriting didn't look female. It was blocky and ragged – it looked like it came from a man. *Why would he write those words?* Elex asked himself. And suddenly it occurred to him to ask someone else. He motioned to his friends that he would return shortly, and he exited to Eddy Street and pulled out his cell phone. *12:08 – Dang!* Maybe it was too late to call. He decided to send a text message and started typing quickly. *"K – u up?"* Elex hit the send button and anxiously waited for the response.

"*Yup*"

"Awesome!" Elex said, pumping his fist. *"can i call u"*

"*Yup*"

Elex searched his electronic address book and called Kristina Abbott as quickly as he could work the buttons. She answered on the first ring. "Hey, Kristina, I'm glad you're up."

"What's up, dude?"

He got right to the point. "What are 'binding leukocytes'?" he asked.

She laughed. "Binding leukocytes? I've never heard of them."

"What about a 'crocentrifuge'?"

Kristina laughed again. "Crocentrifuge?! Have you been drinking?" she asked. Before Elex could defend himself, Kristina rethought her answer. "Do you mean 'microcentrifuge'?"

"Yeah, what is that?" Elex's hopes for elucidation were restored.

"Elex, didn't you ever take biology? A microcentrifuge is a piece of equipment we use in our laboratory to separate small samples. I have one right on my lab bench. You've seen it." Kristina thought a bit further and answered his first question. "Were you reading a protocol or something where there's a step *to* bind leukocytes?"

"Does that make sense?"

"Sure."

Elex threw out the final words he'd seen written on the paper. "Would you use a release fluid to do that?"

"You'd use the release fluid to unbind them. It sounds like some kind of procedure to get leukocytes – that's white blood cells – separated out of a sample. I know that Megan has bought some kits that do that."

"Who's Megan?"

"You know her – a post-doc in the lab. Pretty, blond, slim – until she got pregnant anyway."

He tried to picture all the people from the lab and was able, vaguely, to picture Megan Brack. "I don't remember her being pregnant. Who bopped her?"

"Elex!" Kristina feigned offense. "I'm not exactly sure, but rumor is she's acting as a surrogate for Tom and Lisa."

"You're kidding me. When did that happen?"

"About nine months ago, I guess. She's due in a couple weeks."

"I thought Lisa was, like, the world's cloning expert," Elex jibed. "Why does she need a surrogate when she can just grow babies in a petri dish?"

"Elex, you're profoundly ignorant. You're kidding, right?"

"Sorta, yeah."

"Let's just say we haven't exactly cracked simulating a uterus." Kristina had had enough of science and work for the day. She really wanted to unwind. "Do you want to meet for a drink?"

"I'm whipped. How about later in the week?"

"Deal. G'night."

"Night." Elex was torn between heading back into the bar to finish his beer and going home to bed. As thirsty as he was, the noise, the crush of people and the heat all put him off the former. Relishing the cool, autumn air, he wandered down the hill toward his apartment.

"Must be nice to be rich," Elex said aloud to himself as he turned the last page of the draft Exhibition Catalog. "Wish he'd throw a little of that my way." He had awakened earlier than normal – thanks in part to not reentering Dunbar's and drinking more beer – and now sitting at the kitchen table of his squalid Collegetown apartment, he savored fresh coffee, a stale bagel and the packet Duffield had given him the previous day. Even without a great knowledge of history, he recognized the momentous events in which they had participated. The newspaperman in him fantasized about writing the contemporaneous headlines.

Knights Mangle Becket at Altar
Claim King Ordered, Now in Hiding

Henry V Slaughters French at Agincourt
English Bowman Catch Cavalry in Death Swamp

The Gutenberg test-strike page was his personal favorite of the collection.

Gutenberg Invents New Printing Method
Blockcutters Mock Usefulness and Speed Claims

Elex began considering how to frame the feature article he had to write for the *Sun*. Digging into his backpack he liberated his favorite spiral notebook and flipped through it to find his notes from the Rogers and Duffield interviews. Rogers had spoken little of the items themselves, instead he blathered on about the close relationship with Strater and the (Elex now read from his verbatim notes) "well-deserved, bright shining spotlight of credit and fame now cast upon Cornell's History Department." Rogers had said a lot of things like this, and with Duffield's critique ringing in his ears, Elex could understand why the rotund History Department Chairman might be a tad irritating.

Duffield hadn't said much about the collection either – only the exclamations about all the work he had done and how Rogers hadn't lifted a finger. He had mentioned the Richard the Lionheart relic, and the catalog provided a very lengthy description of this fascinating piece of history. Elex imagined how surprised Richard must have been when the crossbowman found his mark somewhere between Richard's shoulder blade and collarbone. How morbid that they had housed the piece in a reliquary for a thousand years – on the other hand, the bullets which killed JFK were surely kicking around somewhere. Elex hadn't seen the relic yet and wondered whether the blood stains were still visible.

"Jean Flaubert, Rouen" Elex said aloud reading from his notes. This name had stuck in his mind because he had just read *Madame Bovary* by Gustave Flaubert. He had seen the latter Flaubert's name in the Acknowledgements section at the back of the catalog, and he quickly flipped through the stapled packet to check it once more. *What was the other name?* He checked his notes. *Warwick Adams.* Elex ran his finger down the long list of names. *It'd be a lot easier if they were in alphabetical order!* He reached the bottom of the list – this name wasn't there. He rechecked his spiral notebook and the printed sheet once more to make sure he hadn't missed anything. Elex took off his glasses and rubbed his eyes. "If he was such a big expert, why didn't Duffield acknowledge him?" he asked himself, replacing his glasses and rising to refill his mug from the grimy Mr. Coffee carafe. Suspecting he may have heard the name wrong, Elex read carefully through the Acknowledgements looking for anything vaguely similar to Warwick Adams. *Nothing.*

Elex flipped on his computer and did a quick Google search on Warwick Adams. After sifting through a few unlikely hits – a doctor in Colorado, a real estate agent in Kent, and a travel agent in Parramatta – he settled on a likely suspect. ***Warwick Adams – Professor Emeritus, All Souls College, Oxford***. The link took him quickly to an Oxford faculty directory page sporting a picture of a grinning man with thinning gray hair. Elex scanned past the many acronymed degrees and the contact information to find this Adams' *Research Interests*:

> *Professor Adams has extensively researched and widely published on 12th century England and France with a special emphasis on King Richard the First, including his participation in the Third Crusade,*

capture and post-imprisonment reign.

"Bingo!" Elex exclaimed. He looked around for his cell phone, and, remembering that he had used it the night before to call Kristina, sprinted to his bedroom to dig it from a heap of clothing. He then ran back to the kitchen to find Adams' office phone number. Puzzling briefly over which combination of 1's and 0's he ought to dial, Elex opted for trial and error and started tapping the keyboard. It took three tries before he heard a ringing tone at the other end and he patiently waited until one of the double-tones was cut short.

"Eight one six double three four."

"Is this Professor Warwick Adams?" Elex asked. He hadn't figured out what he was going to ask this man yet, but he was confident that it would occur to him very shortly.

"Yes, can I help you?"

"My name is Elex Barnes. I'm a writer and editor for the Cornell University's newspaper, *The Daily Sun*, and I'm doing a story on an upcoming exhibit donated by an alumnus. Do you have a minute to talk to me?"

"Certainly, Mr. Barnes. If I'm not mistaken you're talking about the Strater collection."

Elex was surprised at how quickly Adams had made the connection. "You've heard about it?" he asked.

"My goodness, yes. I have discussed it numerous times with your own Professor Thomas Duffield. He's a smashing fellow, what? Although we haven't spoken for quite a while – I daresay he was very busy during the summer."

"Professor Duffield gave me your name, but I didn't catch which items you specifically collaborated on." Elex was good at fishing.

"We were working on the relic identified as a crossbow bolt – the one that killed Richard the First, or Richard the Lionheart as you usually call him on your side of the pond." Adams always liked being able to bridge the Anglo-American divide.

"That's right, the crossbow bolt. That's pretty neat. Did he show it to you?" Elex remembered the comment about the airport officials and wondered whether Duffield had taken it to England.

Adams inhaled sharply. "Dear me, no. I wouldn't want him carting that around the world. Especially after we found that it wasn't a crossbow bolt at all."

Elex suddenly realized why Adams wasn't mentioned in the Acknowledgements – the Englishman had uncovered the relic as a hoax. Duffield was suppressing knowledge that this collection wasn't all it purported to be. *Now this could be a scoop.* "So it was a hoax?" he asked somewhat hopefully.

"Just the opposite, my dear chap, just the opposite. It's a different kind of weapon altogether – at least it *was* a weapon, until the Romans used it on the wrong person." Figuring he had confused the young reporter, Adams continued, "It's a piece of the True Cross which Saladin had given Richard to end the Crusade. Richard carried it next to his heart until his dying day."

"The True Cross?" Elex asked. "Can you say a little more about that?" He also wanted to probe on Saladin, but the Cross-thing sounded more interesting.

"I suppose you don't call it that – that name's a titch antiquated now. You probably just call it The Cross."

"*The* Cross?" Elex asked, certain that he was missing something.

"Precisely. The Cross on which Jesus Christ was crucified," Adams clarified. He jabbered on while Elex's mind raced wildly. "It's a smashing find. I know that Professor Duffield was well and truly stunned when I shared the research that shattered the centuries-old myth about it being part of the crossbow bolt that killed a King."

Elex had read the catalog's section on the relic very carefully, especially since Duffield specifically referred to it. There hadn't been a word about the Cross – not a single word – and Adams was omitted from the catalog as well. Something strange was going on here and Elex sensed he was onto a big story. He needed to tread carefully as he wrapped his hands around it however. "And you said you shared all this information with Professor Duffield?" he asked.

"Oh, yes. I've sent him everything."

"Thanks, Professor Adams. This has been super helpful."

3

Tom was surprised at how easily he put the finishing touches on the catalog after a relaxing evening and good night's rest. He had nearly forgotten the last event of the previous working day – the irritating meeting with the naïve young reporter. Duffield knew it wasn't the boy's fault. No, it was just one more instance of William Rogers' petty scheming and served as a good reminder that Rogers could never be trusted. Never. Even with a successful Strater Exhibition, Rogers would not let up on his maneuverings and allow Tom a modicum of credit. He resolved to accept that reality and make the most of his work in spite of his boss.

The elusive reference for which Tom hunted the previous day virtually fell into his hand, allowing him to wrap up the work and email it to the printer. Next the catalog would be laid out with high-resolution photographs for the printing, as well as excerpted for placards around the exhibition hall. Tom made note of the time, 9:17am, as he pressed the "Send" button, and he reflected on how it marked the end of nearly a full year of work. How odd, he thought, that the most momentous moments of our lives go nearly unnoticed. Was it so for these people he studied? When Richard chose not to don his armor before riding around Châlus Castle? When Becket chose to defy Henry for what proved to be the last time? When Charles d'Albret, Constable of France, commanded the French cavalry forward into the mucky hollow that would become the killing fields of Agincourt? Certainly finishing the year's labor on the catalog had none of that significance; nonetheless it deserved a triumphant sigh of satisfaction and relief.

The telephone rang halfway into his sigh, and Tom cut his moment short to find out who was at the other end. "Tom Duffield."

"Hi, this is Elex Barnes. I dropped by your office yesterday afternoon, remember?"

Oh God, not again. "Yes, Elex, I recall." Tom contemplated apologizing for his 'hissy fit' but decided he would simply let it slide. "Do you have some questions?"

"You mentioned that the Richard relic broke. Can you tell me a little more about that?"

Shit! What else came out of my mouth? Tom tried to remember whether he had said any other stupid things to the young reporter. He did recall his stipulation. "I mentioned that everything I said was off the record. That should eliminate any need for follow-up questions."

"Sorry, I should've mentioned beforehand that I read through the catalog and was really excited about seeing the collection. I was just wondering if the piece was badly damaged."

"Well, I'd like this to stay out of the paper – as I said yesterday – but yes, the reliquary was knocked over and one of the glass panes shattered. That's really all – a guy at the glassworks here on campus fixed it. You can't see any damage now."

"What happened to the thing inside?" Elex probed.

"The crossbow bolt fragment?"

Elex pushed a little harder. "I thought it was something else."

"No, this was the fragment of the crossbow bolt that killed Richard. I actually had it locked up in my desk in a Ziplock bag until the glass pane was repaired."

"So you actually held it in your hand. Wow!"

"I guess it was pretty cool."

"And is there really blood soaked into it?"

"Well, if you remember, I mentioned in the catalog that that was an unlikely myth." Tom expected that this reference would cause a huge buzz when the exhibition opened. If only people knew the truth about whose blood it was, Tom thought. *Thank God Adams is thousands of miles away.* "Any other questions, Elex?" he asked.

"No, thanks, that'll pretty much do it. See ya," Elex signed off.

Elex was too excited to go to his classes that morning. The story he was chasing was far more interesting than anything he was going to learn about Hardy or *Tess of the d'Urbervilles* in his English Literature course. Even without finishing his second big mug of coffee that morning Elex could feel his heart thumping since he finished the brief conversation with Tom Duffield. All the pieces of a bizarre puzzle were falling into place – yet so bizarre a puzzle that Elex kept scoffing at the plausibility of the conclusion he wanted to draw. It was quite possibly the biggest scoop in two millennia and for that reason alone, he simply couldn't let it drop. He turned to a fresh page in his spiral notebook, laid it before himself on the sticky kitchen table and stared at it for the next fifteen minutes without making a mark. Finally, after letting the ideas swirl madly through his head, he began deliberately snatching them from the tornado of unreason and scribbling them down.

What he knew was that Duffield had physical control of the relic which Adams positively identified as a piece of the Cross on which Jesus Christ was crucified. Duffield had ignored this attribution and obscured Adams participation in the research, leaving him out of the Acknowledgements – despite a significant level of close collaboration. Adams said that they even discussed it face-to-face, yet he didn't have the slightest idea that Duffield didn't accept his research. On the other hand, Duffield acknowledged that the relic might be bloodstained. Duffield also had some kind of handwritten scientific protocol on his desk which involved isolating leukocytes – white blood cells. About ten months ago, Elex had caught Tom Duffield in his wife's deserted lab – deserted because all the students and techs had been taken out by Duffield's wife. And Tom's wife, Lisa Duffield, wasn't just any old scientist; indeed, she was one of the world's experts in reactivating dead cells and creating undifferentiated cells suitable for cloning. Now one of Lisa's post-grads, Megan Brack, was a pregnant surrogate for the two professors.

Elex could no longer refuse the conclusion which had formed in his gut that morning, lodged in his heart for the past twenty minutes and now took hold of his brain. "Holy shit!" he gasped. He said it a second time, separating the words with a thoughtful pause. He suddenly remembered an expression that Lisa Duffield had used during his interview – "playing God". "Talk about playing God!" he said, "They've cloned his son!" A jolt of adrenaline surged through his veins and he leapt to his feet. He didn't want to leave the table, he simply had too much energy to remain seated. Elex cautioned himself to think clearly. All of his journalism training pointed toward fact checking, but he couldn't imagine how to pull that off without risking the discovery of his discovery. If the Duffields knew he was on to them, a preemptive strike on their part could make his story look more ridiculous than it already appeared. He had to take them by surprise.

Or maybe outflank them. Unlike the Professors Duffield, he had never more than greeted Megan Brack. Assuming that she knew what was going on – and it was hard to imagine otherwise – he may be able to catch her off guard and thereby close the loop on his story. He posed some questions out loud to hear how they sounded.

"So, Megan, how does it feel to be carrying the Christ child?" *Way too direct.*

"Hey, Megan, have you ridden on a donkey lately?" *A little too Biblical.*

"Have you made any hotel reservations? Or are you willing to give birth in a barn?" *Snotty.*

Elex knew he needed to be a little more sly if he was going to catch her off guard. And that he might not get the absolute and definitive answer he wanted. He might have to wing it. But what a scoop!

He remembered that Kristina had a class at 11:15 on the western end of the Arts Quad because they often met afterward near the library to go to lunch. It was a ten minute walk from the Biotech building, so that meant that he could go to her lab anywhere between 11 and noon and have an excuse to wait around – and chat with whoever was there. If he went too early they would not be excited about him plopping down for the next hour – if he went too late he might not get far enough into a conversation . . . interview . . . interrogation before Kristina showed up and ended it. He chose 11:45 as the perfect time to roll into the lab and begin snooping.

Elex found it hard to walk slowly as he made his way onto campus and was already five minutes ahead of schedule when he reached the pedestrian bridge over Cascadilla Creek. He walked to the siderail, gazed down into the rushing water sixty feet below and took a deep breath. Elex knew that if he wasn't calm and nonchalant he would most certainly blow his cover. He needed to stroll, not sprint. Besides, it was hot for a September day and he should avoid being sweaty when he arrived at the Duffield laboratory. At 11:38 he resumed the trek, his heart no longer thumping and his breath no longer short.

The young journalist entered a side door of the Biotech building and slipped up a back staircase. He knew that he couldn't afford running into anyone coming out of the lab as they would report that Kristina wasn't there and he would be obliged to turn around rather than continuing up to the lab. He arrived at the third floor without passing a soul, and slowly walked the short distance to the entrance of the Duffield lab. With one final deep breath he entered the lab, stepped into the vestibule and turned left into the student office area. God was smiling on Elex today. Megan Brack sat alone at a desk reading the newspaper.

"Hey," he said, his heart leaping.

She looked up from the paper. "Hi," she responded. "Can I help you?" Megan vaguely recognized him.

"Is Kristina here? I'm her friend, Elex." He could hear his heart pounding.

"I think she has class, or went out to lunch. I'm the only one here."

This is too good to be true. "Do you mind if I wait for her here?" he asked.

"No, its fine, but I'm going back to my bench in a few minutes." She motioned with her head toward the empty chairs. "You can have a seat, if you want."

Elex walked into the room and sat down. "Thanks." He watched Megan return to reading the paper and searched for a conversation starter. "How's the paper?"

"The usual," Megan answered without looking up. "I'm almost done with it. You can have it afterwards."

"That's okay. I've read it already. I'm the Editor."

Megan was relieved she hadn't said anything flippant or critical to Elex's previous question. "Cool," she said, nodding, "good for you." She resumed reading.

Elex was having a tough time engaging her in conversation. After a long, silent pause he asked "Are you pregnant?"

Megan looked down at her bulge. "Ummm . . . yeah." She was trying not to be sarcastic, but given the size of her abdomen this seemed a profoundly stupid question.

"I interviewed Professor Duffield last year for the paper and she was telling me about all the cool stuff she does in the lab here." Elex wondered whether he would have to push further to get her talking about the lab work, and better yet, the baby. When she only looked up and nodded, he added, "What's it called, Ewe Factor?" Elex had reread his notes from the Lisa Duffield interview to prepare for this moment.

Megan answered without thinking, "Yes."

"Does it really work?" he asked.

"Yes." Megan's hand rubbed her belly involuntarily. It was subtle, but Elex noticed it. Conscious that she was speaking in monosyllables, she continued, "We really think so. It's potentially very powerful."

Here we go, Elex thought. "And it can reactivate old cells to grow into, what is it, undifferent . . . undifferentiated cells?" He intentionally tripped over the words to appear less practiced.

"Exactly." Megan was gratified by his understanding of her work. "You remembered that from last year?"

"Yeah, I guess it made an impression." He feigned humility and fibbed. "She said something about using red blood cells."

Megan shook her head. "Not red blood cells, they don't have DNA. You'd have to use white blood cells."

"Leukocytes, right?"

"Right." *Maybe he's not so dense after all*, Megan thought.

"So if I found some old thing with blood on it, could I get the cells off and bring them back to life? Then, you know, like, clone it?" Elex knew the question was direct, but he thought she was off guard.

Megan *had* been off guard, but this question arrested all her senses. She suddenly remembered the Hot and Cold Game she played as a child and imagined that Elex had just wandered close to the desired mark. *Warm.* If not for his easy expression and obvious lack of scientific training she would have been really nervous. "Well, I guess theoretically you could do that, but it would be pretty complicated."

Elex noticed that she was shifting around in her chair. He realized he'd hit a nerve. "So, could you just grow it in a test tube?" *Will she rise to the bait?*

"No, course not. This is very theoretical you know, right?"

Megan wanted to ward him off.

"Sure, sure, but if you couldn't grow it in a test tube, how *would* you do it?"

Megan felt compelled to answer his question, indirectly. "The old fashioned way."

"What do you mean?" He could tell she was evading him.

"In a uterus." She thought of the Hot and Cold Game again. *Very Warm.* She resumed reading the paper, hoping he would stop pestering her.

Elex was now unstoppable. "So if I had something with blood on it from John F. Kennedy or Abraham Lincoln, you could bring them back to life?" he asked.

She looked up from the paper. "I guess so, according to your theory." *Hot.*

"Or some king, from, like a thousand years ago?"

Megan didn't like the way this was going. "Yeah." *Very Hot*

It was time for the make or break question. "Or, say, Jesus Christ?" Elex's heart was pounding as he asked this, but he maintained the happy, gee-whiz expression on his face.

Blazing Hot. Megan could feel a deep blush sweep across her neck and chest and she knew it would be extremely visible to Elex. She looked at her watch. "Oh, gosh, I have to get back to my experiment," she said, standing. "It was nice talking to you." Megan hurried out of the lab office. "I'm sure Kristina will be here any minute," she called over her shoulder.

Even had he not seen the crimson blush, Elex could tell his questions had transformed Megan's placid ease to near panic. There was no question that he had the answer he wanted. And he was prepared to stake his reputation on it.

4

It took Megan several hours to stop fretting over her weird and provocative conversation with Elex. She was deeply rattled at first, and while she to tried to take her mind off it by immersing herself in work, she could not stop wondering whether Elex actually knew something or was merely following a string of logic. Eventually, the panicky feeling wore off as she reasoned that there was no way that the young journalist could piece together enough clues to confidently land at the truth. Now a day later, she felt sure that he had been guessing in the dark. Guessing well, to be sure, but only guessing. Furthermore, he never linked that to her pregnancy.

Megan had decided to work from home that morning and was now making slow progress in typing her grant proposal. It wasn't that she didn't know what she wanted to type, nor that she was a slow typist – indeed, she was lightning-fast. The problem was that the baby kept kicking and she would drop one hand from the keyboard to rub her very taut stomach. Her fingers would then linger on her now "outie" belly button and she would think how weird and cool it was that it pushed out so far. By the time her hand found its way back to the keyboard and the home keys and made the first arrhythmic strokes, the baby would kick again and she would repeat the process. Had Megan calculated that her current pace was about ten minutes per line, she might have been frustrated, but she cherished the peaceful moments alone in her apartment with her computer and her herbal tea – and her baby.

Megan began to doze in the cozy comfort of the warm afternoon when an instant message from *"Kristi#1"* – Kristina Abbott – popped up on the computer screen with a gentle ding.

What's going on with my friend, Elex?
Megan was surprised and baffled by the question and responded with a simple "*?*"

The response was very fast, as if Kristina had already been typing it out. *I just saw a video he put on YouTube*

Megan kept it simple. *So?*

It's about you and your baby

Megan felt a cold chill pass her spine and settle in her legs.

There was something, after all, to yesterday's conversation. Her stomach felt queasy at the same time and the baby's poorly timed kick made her think she was going to vomit. *Where on YouTube?* She queried Kristina.

Can't miss it – Featured Site. Launch YouTube!!!!

Kristina's prompt was completely unnecessary. Megan was already on the internet and her fingers were guiding the mouse to find the YouTube bookmark as quickly as possible. *Hang on*. She stared at the buffering progress bar at the bottom of her screen. "Come on you antiquated piece of shit," she snapped at her computer.

Kristina messaged again as Megan waited. *Is it true?*

Computer's 2 slow! Not there yet As Megan hit the "Send" button the YouTube screen suddenly popped up and she could see Elex's screen shot front and center. The two and a half minute video entitled "God's Back" had been viewed 37,817 times and was rated four and half stars. "Oh, Jesus!" she exclaimed and involuntarily put her hand back on her stomach.

There yet?

"Leave me the hell alone," Megan yelled back, but thinking better of it, she answered simply. *Just a sec* Despite having no doubts about the video's content, she launched it. Again it took a moment to load and then her screen was filled with a head shot of Elex sitting in front of his computer in his bedroom. As he started speaking, Megan thought he seemed slightly drunk.

"Are you all ready for the Second Coming? It's about a week away, and before you close this screen thinking that I'm some kind of crazy, please know that I'm the Editor of Cornell University's *Daily Sun* newspaper and that I would have broken this story on the front page of that esteemed journal. Unfortunately, my editorial board refused to let me publish this 'cuz it seemed too farfetched. But it's true and I can prove it. Listen up.

"Cornell Genetics Professor Lisa Duffield has devised a way

to clone people from their blood – and they have one in process. And it's not just some cool celebrity or a professional athlete or Abraham Lincoln, although that woulda been kinda cool. No, they've gone big time. A certain post-doc is . . . let's just say, very pregnant with a baby cloned from blood found on the Cross. Yes, *The* Cross. It would be capitalized in black and white on newsprint if my stupid editorial board had let me scoop it in the *Sun*. The Cross that Jesus died on after they drove nails through his hands and his feet and cut his side open with a spear. And now he's coming back to us as a little baby. Look up for a bright star, 'cuz one oughta be guiding wise men to Tompkins County, New York. More wise men, that is.

"I hope you're up to date on all your confessions—"

Megan had heard enough. She reached back to the computer's power strip and flipped it off without thinking about Kristina's pending questions. "Shit!" The baby kicked her tender stomach again and she suppressed the urge to throw up. "This is a disaster." She rose from the desk and walked – more like waddled – to the kitchen to find her purse and the cell phone in it. Lisa needed to know what was going on and help her figure out what to do. Nobody was supposed to know all this, and now there were at least thirty-eight thousand people in on the secret. *How did it leak?* she kept asking herself as she quickly dialed Lisa's home number.

"Hello?" It was Tom, who had awakened from a nap to answer the phone.

"Who told?!"

"Megan?" It sounded like her, but Megan wasn't normally given to shouting. Tom had never experienced pregnant women and their legendary hormonal moods. Maybe he was glad Lisa couldn't get pregnant, he thought selfishly.

"Your little science project is all over the internet!" It hadn't occurred to Megan to direct her ire at Tom before she phoned, but now it seemed like a wonderful idea.

Tom was still groggy from dozing. "Megan, what are you talking about?" He recognized that any reference to him and science had something to do with the cloning. He was suddenly very awake. "Megan, what's going on?" he asked anxiously.

"Kristina Abbott's friend, Elex – he's the Editor of the *Daily Sun* – he put a video on YouTube about the baby and who it is. It's already been viewed thirty-eight thousand times and that's just in the last couple of hours."

"That shithead! What did you tell him? He's a newspaper editor for god's sake. They're not exactly known for keeping juicy stories to themselves. They'll even make it up if they don't have anything better to publish." Tom's anxiety had been completely supplanted by anger.

Megan became defensive. "I didn't tell him anything. Do you think I'm crazy? Is Lisa there?"

"Yeah, she's somewhere around, maybe out in the yard. I'll get her." Tom's head was spinning as he quickly worked through the options. "We've got to get out of here. It's going to turn into a circus before we know it. Hang on, I've got a call coming in." Tom looked at the display, recoiling as he read – **F THATCHER 555-2787**. "Holy shit, the Dean's calling me. Megan, listen to me. Pack a bag, we've got to get out of here. We'll call you as soon as we're on the way."

Now thoroughly panicked, Megan was happy to take Tom's clear and confident direction. "Alright. But dammit, Tom, what a mess you've made of this!"

"I know, I'm sorry. Megan, I have to answer this. Just so you know, I am going to lie through my teeth to the Dean. And you have to deny everything as well."

"Okay. Hurry. Bye."

Tom cut over to the other call and tried to sound relaxed. "Hello?"

"Tom? It's Dean Thatcher."

348

"Hello, sir. You shouldn't be working on a Saturday," Tom teasingly admonished as cheerfully as he could. "What can I do for today? Is everything alright with the collection?"

"Well, Tom, I am here with the External Relations staff. They're monitoring some very strange stories that have broken on the internet related to you and your wife and . . . a baby?" The Dean was obviously very uncomfortable with the subject he was about to broach. He decided to try to draw it out of Tom, rather than explain. "Do you know what I am talking about? I mean, have you heard this story?"

Tom didn't want to answer too quickly. "Ummm . . . No. Did you say 'a baby'? No. Can you give me a little more help?" He knew not to push it too far with the Dean, who was both savvy and perceptive.

"This is going to sound a little bit strange, but there's an allegation on YouToo . . . sorry, what's that?" he conferred with someone at his end of the line. "YouTube – that video website. Well, there's an allegation that you and your wife are cloning . . . " Thatcher paused to clear his throat, twice. "There's an allegation that you and your wife are cloning Jesus Christ." He laughed nervously.

Tom laughed louder. "Jesus Christ? You didn't just say what I thought you said, did you?"

"Well, I knew that it sounded farfetched, but we have already had an inquiry from one of those . . . blogging? . . . news sites about whether we had a statement. We thought we should, you know, follow protocol and at least ask you."

"So, you want to hear me deny that we're cloning Jesus Christ?" The revelation that news sites were already chasing the story was all Tom needed to prompt his finding Lisa and begin their hasty escape from Forest Home. He strode down the hall to the nursery. "Dean Thatcher, are you pulling my leg? Do you really have to answer these wackos?"

"I'm sorry, Tom. Yes, we need to deny it."

"And, am I understanding that you mean Jesus Christ, the son of God, sent to redeem us, et cetera, et cetera?"

"Yes, Tom."

Tom had just found Lisa, who was measuring the walls for the Noah's Ark decorative border. She assumed that the call was for her and stood, reaching for the phone and mouthing the question, *Who is it?* Tom didn't hand her the telephone. Instead, he just looked her in the eyes and said, "Well, Dean Thatcher, I appreciate your asking. I can categorically deny that we are cloning Jesus Christ."

Lisa paled instantly and covered her mouth before she could cry out in surprise and blow Tom's calm denial. She grabbed his arm and squeezed tight. Tom continued, "Well, sir, I hope that's what you were looking for."

"Yes, Tom, I am sorry that we had to bother you with such a strange request. We'll take it from here."

"Not a problem. Let me know if there are any other bizarre things my wife and I are accused of doing."

"Will do. I hope this is all. Bye."

Tom had barely signed off and closed the connection before Lisa blurted out, "What the hell is going on?" He grabbed her arm and began steering her back into the main hall.

"Megan called a few minutes ago and said that Elex had posted a video on YouTube about what we're doing and that it's already been viewed by a 'bijillion' people. And then, two seconds later, Dean Thatcher called – he was with the External Relations people – saying that some news website formally inquired as to whether it was true. He was calling for a denial – you heard what I said."

Lisa couldn't count the number of questions that simultaneously popped into her head, some of them appropriate and helpful, others neither. The only one that came out was, "Should we look at the video?" She quickly realized this belonged to the latter set and wished she could replace it with something more sensible, but Tom just jumped on it in his frustration and worry.

"Look at it?! To see if he got the details right? It sounds to me like he's captured the essence. No, we have to get out of here. I told Megan that we would call on our way to pick her up. We need to go!"

"Go where?"

"Away."

Lisa cried all the way to Megan's house, quieting herself only while she called Megan to say that they were on their way, as well as to take a call from Claire. "Sweetie," Claire had said, "the fact that the cloning got out is pretty alarming, but how did they come up with Jesus Christ?" They agreed to continue denying the cloning allegation and that it would probably die away quickly as too preposterous. Lisa ended the call abruptly with a promise to call back as quickly as possible, and as soon as she hung up, began crying again.

They reached Megan's apartment and helped her out to the car with her overnight bag. Tom had already backed out of the driveway and struck out on the road north out of Ithaca before Megan finally asked, "Where are we going?"

Tom reprised his previous answer with slightly less emphasis. "Away."

"That's helpful," Megan responded. Her cell phone rang and she answered before Tom could intercede. "Hello? . . . Hi, Alli . . . What!? Don't be ridiculous . . . Of course I'm pregnant. Did you think I was just putting on weight and carrying it funny? . . A sperm bank . . . Well, thanks for at least asking, I guess . . . Gotta go . . . Bye." Megan and Tom had maintained eye contact via the rear view mirror for the duration of the call. He trusted her, but didn't want to allow any chinks in the armor of their story.

"Nobody should take any more calls," he declared brusquely. "Turn off the cell phones now."

Lisa and Megan complied, but were starting to take exception to Tom's imperious manner. Lisa realized she needed to pull herself together, and that standing up to Tom served as a good prompt to help her do so. "Tom, we're all in this together," she began, deftly avoiding the desire to point out that she thought it was mostly his fault. "Let's stop yelling at each other and ordering each other around." Again, she left out that he was the only one doing this, but only Megan noticed. "I know we are headed 'away', but do you have any idea where exactly?" She reached out and held his hand.

"I haven't figured that out yet," he admitted sheepishly, relieved that he might be able to cede responsibility for the decision to someone else. "It was going to be just a matter of time before the shit hit the fan and we were trapped in Ithaca – and potentially separated from each other. I thought if we got out of reach, we would be able to buy some time and figure out how to make it all go away."

"I don't think this is going to go away – particularly with a baby as perpetual evidence," Lisa replied.

"Then we need a common story. Did we clone? If so, who? Megan just told someone we used a sperm bank. What is Claire going to say? Shit! We need to call her back." Tom's head was still spinning.

"Relax, relax, Claire will use her head. All she has to do is claim patient confidentiality – I'm sure she'll do that." Certain of Claire's reliability, Lisa started to think more clearly. "Let's go to my parents' house in Cansego. It's out in the middle of nowhere and will take a while for anyone to track us there. My folks are down at the lake – they won't care." Lisa's parents still lived in the old farmhouse in which she had grown up. It lay on the outskirts of a small village north of Syracuse.

Before even voicing his agreement to this very good idea,

Tom ran through the route in his mind. Coincidentally, they were already headed in the right general direction, and with a turn at the next intersection, they would be on the fastest route there. Megan spoke up from the backseat, "Do I get a vote on this?"

Tom and Lisa exchanged a look which both understood meant *Not really*, but they simultaneously responded, "Yes."

"I'm less than two weeks from delivering – am I going to have the baby there? Is there a hospital close by?"

Lisa knew the geography best and was quick to reassure her. "Syracuse is only a half hour, and there are a bunch of good hospitals there. Megan, you'll love Cansego. It's really quiet and we'll be out of the spotlight. This is really the best thing for you in these last couple of days. You don't want the phone ringing off the hook and people badgering you." Lisa didn't have to work too hard to sound convincing because she believed this was true.

5

"Senator Massey," Chief of Staff Dave Tinskey whispered tentatively as he inclined just the top half of his head inside the partially-opened door. Only an hour earlier, the senator had retreated to her interior office for a brief nap, still exhausted from a red-eye return from California. She hadn't asked *not* to be awakened, yet Tinskey bore a few scars from similar occasions, and he subconsciously hid his body out of harm's way. When she didn't rouse he repeated her name, "Senator Massey?"

The senator opened one eye without moving a single other muscle in her body. She was thinking *This had better be good*, but answered simply, "Yes?"

Tinskey was relieved. He pushed his head a little further into the open space. "There's a very strange story developing upstate. We thought you ought to know about it." He realized he hadn't figured out how to summarize this story in a way that wouldn't get him fired for insanity. Tinskey paused and turned to look at the two staffers huddled behind him. He considered sending one of them in his stead, but seeing their abject consternation decided he needed to handle this himself.

Senator Dionne Massey, still immobile, prompted him to begin explaining his presence, "What?"

"Well, the story originally broke on the internet –"

"David, please come into the room. You look like you're hiding behind the door."

He stepped into the room. "Do you mind if Katie and Ron join us?"

"Just a minute." She swung her legs off the couch, slid her feet into her shoes, smoothed her skirt and combed her fingers through her shoulder length hair. "Okay." Squeezing her eyes shut for a moment she put on her business face.

Tinskey called the junior staffers in behind him, and like their boss, they quickly straightened their hair and retucked their shirts. The room was quite dark thanks to thick curtains drawn to hold back the bright sunlight. Tinskey reached to flip on the lights, but Senator's quickly upraised hand held him long enough for her to turn on a small desk lamp. He began again, "As I said, the story first broke on the internet." He was stalling for time.

"You said that, David. Get on with it."

"Well, it all began yesterday with a video on YouTube, with the student editor of the Cornell University newspaper . . . Katie, what's it called?"

"The *Cornell Daily Sun*," she answered very quickly.

"Right, the Sun's editor making an allegation that one of the Professors there has cloned a baby – well, it's still in utero with a surrogate – from a human."

"Is it possible to do that? I thought that was still technically impossible."

"The Professor," Tinskey turned to look at Katie, and she answered without his asking.

"Professor Lisa Duffield." She filled in.

"Duffield is a leader in her field of human genetics and has won numerous accolades. It's not out of the realm of possibility – particularly for someone of her expertise and lab capability." The Chief of Staff could tell that the Senator was processing what she had heard and he waited to add more. He knew she liked to direct the conversation.

"What's our position on cloning?"

"We're *for* funding the science to understand the genome, but we're against actual human cloning. The Republicans would stir the Church into a frenzy on that."

"Or the other way around," she said with a smile. "Is it legal?"

"Universities receiving Federal funding aren't allowed to work on it – although we don't know yet that she did it in her lab. On the other hand, this was Republican legislation, we don't have to endorse it."

"New York State law?"

"Pretty confusing – we're still reading through it. It doesn't appear to specifically ban what this YouTube guy says Duffield did."

Senator Massey was quick to drive to action. "So, you want me to make a statement?" she asked.

Tinskey bit his lip. "Dionne, it's a bit more complicated than that."

"Why?"

The staff people exchanged worried looks. Katie and Ron held their breath as Tinskey inhaled deeply. "The issue relates to whom they're cloning."

The senator suddenly looked aghast. "Is it me?" She thought she now understood her staff's strange behavior.

"No, no," Tinskey was quick to answer, "not exactly." He suppressed the urge to chuckle, despite the esteem in which he held the senator from New York. He spoke quickly, both to get it out in one breath, as well as to save the senator from further awkward guesses. "The allegation is that they are cloning Jesus Christ." *There, I've said it*, he thought.

It took her a minute to take in what her Chief had said. "What? Come on!"

"We couldn't make this up. And we certainly wouldn't disturb you for a joke." Tinskey sensed the oncoming wrath and wanted to ward it off. "We know it sounds crazy."

Katie chimed in, "We all got a good laugh when it was first kicking around the internet. But then after initial denials, the University clammed up, and then some reputable news services were picking it up. You know, almost as a just a way to lead into cloning news, which cycles hot and cold."

"But it's just ridiculous," the Senator protested. She looked into the eyes of the three staff people standing around her, searching for a hint of humor. There was none to be seen. "Isn't it?"

Tinskey was relieved by her question. "Not that ridiculous. Duffield has published a number of papers on reconstituting DNA from very small body fluid samples. This is just the next step."

"Yeah? Where exactly does one go to find Christ's body fluids? eBay? Come on guys, you can't chase this crazy stuff. We've got real work to do." She was too tired to chew her staff out further. "Dave, can we look at the afternoon's agenda?"

"Yeah, certainly. But should we just close out the cloning story? Two things –" he wanted to make it brief. "First, the fact that they might be cloning a person still seems plausible and is going to become a lightning rod issue. Secondly, Duffield's husband, Thomas, also teaches at Cornell," Tinskey looked at the reliable Katie momentarily, to ask what subject Tom taught, but remembered it quickly and said it before she could get it out. "European Medieval History. Anyway, he just authored a catalog on a collection of artifacts which were donated to Cornell. Ron's printed out the online version." As Tinskey said this, Ron dutifully held up a thick folder for the senator to see. "They're amazing things – the sword that killed Thomas à Becket, for example – but none of them seemed linked to the Bible. However, we don't know what items may not have been put into the catalog. Guess who donated the collection." He knew the senator would be drawn back in by this item, and he provided it himself when she raised one eyebrow. "John Strater."

"Oh, crap!" Senator Massey and John Strater saw eye-to-eye on very few issues. She didn't know this from personal contact with him – indeed, they had only spoken once, empty pleasantries at a charity fundraising. Instead, she knew this because he had bankrolled the last campaign attempting to unseat her. Despite winning both times, she knew he was still a powerful and wealthy force. "Has our relationship with him warmed?" she asked hopefully.

"Not particularly."

"Tread carefully," she cautioned. "He'll spend a lot to get his way. Wish he'd spend it on us . . . . Anything else?"

"No one can find the Duffields or Megan Brack, a post-doctoral student from Duffield's lab who's been named as the surrogate." This had been the final piece of information which aroused Tinskey's interest when his staff briefed him an hour ago. It had the same effect on Senator Massey.

"Alright, Dave, I see where you're going. Obviously we need to stay close to this one." Tinskey breathed a sigh of relief. "But the Jesus-thing sounds too ludicrous, and we can't lend it any credibility. No statement – and work the Q&A's to be very vague. Let's dig into the Duffields as best we can – you know, phone calls, travel, et cetera. Ron, can I see that file?" She took the file and flipped through the thick wad of print outs, quickly reading snippets from each page. "Strater will certainly get a big tax write off for this. It may be worth checking into that later on. Maybe it's time to check in with some of our friends at IRS." She eyed Tinskey and he nodded, then she handed back the sheaf of papers. "Let's reloop on the cloning story in a couple of hours."

"Yes, Ma'am," the Chief of Staff responded. Their marching orders delivered, the team quickly filed out of the office. "Brief me in an hour," Tinskey added to his subordinates once they were out of the senator's earshot.

<h1 style="text-align:center">6</h1>

Time had been kind to Cansego, but the elements had not. Situated near the eastern edge of Lake Ontario it was hammered by storms rolling east off the vast water – pelting rain in the summer, driving snow in winter and wind year round. Thank goodness the sun was so often masked by clouds, otherwise all the paint would have faded from the few buildings which huddled close to form the village center. Yet the sun was out this warm September afternoon and it cast a charitable light on the white clapboard houses whose glory had been wearing away since the Civil War. The fact that they had any glory remaining after one hundred-forty plus years was a testament to how handsome and proud this village had once been. During the 1830's this part of Upstate New York had been the fertile frontier – the hills were softer and the land less rocky than parts east in New England from where farmers flocked enthusiastically. Here they cheerfully cleared the land to feed the young American democracy, grew prosperous and built hundreds of villages just like Cansego. In a nod to America's still-experimental government, they gave their towns names which recalled ancient Greece and their buildings bore classical architectural styles. Cansego was different only in that it retained the traditional Oneida place name – the white settlers kept that after throwing the natives off the land.

Tom knew to slow the car as soon as they entered the village – not because Lisa wanted to point out to Megan all the sights from her childhood, but rather because there was almost always a cop hiding behind the brick Post Office and he would ticket anyone going a smidgen over the 25 mph speed limit. There was no speed trap today, but Tom crawled through the village anyway. He liked hearing Lisa talk about the village's history, interweaving it with her own recollections of how much things had changed since she was little. There was her church, the town hall where she performed piano recitals and the small general store where she would buy penny candy with her allowance. All three of them enjoyed a break from their worries, and Megan was so completely charmed by this village that she stopped thinking about the mild contractions she had experienced for the last half hour.

They passed through the village in less than a minute – there was no traffic light to slow them down – and proceeded the final mile to Lisa's parent's home. Megan was relieved to finally step out of the car and stretch her legs. She was finding that every position was uncomfortable. If she were standing she wanted to sit and if she were sitting she wanted to stand. Now after ninety minutes she not only needed to move, she was desperate to visit the bathroom and called that out to Lisa who quickly showed her the way. Several minutes later, Megan returned for the proper tour. Tom, who had visited this house many times over the past fifteen years, busied himself with ferrying their bags inside and up the stairs. He decided that he and Lisa would stay in her old room, and they would put Megan in the guest room. As he stood in the latter and peered out the window, he spied the women talking in the front yard, certain of what Lisa was saying even though he couldn't hear them.

"The farm was built in 1835 by my great-great-great grandfather," Lisa said proudly. "Besides being a successful lawyer and merchant, he was already the richest farmer in the county when he bought this property. The soil was so good that it made him even wealthier." Standing in the shade of an enormous oak tree, Lisa pointed across the road. "He tilled the land on that side of the road – that's why the barn and corn crib are over there. The vegetable garden was here in the stone walled space next to the house. He kept the land here behind the house for lumber and hunting." They crossed the road and walked through the outbuildings, all of which were in an immaculate state of repair and tidiness. Crossing back across the deserted road they paused in the shade of the towering oak in the front yard.

"You were so lucky to grow up here. It's beautiful – so peaceful, so wholesome." Megan was enthralled. The day's stresses had evaporated completely. "I can just imagine you swinging under this tree in a little checked dress."

"We've got pictures of it," Lisa laughed. "Let me show you the inside."

They entered the house and toured the ground floor, then the upstairs, the attic and circled down the back stairs, stopping in the kitchen where Tom was boiling the kettle. "Can I offer you a cup of tea?" he asked.

"Is there anything without caffeine?" Megan responded – then wincing, closing her eyes and leaning over she emitted a deep "owwww".

Lisa was just at her side and swiftly grabbed her elbow to support her. "Megan, are you okay?" Tom had come to the other side and they helped her to a chair at the dining table. Megan's eyes had opened but she hadn't yet spoken, so Lisa repeated her question.

"Yeah, yeah. It's passed now. I think it was a contraction."

"Oh my God," Tom exclaimed. "Are you having the baby now?" He had envisioned this happening while they were in Cansego, but pictured himself remaining calm.

Lisa's stern glare put a stopper on his panic. "Don't be ridiculous, Tom. Contractions happen more and more the closer you get to delivering. Right, Megan?"

Megan had regained her breath. "I guess. I was having contractions in the car, but not as strong as that one."

"Why didn't you say anything?" Tom blurted out.

Again, Lisa was the thoughtful one. "Why don't we just give Claire a quick call?" She pulled her cell phone out of her pocket and turned it on. "I've got her cell number in here." Lisa concentrated on the small screen as she scrolled through the choices, found Claire's number and pressed the call button. Within a few seconds she heard Claire's voice at the other end.

"Lisa?" Claire answered somewhat urgently.

"Hi, Claire."

"Where are you guys? Things have gone crazy here. I thought this whole thing would die of its own weight but it seems to be picking up steam. Somebody in your lab told a reporter that I was your – and Megan's – OB and the phone has been ringing off the hook since then. We're having trouble keeping the lines open for our patients." Claire paused to get her breath and then restarted. "What is all this talk about Jesus? I mean, have you heard this stuff? It's kooky! Where are you guys?"

Lisa tried not to be rattled by Claire's apparent panic. "Settle down, Claire. We're up in Cansego at my parents' house. Remember you and Bob came up here with us a couple years ago? Anyway, we need your help as a doctor right now."

Claire couldn't fight off the sarcastic quip. "Isn't that what got us into this?"

"Yeah, okay, I'm sorry. But really, Claire, Megan has had some really sharp contractions over the past couple of hours." Lisa was trying to stay focused.

"Is she there?" Claire asked calmly.

"Yes."

Claire was back in full doctor mode. "Is she having a contraction right now?"

Lisa whispered the question to Megan, who shook her head. "No."

"Can I talk to her?"

"I can relay the questions," Lisa protested.

"I know, Lisa, but she's my patient." Lisa dutifully handed the phone over to Megan.

"Hey, Claire." Megan was now upbeat, the pain having subsided. She explained the nature of her contractions over the past couple of hours – that they were quite irregular and the last one came on after she and Lisa tramped all around the house as well as up and down a couple of sets of stairs. Claire's direction was fairly obvious and straightforward. Stop walking around, lie down and try to take it easy. If the contractions came back and especially if they became more regular, she should call Claire back. When Megan acknowledged that this all made sense and that she would do her best to comply, Claire asked for Lisa again.

"Lisa, please keep an eye on her," Claire said once the phone was passed. "I remember your parents farm being to hell and gone from civilization. If anything goes wrong, please give me a call, okay? Is there a hospital around there?"

"There're a bunch of hospitals in Syracuse and the closest is only twenty – twenty-five minutes at the longest."

With her physician responsibilities out of the way, Claire resumed the line of questions with which she opened the conversation several minutes earlier. "So, Lisa, can you tell me what's going on? This thing about cloning Jesus – what are they talking about?"

Lisa thought for a long time, and at last decided she simply wouldn't answer.

"Okay. Should I read anything into the fact that you won't deny it?" Claire suddenly hoped that the call had dropped and that Lisa was jabbering away at the other end about how ridiculous it was. She imagined Lisa telling her to "get a grip" and then being embarrassed for even asking. Suddenly, Lisa's voice at the other end shattered that hope.

"Claire, Megan *is* going to have a baby. That's all that matters. She needs your help to have it safely. Can we count on that?"

"Of course, Lisa. It's my job. But I just wish you would let me know what you . . . what *we* have gotten ourselves into. I am part of this, you know."

"I'll explain everything when it all calms down. I promise. But now isn't the best time – we'll need more time for the whole story."

Claire allowed an ironic chuckle. "I'll bet we will. Hopefully we won't end up *doing* time."

"Don't talk to the media, Claire."

"Lisa, I'm not an idiot. Besides, it's a matter of patient confidentiality. I'm bound not to say anything."

"I'm sorry we have gotten you into this," Lisa said genuinely. Glancing at Tom she added, "Tom especially." Tom scowled as he heard her say this.

Claire laughed again, "Oh God, say no more. Let's talk tomorrow – and call me beforehand if Megan needs me."

"'Kay, bye."

7

"Gracious me, this is the third call I've received about that artifact. It's most perplexing," said a tired Professor Warwick Adams into the telephone receiver, "You know it's getting quite late in the evening here. Could we possibly chat tomorrow?"

Katie was excited to have tracked the professor down in his home and wasn't going to let him off too quickly. His name and number had shown up repeatedly in Tom Duffield's phone records, suggesting the two men had spoken often. Unfortunately, Duffield had only called his office phone and thus Katie had to call several British Telecom offices to track down Adams' home number. "I'm sorry, sir. We're just hoping you can shed some light on an allegation that this relic is actually a piece of the Cross – the Cross from the Bible, that is. However, Professor Duffield listed it in the collection catalog as part of the arrow that killed Richard the Lionheart. We know you are an expert in this field and thought you could help." Katie looked up to see Dave Tinskey approaching her desk and tapping his watch. She was already fifteen minutes late for their planned reconnect meeting and they were scheduled to see the senator shortly. "It is quite important, sir, I'm sorry."

"Well, it isn't every day that someone from an American senator's staff calls, I must say." Adams went on to explain that his research suggested strongly that this was a piece of the Cross and that he had told Duffield so – indeed, they had discussed it face-to-face. Adams remembered Duffield acting strangely during the discussion. He could not explain why Duffield ignored his new attribution and put it in the catalog per the earlier one. And no, he hadn't known that Duffield had listed it that way until someone called a couple of days ago.

Katie was taking copious notes of what he said and was just about to ask who had called him when Tinskey leaned over her shoulder and whispered, "Let's go," in her ear. Katie nodded and held up one finger to buy another moment.

"So, Professor Adams, is there any doubt in your mind that this is a piece of the Cross?"

"Well, my dear. The years, the people, the legends that stand between us and that fateful day on Golgotha are too numerous to count. But I can tell you that King Richard believed it and because of that altered the course of world events by breaking off his crusade. I suppose it comes down to a matter of faith."

"Thank you for your time, sir. Sorry again for disturbing you at home." Katie hung up the phone and swung around to face Tinskey. "He believes –"

Tinskey cut her off. "The senator wants to see us now. You'll just have to brief us all together." Katie picked up her notebook and hurried after the Chief of Staff to Senator Massey's office. Ron met them at the door and they filed in quietly together, took seats at the conference table and sat in silence as the senator finished a phone call. When she took a seat at the head of the table, Tinskey began the briefing. "Senator, the topline update is that we haven't been able to debunk the story yet. As strange as it sounds, the pieces are actually coming together rather than falling apart. Katie, can you recap what you've learned."

Katie replayed her conversations with William Rogers, Dean Thatcher and Warwick Adams. It all supported a plausible hypothesis that Tom Duffield had both the means and the attitude (the latter according to Rogers) to clone a child, particularly when combined with his wife's capability in the laboratory. The fact that he had suppressed the identity of the Cross relic was extremely suspicious, they agreed. Tinskey then turned it over to Ron, who was charged with tracking down the three fugitives.

"We haven't found them yet," Ron admitted, "but I've enlisted a lot of 'help'. I think it's just a matter of time." As if on cue, his phone rang and he picked it up to see the number. "This could be it, do you mind if I take it?"

Tinskey and Massey simultaneously answered "No" without hesitating.

"Hey, Josh. Whatcha got?" Ron barked. "Yes . . . where? To Dr. Prentiss' office?" Ron nodded at Tinskey. "Got it triangulated? Hang on." He flipped open his notebook and picked up the pen. "What time? And you said between Watertown and Syracuse? Cool. Give me a call if you get anything else. Awesome, dude, thanks." Ron closed his phone and smiled. "We traced a call from Lisa Duffield's cell phone to an obstetrician, Dr. Claire Prentiss. It came from somewhere north of Syracuse."

"What's up there?" Tinskey asked.

"Not much," Ron joked, and then he flipped open a folder. "I think she – Lisa – is from up that way." He quickly scanned a print out of her CV. "Yeah, here it is. Cansego."

"Is that in New York?" Massey asked.

The staffers looked at each other – expressionless. "I think so," said Tinskey, ever diplomatic, "but let's get a map."

"I've got it here," Katie said as she typed the name into her computer and spun the screen around to show the map. "There's not much up there."

"Just the three people we're looking for," Massey said. "I'll bet you dollars to doughnuts they've gone to her home. Can you check whether her parents still live there?"

Ron jumped up from the table. "I'm on it."

"Ron," Senator Massey called out as he was leaving the room, "great work!" Turning back to her Chief of Staff she asked for an update on the media situation.

He explained that the Questions & Answers were prepared but they hadn't received any calls yet. He would cover the message track later on, although he advised that he handle any enquiries so as not to give the story too much credence. Coverage was still focusing on the YouTube story and cloning in general. The Duffields' disappearance with their surrogate mother was getting increased coverage.

"Do you think we're the only ones who know where she is?" Massey asked.

"Yeah, us . . . and Josh, I guess. I'll make sure he stays quiet. There has been one story that Lisa Duffield and Megan Brack are working in a state institution. That part of Cornell is within the New York State University system."

"Please tell me that Lisa Duffield has some NIH grants," Massey pleaded. Katie nodded. "Excellent," Massey said, "so the Federal government has some standing here. Katie, can you get the Governor of New York on the line, please." Katie rose and went to Massey's desk, picked up the receiver and punched several buttons.

Tinskey watched Katie thoughtfully and then tentatively asked Massey, "Can you tell me what you're considering?"

"I think this is a great opportunity for the state and federal government to cooperate on raising a child." She stood and walked to her desk.

"Here she is," Katie said into the receiver and handed it to the senator.

Massey drew her graying hair behind her ear and cleared her throat. "Governor Spangler, hello, it's Dionne Massey. Have you been watching the news?"

8

Tom was the first to rise the next morning. He had awakened at 5 am and tossed and turned for a full thirty minutes before he admitted to himself that trying to fall back asleep was futile. He arose as quietly as possible and crept downstairs to the sitting room, switched on the television and turned to the twenty-four hour news channel. Tom knew the day was going to be difficult when the first thing he saw were the words, "Human Cloning at Cornell?" under the perky newscaster's face and an inset aerial photo of the Biotechnology Building.

" – although the University denied the allegations, the three people named in the potential cloning scandal, married Professors Lisa and Thomas Duffield and their surrogate mother, Megan Brack, a post-doctoral scientist, left Ithaca abruptly and cannot be reached for comment. Their whereabouts are currently unknown. When we come back from this break we'll talk to Medical Ethicist, Dr. Mary Morrison about the human cloning debate. Don't go away."

"Oh my God!" Tom said louder than he wished, given the sleeping women upstairs. He quickly began surfing the channels to find the other news stations. Within thirty minutes Tom found three others, including a local Syracuse station, which were airing the story – each with their own variation. "YouTube's Biggest Scoop Ever" showed a portion of Elex's YouTube video; "Playing God with God?" Interviewed a televangelist about whether Christ *could* be cloned; the third story, "Christ Cloning Hoax?" Featured a "noted" geneticist (from a university Tom had never heard of) who claimed the alleged cloning was impossible. "Shows how much you know, dipshit," Tom said aloud, just as Lisa came down the stairs.

"What are you doing up so early?" she asked, rubbing one eye.

"I'm enjoying our fifteen minutes of fame," he answered grinning.

Lisa looked at the television and her eyes opened wide. "Is it on the television?" she asked, mouth agape.

"Oh, yes! On every news station. Plus we've got bible thumpers, scientists, ethicists jumping on the bandwagon. There's quite a party shaping up."

"What should we do?" She was surprised that Tom did not seem alarmed.

Tom had been working on this question for the last forty-five minutes and had not yet come up with the answer. For Lisa's sake he didn't say so. "Stay here, lie low, hope that some bigger news happens to distract them all."

"And what if they don't get distracted?"

Lisa was always thinking through the possible scenarios, Tom observed. "We'll have Claire come up and deliver the baby here." He shrugged.

"And stay up here forever? We have jobs. You're already missing all your lectures today." Lisa didn't like Tom's plan. "We should just go back to Ithaca and calmly deny everything. We'll say we just wanted to get away for a day and introduce Megan to my parents."

"Morning, guys, did I hear my name?" Megan appeared at the head of the stairs and descended to join them in front of the television. The expressions on Tom and Lisa's faces – and their silence – made her immediately apprehensive. "What's wrong?" Tom described the news coverage and the options he and Lisa had briefly discussed. Megan reflected quietly and then said, "I think going back this morning is the best plan, but I would love to have my baby here."

Nothing over the past two days had struck Lisa with the same thunderclap shock as what Megan just said. *My baby!? My?!* Lisa desperately tried to discern whether Megan had misspoken – she was pregnant, sleepy and trying to manage so much confusing information. It was a bewildering situation, after all. Even so, Lisa felt the need to set the record straight, even if subtly. "*The* baby would probably be better off being born in a hospital," Lisa stated, the only one of the three who heard a gentle emphasis on the word "the". Megan and Tom both nodded their agreement. Lisa went on to suggest that they eat breakfast and then depart. They could be back in Ithaca before noon.

This plan was well in motion – breakfast served, coffee brewed and the trio ready to leave the table and pack their belongings when the phone rang. Lisa instinctively jumped up to answer it – she had always done this growing up – and found her mother at the other end.

"Your father and I have been worried sick about you for the last couple of hours. We thought maybe you'd been kidnapped, by whom we couldn't imagine. You're on the news programs, and they said you'd disappeared. We couldn't reach you on your home phone – "

But for the anxiety in her mother's voice, Lisa almost chuckled. "Mom, Mom, settle down. Who would kidnap us? We're fine. We just came up to get away for an afternoon."

"I didn't have a chance to neaten up for you."

"It's fine. I wish our house were this neat." Lisa exchanged glances with Tom, whom she blamed for all mess at home.

"What's all this news about Jesus? I didn't even think Tom believed in Jesus, isn't that what you told me?"

"Mother, please. First of all, it's all crazy talk. Really, come on. Cloning Jesus? Secondly, Tom does believe in Jesus." Tom harrumphed in the background.

"Well, then, going to church every now and again wouldn't kill him, would it?" Lisa's mother was reliably consistent on certain points. Then picking up another typical line of discussion, she said, "If you all want to stay another day, your father and I can come back and do a nice barbecue or something."

Lisa explained that they were headed back to Ithaca within the hour but thanked her for the offer. Committing to call her mother back over the weekend she hung up the phone. Within seconds, and even before Lisa could step back to the breakfast table, the telephone rang again and Lisa picked it up quickly. "Yes, mother, what did you forget to tell me?"

There was silence at the other end of the line and then a very business-like, "Please hold for Senator Massey." A click, another click. Lisa thought this was one of those recorded pre-election exhortations, although the first voice sounded live. *Is it election time? Not these stupid campaign calls again!* Tom sensed from her expression that it was a telemarketer and told her to hang up – she was just about to do so when a second voice rang out.

"Hello, this is Senator Dionne Massey. With whom am I speaking please?" The greeting was charming and practiced.

Lisa was so stunned that she answered automatically. "This is Lisa Duffield."

Massey was so excited she tingled. "Dr. Duffield, I'm so happy to have reached you."

"Hang up!" Tom repeated from the table, loud enough that Massey could hear it.

"No, please don't hang up, Dr. Duffield. I think it is very important that we speak."

Lisa was rapidly coming to her senses and all five signaled trouble. "What would you like to talk about?" she asked cautiously.

"Thank you for asking. I don't know if you've been watching the news, but there is quite a bit of concern that state and federal money have been used to clone a human being. Now, I think you and I would agree that some of the coverage has gone off the deep end in alleging who the baby might be," Massey had been heavily coached not to say anything specific here, "but there does seem to be evidence that a post-doc in your lab, Dr. Brack I think, is pregnant. Is she there with you?" Massey slid the last question in, hoping to catch Lisa off guard.

"Why don't you go on – tell me why you want to talk to me before I start answering your questions."

"Who is it?" Tom demanded in a stage whisper. Lisa scribbled it down "Sen. Massey" on a note pad and handed it to him.

"Dr. Duffield, I'll get right to the point. We think in order to calm the growing public and media . . . frenzy, that we ought to bring Dr. Brack into state and federal protection."

Lisa's hopes for raising a baby were fading away with every one of Dionne Massey's words. That morning's fears that Megan may be reluctant in giving up the baby seemed insignificant and laughable now that one of the most powerful lawmakers in Washington was suggesting taking Megan into government custody. "I don't think that's necessary. But thank you for your concern," Lisa said.

Massey was not used to being dismissed. "I don't believe that's your choice, Dr. Duffield. May I speak to Dr. Brack? It's really a question for her."

"Did I say she was here?" Lisa looked at Megan, who had read the scribbled note and now held up both hands palms outward to avoid getting drawn into the discussion.

"Please don't toy with me," Massey said, irritated but still calm. "We have some evidence that she is with you and your failure to put her on the line may suggest she is being held against her will." Massey paused to let the subtle threat sink in.

Lisa caught the threat and was angered. "When you find her, you can ask her yourself. Good luck."

"Governor Spangler is prepared to issue an executive order to take her into custody."

"Thanks for the advance notice." Lisa thought she heard a drum beating, and realized it was her own heart pounding blood through her ears. She wondered whether Massey could hear it at the other end.

"You don't know who you're fucking with," Massey snapped.

"Neither do you," Lisa responded. Her legs were shaking so hard that she thought they might give way. She desperately wanted to sit down. "And my mother always told me that word is very unladylike." Lisa enjoyed that immensely. "May I help you with anything else?"

Massey silently took a deep breath. Her more genteel words did not betray the vengeful plans forming in her head. "Thank you for your time this morning, Dr. Duffield. We'll do our level best to keep your location from leaking out to the media. Good day."

Lisa hung up the phone and returned to the table where Tom and Megan waited breathlessly to hear the other half of the conversation. She faithfully reported Massey's terse words, including the profanity, which drew a giggle from Megan, who was shocked that the ever-well-mannered celebrity politician would say such a thing. The trio reviewed the options they had considered earlier and affirmed the decision to return to Ithaca. Claire was there after all, and Lisa was very concerned about bringing the wrong kind of attention to her parents' home. After a few minutes discussion they adjourned to go upstairs and pack up.

Tom was the first one to return downstairs and was just about to exit out the kitchen side door when something out the front window caught his eye. He left his bag by the door and stepped closer to the window, drawing the curtain aside. For an instant, he thought it was Lisa's parents travel van, but then remembered they had sold it last summer. As his eyes adjusted to the bright light he fully realized what he was looking at – a white van with a radio dish on the roof and the letters "WSYA Mobile News – Always First, Always There" emblazoned on the side. It drew to a stop on the grassy verge across the street. Tom knew their escape to Ithaca was now on hold. "Lisa," he called up the stairs, "take your time."

9

True to its promise, the WSYA van was first – several more pulled up within the next two hours – and there. It remained in place throughout the balance of the morning and into the afternoon. Its occupants had been thrilled to transmit live video of Tom, Lisa and Megan peering through the front windows in amazement – and the roving reporter made a dash to the front door to catch them for a live interview. Not surprisingly, however, all three occupants of the Greek Revival farmhouse backed away from the windows, retreated even more swiftly from the summons at the door and took refuge in the rear of the house. From there they could watch the "developing" story on Lisa's parents' ancient television. Every channel now had live feeds from the front-yard and would cut back and forth between reporters at the scene and studio anchors interviewing "relevant experts". Tom was curious how live the coverage really was, and sent Lisa crawling forward to jiggle a curtain while the cameras were trained on the front of the house. They estimated a four second delay and notwithstanding the crisis at hand, agreed that was pretty impressive.

After Tom chased a more emboldened reporter and camera team off the back yard by leaning out the rear door, reminding them this was private property and then adding that no one inside planned any comment to the media, coverage became more skewed to studios. This also coincided with the media's ability to scare up more scientific, religious, medical and ethical experts and bring them in for comment. It was astounding to the three hideouts how many people and groups had a point of view on their story. Even those who neither cared nor put credence in the story of the three people holed up in Cansego, were thrilled to have a spotlight – or for some, an electronic pulpit. There were more than three rings to this circus, Tom observed.

Senator Dionne Massey created another ring to the circus at 2:30pm when the studios cut live to her press conference. She built the drama by deliberately staying in the ready room for five minutes past the promised start time, and then, just as the reporters were running out of inflammatory commentary to mark time, she whisked in cool and solemn. Watching from their sitting room in Cansego, Tom, Lisa and Megan knew this boded poorly for them. Tom muttered the word "bitch" several times but was too tense to say anything else.

"*Good afternoon, everyone,*" Massey began, "*I appreciate your taking time to join me for this brief statement. And I will have to be brief as my plane will be departing shortly for Syracuse.*" There was a stir among the reporters as they realized that their most exciting stories were all tying together. "*I believe some of you are aware of somewhat outlandish allegations coming from that part of New York related to the cloning of a human being.*" Massey was reading from the script Tinskey had prepared. He stood gravely by her side, ready to confer in case any of the questions became thorny. "*Firstly, at this point we believe these allegations to be largely unsupported by rational evidence. While we are informed that Dr. Megan Brack is pregnant and serving as a surrogate mother for Thomas and Lisa Duffield, both professors at Cornell University, we have no evidence that the fetus was not naturally conceived. Unfortunately, however, these three persons have brought some attention to themselves – initially by fleeing their homes in the Ithaca area, and now by refusing to yield themselves to simple public discourse.*"

"Horseshit," Tom blurted out at the television. "We're not obligated to answer any of your nosy questions."

Lisa approached Massey's comments more analytically. Rhetorically she asked, "Since when does simple public discourse involve five television camera crews?" She and Tom returned their attention to the television.

Massey continued, *"Accordingly, they appear to be knowingly fomenting significant controversy and unrest."*

"You're the one who leaked our location!" Megan accused.

"And while none of this is necessarily against the law, we are now very concerned about the health and well-being of the young pregnant woman. We are aware that a call was made to her obstetrician last night, and this morning she was not allowed to take telephone calls." Massey was taking convenient license with the truth. *"Finally, we have some concerns that she's being held against her will."* This provoked a gasp from the crowd of reporters and a flurry of flashes. The crowd was now primed for Massey's self-promotion. *"I have a strong record of standing alongside powerless and often victimized single mothers and mothers-to-be. These are women who are made outcasts of our society, when they should be held up as the society's very core, the prized ones of our towns and cities, lauded and rewarded for the burdens they selflessly bear. A burden irresponsibly heaped upon them by those without the courage to stand in there."*

"What the hell is she talking about?" Lisa called out.

"Consistent with my long track record of defending women like Megan Brack, I have contacted Governor Spangler and gained his cooperation via an Executive Order to welcome her into protective custody. I will be personally escorting Dr. Brack out of the house in Cansego to a joint State and Federal health care team who will ensure that no abuse has taken place and will, at the appropriate time, deliver the baby."

Tom, Megan and Lisa were all dumbstruck. Lisa wished she had really spoken her mind during her telephone conversation that morning, although it probably would have made things even worse.

Tom was stuck on the suggestion of abuse. Megan mourned the loss of her privacy, dwelling on the idea of a team of unknown doctors prodding and poking her for the next ten days.

Massey closed out her prepared statement, "*I am departing shortly for Syracuse and thence with my police escort to the home where young Dr. Brack is being held. I can now take a few questions.*"

"Senator Massey," called out a young reporter in the first rank. "Do you expect any resistance from the people in the house?"

Tinskey had anticipated this question and agreed with the Senator on how she would answer it – she executed perfectly. "*Well, we hope that this can be resolved peacefully and in the best interest –*" She then broke off as rehearsed and leaned to Tinskey who whispered in her ear. She resumed cautiously, "*We know that there are guns registered to that home address, so we will be proceeding with the utmost caution.*"

This was too much for Tom to bear and he angrily stood and turned off the television. "That horrible bitch!" He enunciated the last word with exceeding precision. More profanity surged toward his lips but he held it off while trying to think of something productive to say. Lisa protested his turning off the television but he quickly countered that they had seen enough.

"So what do we do now?" Megan asked, breaking into their discussion.

Tom and Lisa turned and looked at her as if they had forgotten she was there. They turned back to look at one another, each desperately hoping the other had a winning plan. The silence persisted longer than Megan wished. With one hand massaging her stomach, she lifted the other to her forehead and closed her eyes. She prided herself on being able to solve anything, but she realized there was no good solution to what she was now facing. The contractions had returned as well, which alarmed her because she had been resting most of the day – up the stairs once and down the stairs twice, quite slowly each time.

"We can't let them get this baby," Megan declared. "I'm not sure I ever accepted that he's cloned from Jesus, but we know he doesn't have any of the Y-chromosome mutations. None. They'll find the same thing in a matter of days. Do you think Dionne Massey would ever let either one of us have the baby after that?" She shook her head. "I'm not going into protective custody."

"Frankly, Megan, I don't think you're going to have much choice," Tom said.

"I *do* have a choice. Massey said 'welcome her into protective custody' – I don't want it. On what grounds are they going to make me go with them?"

"On the grounds of the Governor's order," Lisa answered.

"But she said 'welcome,'" Megan said petulantly.

"That's only because Massey knows that 'welcome' plays better than 'forcibly seize' when talking about a pregnant woman." Tom had an urge to laugh at his own joke, but he knew the situation was too serious. "I just don't see a way out of this."

Megan was still looking for an alternative. "Do you think that we could stay holed up here and have Claire come and deliver the baby?"

"Here in this house?" Lisa tried not to look aghast.

"Yeah."

"Not if Dionne Massey has anything to do with it."

Megan continued. "I just don't think I can deal with all these strangers inspecting me. I can barely go to the gynecologist – that's why I wanted to meet Claire before I even agreed to all of this. Now I'm going to have the Senator from New York acting as my Lamaze coach for prime time television."

"They don't want you, Megan. They want the baby," Tom said bluntly.

"But the baby's gotta come out of me first, and that's not a public event. It's my body and I don't want to share it with the world." Megan paused and then blurted out, "I haven't even had sex for Christ's sake."

Tom and Lisa were speechless, and so was Megan when she realized what she had said. Only Lisa dared speak. "You've never had sex?" she asked. Megan shook her head. "Why didn't you tell us?" Lisa asked.

"Because it was none of your business." Megan experienced another contraction as she said this, and sank quietly back into her chair. For their part, Tom and Lisa realized, with some mortification, that she was right. The three sat looking at each other dejectedly for several minutes until Lisa stood and walked out of the room. Passing through the door, she caught Tom's eye and twitched her head slightly to the side, signaling for him to come along. Tom, who was still standing in front of the television, quietly followed her out the door. Lost in her own deep concentration and woe, Megan did not seem to notice their departure.

Once in the central hall, Lisa motioned again for Tom to follow her again, leading him toward a door he knew led to the basement. In all his many visits to Lisa's home, Tom had gone down these stairs only a handful of times. He was obviously perplexed and began to ask Lisa what she was doing when she intercepted his query with a finger held to her lips. She depressed the thumb latch carefully and slowly opened the door, directing Tom to go through and down. She followed and closed the door just as carefully and turned to see that Tom had descended only halfway. He stood looking up at her, puzzled. "What are we doing in the basement?" he asked.

"Shhh . . . go down," she said, dismissing his question.

Tom rolled his eyes, shrugged and continued to the bottom of the stairs. He moved to the middle of the quiet, cool space and then looked at Lisa with an exaggerated expectancy. "Lisa, what are we doing down here?"

She approached close and, in a very low voice, stated. "I

have a way out."

"Really?" Although skeptical, Tom was trying not to mock his earnest wife.

"The tunnel!"

Tom's jaw dropped. "Oh my God!" He suddenly remembered his first visit to Lisa's home, when she had dragged him down to the basement and surprised him with the most fascinating mixture of architecture and Americana he had ever seen. Perfectly hidden under the thin granite slabs that made up the basement floor was a tunnel which passed deep below the house and continued under the woods behind. After a straight run of roughly two hundred yards, a small flight of steps brought it to ground level, where a disguised trap door provided the far exit. Another hundred yards from there, again through thick woods, was a small road which ran parallel to that on which their house stood. Lisa had explained that her great-great-grandfather – in addition to being a lawyer and merchant – was a conductor in the Underground Railroad, an ardent abolitionist who enthusiastically broke federal law to help escaped slaves seek freedom in Canada. He built his farm specifically to further the cause and used the tunnel on several occasions to move slaves a little closer to emancipation. Twice in the late 1850's he was visited by slave hunters who suspected him of aiding the "seditious cause". On one of those occasions two slaves ducked into the tunnel just before the vigilantes appeared.

The tunnel became obsolete shortly after cannon balls started flying at Fort Sumter, and other than a brief stint as the family's designated bomb shelter during the early years of the Cold War, it was no more than a curiosity by the time Lisa was born. She opened it up for Tom on that first visit and they clawed their way through cobwebs to emerge at the other end. Tom hadn't thought about it for more than a decade.

"My father keeps it maintained because he's always sure we'll need another escape route."

Tom wanted to laugh at her father's crazy ideas, but for once the old man was absolutely right. "Who knows about it?"

"A few people in town, mostly family friends. We always treated it as a family secret, for some reason."

"That might be a good thing now. Let's take a look. Are there any flashlights down here?" Lisa jumped up and strode quickly to a set of neat metal shelves against the wall where two powerful, spotlight flashlights sat ready on the shelves. As she picked it up, Lisa flicked the switch and a beam shot across the cellar, just glancing one of the half-light windows which provided dim light to the cellar. "Careful!" Tom hissed in a stage whisper. Lisa turned it off quickly, and then picked up the ancient iron crowbar needed to pry loose the covering slab. Handing the tool to Tom, Lisa indicated the nearly imperceptible notch between two adjoining slabs where the tongue of the bar fit perfectly. As if twenty years melted away from the first time he witnessed it, Tom remembered exactly how to lift, pivot and then slide the grey, granite slab away onto the solid surrounding flooring. Lisa's father had waxed the slab's bottom to assist in moving it on the floor, and this also made its movement noiseless.

Tom took the flashlight from Lisa and cast the bright beam into the darkness below. The wooden plank steps were dusty but looked sturdy. There were fewer cobwebs than the last time they had ventured down there, suggesting that Lisa's father had recently performed his upkeep. Tom wasn't given to squeamishness, but he hated the idea of spiders falling on his head or down his shirt. With a deep breath he sat down, swung his legs into the void and tested the first step. Satisfied it would hold him, Tom descended the rest of the way – slowly at first, and then more quickly as he adjusted to the dark and gained confidence in the footing. Now standing at the bottom, Tom peered forward down the long tunnel. The whitewashed plaster walls helped reflect the light farther down the tunnel than the flashlight could illuminate on its own, yet even so it petered out far short of the steps at the other end.

"Do you want me to come down?" Lisa called down into the tunnel. Tom turned to see her backlit head poking down into the hatchway. Although he couldn't discern the expression on her face, he was fairly certain that she didn't appear keen for him to say yes. Lisa had become increasingly claustrophobic over the past several years.

"No, I'm fine. I'm going to check out the other end to make sure we can open it."

"Okay." Her agreement was swift.

Tom set off down the tunnel savoring the earthy musk of the damp ground. The odor was a powerful reminder of the first time he and Lisa had explored the tunnel, and he suddenly remembered that they had stopped halfway and made out for a several minutes. Before long, Tom could begin to see the steps at the other end and he quickened his step. He couldn't believe that he and Lisa might be able to outsmart Massey and her power-hungry cronies – but it all depended on the far end being operational. Tom arrived there seconds later and inspected the steps – like their counterparts at the cellar entrance, they were sound. He now remembered that there was a stone well-house surrounding the hatch above, and a complex drainage system to prevent flooding. Lisa's father had tried to explain it once, but Tom, who was famously un-handy, had just nodded his head and pretended to understand. Once again, he was thankful that Lisa's father worked tirelessly to maintain all of this.

Duffield tested the hatch, slowly, to make sure the opening mechanism worked. Lifting the hatch very slightly, he peeked out on a landscape of bushy undergrowth. He feared seeing the finely pressed trouser leg and polished black shoes of a State Trooper, but was pleased to observe nothing but plants – and one squirrel which scampered up a nearby tree. Tom backed down a step and closed the hatch. Knowing that the hatch worked and that there was no one there was enough. There was no point in disturbing the ground or in any other way attracting attention and giving the tunnel's location away. He waited a moment for his eyes to readjust to the dim light, and then retraced his steps. As he neared the cellar hatch Lisa called out to him again.

"How does it look?"

"Great!"

"Did you test the hatch at the other end?"

"Of course! It works fine."

"That's my father for you." Lisa helped Tom lift himself through the narrow opening. "I'm pretty sure Megan could get through this opening. I was sizing it up while you were gone."

Tom hadn't thought of that, but was relieved his wife (like her father) was so thorough. "Let's close this up until we're ready to use it." With a little teamwork, the two slid the cover slab over the opening and eased it into place with the custom-smithed bar. While Lisa returned the crowbar and the flashlights to their customary places on the shelves, Tom brushed dust back into the cracks around the cover stone. He could still make out the deep seam between this stone and those surrounding it, but decided that the untrained eye would not. Tom joined Lisa on the stairs, and – after making sure that they were out of sight from the small windows – posed the obvious and pressing question, "So how do we do it?"

Lisa grimaced. "I was afraid you were going to ask me that." She drew a wisp of her long blond hair behind her ear as she thought, and then began composing a plan. "Megan can't go alone. She's already having contractions –" Lisa considered saying more but this point was already made. With Tom nodding in agreement, she continued, "And I don't think we can both go. All those reporters out there will be able to tell if the house is deserted. They'll know something's going on."

"So . . . " Tom didn't want to leap to a conclusion as to which of them should go.

Lisa looked him directly in the eye as she gathered her

resolve. "I'll stay here." With that declaration Lisa let go her dream of raising this child. It was the only way Megan and the baby could be free, and that trumped any selfish desire Lisa might harbor. And even though, for all practical purposes, this decision had been made for her already by people and forces outside the old wooden farmhouse, this new plan put the choice on Lisa's terms. She stated it again to leave no doubt in her mind that the decision was clear and final. "I'll stay here."

Tom had not broken off their extended stare and saw, if only momentarily, a deep sadness wash through her eyes. Her jaw, her mouth, her lips gave no hint of what a painful moment this was, but Tom saw it in the eyes that he had known for more than twenty years, and for the first time in a decade realized how callous he had been. He had always likened her desire to have a child as some material object, like a coat or a dishwasher. Tom had never bothered to realize that this was something she needed – more than a coat, more than a career and, maybe, more than him. He had ruined it all through his own jealousy and deceit and he was speechlessly remorseful. All Tom could do was put both arms around this steadfast woman who had cheerfully borne his disregard, and embrace her with his guilt.

They held each other for several moments and as their pain eased, so too did their grip. Their arms fell down to their sides and they each took half a step back. "I guess we ought to ask Megan what she wants to do," Lisa said and Tom nodded. They turned and walked up the stairs and ran into Megan as soon as they emerged into the central hall.

"Where did you guys go?" She looked over their shoulders and wrinkled her nose. "Is that the basement?"

Tom was anxious to share the new plan, but wanted to make sure that they were out of sight via the many windows. After a quick glance around, he judged they were safe. "Megan, we have a way to get you out of here. Are you up for making an escape?"

"Really? How?" She was torn between optimism and skepticism, hoping the former would be satisfied.

Lisa explained the tunnel and its history, and Tom described how he had just walked the length of it and tested the hatchway at the other end. Megan's hopes lifted with each word, yet her analytical nature was still seeking flaws in the plan. When Tom finished she asked the most pressing and obvious question. "What are we going to do when we pop out the other end? It's not like I can move very far or fast. Where will we go from there?"

"We'll need to put a car at the other end," Lisa answered.

Megan continued, "So how do we stall until then? Dionne Massey is about to pull up to the front door in her motorcade and invite me for a ride."

"We have to wait until dark anyway," Tom said soberly, "Despite how thick the underbrush is back there, they might see us if we go before sunset." He closed his eyes and pursed his lips. "We need some help."

"With all this holiness floating around, don't you have a guardian angel you could call on?" Megan teased.

Tom's eyes lit up. "Strater!"

"Huh?" Both Lisa and Megan said together.

"Dean Thatcher called him that – my 'guardian angel' – months ago when he saved me from getting canned. Maybe he can come to the rescue again." Tom reached into his pocket, pulled out his cell phone and dialed Strater's number. "Please answer, John," he whispered as he could hear the call going through and the ringing begin at the other end. John answered on the third ring.

"Tom, what's going on up there?" John asked without waiting for Tom's greeting.

"John, we need your help."

"To hear the media right now, you have powers on your side far beyond what I could muster." Strater chuckled at his own joke. "I talked to Adams, you know, right after the story broke on the internet. And frankly I can't figure out whether I am pleased that I paid so little for that relic or bothered that my attribution was so far off the mark."

Tom didn't have time for Strater's rhetoric. "John, don't let them get this baby."

Strater detected Tom's anxiety and became serious. "You didn't actually clone from the relic, did you?"

"Yes – but long before I spoke to Adams."

"And you think the baby is . . . holy?"

"I know it." There was silence at the other end of the line. Only the eventual sound of light breathing at the other end told Tom that Strater was still there.

"You know I respect you immensely, Tom Duffield. Are you saying what I think you're saying?"

"Yes." And then after a pause, "Don't let them get this baby," he reiterated.

Strater's demeanor changed completely. Were he given to self-awareness, he would have noticed that his hands began trembling slightly. "What can I do?"

Tom had hoped that Strater would have sparked to an idea first, but it didn't take him long to answer. "I need you to hold off Dionne Massey and her lap dog, Spangler, for a couple of hours." He looked at his watch. "Until nine o'clock tonight, minimum."

"Tell me one thing, Tom. What does the girl want?"

"Megan? She's here. Do you want to talk to her yourself?" Tom held out the phone to Megan who anxiously took the phone.

"Hello? This is Megan Brack." she said, pulling back her blond hair so she could put the receiver close to her ear.

"Hello, my dear, this is John Strater. Is this what you want – delay Massey until tonight?"

"Yes."

"That's all I need to know. Let me get to work. This isn't going to be easy." He disconnected, and Megan handed the phone back to Tom.

Lisa had been paying half attention to Tom and Megan as she worked on the other problem – the getaway car – and she believed she had a solution. "Megan do you have your cell phone?" Megan retrieved it from the overnight bag which had been sitting nearby on the floor since their aborted trip to Ithaca. "Do you have Claire's number in there?"

"Yeah, I think so." She turned it on and searched through her address book. "Yeah, here."

Lisa took the phone and called their friend and doctor. Like Tom, she breathlessly waited for the other end to connect, and fortunately, the wait was short. "Hi, Claire. It's the fugitives calling."

"You guys are having quite a party up there. How's the patient doing?" Claire's irritation from the previous evening faded as her professional instincts kicked in.

"She's doing well. She hasn't gone out today." Lisa paused to imagine a rim shot underscore her ironic humor. "Can you come up here?"

"Yes, if I need to."

"Only if Bob can come also *and* you can loan us a car."

Claire didn't see that coming. "Huh?"

"We need you to leave a car."

"Leave?"

"For us to use."

"Aren't you surrounded by about five hundred camera crews?!" Claire asked, incredulous.

"We have a plan." Lisa figured the less Claire knew the better.

Claire quickly came to the same conclusion. "Should I ask any questions? Or should I just ask for directions?"

Lisa felt guilty for asking her friend to do this, but saw no other way. "Just directions." She described the best and fastest way to drive to her parents' house, but then became tripped up trying to make sure that Claire moved to the back roads before hitting the growing traffic jam around their small farm.

Megan was listening in and could tell Lisa was having trouble describing exactly where to leave the car. She waved her hand in Lisa's face, and capturing her attention asked, "Do they have a GPS system?"

"Do you have a GPS system?" Lisa repeated into the phone.

"Bob does." Claire answered and Lisa repeated to Megan, waiting for further instructions.

"Do your parents have a computer and internet?" Megan asked.

Tom cut in, "Yeah, I helped them put it in last year. It's up in their room."

"Great," Megan said, "tell them to get going and we'll text the GPS coordinates to her cell phone."

Tom and Megan headed up the stairs, he two at a time and she somewhat slower, as Lisa reiterated the routing and clarified how to find the road parallel to and behind theirs. Claire promised that she and Bob would hit the road within the next twenty minutes, which put them in Cansego, barring any problems, by five-thirty. Lisa wasn't sure whether to thank her or apologize, so she did both, profusely, and when she signed off, leapt up the stairs to join Megan and Tom. The computer was finishing its boot up, and Megan was anxiously fingering the mouse. "I'm going to use Google Maps to find the exact latitude and longitude of where we want the car to go, and then we'll pass those coordinates to Claire and Bob," Megan said. Lisa and Tom, who were computer literate, but not altogether "tech-savvy", smiled in agreement. "I'll just need you to guide me to find where we are now," she said, looking back at the computer and navigating to Google Maps. Within seconds Megan had zeroed in on Cansego, then Lisa and Tom both started calling out directions.

"Go up"

"A little more . . . left. Not so far."

"Right there. Now zoom in. Wow."

"There's the house," Megan declared.

"But where are all the camera vans?" Lisa asked hopefully. "Have they left?"

Tom bit his tongue, but Megan started laughing. "It's not live, Lisa." This was the first time she was amused all day. Lisa felt the emotional release and was happy to ease the tension they had been feeling all day. Even so, she was eager to change the subject.

"That's the Case's house, and the Millar's. Wow, this is amazing," she said.

"Ok, now help me find the back road," Megan cut in. "Is it back here?"

Tom reached for the mouse, which Megan yielded, and he put the cursor on the edge of the back road closest to the tunnel exit. The precise latitude and longitude showed on the screen. "That's it exactly," he said, grabbing a pencil and writing it down on a slip of note paper. "Let's get this to Claire." Lisa had set Megan's phone down on the table, and Megan had already picked it up and begun texting the info faster than Tom could write.

"Done." Megan said proudly. A moment later a text came back, "Got it." Megan was pleased to have regained a measure of control of her situation and was quite hopeful that their plan would succeed. At least they had a plan, she thought. Her contractions had eased and she associated that with the excitement of escaping. "What do we do now?"

"Wait!" Tom and Lisa said in unison.

10

Waiting proved tedious at best and extinguished much of the tingly anticipation all three felt after they contacted Claire and Strater to set the escape plan in motion. Tom figured it would take Massey two and a half to three hours to travel from Washington, given the ninety minute flight and the driving at either end. The media was making it very easy to track the Senator's progress, since the networks were all now broadcasting live from Syracuse Airport and still waiting for her to land. The journalists had been joined by a mix of protestors (Leave them alone!) and supporters (Support Young Mothers!), and, somewhat inexplicably, Animal Rights people who sniffed the opportunity to thrust their ideology in front of idle cameras. Ironically, their effort was paying dividends. Tom prayed Massey would feel the need to make another statement, which in turn would provide Strater a little more time to intercede. The fact that John hadn't called him back was becoming increasingly worrisome, and Tom started wondering whether he ought to call to check on progress. In the meantime, he turned to paging through a gazetteer of Upstate New York and trying to figure out where he could escape with Megan. Canada was the most obvious choice, so he scoured the map for where the border might prove porous.

At 5pm Senator Massey's flight touched down and within a few minutes the cameras showed her zipping past in her motorcade with State Troopers escorting fore and aft. Tom cursed her for not stopping to drop a few more inflammatory remarks about him and his wife, both because it would slow her down, and because it would irritate him enough for the battle that may ensue if Strater were not to come through. Lisa, who kept crawling to the front of the house to peek through the windows, reported that a large number of police had shown up and had sealed the road at either end with orange barrels. She was just about to crawl back for another look when the doorbell rang, and all three looked at each other with horror.

"Is it Massey?" Megan asked what all three were wondering.

Tom checked his watch. It was only 5:15 – there was no way she could have made it that quickly. He shook his head and then lit up as he realized who it was. "Claire!" He and Lisa jumped up, ran to the front door and threw it open once they confirmed it was their friend, doctor, and now, co-conspirator. She stood on the front porch with Bob, as five policemen hovered fifteen feet behind them.

"Come in," was all Lisa said given their worldwide audience, and the two newcomers swiftly obliged. As soon as the door was closed behind them, all four round-robin hugged each other and exchanged greetings in a flurry of energy. Lisa began thanking and apologizing all over again until Claire held up a hand for her to stop.

"Don't worry about it. We're friends and we know you would have done the same for us," she said.

Bob, apparently thrilled by the situation, then cut in, "We left the car exactly where you said. Locked it, but keys are on the passenger's side, front tire. We don't think anyone noticed, but there are a lot of cars around, even a couple on that back road."

Megan had made her way out to the front hall and greeted Claire and then Bob. Claire sized her up in a minute and then stated, "Honey, are you sure you're up to crawling through those woods in the dark?" Claire's skeptical look betrayed her view of the matter, but she realized that Megan was headstrong.

"I'm up for our plan," was Megan's cryptic response.

"Let's go into the TV room for me to take a look at you," Claire said. She knew Megan would not turn that aside.

However, Tom was more worried about Massey's impending arrival and unveiled his backup plan in case Strater did not appear in the next few minutes. "Claire, do you think you can hold off Massey until dark? You know, tell her that Megan can't be moved right now or something like that?"

Claire rolled her eyes and took a deep breath. "Is there any way someone else can do that? I'm already up to my neck in issues that'll threaten my license. Now you're asking me to lie to a U.S. Senator?"

Tom didn't answer because they could suddenly make out the sound of a siren far in the distance. "That's her."

"I'll just tell her that I'm not going with her – that they'll have to come subdue me," Megan burst out defiantly. The hours of waiting had galvanized her decision not to go into custody.

Her statement was cut off by a cell phone ring tone. All five of the people in the room reached into their pockets, but only Tom pulled out the one that was sounding. A quick glance at the screen confirmed that Strater was on the other end and Tom answered breathlessly, "Hello, John."

"Hi, Tom. Did Massey get there yet?"

"She's close – we think we can hear the sirens of her escort."

"Can you hear a helicopter?"

"Oh, God, don't tell me they have helicopters, too!" Tom could sense their plan was about to disintegrate. The others standing in the gloomy front hall heard him say this and repeated "helicopters" in a nervous, questioning whisper.

"I'm not getting in a helicopter," Megan said.

Strater cut back in, "The helicopter is mine. I took off from home within a few minutes of your call. I think I'm coming in range now."

Tom could hear the *whump-whump-whump* of the helicopter, but just barely over the din of the police siren. By the sound of the latter, he judged Massey to be drawing up just in front of the house. "I can hear you now, John, but you need to hurry."

All eight eyes were on Tom as he said this, and all eight simultaneously lit up with the hope of a reprieve. Megan clasped her hands together over her prominent bulge, and Lisa and Claire both threw an arm around her from each side. Two of them whispered what the others were thinking, "Thank God."

"All those flashing lights made it pretty easy to find you," Strater said. "Can I land in the field next to the barn?"

"Yes, yes." Tom had no idea what Strater might have up his sleeve, but he was confident it would work. He ran to the front window and pulled away the lacy curtain to view the front lawn. As expected, Massey's black limousine was parked in the middle of the two-lane road, directly across from the front door. A man emerged first out of the back seat, and like the others – the camera crews, reporters and police officers – was looking up at the eastern sky. Every few seconds he leaned down to shout something to people inside over the din of both the sirens and the helicopter engine which was becoming progressively louder. Fortunately, the police shut down their half of the noise, and now just the chopper provided the soundtrack to what twenty-four hours earlier had featured only crickets and song birds. Tom saw first the shadow of the helicopter flash across the lawn, and within another couple seconds the dark shape appeared overhead.

"I'll hang up now, Tom. Just tell Dionne I'll be there in a minute." Strater had a touch of smug triumph in his voice.

Tom dropped his phone back into his pocket and resumed watching the proceedings in front of the house. The others had followed him, each taking a position at a different window, except for Lisa and Megan who were doubled up next to Tom. They watched Massey exit the sleek, black car with tinted windows and stare after the helicopter which had circled once around the barn and was now hovering above a grassy field. She appeared to be in an animated conversation with the man they recognized from the podium at her press conference. Massey repeatedly pointed toward the helicopter and the man kept shrugging and shaking his head. While glad to be safely inside the farmhouse, Tom and Lisa both wished they could hear what Senator Massey was saying.

"Goddammit, Dave, I thought the police were going to secure this area!" Dionne Massey barked at her Chief of Staff.

"We asked them to secure the road, which they've done. We weren't expecting helicopters out here," he answered, fighting off the urge to appear sheepish given all the cameras trained on him.

"*You* weren't expecting helicopters. What if we'd come in a helicopter? We'd be trying not to collide with each other," she responded with a sneer.

"If we'd come in a helicopter, we would have had the police secure the air. That's our protocol." Tinskey knew the protocol, largely because he authored it. "It's probably just another reporter."

"Well, find out who it is and cut them off our list – no more interviews. They screwed up our whole entrance here." Massey reflected on her pronouncement. "Unless it's Couric." They watched the helicopter finish settling down and cut the engine. The din and rotor breeze died away immediately. "Alright, let's get going, the cameras are waiting for us to fetch the woman. Do you have the Governor's order?" She straightened up, brushed her skirt down with both hands and put on her camera face.

"Yes, Ma'am." Tinskey held up a folder.

"Let me go first, you stay a few steps behind." Massey stepped off briskly, hesitating an instant later when she heard a shout behind her. It was Strater, who had jumped out of the helicopter and was sprinting across the field.

"Senator Massey, Senator Massey! Just a minute." He was waving a piece of paper above his head.

Massey looked back in his direction, squinting into the afternoon sun. She raised a hand to shield her eyes, but could not make out the figure running toward them. Tinskey, a step closer, was doing the same. "Who is that David?"

Tinskey recognized Strater almost immediately and was overcome with nausea and dread. The grand plan was crumbling around him and he was going to take the blame. "It's not Couric," he said feigning ignorance.

"I know *that*! Oh my God, it's . . . it's . . . ."

"John Strater." Tinskey figured he might as well deliver the bad news himself.

"That son of a bitch! What's he doing here?"

Strater had drawn up within twenty feet and the police, ignorant of his identity and purpose, closed in toward him, nervously fingering their holsters. "It's okay, gentlemen," he called out cheerfully. "I come myself as an agent of the law." The policemen looked back at Massey and she begrudgingly nodded in acknowledgement. "Hello, Dionne, gosh it's been a long time."

Massey wished it had been a half hour longer. "Yes, John, it has. I'm actually very busy here, John."

"Well that's just it, Senator, you may not be as busy as you thought. The U.S. District Court of Northern New York has put the brakes on your little operation." He held out the paper he had been waving above his head.

Massey was too irritated to take it out of his grasp. "What is that?" she asked sharply.

"It's an injunction. The Court doesn't think there's probable cause for this woman to be taken into custody against her will. Plus, this State and Federal thing you've put together is a little out of the ordinary."

"How do you know this girl isn't being held against her will right now? How do you know that she's not in danger?"

"I talked to her myself a couple of hours ago." Strater flashed an exaggerated smile.

"Give me that," she said, grabbing the paper out of his hand. She scanned down the fax sheet, looking for the slightest error which might invalidate it. "Where did you get this?"

"It was faxed to my helicopter twenty-five minutes ago. There's a hard copy coming up from Syracuse as we speak. But I think this copy is official enough, plus the fact that three police officers and bunch of television news cameras just witnessed you read it makes it pretty awkward for you to ignore." Massey tried to hand it back to Strater. "That's okay, keep it for your scrapbook," he said.

Massey shoved the paper at Tinskey and he was quick to accept it. Her face had turned scarlet and Tinskey wanted to do everything to stay clear of her wrath, if that was still possible. "You know this is just a speedbump for me, Strater," she said low enough that the reporters would not be able to hear. "When Spangler and I steamroll right over it, I hope there isn't a lot of collateral damage to those skulking nearby. In fact, you may want to climb back in that helicopter of yours and get out of here – now that your little stunt is over."

"You mean pass up the opportunity to visit with my friends inside?"

"You're standing into danger. Can you afford to get wrapped up with these people?" Massey said this flatly, but the tiniest twinkle in her eye betrayed the fact she hoped her threat would go unheeded.

Strater kept his poise, and was amused by Massey's choice of words. "Afford it? Frankly, yes. I have yet to find something I can't afford." He brushed past her and strode the remaining twenty feet up the stone path toward the front door, which swung open just as he mounted the neatly-cut granite stoop. Although Strater half-expected to be stopped by Massey or the police, and thus held his breath and had his ears cocked backwards to hear the command to halt, he continued into the house and saw the door swing closed behind him.

Massey and Tinskey silently watched Strater disappear into the house and then turned to look at each other. The Chief of Staff tried hard not to look as if he expected to be hit with a two-by-four; his boss tried hard not to look like she was about to swing one. Both were only partially successful, but that was quickly moot as Massey glanced around at the multitude of cameras trained on her face. "Let's discuss this in the car." A broad and practiced smile spread across her thin lips and she retreated to her limousine, opened the door and climbed in. Tinskey circled around to the other side, and, just before sitting next to the furious lawmaker, mimicked Massey's smile to the cameras.

11

Strater had joined the five others standing silently at the front windows to watch Massey's return to her car, and as soon as Tinskey's door closed, he straightened up and declared, "I'd love to hear what's going on in there." He laughed out loud. "Someone's getting an earful. Gosh that was fun!" And then after a moment of reflection, he added, "I really do hate that woman."

Tom was the first to approach Strater, his hand extended. "Thank you, my friend," he said earnestly. "You can't possibly understand how much we appreciate your saving us from . . . them."

"I appreciate it especially," Megan said, stepping up to give him a warm but physically awkward hug.

"It's the least I could do. I'm very pleased to meet you, Dr. Brack."

"Megan, please," the pregnant woman said. She and Tom introduced the others to Strater and after the brief greetings and handshakes she voiced the question each of them was thinking, "How much time have you bought us?"

Strater's grin faded as he considered her question. "It's not going to hold them off forever, or, for that matter," he glanced at Megan's belly, "until that baby needs to come out." He saw the fear wash over Megan's face and amended his response. "But I've got a few more tricks up my sleeve. It all depends on what you want to do. Do you want to deliver the baby here?" he asked looking at Megan and then at Claire.

Claire turned the question back Megan, who was just about to answer when Lisa spoke out, "We were thinking we would sleep on it tonight and make a decision in the morning." She looked directly at Megan as she said this and successfully caught her eye.

Megan added, "It's been a really long and stressful day, as you can imagine. Just knowing that we can have a quiet evening makes a huge difference."

Lisa put her arm around Megan, partly to thank her for

playing along, and partly to manage her through the next bluff. "Claire and Bob, thanks for bringing the extra car, but I don't think there's any way we could sneak out the back door at this point."

"Everyone's welcome to stay," Tom added. "The fridge is full of food and there are a couple of nice bottles of wine. Let's go back to the family room." Strater quickly agreed to overnight with them, and Claire and Bob conferred quietly a few steps removed. Tom was listening closely, and for a brief and troubling moment he was afraid Bob might leave, given the "getaway" car was not required. However, walking past the cameras and police barricades to get the other car seemed too daunting and so they, too, agreed to spend the night. He ushered the group toward the rear of the house, sliding around them to grab the road atlas he had left lying on the couch. It was still open to the map of Northern New York and Tom, already comprehending Lisa's intention to keep the escape plan secret, did not want to arouse suspicion. "This is where we've been holed up all day, watching ourselves on national television. It's really quite interesting – let's see what's going on now." He picked up the remote and turned on the TV. No one was too surprised that the first image that came into focus was their neat, white clapboard house with its green shutters. A perky, young reporter in the foreground, prompted by questions from the headquarters anchor, was speculating on what had just transpired between Massey and Strater. While this may not have been simply a stall tactic, she conveniently drew her explanation to a close as the coverage cut back to the anchor desk for a short biography of John Strater, the "eccentric philanthropist". John was mostly pleased by the attention, although most of the B-roll video they showed was old and the people they interviewed were political opponents or business competitors.

"I'm surprised they didn't ring up Dionne Massey for her point of view," he sniped as the segment finished. "They're probably working on that now."

Megan was still stuck on the reports of his wealth. "I don't mean to be rude, but do you really have five billion dollars?"

Strater considered the question and shrugged. "Something like that – give or take a couple hundred million." The news coverage cut back to the house and the group hushed as they watched Massey's car pull away from the house and motor down the road. Unfortunately the police remained and began pushing back the camera trucks and cordoning off the area in front of the house. "That's round one, folks. But don't count her out. Senator Massey might not get her way, but in trying she'll leave a few bodies in the wake."

Lisa stood and walked to the door. "I'm going to figure out dinner. I assume you're all staying," she said with a smirk. "Tom, could you come give me a hand? Maybe find some wine or beer or something?" Tom jumped up and followed her out. This cued Claire to suggest she give Megan a quick checkup, and the two women moved upstairs for privacy.

"We can't tell them what we're going to do," Lisa said quietly as soon as they reached the kitchen.

"Okay," Tom answered.

"Claire will be opposed to it on account of Megan's state, and Strater may feel like he's being made an accomplice."

"I agree."

She continued as if she were still trying to convince him, "And if they don't know what happened then they can't give it away."

Tom grabbed her by the shoulders. "Lisa, I agree with you. Get a grip." He leaned forward to give her a kiss on the cheek. She relaxed visibly and he resumed talking in a whisper. "I took a look at the map. It'll take about four hours to reach the area along the Canadian border where I think we can cross – you know, through the woods – so I was thinking we need to get out of here by ten so it's still the middle of the night when we get there. Plus, I don't want to spend any more time here than necessary. Remember how the Feds snatched that little Cuban kid in the middle of the night?"

"Do you have everything under control here? I'll serve some drinks quickly, but I want to put together a bag with all the stuff we'll need and get it down to the basement." Tom and Lisa brainstormed the rest of their plan quickly – they would move everyone into the front dining room for dinner and then linger there for a long time – all in plain sight through the front windows – and then have Tom and Megan excuse themselves, ostensibly to go to sleep. Instead they would steal downstairs where Tom would muscle aside the covering slab, help Megan into the tunnel and then close the opening behind them. This would not be easy, they agreed, but Tom was confident he could do it. The rest of the party needed to stay at the table for at least another hour.

Lisa busied herself with putting together a dinner party while Tom, after opening the bar and making sure his guests were distracted by the television news, lined up everything he thought he would need to escort Megan to the northernmost reaches of New York and through the woods of Quebec. He logged back on to the internet and printed out satellite images of the area he thought best, then he went back into the garage to scan the tools. Lisa's father had every kind of implement one could ever need, and Tom picked through the tools quickly to find the few that might prove useful. Too many of them he didn't recognize at all, and while that made his selection simpler, it troubled him as a man. He reminded himself that he was a social scientist and not a tradesman or engineer.

Megan returned downstairs, joined Lisa in the kitchen and reported that Claire thought she could give birth at any time, although it was not necessarily imminent. Claire had said she could probably move it along faster if that is what Megan wanted, to which Megan replied, as earlier, that she would like to sleep on it. Lisa, in turn, briefed her on the newest details of the escape plan, and Megan agreed that they should shield the others from knowing their plan – the fewer insiders the better. They schemed a way to switch places at the dinner table later that evening and the first step was for them to put on their (purely coincidentally) matching red sweatshirts and tie their hair in pony tails. Lisa ran upstairs to fetch both sweatshirts from their overnight bags, as well as grab the other items Megan wanted stuffed into Tom's pack, and she came back to the kitchen to find Tom and Megan discussing the final plan in detail. There was something reassuring to all three of them to see the confidence of the others, to hear someone else articulate the plan and to see that another person – another smart person – actually believed it might work.

Mindful that they had been away from the others for nearly a half hour, Megan, Tom and Lisa came out of the kitchen and entered the family room together where Claire, her husband and John Strater were watching continued coverage of the "developing story". Ever the leader, Strater had taken possession of the remote control and had been surfing through the channels and giving the others a running commentary of the news personalities they were watching. John explained to the newcomers that the media was now informed of the injunction Strater had won from the District Court and a couple of channels were trying to penetrate the legal wrangling which must now be in play. Nancy Grace, in particular, had sunk her teeth into the story as the legal battle of all-time. "Who Owns God" was the prominent subtitle adorning the bottom quarter of the screen; above it were an august handful of lawyer celebrities wrangling the conundrum in primetime. It was not clear whether they would resolve the question before the regularly scheduled end of the program, though Nancy might be able to swing extra coverage on this story. On PBS the question was being handled at a slightly higher level. Many clerics had declared this the Second Coming and the faithful were pouring into churches around the world to begin a vigil. Stopped by reporters at church doorways, they were happy to voice opposition to government custody of the young mother and baby. Other clerics were bitterly resentful that science could hijack religion, although they had trouble answering why scientists would reproduce Christ if they did not believe in him. Still other men and women of the cloth believed the whole thing was a scandalous and blasphemous hoax. BBC World News was following the reaction of foreign leaders, the most dramatic of which was from Russia's president who vigorously denounced the idea that God would choose America for the Second Coming.

When it finally seemed that all angles of the story had been explored, Lisa came in to announce that dinner was ready. John dutifully turned off the television and all six stood looking at each other for a prolonged time, every one of them thinking how odd it was that the whole world was abuzz with what was going on this tiny house, yet they themselves were blithely trooping off to the dinner table. Excepting the television news (and the cameras lined up outside which made it possible) everything seemed so normal that they all had the sense that they were dreaming. "This way," Lisa said, turning back through the door, leading them through the darkening hallway and left into the dining room. "Megan, why don't you take the seat right here? It's a little more comfortable, plus you don't have to face the windows." Megan peered through the windows and smiled for the cameras before she turned her back and sat at the prearranged place.

"Don't you want to draw the curtains?" Claire asked. "A hundred million people are going to watch us chow down."

"No, no," Tom was quick to answer. "It'll be good for them to see that all is normal here."

Claire shrugged and leaned over to Bob, "Don't eat with your mouth open."

As soon as everyone was seated – except for Tom, who was circling the table pouring from a bottle of Chianti – Lisa initiated the family-style self-service and there ensued a flurry of passing dishes before they were all ready to tuck into their spaghetti bolognese and salad. Just after the last plate filled and the final serving dish returned to the center of the table, they looked at Lisa for the signal to begin. Not once in all the years she had eaten dinner at this table had Lisa skipped saying grace, but now, as the others waited for her to lift her fork, she struggled with what to do. Did you need to praise and thank God when his presence already graced the table and would partake in the meal? Or was this the moment where his blessing was most acutely required? What signal would they send the watching world if they bowed their heads in prayer? Her deliberation lasted a moment too long, and Tom, anxious to move the evening plan along, called out, "Bon Appetit!" and downed a large mouthful of spaghetti. Lisa prayed quietly to herself and began eating.

Moods and apprehensions lightened as the food, and perhaps more importantly (for all but Megan and Tom) the wine, made their mark on the dinner party. John Strater fell into his usual role as Master of Ceremonies and entertained the others through the combination of his charm and fascinating life experiences. Yet John, like the others, was unusually conscious of Megan's pregnant presence at the table. He noticed that the others were often looking at the young woman and her bulge in particular, through the corners of their eyes. On the couple of occasions he swore, either as a quote from the story he was telling or as a matter of emotional emphasis, he looked quickly at her to gauge whether offense was taken. He excused himself once when he said the word "shithead", but Megan had no idea the apology was directed at her and thus did not bother to acknowledge it. Enthralled by Strater and his palpable ego, Megan failed to recognize that she was the center of attention, not just of the other five people sitting around the oblong table, but by millions of others watching her from behind via satellite broadcast. For her, this delicious meal and congenial company provided such an escape from her anxiety of the past two days that she completely forgot the terrifying spotlight into which she had been thrust. Her only regret was the baby's pressure on her stomach made her feel full far too quickly.

The next two and a half hours sped by and just as energy seemed to fade and her dinner guests – at least those not involved in the escape – appeared restless, Lisa brought out the brownies and ice cream for dessert and Tom opened a very nice bottle of port. Tom had paced his drinking through the night, as he was anxious to be alert and functional through the escape and the long evening that would follow. Even so, he allowed himself a suitable tot of this port, seeking both the courage and the energy it could provide. Right on the heels of the first round of port, Lisa brought out playing cards and coaxed the others into playing a few hands. This was Tom's cue to beg off and say that he was going to bed, and Megan's cue to ask Lisa whether she could stretch out on the Victorian loveseat in the near corner of the dining room.

Megan dropped her napkin on the floor as she was asking this question and leaned over to pick it up as she left her chair. Lisa leaned over to pick it up as well, and the two passed low next to the table – Megan moving directly to the loveseat and Lisa coming up in the chair which Megan vacated. Thanks to their matching sweatshirts and ponytails, observers outside would perceive that Megan had leaned over to pick something up and had now straightened up in her seat. To those inside the dining room, Lisa had come closer to the others to play bridge. Megan was now tucked in the corner of the room closest the door and would only have to stay a few minutes before slinking away. Their switch was perfect and both women fought off the urge to give any sign to the other. In fact, Lisa had to be careful not to turn her head in profile lest those watching would realize that Megan was no longer there.

Without monitoring her watch, Megan waited the prescribed five minutes before announcing she needed to go to bed. In order to keep the others from following her lead, she made the announcement just as they were in the midst of a close hand and as Lisa refilled the port glasses. Only Megan and Lisa knew this was "goodbye" and not "goodnight", and both struggled with how easily the moment passed for the others. Megan wanted desperately to hug Lisa, Claire and John and tell them how much she loved them and how much she appreciated everything they had done to protect her. Yet she needed to move quickly so the others would not be seen facing and talking to her for very long – she needed to minimize the chances of them saying her name or asking about the baby, just in case someone watching could read their lips and recognize the incongruity. Lisa felt the pain of losing both the baby she had dreamed was hers and a true friend and protégé. In a way she was relieved to not be allowed to turn or look toward the door as Megan walked out, as doing so would make her visible to those outside – she knew her emotions would not be checked. Claire noticed that Lisa did not look up from her cards as Megan slipped through the door, and while it struck her as odd, she chalked it up to Lisa's engagement in the card game.

12

Megan made a quick stop in the bathroom off the darkened hall before she quietly opened the door to the basement, stepped through, and closed it behind her. She waited a moment for her eyes to adjust to the light and then, tightly holding the banister, stepped cautiously down the wooden steps. Tom was standing at the bottom with a flashlight held up against his chest. It cast just enough light for her to make out the edges of the steps, which creaked faintly as she trod. When she reached the bottom of the ancient staircase, Tom switched off his light and then took her elbow and guided her toward the opening in the floor. Megan's eyes had adjusted to the light by this time and she could see the glow from the news vans outside through the half-light windows along the front wall. She and Tom were out of sight, yet she crouched as much as her pregnant frame would allow while crossing the stone floor.

Tom stooped by the opening to the tunnel and switched on his light to cast a beam into the tunnel. "Here it is. Can you sit on the edge?" he whispered. She sat on the floor and swung her legs into the dark void. Tom switched off the light again to make sure he did not inadvertently send a beam across the cellar or through one of the front windows. Megan was far more spry than Tom expected, and not only did she sit on the edge, but she tested the first step and then made her way to the bottom. "You okay?" he whispered, peering down the hole.

"Yeah, come on." Megan was anxious to get away from the house and the potential captors who waited outside. Her heart pounded as she waited for Tom, whose body was silhouetted above in the dim light. "Come on," she repeated.

Tom handed down the backpack and followed quickly. "Give me a sec while I close this," he said looking down at her. Standing halfway down the ladder he grappled the heavy slab and slid it closer to the opening. He wasn't sure he could bear the full weight of the stone above his head, but if he lined it up properly he thought it would work. Lisa had agreed to come down in the middle of the night and fix the stone if he could not manage it, but Tom keenly desired a clean getaway. He took another step down as he pulled the stone closer to its home position. Just before he took the full weight he breathed in deeply and bent his knees. *Klunk.* The stone fell just as he hoped, plunging them into complete darkness. "Yes!" he called out, relieved. Tom pulled the light out of his back pocket and switched it on without fear. "Let's go."

Megan needed no further prompting and she turned and made her way along the damp tunnel, Tom following close behind. He was surprised by how quickly she went, and considered suggesting she slow down. Yet his own adrenaline was surging through his veins and his apprehension about escaping at the other end drove him to scurry just as fast. "I can't believe how long this is!" she called out without turning back to look at him.

"Be glad. The worse thing would be to pop out of the ground in the middle of the reporters," he answered. The tunnel seemed longer than it had during the afternoon, but he knew that impatience was clouding his perception. Tom worried whether he should have drunk that whole glass of port. Within a few moments, his light caught the bottom of the ladder at the far end, and the two actually quickened their step. "Here, let me go first," Tom said, handing her his pack and turning off the flashlight. He climbed carefully up the steps and opened the hatch even more cautiously than he had several hours earlier. Moonlight entered the dark tunnel, but it was dim and quiet, which gave Tom confidence this part of the property remained deserted. He raised the hatch a little higher and looked all around. Still empty, they were in the clear, he thought. "You ready to come up? We need to do it fast," he called down in a hushed voice.

"I'm ready! Let's go!" she exhorted.

It was Tom's turn to move with alacrity. He thrust the hatch open and leapt up the last few steps, and then he swung around the side and reached down for his pack. As soon as he pulled that clear and flung it aside, he reached back down for Megan and helped her up by the elbow. Her own adrenaline was pumping and she came up the steps at nearly the same speed as Tom. Tom now circled around the back of the hatch, found the heavy iron ring on the lid to begin dropping it back into its original position.

Megan stood pressed against the metal grate as Tom was lowering the trapdoor. When she heard the *klunk* of the latch mechanism, she stood back to the other side, allowing Tom to step forward in the cramped well house. For not having rehearsed all of these movements, the two seemed perfectly choreographed. In the dim moonlight, dimmed further by the structure around them, Megan could see the ring of limestone topping the trapdoor fashioned to look like an old well head. She wanted to remark how clever a disguise it was, but that seemed superfluous – they were not sightseeing, they were in the midst of an escape, and the entire tunnel system was designed to protect runaway slaves from people who would do them real harm. She wondered how many bad people the tunnel had fooled over the last one hundred-sixty some years. And how many had it saved?

Tom fumbled for the catch above the grate, wincing as he felt a tacky tangle of cobwebs. The cool iron handle finally met his grasp, and lifting it, he swung the grate free. The wrought hinges sighed only lightly – Lisa's father had kept them well greased – and Tom stepped out into the night air, swinging his head from side to side. "Come on!" he whispered into the gloom. It was all the coaxing Megan needed and she stepped promptly onto dry leaves covering the ground. While closing the grate, Tom pointed to the glow above the dense yews planted in enfilade around the well house.

"That's the front of the house," he said, and then pointing in the opposite direction, "Bob's car should be directly back this way." Tom began picking his way over small fallen branches and shin-high shrubs. Megan followed closely behind, her heart pounding at the prospect of making a clean getaway. They zigzagged through a set of yews, planted like those on the other side to obscure the well house without looking like a planned hedge, and continued another hundred yards through dark woods now lit only by the moon.

Passing through one last set of yews, Megan and Tom saw the dark shape of Bob's car parked alongside the deserted dirt road. Tom jogged forward and knelt down by the right front tire, reaching up under the wheel housing to find the keys Bob had left as originally directed. There was nothing there. "Shit!" he said under his breath. Tom inhaled, once and slowly, to calm himself, then felt for the keys again. Nothing. "Shit," he said this time to Megan. "They're not here. Bob said that he left them"

"Maybe they fell on the ground," Megan suggested.

Tom pulled out his flashlight and held it up against his body as he switched it on, and then cast a thin beam through his fingers.

Still seeing nothing, he shone an unfiltered beam at the ground behind the wheel. He looked long and carefully and even shot the light across to look behind the wheel on the driver's side – all to no avail. Bob had forgotten to leave the keys.

"See anything?" Megan asked hopefully.

Before Tom could answer, they heard a jingle behind them, accompanied by a familiar voice posing the question, "Looking for these?" Tom knew the voice, but needed to see the swollen visage from which it came. He pointed the flashlight beam directly in William Rogers' eyes, fully mindful of the discomfort the bright light caused his hated boss. Rogers shielded his face with the hand holding the keys, causing them to jingle again. Tom turned out the light, not because of its effect on Rogers, rather, he wanted to manage this new obstacle in the dark.

"William," Tom said, mustering all of his patience and self-control, "give me the keys."

"Oh, come, come, Tom – and you must be Dr. Brack, judging by your shape – don't you want to hear how I figured out where to find you?" William's voice oozed with self-satisfaction, and while he could not see it in the dark, Tom could picture the smug look on Rogers' face.

As a matter of fact, Tom was very curious at how Rogers had discovered the back entrance to the tunnel, yet his need to take back the keys and hit the road were far more important to him. "William, I don't really give a shit as to what you think you're doing here, but I need you to give me those keys."

"When I heard Cansego I recognized it as a station on the Underground Railroad and Lisa's maiden name matched the name of the local conductor. Tom, you *do* remember I used to teach an Honors Course on Slavery in America. I knew a lot of these houses had escape tunnels so thought I'd troll this back road —"

"Give me the keys!"

"Lo and behold, here was this car which just happened to

have an Ithaca dealer's license plate frame. I put two and two together and ventured into the woods, where I saw the well house. Rather than share my discovery with any one of the thousand reporters out there, I thought I would wait here and see what happened next." Rogers was excessively pleased with himself.

Tom stepped closer to Rogers. "William, give me the keys!" he said firmly and without emotion. Megan took a step back and remained silent.

William was surprised at Tom's tone. He did not realize that Tom would not engage in the usual testy banter which the two had always practiced, and which William always held the upper hand – thanks to his rank. He edged back toward his car, whose dark shape Tom could now see parked twenty-five feet back along the road. "It sounds like real historian work to me, don't you think, Tom?"

"Give me the keys, William," Tom said with a growl. "I am not kidding around here," he added, just in case William had underestimated his intent. He took another step toward William, who was still ten paces away.

"Tom, don't try to play tough with me. You know you're still on thin ice, especially after this episode." As usual, Rogers resorted to threats when he himself felt threatened. He was the classic bully, and realizing that angered Duffield even more.

"William, you have no power over me." He took a step closer. "I need you to give me those fucking car keys, or I will take them from you." Tom judged that with a quick sprint he could catch William in a matter of seconds.

William was rattled. Somehow his petty and mean-spirited mind had not contemplated the confrontation which was now brewing. Somehow he trusted the power he had always wielded indiscriminately to his whim and advantage. He looked back at his car and realized it offered a safe haven from the angry man approaching him. The most obvious means of defusing the situation – simply giving Tom the keys – was trapped behind William's obstinacy. In his mind, William had won every encounter with Tom and he was not about to give in on this, perhaps most important, dispute. He turned quickly, given his large size, and leapt toward his car, his large stomach swinging side-to-side.

Although Tom was just about to pounce, Rogers' quick turn surprised him and he watched awestruck as the obese man ran toward the far car. Tom did not linger long, however, and he, too, sprinted after the lumbering figure, catching up to him halfway between the two cars. Duffield grabbed Rogers trailing arm and swung him around, reaching blindly for the keys which Rogers carried in the other hand. William was quick to protect them however, and pushed Tom hard, knocking him to the ground. He started again toward his car, with Tom, now angrier than ever, quickly at his heels. This time, Duffield went directly for the keys, grabbing at the black fob dangling from Rogers' enclosed fist. He got it on the first try and attempted to tug them free, but Rogers wasn't letting go. Now panicked and threatened, Rogers stopped, turned and swung at Tom with his free hand – wildly and slowly enough for Tom to duck clear. Tom remained focused on freeing the keys and began using his other hand to pry them free. Rather than taking another swing, Rogers brought his free hand to bear on loosening Tom's grip. The two men grunted and pulled at each other, Tom increasingly fearful that one of them might squeeze the fob buttons too tightly and trip the car alarm. This had to end now, and it had to end quietly. Duffield turned his shoulder into Rogers and began using his legs to drive the bigger man backward.

What happened next would have been clichéd if the two had been struggling for control of a pistol – a shot rings out, both men freeze and then one slinks to the ground mortally wounded. But in this case the men were fighting over a car key and its electronic fob, and only one of the men froze – William Rogers. A deep aching pain had paralyzed his left arm loosening his grip on the keys and causing him to emit a deep groan. The pain then shot down his entire left side and concentrated as a crushing weight in his chest. He released the keys entirely and staggered backwards, silent and staring at Tom.

At first Tom felt joy for having wrested the keys free and thought only of sprinting back to Bob's car, helping Megan get in and speeding away. Yet there was something in the look on William's face which gave Tom pause, and he found himself staring at the other man and trying to decipher what was happening. William wore a look of both surprise and fear – his mouth moved as if he were trying to say something, but no sound escaped his twisting lips. And then he fell to the ground with a thud.

"William?" Tom called out. "Are you alright?" There was no answer – not even the sound of labored breathing which Tom always associated with his boss.

Megan stepped up next to Tom. "What happened?" she asked.

"I don't know . . . I think he just had a heart attack."

"Well . . . do something. Do you know CPR?"

Tom was exasperated. William Rogers always found a way to screw things up, first showing up at the getaway car, then taking the keys and finally – now – collapsing with a heart attack. "Son of a bitch!" he muttered under his breath as he stuffed the keys into his pocket and knelt next to Rogers' crumpled mass. Tom began untangling Rogers' limbs and laying him out on his back. He leaned close to the still man's face to sense whether he was breathing, and then felt his neck for a pulse. There were no signs of life. He muttered again to himself – more of a harrumph than actual words – and began the process of compressing Rogers' chest and giving him mouth-to-mouth resuscitation. The latter disgusted him completely, but somehow he put aside both his abhorrence for the man and his original objective of escaping Cansego, and faithfully tried to bring the stationary heap back to life.

After two or three minutes Tom checked again for a sign that his efforts were doing anything. Finding nothing he looked up at Megan. "He's dead as a door nail. Even if I ran for help right now, I don't think they'd be able to bring him back. It'd take me ten to fifteen minutes."

"So what do we do?" Megan had never seen anyone die before, and despite the brave face she put on, she was completely shaken by the experience.

Tom was trying to stave off panic and think his way through the immense problem at hand. He looked at the keys in his hand, and then up and down the road at the two cars. Then he looked back toward the moonlit woods and the tunnel. "I think I have a solution. Can you drive?"

"Me?"

"Yes, Megan, you. Do you think you can drive?"

She shrugged. "Yeah, I guess so. What are you going to do?"

"We can't leave his body here next to the road, nor all these cars. With all the traffic around here we're lucky no one has come down this road for the last ten minutes."

She pressed for an answer to her question. "What are you going to do?"

"I'm going to get the body back away from the road. But that's going to take a while. You need to go on without me. Can you do that?"

"I guess . . . if I have to."

"If you take his car, and leave it where we talked about, you know, near the border, no one will ever know what happened to him. It's much better than abandoning Bob's car up there, because it'd get traced back to us so quickly."

Megan nodded. "I get it." The shock of William's death was easing, particularly as she focused back on escaping government custody. Tom began fishing through Rogers' pockets to find the keys to the dead man's car, and when he found them ran to its trunk and opened it up. Megan followed more slowly behind him, and asked as she caught up, "What are you looking for?"

Tom's eyes fell on it as she asked, and he pulled it out. "A stadium blanket."

"You can't wrap him in that. It'll hardly get around him."

"I'm not wrapping him – I need something to drag him on. I don't think I could budge him very far otherwise." Tom closed the trunk and squared to Megan. "You need to get going. Can you do this?"

Megan found her resolve. "Yes. I can do this." Repeating it back reinforced her confidence. "I will."

"Okay, you take the backpack. It has all the maps we looked at before dinner. Remember, I numbered them?" She nodded. "Let's see if there's gas in the car." He opened the driver's side door, leaned in and turned the key in the ignition. It started promptly, and the fuel gauge jumped to near full. "Excellent, you should make it without having to fill up." He straightened up and moved aside for Megan to toss their pack to the passenger seat and take her place behind the wheel. She quickly checked her mirrors and the controls around the steering wheel, and then looked up at her escape companion.

"Thanks, Tom."

Duffield was touched that she thanked him after all the trouble he had caused. "I wish you all the best. Lisa and I are going to miss you. Drive carefully – you've gotta take care of yourself – and your baby."

"I promise I will. I'd better get going."

"Yes, go this way until the first right, and then follow the signs for 81 North. At Watertown you'll break off east on 11 toward Malone."

"I remember. I was paying attention."

Tom paused to consider the right words to bid farewell. He leaned in and hugged her around the shoulders. "Godspeed," he said tenderly.

Megan suppressed the urge to hug Tom too tightly and betray her apprehensions. "You, too." She felt a mild contraction. "Bye."

"Bye." He looked deep into her eyes and then withdrew from the car, firmly but quietly shutting the door. Once he stepped away, Megan put the car in gear, switched on the headlights and pulled away down the road. Tom didn't watch her for long. Although he chose not to tell Megan, he had decided to slide Rogers' body all the way back into the tunnel, and that was going to take a long time. He approached the lifeless body, laid out the blanket alongside, and began the arduous task of rolling the body onto the blanket and dragging it back into the dark forest.

13

Megan had no trouble finding her route and gained the interstate within twenty minutes. She passed a number of police cars along the way – local and state troopers, and unmarked cars she took to be FBI. Fortunately, none of them paid any attention to her as she motored past and made her way north to freedom. Megan kept imagining that police cars were tailing her and looked repeatedly in the rearview mirror. Yet once she was twenty miles up the interstate her concerns eased and she began to revel in the thought that she was going to escape. She turned off the interstate highway in Watertown and continued northeast on Route 11. Thanks to the late hour, the midweek traffic was very light and she made better than expected time. She did not speed, however, as she could think of nothing more ridiculous than getting all this way and being stopped for a traffic violation.

Megan's emotional revelry ceased abruptly near midnight as she closed in on Malone, New York. A sharp contraction belted through her abdomen and held on much longer than any she had felt before. She managed to concentrate on driving, but sensed that her pregnancy was entering its very last phase. Megan reminded herself of her commitment to crossing the border and hoped her resolve would put premature labor in check. Five minutes later, another contraction pulsed through her groin and she felt the need to find a toilet, and pretty soon. She was almost to the town center, where she would break north for the last fifteen miles, when a third contraction hit. Megan had been paying attention to the clock on the dashboard and could see that this contraction, like the one before it, had a five minute interval. She realized that she needed more than a bathroom, she needed a doctor. She pulled over to hunt for a nearby physician online, but was disappointed to have no cell coverage.

Ahead on the right was a sign pointing the way to a Family Restaurant nearby, and Megan figured she could find both a restroom and, with luck, a phone book. She made the turn and saw the restaurant just ahead. The lights were on, but dimmed, so she supposed the staff might still closing up. Megan parked, and judging that she had three minutes before the next contraction, decided to try to make the restroom first, weather the contraction, and then come out to ask for a phone book. Spotting an older woman wiping down the counter, Megan exited the car and made her way to the door. *Thump, thump, thump.* "Hello?" Megan called to her.

The woman started and looked up, pausing as her eyes adjusted to the dimmer light outside. Once she realized it was a woman standing outside, and not some thieving hoodlum, she relaxed and called out, "We're closed! Ten PM!"

Megan pointed to her pregnant bulge. "I just have to go to the bathroom. Please?" The woman immediately took pity on Megan and made her way to the door. She unlocked and held it open for Megan to come in.

"I'm sorry, honey, I didn't see you were pregnant. My gracious, you're due pretty soon," she said, her eyes wide. "I remember going to the bathroom every ten minutes back when I was like that." She pointed to the right. "It's over there."

"Thanks, so much." Megan made a bee line past the woman,

nervous that she would double over with the next contraction before she made it. The door was charmingly signed as "Girls" and Megan yanked open the door, entered, and quickly found the nearest stall. She sat and emptied her bladder and bowels just before the next contraction kicked in. While no less intense, it was less uncomfortable without the other pressures. She tried to breathe in deeply and relax all the other muscles in her body as the ones around her pelvis strained involuntarily. After about a minute, the pain subsided and she cleaned up and went back out the counter where the woman was back at work. "Thanks again. Hey, would you happen to have a phone book I could look at real quick?" Megan asked.

The woman eyed Megan a little suspiciously, but answered, "Sure." She turned and reached under the counter, sifted through some papers and books, and pulled out a dog-eared local directory. "Can I help you find someone? I know darn near everybody in Malone."

"No thanks. I was driving in town the other day and thought I saw an old friend from school, so I thought I'd see if they lived here." Megan marveled at how quickly she had come up with that story – she had never been a good liar. She was skimming down through the names to find any titled "Dr."

"Honey, do you live around here?" the woman asked.

"We're from downstate, but my husband and I are renting a cabin near Trout River. They say you need to live it up before the first baby comes." Megan wondered briefly what her husband looked like and what he did for a living.

"Ain't that so!" the woman exclaimed. She wanted to ask Megan what she was doing out so late, but feared she had already asked too many questions.

Megan kept her eyes skimming down the page. *Success! Dr. Peter Lynch, Sand Road, Trout River.* She quickly memorized the phone number, although she was not sure she could depend on cell coverage. "Where's Sand Road?" she asked.

"After Constable, it's about halfway to Trout River, off on the left." She was about to ask Megan for the person's name but Megan, mindful that her next contraction might come momentarily, closed the phone book and thanked the woman for her help. "Come in and see us for a meal!" The woman called out as Megan slipped outside and got in her car.

Megan had just cleared the town limits when a contraction brought a warm gush between her legs. It took her a moment to realize that her water had broken, and that it was just a matter of time before the baby would follow. There was no way she was going to trek through the woods without endangering herself and the baby. She needed to find Dr. Lynch's house and pray that he was there. Each contraction seemed slightly more intense than the one before and it was becoming increasingly difficult to drive. Just after she passed through the collection of houses called Constable, she pulled over to the side of the road for the next wave of pain then continued on.

The sign for Sand Road popped out of the darkness and Megan followed it anxiously. There were few houses – maybe one every quarter mile – and Megan wondered how long she might have to drive before finding the house she was looking for. The phone book showed no house number for Dr. Lynch and she had worried about locating it, yet all the mailboxes so far displayed family names. She slowed while passing each one to make them out. *McGovern, Weagle, Sabatelli.* After a long stretch with no houses, the road bent slightly to the right and revealed another driveway ahead. Just as another contraction came on – this one causing her to lose her breath – Megan could see the word "Lynch" stenciled neatly on a mailbox. She stopped to ride out the contraction, and then muttered "Thank God!" as she turned into the gravel driveway. The house was set a hundred yards back and lights still shone in some of the downstairs windows. Megan sped along, fearing they would be extinguished in the next thirty seconds and leave her abandoned at the door.

She pulled to a stop behind a black Range Rover and climbed out of the car. She was happy to leave the damp leather seat soaked with amniotic fluid, although her sweat pants were drenched and hung heavily from the high waist band. Even her socks and sneakers dripped as she ascended the few steps to the front door. Standing at the stoop she looked through the glass panes for anyone inside. Megan realized that she had taken the lights to mean that someone was there – peering through the window she could see no one. *Bam, bam, bam* She knocked on the wooden door anyway. "Hello?!"

The house was modern and open in its layout, but rustic and woodsy in its appointments. The interior walls were paneled with pine and adorned with mounted trout. Apparently, Dr. Lynch was an avid fisherman. Hopefully this wasn't just a weekend retreat. Just as she prepared to knock a second time, a flicker caught Megan's eye and she realized that it came from a television in the farthest room. She didn't see anyone watching, but there was a large armchair with its back to the door. Megan rapped once more, this time willing for someone to rise from that chair and come rescue her. Her prayers were answered. The chair shook as its occupant sat up, revealing to Megan a shock of gray hair above the chair's crest. *Bam, bam, bam.* "Hello? Dr. Lynch?"

An old man swung his head around the side of the chair and looked directly at Megan. Clearly he was surprised to have a visitor, yet unlike the woman at the restaurant, he didn't fear mischief. He looked kindly, Megan thought, but slightly confused by what was going on. She assumed he had fallen asleep in front of the television and was still groggy. "Come on, wake up," she said out loud, though not loud enough for him to hear. *Bam, bam, bam.* "I need your help," she called out.

The word "help" seemed to stir Peter Lynch to life and he shook his head once and then, with some effort, raised himself out of the overstuffed chair. He raised a hand as if to signal he was on his way, and approached the door. Lynch's gait made it look as if he was hurrying, but it seemed agonizingly slow to Megan, who began to expect her next contraction. Lynch reached the door and pulled it open. This surprised Megan as she assumed it would be locked, and was amused that she had not tried to open it herself. As a result, she lost track of what she had planned to say, and stood looking at Lynch.

He was the first to speak. "Can I help you?" Megan thought he could be typecast in commercials as the friendly grandfather.

"Are you Doctor Lynch?" she asked.

"Yes."

"I need your help. I'm in labor and my water just broke. Can you deliver a baby?"

"Goodness me, come in, come in." He ushered her inside and took note of her dripping sweat pants. "I've delivered hundreds of babies in my day, but I've been retired for fifteen years. Here, come to the sitting area." He guided her back toward the room with the television and pointed her toward a couch. "Lie down there."

"But I'm soaked."

After forty years of practicing family medicine, Lynch was not given to squeamishness. But he knew most people were much more delicate, and he had always been in the business of making others comfortable, physically and psychologically. "Oh, yes. Well, do you mind taking off what's wet while I get some towels?"

Megan trusted this older gentleman. "Thanks, that would be nice." She began kicking off her sneakers.

"Let me turn this on, it'll make it cozier in here." Lynch flipped a switch on the wall and the gas fireplace sparked to a warm, blue glow. He left the room while Megan continued stripping off her wet clothes. She left on only her sweatshirt and her underpants and lay down on the couch just as another contraction pulsed through her midsection. She groaned quietly with the pain, and clenched her eyes shut, opening them a moment later to see Lynch standing in front of her. "Another contraction?" he asked. She nodded. "How far apart are they?"

"Maybe three or four minutes."

"Is this your first child?"

"Yes."

Lynch slid a thick cotton towel under Megan's bottom and legs. "Has your pregnancy been normal?"

Megan laughed. "Yes," she answered with the first smile to grace her face in hours.

Lynch excused himself again to leave the room and came back carrying a black medical bag, a pillow and a bathrobe. "This was my late wife's robe, and although she died almost five years ago, I haven't been able to part with it. Do you want to put it on?" Megan accepted it gratefully, sat up and donned the terrycloth robe while Lynch set down the pillows for her head. "As a career physician I have learned not to ask too many questions, but I can't understand how you found me." Once he got that out, follow-on questions came out more easily. "And what are you doing out here? Were you lost?"

Megan started to answer, but winced as another contraction tore through her. Lynch reached out to hold her hand and she grasped it tightly. As the contraction began to subside, she weighed the questions he had asked. "It's really a very long story. Can we leave it until after the baby is born?"

"Of course, but I don't even know your name."

Megan could see the television out the corner of her eye and wondered whether he was up-to-date with the news. "Marie," she answered using her middle name.

"Well, Marie. I'm glad you found me. Now if you're ready, let's see how this baby is doing." He eased off her underwear, pulled on a pair of latex gloves and gave her a quick examination. "You're almost fully dilated. It shouldn't be very long. I can feel the baby's head and it seems to be in the right position." But for the discomfort of the contractions, Megan was becoming excited to see her baby face-to-face.

The labor progressed quickly and within twenty minutes, Lynch was coaching Megan to breathe and push and keep her spirits high. "You're doing great," he said at periodic intervals. In her clearer moments Megan wondered whether he really meant it or whether it was simply professional habit. "Okay, here's the head. Stop pushing, stop pushing." Lynch supported the head and turned the baby just slightly to ease out a shoulder. From there the baby slid out quickly into Lynch's grasp. He laid the baby on a towel on the sofa, and seized a rubber bulb to suck mucus out of the baby's nose and mouth. Within seconds the baby began spluttering and then crying with the high-note of newborns. "It's a boy. Did you know that already?"

Megan collapsed back on the pillows, panting from exhaustion. "Yes."

Lynch grabbed the pair of surgical scissors he had readied, and clamped and then snipped the umbilical cord. He then picked up a spare towel to begin softly rubbing the baby. Megan lifted her head to watch him and was dismayed at the sight of the infant. "Is he okay? What's all that white stuff?"

"He's fine, just fine. It's just vernix. It protects the baby's skin from the fluid in the womb. Let me just clean him up a little and I'll hand him up to you." Lynch said this above the baby's pathetic cries and then began talking gently to calm the newborn. Megan was amused at the sight of this old man cooing at the shrieking baby and she giggled. Suddenly the events of the past two days, together with the relief of having escaped Cansego and safely delivered the baby washed over her. Tears began streaming down her smiling cheeks.

"The two of you are going to make *me* cry," Lynch said and his eyes glistened. "That should do it," he said putting one towel aside and lifting a clean one from the stack. "Let me just swaddle him." Still crying, Megan watched as the old doctor deftly laid the baby on the clean towel and wrapped it tightly around him. He lifted the baby toward her, "Here he is, Marie." She gently took the baby and laid him on her chest, their faces inches apart.

The infant's crying subsided. With the warm glow of the fire twinkling in his eyes, he gazed peacefully into his mother's weary face – and she beamed with joy at the sight of her child.

"He's a beautiful baby, Marie. Congratulations," Lynch said softly.

Megan stroked the baby's cheek with her thumb and leaned forward to kiss his forehead. "He's perfect."

Epilogue

1

Tom was awake and staring at the ceiling when the first rays of a dazzling sunrise streamed through the window and transformed the dreary gray to golden yellow. He found the moment strangely reassuring after five hours of covering his tracks and worrying about whether Megan had made it safely across the border. If he had slept at all, it was not for more than a few minutes.

Earlier that evening, after wrestling William Rogers' lifeless body down the ladder and into the tunnel, Tom drove Bob's car a mile down the still-quiet road and jogged back to the tunnel. He did his best to obscure any marks which Megan, Rogers and he had made on the ground, particularly in the area surrounding the well house, and then closed himself inside. Exhausted both physically and emotionally from the last couple of hours, he sat on the steps of the ladder and stared at Rogers. The contempt he had felt for so many years had given way to pity, and he actually regretted having to leave the body here in the tunnel, probably for a very long time. After covering the corpse with the stadium blanket, he made his way back to the cellar.

Once there, Tom tried to eliminate any sign of Megan's escape. Not only did he replace the tunnel entrance's slab covering, but he also took fine sand and potting soil, which Lisa's father kept among the gardening supplies, and fed it into the cracks between the slabs. Finally, as the step which he found most clever, Tom rigged a fan at the top of the basement stairs and threw a small handful of plaster mix into the blades' wash. As far as anyone could tell, no one had trodden on that cellar floor for weeks.

Tom was unable to sneak into the bedroom without waking Lisa and in a hushed whisper he described everything that had happened. She was horrified by Rogers' death, and amazed that Tom had attempted CPR. They argued at some length about leaving the body in the tunnel, but Tom was finally able to convince her it was the only option. Then he proposed a simple cover story – Megan had, without the knowledge of the others, exited the farmhouse through the backdoor while everyone was sleeping. In his bone-weary fatigue, it was the best story Tom could conjure.

Lisa's voice now jolted him further awake. "Did you sleep?" she asked.

"I don't think so," he replied.

"Are you sticking with the story?"

"Got a better one?" Tom had been pondering it the whole night and identified most of the flaws. The idea that Megan had slipped by the media and police in the dead of night seemed somewhat implausible, although when he had gone upstairs to bed around 2:30 am, he had noted how dark it was in the backyard. Moving Bob's car was another risk, as he and Claire might notice when they went to pick it up on their way back to Ithaca. On the other hand, Tom could not risk them being followed and raising suspicion about the area where the car had originally been left. He was pretty certain they would be distracted by the crazy events of the last two days and simply keep driving on the back road until they came upon it. Most concerning was the inevitable recognition of Rogers' disappearance. On this point, Tom had to rely on the fact that Rogers lived alone and was unlikely to have told anyone that he was leaving Ithaca. If Megan had taken any care in hiding Rogers' car, it would be weeks before anyone put all the clues together. As for the body, Tom hoped for a speedy decomposition. In any event, Rogers had died of natural causes and Tom had tried to revive him.

Tom and Lisa went downstairs and turned on the television. Their story was still filling the airwaves, with occasional "LIVE" satellite feeds from the media vigil outside. They were pleased and relieved that Megan had not been apprehended. Unless the authorities were covering it up, they reasoned that she must surely have made it to Canada.

Claire was next entering the family room. "Is Megan up yet?"

"She's gone," Tom said. He and Lisa had agreed that he would be best at carrying off the story. "We looked in on her this morning and her bed was empty. There's also a missing backpack. She must have sneaked out the backdoor in the middle of the night. Judging by the news, she got away."

"She was in no state to drive, let alone walk very far. My god, I hope she's okay." Bob entered the room and Claire reached out for his hand. "Megan sneaked out overnight. She's gone, she got away."

"I thought something was going on when she slipped out from dinner last night. Did she take our car?" Bob asked. "Are we done for when they find her driving it?" He grimaced.

Lisa and Tom exchanged glances and she piped up, "Megan's smart and she's strong. She's gotten away and she's going to be fine! And the baby, too!" Lisa hoped saying this might help it become true. "Besides, there's no evidence that we have done anything wrong, is there? Who knows how she got pregnant? Plus, they'll be hard pressed to say that she was being held here against her will. Just this morning they aired video of us having dinner together last night. In the clip they showed, Megan was laughing her head off."

Claire added a reassuring piece of news. "I have to admit that I wasn't too detailed with her medical records. They won't get much from them."

With John Strater rounding out the party over the next half hour, the group aligned on a plan of telling the authorities that Megan was gone and inviting them into the house. They felt confident that they couldn't be charged with any offense, particularly as Massey's court order was specific regarding simply taking Megan into custody – Tom and Lisa were not formally named. For all the grandstanding the senator had done in her press conference, she would be challenged to press charges against any of them. Tom crossed his fingers that the police would not find the tunnel in the basement. Discovering Rogers' body would be particularly inconvenient.

At nine o'clock, the agreed time, Strater opened the front door, stepped out into the crisp autumn air and called out to the groggy state troopers who had spent the night in their cruisers, "Officers, may I have a word?"

2

"Good morning, my dear, how did you sleep?" Dr. Peter Lynch asked as he peered into the guest bedroom. Megan looked up sleepily from the bed where she was nursing the baby.

"As peacefully as possible with him crying every couple of hours." She smiled and looked down at the baby. "I hope I'm doing this right."

Peter did not have to work hard to muster his reassuring bedside manner. "You're a natural. If it seems like it's working, it probably is." He stepped back out of the door and was about to continue along the hall when he paused and turned back toward Megan. "I was watching the news this morning and saw a story about a girl who could pass for your twin. Her name is Megan and I'll be darned but she's having a baby, too. Unfortunately, she's been cornered in a house down in Cansego by that witch, Dionne Massey." Megan went cold as he said this and desperately sought something to say. Peter continued, "I've moved your car behind the house. The neighbors can be kind of nosy. They won't see it there."

Megan's fears began to ease. "Do you think that I –" she looked down at the baby and corrected herself, "*we* could stay here for a little while?"

"Marie, you are both welcome to stay as long as you like. My wife and I were never so lucky as to have a child. Now it's like gaining a daughter and a grandson all at once." He blushed. "If you don't mind my saying that."
"I can't thank you enough." The baby cooed softly and continued nursing.

3

"David, just listen to yourself. People don't simply disappear! You're being an idiot." Massey was still furious with her Chief of Staff after yesterday's global media event featuring John Strater, a helicopter and a last-minute injunction. "Now, let's get on with salvaging my reputation and your job. Is the speech loaded in the teleprompter?"

Tinskey was relieved for Massey to be done with the condemnation. "Yes, I checked it myself for your latest edits. We've dialed up the whole 'worried about the young lady' angle as discussed." He decided not to mention again the fact that the state police could not find any evidence of where Megan had gone. "We are still waiting to hear back from Megan's parents about meeting with you. We'll have the staff photographer and some local press cover it."

The door opened and a staffer peaked her head in, "The press corps is assembled. We're ready for you, Senator Massey."

Massey thanked her with a smile and then turned and glared at Tinskey. "Go find that baby!"

Made in the USA
Middletown, DE
14 December 2015